Praise for Lin Anderson

'[A] sexy new rival for old Rebus . . .'

Scotsman

'A fast-paced, gripping tale that grabs the reader's attention right from the very first page'

Sun

'Lin Anderson is one of Scotland's national treasures – don't be fooled by comparisons, her writing is unique, bringing warmth and depth to even the seediest parts of Glasgow. Lin's Rhona MacLeod is a complex and compelling heroine who just gets better with every outing.'
Stuart MacBride, author of *Cold Granite* and *Dying Light*'

'A flat-out sprint . . . a complex and engaging protagonist . . . definitely a cut above the average: vivid and atmospheric, with an enthralling chase through the city's sewers towards a thrilling denouement.'

Guardian

'Forget Las Vegas, forget Miami, this is CSI Dowanhill and it'll keep your adrenalin pumping from the first terrifying page until the last.'

Daily Record

'I was absolutely gripped . . . very enjoyable and truly, truly disturbing . . .'   *Radio 5 Live*

'Chills the blood . . . would make Ian Rankin's old man Rebus choke on his whisky chaser.'   *Big Issue*

LIN ANDERSON

Torch

and

Deadly Code

HODDER

Torch Copyright © Lin Anderson 2004
Deadly Code Copyright © Lin Anderson 2005

Torch first published in Great Britain in 2004
by Luath Press Ltd
First published in paperback in 2007 by Hodder & Stoughton
Deadly Code first published in Great Britain in 2005
by Luath Press Ltd
First published in paperback in 2007 by Hodder & Stoughton
An Hachette UK company

This Hodder paperback edition 2009

1

A CIP catalogue record for this title is available from the British Library

ISBN 978 0 340 99386 6

Printed and bound in Great Britain by
Mackays of Chatham Ltd, Chatham, Kent

Hodder & Stoughton policy is to use papers that are natural, renewable and
recyclable products and made from wood grown in sustainable forests. The
logging and manufacturing processes are expected to conform to the
environmental regulations of the country of origin.

Hodder & Stoughton
338 Euston Road
London NW1 3BH

www.hodder.co.uk

LIN ANDERSON

Torch

HODDER

Thanks to Emma R. Hart,
BSc, MSc, Forensic Science for her inside knowledge.

To Detective Inspector Bill Mitchell

I

IT WAS STARTING to rain. Emperor looked up reproachfully as an icy drop hit his muzzle.

'Okay, boy.'

Karen slipped the penny whistle into her pack and rolled up the blanket. She counted the money in the hat. Shit! Ten pence short.

The Alsatian was pacing, anxious to be away, anticipating a meal. She set off, head down, into the rain. There was an empty building near the west end of Princes Street. She had been sleeping behind the hoarding for the past couple of weeks.

The dog started to jump about as they got near Burger King; tongue hanging out, eyes bright with excitement.

The door opened and a guy came out, stumbling over Emperor, nearly dropping the precious cardboard box. He smiled when he saw her.

'Hey, Karen! You eating?'

It was the *Big Issue* seller from outside Waverley Station. He'd told her his name. Jaz. She liked that he was named after music. He'd asked her name and she'd told him. But that was all.

Karen shook her head.

'What about Emperor?'

'He's eaten.'

Emperor was sniffing the box, so she started to walk on.

'I'll see you later,' Jaz shouted after her. When she was far enough away, she hugged Emperor and he licked her face. 'I promise, Emps. Tomorrow. First thing. Ten pence more, and it's yours.'

The hoarding was plastered with posters advertising Edinburgh's New Year. She waited until no one was looking, then slipped in behind, swept the litter off the step and spread out the blanket. Emperor waited patiently while she settled herself, then lay down beside her.

Through a hole in the hoarding, an illuminated Edinburgh Castle looked down on her like a picture in a fairy tale.

When she opened her eyes Emperor was alert beside her, his ears pricked up, a low growl in his throat. Someone was moving about behind the door.

'Easy boy,' she whispered.

She waited, a hand on Emperor's head. A security guard would check the door then go away, and they could go back to sleep.

As the door opened, she quickly reached for her pack and blanket.

'Go, Emps.'

She was about to follow when she was grabbed from behind.

'Not so fucking fast!'

Emps had heard her scream and was coming back, but he was too late. The man yanked her inside and kicked the door shut in the dog's face.

'Look what I found.'

The other two men turned and stared at her. The smile on the blond one's face turned her stomach. The one in the leather jacket was excited about something, but it wasn't her. Behind them, Emperor was barking and scraping at the door.

Leather Jacket said: 'Get the dog!'

The blond one picked up a metal bar and opened the door, just enough to let Emps get his head in. The agonised yelp as the bar hit the dog's muzzle brought Karen to her knees.

Now he was finished with the dog, the blond guy was looking her up and down.

'Seems a shame to waste her.'

Leather Jacket was walking away, his mind on something else. 'Make it fast,' he shouted.

The one holding her laughed. 'Only way he knows.'

'Shut the fuck up!'

Karen felt spittle hit her face as he climbed on, pinning her arms to the floor. The one behind pulled up her jumper and stuffed it in her mouth. She wasn't going to scream anyway. If Emperor was dead she didn't care what they did to her.

When she came to, the room was thick with smoke.

She dragged herself onto her knees and crawled towards the door, hauling herself up by the handle, praying it wasn't locked. When she pulled it open, a long cold surge of oxygen smacked her face.

As the air rushed past, there was a high whistling sound like a train going through a tunnel. Seconds later the backdraft hit her, demolishing the hoarding and propelling her forward in a ball of flame.

2

DR RHONA MACLEOD switched on the data projector, inserted the crime scene tape in the video recorder and pressed 'Play'.

The output on the large wall-screen was as good as if she had been at the cinema. Police photographers routinely recorded a body's position and injuries, sometimes catching those who moved quietly in the background – the scene of crime officers, the pathologist, the forensic expert like herself.

The body on the screen was that of a young male. He lay in the pugilistic attitude typical of fire victims; the arms extended from the shoulders, the forearms partially flexed in a boxer's stance. In close up, his skin had odd white patches left unburnt, although intense heat had ruptured his skull and split his ankle joint, so that the right foot was free of his leg.

She had examined fluid from his blistered skin but the results were puzzling. Some behaved as if they had been made after death, with little fluid to extract and no positive protein reaction on test-tube heating. Others behaved as though they had been created while he was still alive.

It was common for murderers to believe they could

cover a death with fire, but fire did not consume everything. Even the slightest traces of accelerant could be sampled and identified. The difficulty lay in deciding whether a chemical detected at the scene was there normally, or for the purpose of starting the fire.

Rhona stopped the tape and switched it for the home video Detective Inspector Bill Wilson had sent round. While the hullabaloo was going on round the burning Glasgow tenement, someone in the crowd had had the sense or the morbid curiosity to capture it on video.

She might have been watching a television drama, except that the expressions of fear and determination on the faces of the firemen were real and the flames that roared from the roof of this building were not computer-enhanced.

The owner of the camcorder had zoomed in on a couple on the second floor. The man was holding a baby out of the window in a desperate attempt to help it breathe. The look of terror on the woman's face distressed Rhona, even though she knew all three members of the household had escaped unharmed.

Rhona concentrated on the flames, their colour, shape, direction and intensity. The characteristics of a fire could provide clues to its origin. She played the tape through once more, pausing periodically, taking notes, knowing someone in the fire department would be doing exactly the same thing.

Chrissy McInsh, her scientific officer, stuck her red head round the door at seven.

'I'm starving. Fancy something to eat?

'We could try the new Chinese takeaway on Gibson Street?'

'What do you fancy?'

Rhona shrugged. 'You decide.'

While Chrissy went to order, she began to clear away the debris of the day. She checked her email once more in case there was a message from Chemistry about the tests on the fire debris, knowing it was too soon. This was the time in an investigation when patience was most needed. And when she had it least. Outside, midwinter darkness enveloped the Kelvingrove Museum and Art Gallery and the neighbouring park. The park was frequented by families during the day, but it became the location for a different type of pleasure after dark. Tonight the ill-lit paths were deserted.

There was one message in her inbox. No subject title, and she didn't recognise the address. She contemplated dumping it. In an attempt to cut down on the spread of viruses IT services had advised the deletion of any unofficial looking mail, but curiosity got the better of her. It was a string of capital letters. I C H B U N R T E B T H.

She'd had two like this already and deleted them both. She tried for a couple of minutes to make the characters into a word, then gave up and saved it. If another one arrived, she would try and puzzle it out.

'It's got to involve drugs,' Rhona said.

Chrissy looked up from her lemon chicken.

'Because in that part of Glasgow it usually does?'

Rhona nodded. 'If I'm right and the blistering on the victim's wrists was nothing to do with the fire, what does that suggest to you?'

Chrissy shook her head. 'No idea.'

'Drug barons like to control their patch. Beatings and torture are ways of doing that.'

'Dr Sissons said the death looked like a heart attack.'

'Or a heroin overdose.'

Chrissy pushed her food away.

'Can we leave the post-mortem for tonight? My stomach feels funny.'

'I think it's the chicken.' Rhona made a face and gestured towards the bin.

The flat was in darkness when Rhona got home. Sean would have already left for his gig at the Ultimate Jazz Club. The ansaphone was flashing in the hall and there was a note beside it. There was fresh pasta in the fridge if she was hungry. He'd see her at the club.

She pressed the button to save the messages and went through to the kitchen, wishing she hadn't succumbed to the Chinese takeaway.

A full bottle of red wine was uncorked and waiting for her. Sean never drank before a gig. Playing the saxophone was his high. That, sex and cooking in equal proportions, and sometimes at the same time.

She opened the bedroom window a little and pulled the curtains, got undressed and climbed into bed.

Rhona felt the cat before she heard it; a long soft tail brushing her face, then the press of paws as it settled on her chest. She opened her mouth to protest and a hand slid over it, smothering her complaint. The cat jumped with an angry miaow to the floor.

'Ssh, now. You can't blame the cat for lying where it did.'

'Sean!'

'Who else would it be?'

'What time is it?'

'Nearly three.' He touched her lips.

'You're frozen,' she protested.

'You can warm me up.'

He quickly pulled off his clothes. She caught a glimpse of chest, of thigh. The duvet flicked back, there was a rush of cool air and then Sean pressed his naked body against hers. She shivered with pleasure and cold.

'You shouldn't go to bed and leave the window open,' he whispered into her hair. 'It's not safe.'

'We look down on a convent. God will protect us.'

He laughed. 'Who's the Irish Catholic here?' and buried his face in her neck.

His chilled lips travelled downwards to draw in her nipple and suck it. A ripple of anticipation encircled her hips. She felt him stir against her and traced his thigh with her fingers.

He flipped her, pinning her below him.

'I want to play a tune.'

She smiled. 'What's wrong with your saxophone?'

'Your notes are sweeter.'

Rhona rolled over and flicked on the light.

'I was going to tell you,' Sean said evenly.

'When? After we had sex?' she asked accusingly.

'I only got confirmation this morning.' He was placating her, as usual. 'You said you were coming to the club. I would have told you then.'

Rhona was silent.

'It's a good gig, Rhona. I'll only be away a few days.'

'I know. It's just . . .'

'What?'

He waited, sensing something else was wrong.

'I've arranged to meet Liam,' she said quietly.

The name of her son hung between them.

'He's coming north to visit a school friend before he leaves for his gap year in Africa.' She paused. 'He wants to meet me.'

Sean was struggling to understand her distress.

'But you've wanted this for so long,' he said, puzzled.

'And now it's happened . . .' her voice tailed off. She couldn't articulate her fear, even to Sean. What if Liam didn't like her? What if he hated her for what she'd done?

'Your son will love you.'

She wondered if he believed that or was saying it to avoid any further discussion.

'Love the mother who gave him away?'

He pulled her to him, pressing her head to his chest. His heart beat gently in her ear.

'It'll be okay,' he murmured.

Sean's answer to everything.

'And if it's not?' she insisted.

There was no reply as Sean drifted into post-coital sleep, his mind already in Amsterdam.

A knot had formed in her chest. She shouldn't have mentioned meeting Liam. What if it all went wrong?

She waited until she heard the soft measured sound of sleep, then extracted herself carefully from beneath Sean's arm and got up.

Rain splattered the window so that the lights of Glasgow ran into one another like a watery kaleidoscope. Her naked shadow stood alone, reflected in the glass. She mouthed the words, *we are born alone and we die alone*, even as something inside her wished Sean had said, 'You'll always have me.'

3

WHEN DI BILL Wilson contacted her early the next morning, they had to transfer the call to the Chemistry Lab where she'd been with Dr Spenser since first thing.

Spenser was definite. It was a Class A fire.

'So, mainly paper, wood and fabric?' Rhona suggested.

The forensic chemist nodded. Rhona wondered if the long granite face would ever be split by a smile. 'And no evidence of hydrocarbons?' He shook his head. 'Only the normal traces from household goods.'

'In the video,' Rhona paused, already knowing he would put her down, 'I thought the smoke looked black.'

He gave her a sideways look. 'You've been studying too many American flame charts.'

'So how do you think the fire started?'

'You'll have to discuss that with the fire investigator. As far as I'm concerned there is nothing chemical to suggest that this was a wilful fire incident.' Rhona tried another tack. 'We found evidence of alcohol in the remains of the victim's jacket, especially round the wrists.'

'Maybe he couldn't hold his drink.'

Rhona didn't laugh. Spenser never made jokes intentionally.

'Drugs?'

'We're still running tests, but there's nothing to suggest there were any on the premises.'

When Spenser's equally dour assistant called her to the phone she found Bill's friendly voice a pleasant relief.

'How's cheerful Charlie?' Bill asked.

Rhona kept her voice neutral, for the sake of inter-lab relations. 'Same as usual.'

'And the tests on the fire debris?'

'No evidence to suggest an accelerant was used,' she told him.

'The pathology report says the victim died of an overdose.'

'And the fire?'

'He dropped a cigarette, and whoosh?'

It didn't sound right to her. 'What about the blisters on his wrists?'

'Accidental.'

Bill was baiting her to see what she would come up with.

'You and I both know another accidental fire in three months in an area up for redevelopment is suspiciously convenient.'

'We have nothing to substantiate that at this stage.'

That would be just what his superior would say.

'So why did you phone?'

'I was coming to that.'

Rhona had worked with Bill on many cases since

she'd arrived in Glasgow after her stint in the DNA Laboratory in Birmingham. She had thrown herself into the new job, relishing the responsibility for drawing the different branches of forensics together. The relationship between the forensic department and the CID was good because of Bill.

'Dave Gallagher's had a heart attack,' he told her.

'My God. Is he okay?'

'He's out of danger, but he'll be off work for six weeks at least.' He paused. 'He's been working on the recent Edinburgh fires. There was another one last night.'

'I heard on the news this morning.'

She knew what he was going to ask.

'I'm pretty tied up here, Bill.'

'I know.' He sounded apologetic but resolved. 'But if there's even a remote chance there's a link between their fires and ours . . .'

He waited.

'Okay,' she conceded. Wilful fire-raising at the same time in Scotland's two major cities was unlikely to be coincidence.

'Great.' Bill's voice had grown cautious. 'Severino MacRae is the chief fire investigator. You'll be working with him.'

The best thing to come out of Edinburgh is the train to Glasgow, or so say the citizens of the dear green place. Of course, that can be reversed. Cities forty-six miles apart, one wholly respectable and the other totally irreverent, the dichotomy of the Scottish urban psyche.

Rhona turned from the train window and refused the offer of coffee from the trolley. The lemon chicken from the night before was taking its toll.

She had called Sean from the station to explain her sudden departure to Edinburgh.

'Will you be back before I leave for Amsterdam?'

'I don't think so.'

'I'll give you a call when I get there.'

'I'm staying at Greg's.'

'Okay. I'll see you in a week, then.'

The call had ended in awkward silence.

Rhona turned to the window as the train drew away from Linlithgow Station. Low December sunlight brushed the imposing walls of Linlithgow Palace and danced on the choppy waters of the nearby loch. One summer when she was eight or nine, her father had brought her here for the day. She'd stood in the big courtyard with its wonderful fountain and tried to imagine what it was like to be the princess destined to be Queen of Scots.

She wondered, not for the first time, what her beloved adoptive parents would think of her now, had they been alive. They had never known about Liam. She'd kept her pregnancy a secret because Edward, her lover at the time, wasn't ready to be a father. She had to finish her degree and establish her career. Their relationship had been washed away in the misery and guilt she'd felt after giving up her baby for adoption. Like her, Liam had had adoptive parents who loved him. For her, it had been enough. But for Liam?

Edinburgh Waverley was busy with tourists in town for *The Biggest Hogmanay Party in the World*. A young guy was selling the *Big Issue* on the Waverley steps. Rhona thrust a two pound coin into his hand. He tried to give her change, but she waved it away and he smiled his thanks.

The east end of Princes Street was almost devoid of traffic. A little way along she realised why. The police had cordoned off a section of road and were directing traffic onto George Street.

When Rhona reached the cordon she showed the constable on duty her ID then headed for the incident tent.

4

SEVERINO MACRAE REACHED for the phone on the third ring, an Americanism he'd picked up at some stupid management course they'd insisted he go on. Never before the third ring, never after. The habit had stuck.

'Of course I'm up,' Sev threw back the covers. 'Already been for a jog.' He lifted the open whisky bottle from the bedside cabinet with his left hand and threw some into a nearby glass. 'It's better than sex, Sergeant. You should try it.' He moved the receiver out of the way. The alarm clock showed nine. 'I've an appointment at eleven thirty.' He held the phone in the crook of his neck while he poured another shot. 'Okay, I'll be there. Just tell them to touch nothing. Got that? Nothing. And Sergeant? Tell MacFarlane not to piss on the embers or I'll cut off his dick.'

The bottle was empty. He threw it in the bin on his way to the shower. There was always a chance Gillian might come round. He didn't want her to think he lived like a pig just because she had left him and taken their daughter Amy with her.

The water on his head woke him up enough to remember Gallagher was still in hospital recovering from his heart attack. Looking at Gallagher's colour last night, Sev guessed his colleague would be out of the game for at least six weeks. So no forensic, or at least no forensic with Gallagher's experience of fires. It was as if this particular fire-raiser knew he had a clear run.

Sev dried himself and looked for a clean shirt. The hangers in the wardrobe stared emptily back at him. Shit. He'd left the six new non-iron shirts from Marks and Spencer in his office. He picked last night's off the floor and sniffed it. If he kept his jacket on he might avoid knocking anyone out.

Before he left, he phoned Gillian. He knew before he started to speak it was a hopeless case. There was frost forming on the other end of the line.

'What makes you think I would cancel?' He tried to sound offended.

Silence.

'I might be a bit late, that's all.' Sev looked at the clock. 'Look, I'll be there. Right? Eleven thirty.'

He rang off and headed for the door. The postman had already delivered an ominous pile of mail. Sev kicked the half dozen brown envelopes out of the way and a small white one slipped into view. He picked it up, thinking the big round writing might be Amy's. Since his ejection from the family home, Amy had taken to sending him small notes with big illustrations. Mostly they consisted of tales of her hamster and its various methods of escape. Every time one arrived, Sev's guts twisted a little tighter.

The writing wasn't Amy's, and there was no postage stamp. Sev opened the door and looked out, trying to remember when he'd heard the letter-box rattle. When he was on the phone to Gillian? The stairwell stared back at him, silent and empty. Whoever delivered the letter was long gone.

Sev waited until he was in the car before he opened it, his mind already assimilating this latest development in the letter saga. So now the bastard knew where he lived? Sev examined the last few days. Where he had gone, when he had come home, the people he'd talked to. Had he been followed, watched, as he muddled his way through what had become his life since Gillian threw him out? He began to unfold the white paper, already knowing what it would say. The texture felt strange, as if something had been spilt on it. He held the paper to his nose and sniffed.

'Jesus!'

Thank God Gillian had thrown him out. If she hadn't, some crazy bastard would have been pushing semen-encrusted letters through her letter-box instead of his.

The usual message spewed across the stiffened paper. All the key words were there. Fire. Bitches. Sex. This one hated women so much he needed an inferno to get a hard-on. And that's exactly what he had done last night: lit one.

Sev parked his old Saab next to the mortuary van, wondering why the sergeant hadn't mentioned any bodies when he called him, just the extent of the fire and its prominent position on Princes Street. The building had been lying empty for months. Rumour had it development was being held up because the original façade had to be retained. An expensive investment for somebody.

Detective Inspector Peter MacFarlane came towards him as he climbed out of the Saab.

MacFarlane looked in need of a good night's sleep. The mortuary van might have been there for him. Sev stepped over the yellow incident ribbon and nodded in the direction of the police tent, constructed over the pavement that bordered the famous Princes Street Gardens.

'There was a body,' MacFarlane told them as they walked. 'A young girl. She must have been nearby when it blew. ' MacFarlane looked sick.

The mental picture hadn't escaped Sev either.

He turned on the first retch, thinking MacFarlane was emptying his stomach, but MacFarlane wasn't the one being sick. To their left a gate led into the Gardens where a path cut through a bed of roses, a riot of colour for summer tourists but in December bare, pruned and colourless, except for the blonde head and blue jacket among the bushes.

'She took a look inside the tent while she was waiting for you.'

'Waiting for me?'

'That's right.' Sev could hear caution in MacFarlane's voice. 'Visiting forensic from Glasgow.'

Sev didn't like the sound of that, particularly not after the latest epistle from the arsonist.

'Send her home,' he said.

'What?'

'I said send her home.' Sev wasn't in the mood to go into details. 'I don't want a woman on this case.'

MacFarlane was getting shirty. 'You need a forensic. She's been working on the Glasgow fires. There may be a link . . .'

'I don't care. I don't want a woman,' Sev said.

'I thought sexism was only rife in the Police Force.'

'Leave it out, MacFarlane. I have my reasons.'

'Well now's your chance to tell them directly to Dr MacLeod.'

The woman coming towards him was exactly what Sev didn't want. Sexy, her intelligent eyes meeting his, examining him.

Rhona sat at a table while MacRae went to get some coffee. Even the furniture in the café smelt deep-fried. She concentrated on breathing as shallowly as possible. The toilets were right behind her. Close enough for an emergency.

When MacRae came back he was carrying a tray with two cups, a pot of coffee and the full works; bacon, sausage, black pudding, fried bread and a double portion of eggs. He laid the tray on the table and made a big show of splashing tomato sauce over everything.

'Sure you don't want some?'

Rhona shook her head. 'No thanks. I've eaten.'

'It didn't stay down long.' He forked a sausage. 'You going to do that when we get inside the building?' He wagged the burnt sausage in her face then plunged it in the tomato sauce.

Rhona ignored the jibe.

'So, how long have you been doing this job?'

'I've been in Glasgow three years . . .' She began the usual answer but he didn't give her a chance to finish.

'Three years. Wow. Long time.' She ignored the sarcasm. 'I was seven years at the Forensic Lab in Birmingham before that.'

He took another bite of the sausage. 'You married?'

She hadn't been expecting that one.

'Thought not,' he said when she didn't answer.

'What's that supposed to mean?'

'No time?' he suggested, the sarcasm back.

'No inclination,' she said firmly.

He laid down the knife and fork and reached for her hand, catching her completely off guard. The hand that held hers was warm and dry, the grasp firm but not tight. He pulled it towards the coffee pot and held it there for a moment.

'Ever been burned?'

She pulled free.

'Yes . . . no . . . not really.'

'What does that mean, not really?'

'It means, nothing serious.'

He shook his head. 'You don't know fire until you've been burned.'

'I disagree.'

'Gallagher had ten years' experience in this game.'

'And *he's* a man.'

'With a strong stomach.'

If she hadn't been so angry, Rhona would have laughed. 'I wasn't sick because of the body.'

'This isn't a job for a pregnant woman. There are fumes, asbestos dust . . .'

He was unbelievable. Rhona lifted her coat from the back of the chair.

'Where are you going?'

This time she had caught him off guard.

'I'm going to do what I came to do. My job.'

MacRae wasn't defeated yet.

'No assistant of mine goes into that building until it's structurally safe.'

Rhona was aware that at least half the café was listening to their argument. She raised her voice for the benefit of the other half.

'You'd better find your assistant and tell them that, then.'

'Look, lady . . .'

'No, you look, Mr MacRae. I am not your "lady" assistant. I am a forensic scientist. You, I believe, are a fire investigator. Together we can find out why and how this fire happened or I can catch the next train to Glasgow. Either way I'm happy, although I think your superiors may not be pleased if I choose the second option.'

MacRae's expression didn't change. He stood up and looked at his watch.

'I have an appointment to keep,' he said. 'No one goes into the building until I get back.'

Rhona watched him leave, irritated with herself for handling things badly. MacRae didn't want her there, that was obvious. Exactly why, she wasn't so sure.

*   *   *

Sev got to the Family Reconciliation Office at eleven thirty-five. It wasn't soon enough for Gillian. The meeting had started badly and was deteriorating every time he opened his mouth. The counsellor was doing her best, but what a sixty-year-old woman with hair like the Queen could tell him about marriage wasn't what he wanted to know. He wanted to see Gillian alone, not as part of a family reconciliation sandwich.

The counsellor wasn't giving up. Awkward customers like him were her bread and butter.

'Mr MacRae. I believe you would like to discuss your daughter.'

That was rich.

'No. I'd like to see my daughter.'

Gillian wasn't letting him away with that.

'You do see Amy. You see her more now than when you were at home.'

The way she said it sounded as if he had left home by choice. Sev stopped himself blurting that out, just as a fire engine went past, siren blaring. His impulse was to go to the window but he already knew which direction it was heading. Besides, Gillian would be watching his reaction, ready to jump on it like a dog on a bone. He sat still.

'You're not listening,' she said.

He tried to keep his tone patient. He sounded long-suffering. 'I am listening.'

'Not to us.'

It was the counsellor's turn.

'Mr MacRae, your wife is concerned about the effect your work has on your family.'

'I have to work,' he said. 'Everyone has to work.'

'Not twenty-four hours a day.'

Gillian was right but it didn't make it any easier.

Sev was waiting for the other fire engine, knowing it was only a matter of time. Tollcross was a good unit. Fast. The second engine would be right behind the first. It was.

'Like now,' Gillian said, vindicated.

Sev tried to smile, feeling his face shift under the weight of it. Gillian was right. He was working just now. He was working out what the addition of a female forensic would do to the fire-raiser's view of the current situation. If the fire-raiser liked watching him, he would like watching the woman even more.

MacRae dragged himself back to the present. 'I'm not working right now,' he lied.

'No, but you're thinking about work right now.'

The counsellor came back in like a diligent referee. 'It would seem important to both of you that the issue of your daughter is resolved,' she suggested.

'That's why we should discuss custody.' Sev watched fear blossom in Gillian's eyes as he said this, and was sorry. But he wasn't going to back down on this one. Gillian might be giving up on him but he couldn't live without his daughter.

'It's not called custody now, Mr MacRae. It's called residence and . . .'

Sev wasn't interested in what it was called.

'If she wants to break up the marriage, then I want to look after Amy.'

'That wouldn't work.'

He willed Gillian to see how he really felt behind the anger and the bravado and the hurt. 'I don't want to be a part-time father,' he said, and meant it.

But Gillian was there before he finished the sentence.

'You always were.'

The drill of his mobile saved the counsellor the bother of another intervention. It was MacFarlane. Sev had left him in charge of the scene and Dr MacLeod until he got back. He suspected MacFarlane had his work cut out.

'Just keep her away from the building until I get there.'

When he turned back, Gillian was on her feet.

'I take it you're leaving?' she asked.

'I can wait till we're finished.'

'We're finished now.'

'I suggest,' the counsellor was brisk, 'we start ten minutes earlier next time. Make up the time lost today.'

Sev followed Gillian down the steps. He could tell how bad she felt by the stiffness of her back. He wanted to put his arm around her, hold her. Instead, he stood beside her on the pavement with his hands in his pockets.

'I'll see you Friday then.'

Gillian nodded and turned to go.

'If you want to see Amy before then . . .' she looked back at him, 'she's been asking for you.'

'I'll phone and arrange something for tonight,' he promised.

'Just because we're in a mess, doesn't mean Amy has to be,' Gillian said quietly.

Her vulnerability made MacRae take her hand. She didn't pull it away.

'Gillian . . .' he began.

His mobile vibrated against his chest. He swore. It would be MacFarlane again.

Gillian's voice was resigned. 'You'd better answer it.'

'I don't have to.' He sounded desperately torn, even to himself.

Gillian gave him a look that suggested that in the end he didn't have any real choice.

'Okay,' he reached in his jacket. 'Give me a minute.'

She nodded, but when he turned back after speaking to MacFarlane she had gone.

5

JAZ WALKED THROUGH the railway station, shouting a 'Hi' to the woman on the WH Smith counter. He bought a coffee at the kiosk on the corner and sat down on a bench to drink it. He was later than usual this morning and the rush was over. Rush hour wasn't good for him anyway. The punters were in too much of a hurry to get to work. He just got in the way.

Now was the time for shoppers and tourists. Most of the shoppers were regular as clockwork. He even knew some of their names. Mrs Paterson from Musselburgh, off the train every Monday at eleven o'clock. She always bought a *Big Issue* from him. Sometimes she gave him a home-baked scone or cake. Even complained to him about her husband. Jaz didn't mind. At least Mrs Paterson spoke to him like he was a human being.

He finished his coffee and made for the exit, just as the 10.20 from Glasgow pulled in. He wanted to be ready with the magazines. Glaswegians had a reputation for generosity.

From his pitch he could see the Edinburgh skyline. The castle and law courts to the left, the central sweep of the gardens leading to the art gallery, and on the right the Scott Monument. Tourists loved this view. Jaz would watch them emerge from the bowels of the station into daylight and the sudden splendour of the city. The Athens of the north, he'd read that somewhere. In summer it was occasionally true.

Today was dull, with a cold wind from the east and the odd spit of rain. The tourists didn't care. As soon as they spotted the castle, the cameras were out. If only he had ten pence for every photo taken of Edinburgh Castle, Jaz thought.

It was then he noticed the smoke. A blanket of it lay to the north-west of the city. He was so busy staring at it, he didn't notice the pretty blonde woman trying to buy a magazine. She handed him a two pound coin and he tried to give her change but she wouldn't take it.

He stayed on his pitch until curiosity got the better of him. At least half a dozen of his regulars had already asked if he'd heard about the fire on Princes Street. The police had cordoned off part of the road but you could get a view from the Gardens, they said.

It seemed he wasn't the only one keen to get a look. Around the Ross Bandstand half of Edinburgh seemed to be spending lunchtime in the Gardens, despite the cold weather.

Jaz wasn't surprised to see Emperor standing by the railing at the top of the steep bank of roses. He'd half-expected to see Karen in the Gardens anyway. She usually brought Emps in for a run during the day. But not as early as this. Lunchtime was busy for her. People strolling along Rose Street liked to hear her play.

The dog started to howl, a mournful sound. Jaz hurried up the steep bank. A tent was erected on the pavement, and just left of it the dog was tied to a railing.

Jaz stuck his hand through and rubbed the dog's ears. 'Hey, Emps.'

'Watch out, son. He might bite.' A policeman had emerged from the tent and was coming towards him.

'No he won't. Will you, boy?'

The dog stopped whining and started to growl as the policeman approached.

'Where's Karen?' Jaz was talking to the dog but it was the policeman who answered.

'Who's Karen?'

Jaz stood up. 'Emps belongs to a girl called Karen.'

The policeman was interested. 'Is this Karen a friend of yours?'

'I know her.'

'Could you come round here and tell us a bit more about Karen?'

'Why? What's happened?' Jaz was suddenly frightened. Karen wouldn't tie Emps to a railing and abandon him. There was a funny look on the policeman's face. 'A girl . . . we think she was asleep in the doorway when the fire . . .'

'Karen's dead?' Jaz felt dazed. A picture of Karen formed in his mind, her fingers coaxing music from the whistle, her eyes closed, her mind somewhere else. Always somewhere away from here and now.

'We need to contact her family to identify . . .'

Jaz's brain was stupid with pain. 'Karen hasn't got a family.'

'Everybody's got a family, son.'

'That's shite!' The shout caught in his throat. 'Karen had no one,' he looked down, 'except Emperor.' The dog whined and pawed at his leg.

'What's going to happen to Emperor?'

'We've called the RSPCA.'

'They'll put him down.'

The policeman was getting out his notebook. 'Look son. You give me your name and address. If we can't find a relative, maybe you could identify the girl.'

Jaz spoke quietly, his mind already made up. 'Give me the dog.'

'I can't do that . . .'

Jaz was on his knees, his hands through the railings, wrestling with the rope attached to Emperor's collar. The dog was jumping about, pulling at the rope. Another policeman was on his way over. The one beside him was trying persuasion tactics.

'Look, son. Come over and give us a contact address. I'll tell the RSPCA that you're interested in the dog and . . .'

The rope was almost free.

'Come on, Emps. Come on, boy.'

Jaz started to run.

Behind him the dog, suddenly frantic, tore at the remains of the knot. Jaz heard the policeman shout as Emps cleared the spikes and landed in the rose bushes. Jaz kept on running.

6

RHONA HAD BEEN hanging around now for almost an hour. DI MacFarlane had been pleasant but firm. No one was permitted to enter the building until they were sure it wasn't in imminent danger of collapse.

They weren't waiting for an inspection team to give the all-clear. Rhona was sure of that. They were waiting for MacRae to return from wherever he had disappeared to an hour before. She'd spotted MacFarlane on the phone, decidedly rattled. No doubt checking in with his lord and master, she thought unkindly.

After walking round the building a couple of times, she retired to a police car with a cup of coffee from a doughnut vendor. Through the windscreen, she watched scene of crime officers sifting through the piles of sodden debris that littered the pavement, an unpleasant but necessary business. At least MacRae had let them make a start on that. She'd already introduced herself to the two men involved. They'd worked with Gallagher and seemed to know what they were doing.

Her meeting with the pathologist had been less satisfactory. Brisk and professional, he gave nothing away. She'd eventually mentioned her work with Dr

Sissons. At the name of his Glasgow counterpart, the doctor raised an eyebrow.

The voice was old school Edinburgh. Chances were he had never been to Glasgow in his life.

'You've come through from the west to help us.'

It made her sound like the cavalry.

'There may be a link between the two spates of fire-raising.'

'I take it your main concern is the fire and not the death of the girl.' 'Well,' she hesitated, knowing what she was about to ask was not strictly protocol. 'The two are related.' He waited while she chose her words. 'I was hoping I might sit in on the post-mortem.' 'Is that absolutely necessary?' The man looked as though he had just discovered a bad smell.

'It might help.'

He stared at her, then nodded.

'I have two to do today. It won't be until tomorrow morning. 7.30.'

Chrissy wasn't telling her anything she didn't know already. Rhona moved the mobile to her other ear and reached for the coffee cup she'd stuck in the door pocket.

'Okay, Chrissy, but you haven't met the man. I'm going to insist all samples come through to you. That way I won't have Valentino breathing down my neck. And no, I do *not* think he's sexy. If you saw him dipping a charred sausage in a blob of tomato sauce you wouldn't think so either.'

The noises on the other end of the phone suggested

Chrissy did not believe her. Denials always made matters worse with Chrissy.

'I'll have to go. My caveman's back. And Chrissy. Don't buy any more of those takeaways. I spent half the morning being sick.'

Rhona dropped the window on MacRae's second knock.

The voice was irritated. 'You ready?'

'Of course.'

'Let's go then.'

Rhona wondered if the anger radiating from his body was specifically directed at her.

He turned back as she shut the door of the police car.

'I suggest you bring a plastic bag. No one is allowed to pee, spit, shit, cough or vomit once inside the building.'

Rafters gaped above Rhona like the broken ribs of a huge whale. Underfoot, the floor was a spongy mass of sodden debris.

MacRae led the way, followed by MacFarlane who joined them at the door. The acrid smell caught at Rhona's throat. Despite being familiar with fire scenes, the devastation fire wrought always surprised her. At a normal murder scene it was the victim that lay mutilated. Here, the building was the victim.

Along the wall of what must have been a reception area, a set of metal shelves were twisted by the strength of the fire. A filing cabinet stood open, buckled by the heat.

MacFarlane spoke first.

'One of the firemen said the colour of the flames was wrong.'

'Whatever was burning wasn't what should have been in here?' Rhona asked.

MacFarlane nodded.

'The building was being renovated and the owner was taking a long time about it. The preservation people were being awkward.'

'You think it might be an insurance job?'

They both looked at MacRae for confirmation.

'I don't think anything. But I sure as hell smell something.'

MacFarlane had picked his way across the debris to the remains of a doorway on the left.

'Take a look at this, Sev.'

Straight ahead was a wide staircase. To the left and right, archways led into other rooms. MacFarlane was standing in the remains of the left-hand arch. MacRae followed him through. In the centre of the room was a pile of debris. MacRae knelt beside it and nodded at Rhona to bring the fire investigation kit.

'It smells like . . .' MacFarlane began.

'Don't bother, MacFarlane. You haven't the nose for it.'

MacRae filled the bag and handed it back to Rhona.

'Have they checked the windows?'

'All the ground floor ones were blown out with the blast,' MacFarlane told him. 'Gas and electricity have been off for the past year, so it wasn't a gas explosion.' He looked about. 'It'll be difficult to prove a break-in.'

A line of scorch marks was visible on the bare floorboards. Rhona followed it back to the archway.

'Don't wander about.' MacRae's voice followed her. 'Not until we're sure it's safe.'

'The fire ran this way.'

The scorch marks led to the foot of the staircase. Rhona wondered why she had missed them on her way in, but then her eyes had been on the ceiling, or what was left of it.

'I think someone piled bits of old shop fittings where you are now and splashed petrol about, then dripped it through here and up the stairs and back to the front door. When he lit it, the fire ran back into the side room.'

'Christ, MacFarlane, tell her!' The voice was sharp with exasperation.

Rhona noted MacFarlane's concerned face before she started up the stairs, but she had wanted to be sure. The first and second steps were burned through but the third and fourth showed the signs she was looking for.

'He's right,' MacFarlane tried.

'The petrol had already vaporised, that's what caused the explosion,' she looked back at them pleased.

'Shit!' MacRae was coming towards her but she was too engrossed in her explanation to care.

'The chemical reaction absorbed the majority of oxygen in the atmosphere so the fire . . .'

'Watch out!'

MacRae pulled her down the stairs and into the relative shelter of the archway as a section of ceiling gave way.

She would have apologised if he'd given her the chance but as soon as the noise stopped he headed for the entrance. MacFarlane shot her a look that suggested it would be better to keep her mouth shut, and followed MacRae out.

He was already dishing out orders.

'We need a scaffolding gantry before we put a full team in. No one, I repeat, no one, is to go back in there until we're sure of the ceiling. And MacFarlane, this is an old building. I bet most of the joists survived the fire. I'd like a proper look at them once the place is cleared.'

MacFarlane moved off towards the police tent, throwing Rhona an encouraging look as he left.

'So, what do we do now?' she asked MacRae.

'I wait until they make it safe.'

Rhona ignored the singular pronoun.

'How long will that take?'

His voice was clipped. 'Twenty-four hours, maybe more.'

She held up the sample bag. 'I'll send this to the lab. Get them to check for an agent.'

'Suit yourself.' He turned away.

'You think it was petrol?'

'I know it was.'

'You can't be sure until it's tested.'

'Look, lady . . .'

'My name's Rhona.'

'You play around with your chemical reactions all you like. That fire didn't just happen. Someone made it happen and that someone made it big and powerful enough to blow a young girl halfway across Princes Street.'

The *Big Issue* seller from Waverley was hovering on the edge of their conversation. An Alsatian stood alert beside him, looking like a police dog awaiting a command. On their right, MacFarlane emerged from the operations tent with a mobile held to his ear.

'MacFarlane!'

In broad daylight, MacFarlane looked worse than Rhona felt. He had probably been up all night.

'Who's the guy?' MacRae motioned behind him.

'Where?' The DI's tiredness was turning to stupidity.

'With the dog.'

'Oh, him. Name's Jaz. He knew the victim. That's her dog. He ran off with it, then changed his mind and came back. He offered to identify the body for us, while we try and find her family.'

MacRae turned. 'Come here, son.'

Jaz hesitated.

'Does the dog like chips?'

'Salt and sauce?'

'Of course.'

MacRae opened the Saab door. He grabbed a chip poke from the passenger seat and emptied its contents onto the road.

Emps looked up at Jaz.

'Go on!'

They watched as the dog devoured the chips, licking up the sauce like a pro.

'DI MacFarlane here says you knew the girl.'

'Karen didn't really know anybody. She liked to be

alone, except for Emperor. I spoke to her now and again. Offered her food. She never took it. She wouldn't beg either. She played the penny whistle for money. Rose Street mainly . . . she was good.'

Rhona bent and rubbed the dog's ears.

'Had Karen been sleeping round behind the hoarding?' she asked.

'I don't know. She could have been.' Jaz looked straight at Rhona. 'You think somebody started that fire deliberately, don't you?'

Rhona glanced at MacRae, but he said nothing.

'We don't know that yet.'

'That's murder.' The boy's voice was angry and the dog's head came up, neck hair bristling.

'Have you seen anyone hanging about the building?' Rhona asked.

He shook his head.

'We'll be back tomorrow. If you think of something you could speak to us then.'

The boy nodded and walked away, the dog at his heels.

MacRae was climbing back into the car. She asked where he was going. It was like a red rag to a bull.

'You're beginning to sound like my ex-wife. Correction, my estranged wife. For your information, I'm going to the scene of the last fire. The one that gave Gallagher a heart attack and landed me with you.'

Rhona kept her voice calm. He was not going to get her as rattled as he was. 'I'd like to come.'

'Suit yourself.'

The dog's chips weren't the only fast food in the car.

Rhona swept the remains of three other fish suppers onto the floor before getting in. The stereo was blasting out an old Marvin Gaye number. MacRae reached across and turned it up even louder.

Rhona kept her eyes on the road. Once you got used to the level, the music was alright. All those songs that sink into your brain so that years later you find yourself mouthing words you never knew you knew.

MacRae's face was as tired as MacFarlane's. Or else he had a hangover. Probably chronic. He drove like a maniac.

Ten minutes later they reached a burned-out office block.

'When did this happen?'

'Thursday last week.' He waved at the approaching security guard, who nodded and unlocked the entrance chain. MacRae held the temporary door to one side and Rhona stepped in. She was in a large, domed entrance hall. Ahead of her, a broad stairway spiralled upwards to a further two floors.

'It used to be a town house, then offices. Some computer consultancy firm had the first floor. An investment company had the top and the ground was an advertising company.'

'It must have been beautiful. That staircase especially.'

Despite the damage, the hall retained an elegance, its marble flooring blackened but intact.

'Can we use the stairs?'

'Not if you want to live.'

Behind the staircase a ladder had been erected through to the upper level. He motioned her to go first.

'Better you land on me, than me on you.'

Rhona wasn't convinced that was the only reason for the chivalry.

When she was halfway up he followed. She waited for him at the top. This time she wasn't going to wander.

He pointed at a pile of debris to the left of the door.

'He started it where we came up, burning a hole through the ceiling, then spread the accelerant out the door and down your nice staircase.'

'An insurance job?'

'The insurance company doesn't think so. The building was in the process of being sold for a good price. There was planning permission to convert it into flats.'

'Vandals?'

'I don't think so.'

MacRae went back down the ladder first, then watched her descent with interest. Wearing a skirt had been a bad choice, Rhona thought.

They walked back to the car.

'Any chance we could give the music a miss this time?'

The grin took her by surprise. MacRae looked completely different when he smiled.

'That bad?'

'That loud,' she said, returning his smile.

He switched off the stereo and started the car. This time the pace was slower.

'What does MacFarlane think about the fires?'

'MacFarlane thinks we have a nutter on our hands.'

'And you?'

The smile had gone. 'I don't know why the places were torched, but I'd risk my neck and say they were torched by the same person or persons. The jobs are professional. Same level of organisation and sophistication.'

'Do you have any idea who it might be?'

He reached across her and for a moment she thought he was going to turn on the stereo again. Instead he opened the glove compartment, brought out a letter and tossed it in her lap.

'This arrived this morning, delivered by hand to my flat.'

She opened it and read it. 'Whoever wrote this doesn't like you very much.'

'He likes women even less.'

Threatening letters were notoriously difficult to trace. It could take weeks, months of police time. In most cases the threat never materialised anyway. Frightening the recipient was usually enough for the letter-writer.

Rhona held the paper up to the light. Something had been spilt on it. She sniffed.

'Semen?'

'I would say so.'

Leaving evidence lying like this in a glove compartment with a half drunk bottle of whisky wasn't a good idea. She told him so. 'You should have given this to Forensic.'

'I just have.'

She held her tongue. She was beginning to learn confrontation didn't work with MacRae.

'I'll have it DNA sampled. We might get a match.'

He shook his head. 'If he was on file, he wouldn't have sent it.'

He might be right. DNA fingerprinting had become common knowledge, thanks to television.

She thought for a moment. 'The person who sent this may not be the one lighting the fires.'

His face was stubborn. 'He is.'

'Just once, you might be wrong.'

He was adamant. 'Not this time.'

They drove to his office in silence. At first glance, Rhona thought, there was no evidence to suggest the fires in the two cities were connected. Here, prominent buildings had been set on fire, not rundown council housing. If the fire-raiser had written that letter, then there was both a sexual element to his crimes and a desire to persecute and outwit the fire investigation team, ie MacRae. She glanced sideways. MacRae was obviously under a lot of pressure, and not just from the job. He was edgy, irritable and, judging from the bottle in the glove compartment, drinking too much. But he did have years of experience of fire investigation. She might be skilled in forensics, but he, like all fire investigators, had worked his way up from the ranks. He had fought numerous fires. He knew how they behaved.

MacRae's office was on the third floor of the red sandstone building that housed the headquarters of

Lothian and Borders Fire Brigade. The receptionist smiled at MacRae and gave Rhona the once-over.

'Any calls?'

'DI MacFarlane. Half an hour ago,' she told him.

They passed a display of old fire equipment and climbed the stairs. MacRae's office was small, with a desk, a filing cabinet and two easy chairs, both piled with papers. MacRae lifted a pile and motioned Rhona to sit down, then disappeared into the back room. On the desk, alongside three empty coffee cups, stood a photograph of a pretty, dark-haired woman and a girl of about six. Rhona wondered what had caused the separation and whether MacRae's drinking and chauvinistic attitude were the result or the cause.

MacRae called from the back room.

'Take a look in the top drawer of the filing cabinet, under miscellaneous.'

She pulled open the drawer. There were, at a guess, a dozen other letters. If these had anything to do with this investigation, then MacRae had been withholding evidence.

He was standing at the door, bare-chested, with a package in his hand. He tore the plastic wrapper off the new shirt and shook it loose.

'Does Gallagher know about these?' she asked, annoyed.

'I didn't want to be the one responsible for another heart attack.'

'That's not funny.'

'Who's laughing?'

MacRae turned away and Rhona's breath caught in

her throat. She had never seen such a badly burned body before, at least not one that had survived. Even the deep tan couldn't disguise the mass of mottled tissue that stretched from shoulder to shoulder.

Rhona forced herself to speak.

'You should have given these letters to Forensic,' she said.

MacRae was buttoning up the shirt. If he had sensed her reaction to his back, he chose to ignore it.

'We had that conversation, remember? Anyway, they're not all from the same bloke.' He shrugged. 'People don't like me prying into their fires. I might worry the insurance company enough not to pay out. So they write me letters.'

'They threaten you?'

'Some do. Others claim to have started the fire or think the fire was a sign of God's wrath.' He reached for a tie from the back of the chair. 'Take the letters with you if you like. They make good bedtime reading. See if you can pick out the ones from our friend, the wanker.'

He was putting on his jacket. 'MacFarlane said you were staying over. Can I ask where?'

'With a friend.'

'Male?

'I don't see . . .'

'Easy. You can stay with a transvestite poodle for all I care. Provided it has a loud bark.'

He had come right up to her. She could smell the pressed cotton of the new shirt.

'What do you mean?'

'The arsonist sees us as the enemy. For the moment he's outwitting us. If he thinks we're getting too close . . .'

She interrupted him. 'I've only been here a day.'

'Long enough.'

He headed for the door. 'If you want a lift, we have to go now. I have a date and I'm late already.'

The traffic was heavy in the city centre but MacRae dodged through it, oblivious to angry shouts and blasting horns. Rhona began to wish she had taken a taxi. She suggested he could drop her at the west end of Princes Street and she would find her own way to Greg's flat from there.

'I'll take you right to the door after I pick up my date,' was the curt reply.

Whoever the woman was, MacRae didn't want to be late for her. And she had been feeling sorry for him because he was separated from his wife and family!

They reached the house ten minutes later. MacRae sounded the horn and Rhona caught sight of a figure at the window, then the door opened and the wee girl in the photograph came running down the path.

The child waited until MacRae rolled down the window then gave him a good telling-off.

'You're late and Mum's angry.'

MacRae's wife was following her daughter.

'Amy's been ready for half an hour,' she said sharply.

'It's okay, Gillian, we've got plenty of time. The film doesn't start till 5.30.' He turned to Amy who was settling herself happily in the back seat. 'Amy, this is Dr MacLeod. She's helping me while Mr Gallagher's in hospital.'

'Hello, Dr MacLeod.'

'Hello, Amy.'

'You didn't say anyone else was going.'

The suggestion was all too obvious.

'I'm not going to the film, Mrs MacRae.' Rhona hoped she didn't sound as embarrassed as she felt. 'Mr MacRae just offered me a lift back to my flat.'

'Did he?'

MacRae was rolling up the window. 'I'll have Amy back by eight.'

'You'd better.'

The only one who talked on the way to Greg's was Amy. She chatted on about school, her best friend Katie and her pet hamster.

Rhona sat seething. MacRae had deliberately misled her into thinking he was meeting a woman when he was collecting his child. Then he deliberately embarrassed her by making his wife think he was going out with her. The fact that she knew she was exaggerating the situation didn't make any difference. One thing was sure. MacRae couldn't care less about other people's feelings.

The journey took too long for Rhona and when they got there she had to endure the expression on Mac-Rae's face as he looked up at the luxury block.

'Isn't this the street where a flat went for half a million recently?'

'I have no idea.'

'Quite a catch.'

'Greg is gay,' Rhona said defensively.

She got out and shut the door.

'I'll see you tomorrow.'

'Sure.'

She turned to go.

'Are you eating out?' The cynical tone had gone.

'Why?'

'Stay clear of the Italian on the corner. It's over-priced and the food's crap. And take your gay friend with you. For safety's sake.'

7

THE FLAT WAS empty, but Greg had left the hall light on and there was a note from him beside the phone.

Make yourself at home. There's food in the fridge but if you can't be bothered cooking, there's an Italian on the corner.

Rhona went into the spare room. She emptied her bag on the bed, grabbed her dressing-gown and shampoo and headed for the shower.

She didn't hear the phone at first. When she did, she assumed Greg's ansaphone would click on, but it didn't and the phone went on ringing. She climbed out of the shower and grabbed a towel.

The line clicked dead as soon as she said hello. Rhona tried 1471 but the number had been withheld.

She thought for a moment, then threw the bolt on the front door and unbolted it again seconds later. She would not let Severino MacRae unnerve her.

She was halfway through drying her hair when the phone rang again. She was there on the third ring.

'Who is it?' she shouted.

'Hey. Take it easy.' It was Chrissy.

'Sorry. I had the hairdryer on. It deafens me.'

'You sound more like pissed off. Bad day?'

'I've had better.'

'The samples arrived. I sent most of them to Chemistry,' Chrissy said accusingly.

'I'm sending through a letter . . .'

'Not handwriting analysis?'

Chrissy's voice was a mixture of disappointment and cynicism. Handwriting specialists came a little lower than forensic chemists in Chrissy's scheme of things.

'I want you to look at it first,' Rhona said. 'It's impregnated with something.'

Chrissy was interested now. 'Blood? Perfume?'

'Possibly semen. Can you check it on the DNA database?'

'Sure. Bit of a long shot though.'

'I know. MacRae had other letters in his filing cabinet that Forensic haven't seen. Some of them may be from the same man. I want to read them, before I send them through. Anything on the Glasgow fire?'

'Are you familiar with thallium poisoning?'

'I've seen it once before. Why?'

'The victim was at the doctor's last week with a crop of symptoms that might have been caused by thallium poisoning. We're running some tests. I'll have more when you get back. When is that likely to be?'

'As soon as possible.'

The restaurant was too upmarket for Rhona, but it had been difficult to retreat. The young man at the desk gave her the once-over, then asked pointedly if there would be one or two persons eating. When she said one, he raised his eyebrows and escorted her to a corner table inches from the kitchen entrance. The other diners, mostly couples, glanced briefly in her direction then went back to their conversations.

Rhona wondered whether reading the forensic magazine she'd brought with her would make her more conspicuous, then decided it was better than staring into space. When the waiter arrived she ordered a pasta dish and a half bottle of house white. She was absorbed in an article about cocaine residue on American bank notes when she noticed MacRae standing at the entrance impatiently scanning the diners.

Rhona buried her face in her magazine, praying he wouldn't spot her.

No such luck.

He removed a chair from a nearby table and sat opposite her. 'I thought I told you not to eat here.'

Rhona avoided catching his eye. 'I don't think it's part of the job of the fire investigator to tell the forensic where to eat.'

'So you don't accept advice? Even from a expert?'

The waiter was offering MacRae a menu. He ignored it. Rhona shook her head and the waiter gave her a knowing look. Lovers' tiff, it said.

'So what's so important you came looking for me?' she asked, trying to be reasonable.

MacRae stood up. 'I'll explain on the way.'

'I can't just leave.' This was ridiculous. Did he think

he just had to call and she would follow him about like a pet dog?

'Why not?'

'I've not finished my wine.'

He reached for the bottle. 'We'll take it with us.'

'No.' She grabbed it back. 'I haven't paid for it yet. Anyway,' she topped up her glass, 'I've already ordered.'

'You've what?'

'Keep your voice down.'

'If you don't come,' he whispered dramatically, 'I'll be forced to tell all these people about the aubergines.'

'Don't be stupid.'

He shrugged and stood up. 'Ladies and gentlemen, I'm sorry to interrupt your meal but being from the Department of Public Health I feel it only fair to warn you about the sexual predilections of the current chef of this establishment, which involve aubergines . . .'

Rhona lifted her jacket from the back of the chair, left money on the table for the astonished waiter and headed for the door.

When MacRae opened the car, the music was on full blast. He turned it down before she got in. The chip pokes had gone.

'My daughter doesn't like an untidy car. Takes after her mother in that respect.'

Rhona ignored his attempts at conversation and looked pointedly out of the window. They had left the city centre and were heading north, towards the Forth. She refused to ask MacRae where he was taking her, but whatever he wanted her to see, it had better be good.

8

IT TOOK TEN minutes to get to the important place that had spoiled her dinner. On her right hand side was a small harbour, half a dozen boats beached on the mud. On her left a long, low white building with bright red signs. Rhona stared out of the window in disbelief.

'What's this?'

'A *real* restaurant. Best fish and chips in Edinburgh.' MacRae was actually grinning at her. 'It's impossible to get a table here on a Friday night. Ian promised to hold one for fifteen minutes, no more.'

'This is why you embarrassed me and dragged me from my meal?'

MacRae shrugged his shoulders. 'It got you here, didn't it?'

He was already out of the car.

'Come on. I've removed you from hell and taken you to heaven. What more do you want?'

The smile MacRae got from the waitress was verging on a come-on. She twinkled and bobbed and escorted them to their table with a swing of her hips.

'Amy likes it here,' said MacRae, handing Rhona the menu. 'They make a fuss of her.'

'They make a fuss of her father too.'

For the first time MacRae looked embarrassed, but the look disappeared so quickly Rhona wondered if she'd imagined it.

'Okay, what is it you wanted to show me?' she insisted.

'After you sample some real fish and chips.'

Rhona refilled her cup from the large teapot and sat back in the chair. MacRae had been in the kitchen for the past five minutes. As he disappeared through the doors he had been greeted with cries of welcome. It made her think. MacRae was different tonight. Seeing his daughter had done him good. This morning he had been coiled and tense. Tonight he was relaxed.

He emerged, laughing. Behind him a handsome male face grinned out.

'Jamie sends his love.' MacRae sat down. 'I told him you're not interested.'

'What makes you think that?'

'No time,' he smiled, 'or was it no inclination?'

He held her eyes until she looked away.

'Why did you bring me here?'

His face grew serious.

'This was on my windscreen when I came out of the cinema.'

He handed her a typed note.

She read out the words. 'I hope you'll be at the party?'

MacRae's face confirmed her suspicions.

'He means the Hogmanay street party, doesn't he?'

'The arsonist profiles as power-assertive. He achieves a sense of superiority through expressing exploitative control, dominance and intrusive violations of the law. In layman's terms, he gets his kicks from mayhem. With the crowds that'll turn out over New Year, he'll have his biggest audience to date.'

'You're certain the fires weren't insurance or fraud jobs?'

'If a building is set on fire for insurance purposes, no one lets us know, before or after the event.'

If the person responsible for the fires had no more reason for lighting them than pleasure, it would make him almost impossible to catch.

MacRae was reading her mind. 'The worst kind to find.'

The ring of his mobile broke the silence that followed. As he listened to the caller, his expression became fraught with worry.

'I'm on my way.'

He was on his feet.

'What's wrong?'

His voice was hardly more than a whisper.

'Someone threw a petrol bomb through Amy's bedroom window.'

MacRae ignored the No Waiting sign and the double yellow lines and swept into an ambulance space outside Casualty. It had taken twenty minutes to get to the hospital. MacRae had ignored every red light and kept his horn on full blast most of the way. Rhona had expected a police car to stop them at any time. When she offered to park the car, MacRae threw the keys in her lap without speaking.

Rhona sat for a while in the car park trying to decide whether to go in to the hospital or not. She desperately wanted to know if Amy was okay, but if Gillian was there it would look bad. She didn't want to cause any trouble between MacRae and his wife, especially now.

When she entered reception, MacRae was standing alone, but almost immediately the lift door opened and Gillian emerged. Rhona waited at the entrance but MacRae caught sight of her and motioned her over.

The words were tumbling out of Gillian.

'Amy was in bed. She was tired after the cinema. I heard a crash, then Amy screaming. By the time I got to her the room was full of smoke. I got her downstairs and outside. Mr Fraser next door phoned the Fire Brigade.'

'Where's Amy?'

'Ward 7. She'll be alright.' Her relief was inflected with anger. 'I knew something like this would happen but you would never believe the threats. The job always came first.'

MacRae's knuckles were clenched white.

'This isn't the time to discuss my job.'

'Your job almost killed our daughter.'

MacRae looked stricken.

'Gillian, please . . . why don't you and Amy come back and stay with me in the flat?'

Gillian was staring at Rhona.

'Wouldn't that be a little crowded?'

MacRae looked weary. 'Dr MacLeod is covering

Gallagher's job. She's staying at a friend's flat, not mine.'

Gillian was unconvinced.

'*You* threw *me* out, Gillian. Remember?'

'It seems throwing you out wasn't enough.'

MacRae turned to Rhona. 'I'm going to see Amy. Can you take a taxi back?'

She nodded. 'Of course.'

Gillian threw Rhona a look as MacRae entered the lift. Rhona wondered if her presumption of infidelity was based on past experience. Or was it the sense that she could never come before the job in Severino's life?

9

JAZ COULDN'T SLEEP. He rolled out of bed and went to stand at the window. The lights of Edinburgh stared back at him. He had been in this flat for three months and he still loved it with a passion he would have found impossible to describe. The only people who could ever understand what this flat meant to him had been homeless themselves.

He left the window and went into the tiny kitchenette, filled the kettle and popped a tea-bag into a cup. He didn't bother with milk. Without a fridge it went off too quickly. He scooped two teaspoonfuls of sugar into the cup and poured in the boiling water.

The dog was awake and when Jaz sat down it came and laid its head in his lap. Emperor was missing Karen. Every time he heard a female voice on the stairs, he was up and at the door.

Jaz was the same, even though Karen had never been in the flat. He'd offered her a bed one night when it was really cold, but she'd refused.

'Emps keeps me warm,' she told him.

He'd gone back with the dog and the policeman had taken a note of his address and told him he could hang on to Emps for now. Jaz had offered to look at the body, check if it was Karen. They'd agreed because they knew it would take time to locate a relative, if they managed at all. Kids like Karen were running from someone or something, and it wasn't usually concerned families.

The blast had hit her back, so her face was recognisable. It only took a second but the smell of burnt flesh stayed in his nostrils. That and a terrible feeling of anger.

It wouldn't be light for another hour. Jaz rinsed his cup at the sink. It was a good time to find the people he needed to talk to. The ones who might have seen someone hanging about the empty building. The people nobody noticed or if they did they looked straight ahead and pretended they hadn't. The people who were an embarrassment to the good folks of Edinburgh. People like him.

Outside the streets were glistening in a light frost. Jaz stuck his hands in his pockets, whistled lightly to Emps to follow and set off for the Grassmarket.

To the tourists, the Grassmarket meant pubs and eateries. To Jaz, the down-and-outs who sat begging from passers-by gave the place its character. At night they clogged the alleys and jammed the doorways. These were the long-stay patrons of Edinburgh's underbelly; the ex-servicemen whose lives had fallen apart, the drunks and the addicts.

Traffic was beginning to flow along Chambers Street as he passed the Museum of Scotland and headed down by Greyfriars churchyard to the Cowgate. The men's hostel on the corner was closed but there was an old guy coughing up spit on the front steps. Jaz recognised him.

The Bruce wasn't one to miss a chance. He had his hand out right away.

'Any change, Mister?'

Jaz dropped a pound coin plus fifty pence in the dirty palm and the face lit up. The price of a can of extra-strong lager. Breakfast had arrived.

'Ah, you're alright son.'

'It's me. Jaz.'

The old guy's face worked hard on focusing.

'I'm looking for Mary,' Jaz explained.

The face changed to suspicion. 'What d'you want the Queen for?'

'I need to talk to her.'

'The Queen doesn't talk. Not sense anyway.'

The old guy was shuffling off towards a High Street newsagent and off-licence open early enough for breakfast. Jaz walked beside him.

'I heard Mary had a little trouble.'

'What's it to you?'

They were nearing the shop. There was anticipation in the old man's step. In his head he was already swallowing the lager, feeling the surge as the alcohol met his brain. He might be a drunk, but he was shrewd. If Jaz wanted information, he would pay for it.

The owner was pulling up the safety grille, lifting the big bags of delivered rolls from the shop doorway.

'We could buy four cans and a couple of rolls,' Jaz said. 'Keep you going for a while.'

The old guy was summing up the offer. 'Forget the fuckin' rolls and make it six cans.'

Jaz nodded. It would skin him, but he needed to talk to Mary. If what he'd heard was true, she might know who lit the fire.

The Bruce waited till the money was across the counter and the pack of lager in his hands.

'The Queen's in the Infirmary. Some bastard tried to get her out of a squat. She wouldn't budge, so he set her hair alight.'

'Was it the same guy she told the Wallace about?'

'The same one.' The Bruce laughed. 'Stupid bitch is cracking up. No drink allowed in the hospital.' His laugh sounded like dirty water going down a blocked drain. 'She wants the Wallace and me to rescue her.' Then he was off across the road to a wooden bench.

There was no point turning up at the hospital until nearer official visiting time. If Queen Mary knew anything, he would find out soon enough. Jaz headed for his pitch outside Waverley, turning over in his mind what he should do after that. All he knew was that Karen shouldn't have died. Whoever lit that fire was responsible for her death. If the police didn't find him, he would do it himself.

10

'WE FOUND A leather pouch round her waist. The pocket was at the front so it escaped much of the heat. It held some coins . . . and this.'

Dr MacKenzie handed Rhona a photograph. The bright young face stared out at her, side by side with the Alsatian. Rhona wondered how the girl had persuaded the dog into the booth, then made it sit in such a way they were both visible for the flash. The dog's tongue hung out, long and pink and dripping. It had a grin on to match its mistress's.

'She had just about enough money for her next meal, a penny whistle and a change of clothing, plus the remains of the tartan blanket.' The pathologist nodded to the bagged items behind him. 'According to eye-witnesses, the blast from the backdraft was extensive. From the state of the body, she must have been facing away from the fire, but directly in its path. The lacerations to the back of the skull suggest intense heat. Her front is relatively unmarked except for the genital area.'

'What do you mean?'

He motioned her forward.

'The pubic hair is burned away, the genitals blistered, yet this area would have been shielded from the blast.'

'Do you mean these burns were inflicted before the explosion?'

He nodded. If that was true, it was the first link between the Glasgow fire and this one.

'I take it you want to stay while we open her up?'
Rhona nodded.

The doctor reached for an array of instruments beside him. Each pathologist had his own systematic procedure for post-mortem. Rhona watched as Dr MacKenzie chose the favoured way, a simple incision down the middle of the body from the neck to the pubis, making a detour round the tougher skin of the navel.

'The usual samples have already gone to the lab,' he said. 'You may speak to my assistant about those if you wish. Apart from the genital burns, there is no sugges-tion of violent injury prior to death. However, there was evidence of recent sexual contact, which may or may not have been consensual.' He paused as he lifted the stomach clear of the body and manoeuvred it over a container. 'And if I'm not mistaken, nothing to eat for some time.'

The scissors bit through the stomach wall, releasing the meagre contents into the container with a soft plop.

The girl had been living on fresh air. Whatever she had earned from playing the whistle had not been spent on food.

'Maybe she was feeding a habit?' Rhona suggested.

'More likely feeding the dog. A dog that size needs

copious amounts of food and seeing it tied up outside the tent, it was well looked after. Anyway, we'll know about drugs once we get the results of the urine tests.'

'She was very young,' Rhona said, thinking about the face in the picture.

'I would suggest a little over fifteen. The breasts are small and not, I think, fully formed. We'll be able to tell from the hair samples, but I'm fairly sure she hadn't reached late teens.'

'Jaz, the boy who took her dog, said she had no family.' It hardly seemed possible that a fifteen-year-old girl could be sleeping rough on the streets of their capital city and no one had reported her missing.

Dr MacKenzie's tone was tart. 'I take it there are no homeless girls on the streets of Glasgow?'

'They don't usually make their living playing the penny whistle,' Rhona said.

'This one may not have either if the semen is anything to go by.'

'I'd like to check your DNA findings against a seminal fluid sample we have already.'

'Of course.'

Rhona was glad to leave the sterile atmosphere of the Pathology Lab and breathe in Edinburgh's pollution instead. She stood on the steps outside, clearing her head of the scent of death. The police car was waiting at the kerb. She would pick up her things and head back to Glasgow. The message from her lab via Mac-Farlane had simply stated she was needed.

She thought briefly about calling the hospital to

check on Amy then decided against it. If Gillian was there, it might make things worse. Judging by Gillian's reaction the previous night, it was time for MacRae to choose between his family and his work.

When or if she returned to Edinburgh, the chances were she would find herself working with someone other than Severino MacRae. Rhona was surprised by her sudden feeling of disappointment and quickly dismissed it. She didn't like working with MacRae and he didn't like working with her. It would be easier for both of them if the investigation passed to someone else. But what if the warning on the windscreen was for real?

Hogmanay tourists thronged the north side of Princes Street, ambling in and out of souvenir shops, stopping to take pictures of the castle. Traffic was flowing again, the incident tent was down. To her left the shattered building was a hive of activity. The scaffolding was up and a team at work inside. A white suit emerged as the police car passed, face encased in a cartridge respirator. MacRae wasn't taking any chances. Buildings like these were often lined with asbestos, and sifting through the debris risked disturbing particles of the lethal substance. Then there were the noxious gases trapped under deposits which might be released during excavation.

The car rolled down the ramp into Waverley station.

'Mr MacRae said he'll call you later,' the driver told her.

'I didn't tell Mr MacRae I had to go back to Glasgow,' she said, puzzled.

'He asked me to give you this.'

The driver handed Rhona a brown envelope with 'for the Lady Scientist' scrawled roughly over it.

Rhona settled herself in a window seat. The train was quiet. It wasn't a peak time for travelling between the two cities. She placed the envelope face up on the table in front of her and for once the title 'Lady' didn't irritate her. She wondered what effect the contents of the envelope would have.

After returning from the hospital, she'd read through the bundle of letters from MacRae's filing cabinet. When Greg arrived back around two she was still up, mulling over them. Some were general complaints and acts of God. Four looked as though they came from 'the wanker', as MacRae called him. The front door opening and muffled laughter from the hall had broken into her thoughts. Greg stuck his head round her bedroom door, his eyes hazy with drink.

'Didn't think you'd be awake. I've brought someone back with me. Hope you don't mind?'

'Of course not.'

'We won't make a noise,' he promised.

He was true to his word. Either the walls were soundproof or it was the quietest lovemaking on the planet. Rhona turned up the stereo to stop herself thinking about sex.

It was the sight and smell of death that did it. Rhona had experienced the feeling many times before. The need to prove to herself that she was alive to shake off the presence of death.

She picked up the four separate letters and laid them one by one across the bed.

Fire aroused the arsonist. Made him feel alive, when nothing else could. But this wasn't a roll on the rug in front of a log fire. His fires had caused devastation on a grand scale, and now death.

The sound of traffic outside had dwindled to an occasional hum. Rhona rose and stood at the window, wishing Sean would call her. She desperately wanted to hear his voice. No. She wanted his weight on her, his breath in her hair. She wanted the smell of sex in her nostrils.

The street was deserted, save for a man with a dog. The figure paused and looked up and Rhona strained to make out the face in the orange glow of the street light. The dog lifted its leg and marked the lamp post, then with a small yelp urged its master on.

11

'WHAT THE HELL is going on, MacFarlane?'

'Take it easy, Sev. We're on the case. All known punks . . .' MacFarlane didn't get to finish. Severino threw the electric razor on the desk. Shaving hadn't made him look any better. Bed and sleep were both an elusive dream.

'Cut the crap. You and I both know who did it.'

'We don't know for certain,' MacFarlane countered.

'Correction. This arrived this morning.' Severino threw an envelope across the desk. 'The bastard knows everything about me and our lady forensic. Gillian's talking about taking Amy north to her mother's. As far away from me as possible.'

MacFarlane said: 'I'm sorry.'

Severino paused before the next barb. It wasn't MacFarlane's fault. He was doing his best. But it wasn't enough. If it were just himself, it would be different. But not Amy.

'Look, I investigate fires. I'm not responsible for finding the people who set them. That's your job.'

'If he hits during the street party we have to be ready for him.'

'You're talking to the wrong man, MacFarlane,' he said firmly. 'You want fire *prevention*.'

The DI wasn't giving up. 'There will be a lot of people about.'

MacFarlane was putting words to the pictures in Sev's own head.

'Cancel the celebrations. You would cancel for a terrorist threat. Edinburgh's become fireworks city. It thinks it's fucking Disneyland.'

'You know we can't do that. Not on what we have.' MacFarlane looked apologetic. 'The three days are a sell-out. Sky's covering the whole event.'

Sev shrugged his shoulders.

'Suit yourself. It's nothing to do with me.'

'But you know how he thinks.' MacFarlane was like a dog with a bone.

'In case you haven't noticed,' Sev said, 'I always get there after the event.'

'He's never warned us before.'

Sev ran his hand through his hair. It didn't help his brain. He had gone over the same idea a hundred times. It still didn't fit.

'Has it never occurred to you that's what's wrong?'

In the distance the castle dominated the skyline, Union Jack fluttering in the breeze. Her Majesty's garrison in Scotland. If the bastard had his mind set on the city centre, the castle might be the only safe place this weekend.

'While we all run round trying to figure out if, where and when during the Hogmanay party he's going to perform,' he went on grimly, 'the bastard will be somewhere else.'

'We have to take that chance.'

'No. You have to take that chance.' Sev picked up a buff folder. 'Here's my report.' He shoved it in Mac-Farlane's face. 'The last four fires in the city centre have been started deliberately, I believe by the same person or persons. All the details are there.'

He turned to leave.

'Where are you going?'

'A drink, home and bed. In that order.'

His jacket was behind the door. MacRae pulled it off the hook, slung it over his shoulder and swung round. He wanted to be sure of one thing before he left.

'She got the message?'

'She was on the twelve o'clock to Glasgow. I'll make sure she doesn't come back.'

'Thanks.'

MacFarlane looked gloomily resigned: 'She'll be safer in Glasgow.'

'We'd all be safer in Glasgow.'

12

SEV DIDN'T LOOK up when Jaz entered the bar. Instead he drained his whisky glass and waved it for a refill. He wasn't in the mood to talk to anyone, least of all him.

When he left the office, he'd made for the centre of town rather than the flat. There was no need to visit the fire scene again. He'd signed off. He'd kept his promise to Gillian. But it wasn't Gillian's frightened demands the night before that had made up his mind. It was standing in the ward looking at Amy's pale face, the dark shadows under her eyes. His wee girl. She was okay, they'd told him. She was being kept in overnight only as a precaution. That hadn't made him feel any better.

The whisky slid down his throat and bit at his chest. It numbed his thoughts but it didn't drown them out. When he'd arrived at the building this morning, his whole team had known about what had happened at Gillian's. He could tell by their faces, the dropped looks, the caution in the voices. He had ignored it all and they'd got started, glad not to have to say anything. They would systematically comb the debris, bit by bit, just as he had told them. But it was probably all a complete waste of time. While they were tied up analysing this job, the arsonist would be planning his next strike.

Jaz was standing behind him. He heard the scuffle of the dog's claws on the floor as it sat at the boy's command.

'Hey.'

Sev turned. 'Hey.' He patted the dog and it licked his hand.

'Buy you a drink?'

'No thanks.'

'Not your drug, eh?'

Jaz ignored the taunt.

'Have you found out who it was that killed Karen?'

'You're talking to the wrong man,' Sev heard himself say. 'You want DI MacFarlane of Lothian and Borders Police.'

'What if the same guy hurt your little girl?'

Sev grabbed him by the jacket. Jaz didn't resist. His back pressed against the counter, he stared at Sev, his eyes accusing.

'Who told you that?' Sev tightened his grip. The dog growled.

Suddenly Sev's anger drained as quickly as it had erupted. He loosened his hold and Jaz stumbled free.

Sev picked up his glass, his hand shaking. He was losing it, he realised with a flash of clarity. The image of Amy's face in that hospital bed kept swamping his mind. The thought that she could have been badly burned, or worse still, lying in a coffin, made him sick with fear.

'Go away,' he said brusquely.

But this one was as stubborn as MacFarlane.

'Don't you want to nail the bastard?' Jaz said.

'I'll nail him with my evidence,' Sev said quietly.

'You have to catch him first.'

The guy was like a fly buzzing round his head. Swatting him hadn't worked. What now? Sev looked Jaz up and down. The ponytail, the combat gear, the big boots, the determined face.

'I know who he is.'

'What?'

'A mate of mine, Mary Queen of Scots, hangs about the Gardens with two old guys, the Bruce and the Wallace . . .'

That was all he needed. The demented drunken ravings of resurrected Scottish heroes. Sev stopped him mid-sentence. 'Alkies.' He waved at the barman for a refill.

Jaz slid his eyes pointedly to the glass. Sev got the message.

Jaz went on: 'This guy told Mary to move from her squat last Friday night or he'd torch her. He came back when she was asleep and set her hair alight. The Wallace and the Bruce heard her screaming. The hospital kept her in for a week and she didn't get any drink . . .'

'I can sympathise with that.'

The boy ignored the cynical remark. 'She's been on the bevvy ever since,' he went on. 'She's shit-scared he'll come back and get her.'

'Maybe this guy just doesn't like smelly old alkies squatting in his building.'

'He isn't the owner.'

Sev knew he should stop listening now. Tell the boy to take his story to MacFarlane, keep out of it. But the story was planting itself in his brain, burrowing down.

'So where's this building, then?' he asked finally.

'I wrote down the address.' Jaz pulled a piece of paper from his pocket and flattened it on the counter.

Below the address was a pencil drawing of a face. 'What's this?'

'Mary described the guy, so I drew him. It took a few tries, but she swears this looks just like him. And she might be an alkie, but she never forgets a face.' The boy's voice was anxious.

Sev examined the drawing. It was impossible to know if it caught a likeness, but if it did, he would know this face again. 'You *are* a wee smart-arse.'

The boy looked pleased. 'He's about heights with me. Twenties. She says he smells nice.'

Sev looked him up and down. 'Not on the streets then?'

'You don't smell so sweet yourself.' Jaz was giving as good as he got.

'I've been up all night.'

'At least you've got a bed to go to.'

Sev nodded at the picture. 'Can I keep this?'

'If you like. I've got a spare.'

He folded the sketch and put it in his pocket, then put some money on the counter for his drinks. Jaz was watching him. Sev suddenly remembered what the pathologist had said when he phoned about the post-mortem. The dead girl had been living on fresh air.

'You hungry?'

The chin was up, defensive and proud. 'I don't need your money.'

MacRae looked down at the dog. 'Buy my friend some chips then.' He pushed some change across the counter. 'And don't forget the salt and sauce.'

13

CHRISSY LOOKED UP from the forensic journal.

'It says here that one gram of thallium sulphate constitutes a lethal dose in an adult. With doses greater than two grams, the illness progresses rapidly to cardiovascular shock, coma and death within 24 hours.'

'If someone wanted rid of him, why not give him a straightforward overdose?', Rhona suggested.

Chrissy shrugged. 'A waste of good cocaine?' She slammed the book shut. 'Neat stuff, eh? Colourless, tasteless and odourless. Found as a contaminant in some Chinese herbal medicines, rodenticide and green fireworks, can be mistaken for cocaine and sniffed . . .'

'What did you say?'

'I said lots of things. Which one?'

'You said something about fireworks.'

'Green fireworks. It's in green-emitting fireworks.'

Chrissy gave her a look that accused her mind of being elsewhere, which it was.

'Visited the drug centre a week before he died complaining of nausea, vomiting and abdominal pain,' Rhona read from the report. 'The doctor there reported him as manifesting acute nervous and gastro-intestinal symptoms. He wanted to admit him to hospital. He refused and was persuaded to give urine and blood samples. He then left.'

'One week later he's found dead of an apparent overdose in a burned out building,' Chrissy added.

'The general lab tests on the urine and blood showed nothing,' said Rhona thoughtfully, 'but then they weren't looking for thallium.'

'By the pricking of my thumbs, something wicked this way comes,' said Chrissy darkly.

Rhona laughed despite herself. 'I didn't know you were a Shakespearean scholar.'

'I'm not. It's from a Ray Bradbury book.' Chrissy shook her head. 'Let's face it. Something smells like shite.'

'You're sure about the hair?'

'Come and see for yourself,' Chrissy offered. 'Most of the hair was singed but I got some from the back of the head. Of course, we don't have a control sample from before death but . . .'

Under the polarised light, the dark bands and distorted anagen roots supported Chrissy's diagnosis of thallium poisoning. Rhona glanced up. 'The urine and blood taken after death?'

'We're working on that now.' Chrissy's self-satisfied tone suggested that life went on as usual even if the Captain had left the ship.

'I'd better call Bill.'

Bill wasn't mincing his words. 'They don't want you back.'

'Why not?' She tried to sound disinterested.

'Apparently you're difficult to work with.' He paused and when she didn't reply, felt safe to go on. 'Anyway,' he said placatingly, 'you've got your hands full here.'

Rhona came back at him. 'And you agreed?'

'It isn't up to me.'

'So what's to stop me going back?'

'Saving your sanity?' he suggested.

Bill was right. There was no reason to return. The samples from the Princes Street blaze had been tested and confirmed the use of an accelerant. They were still waiting on an exact breakdown but that would arrive soon. The presence of an accelerant was all they needed. The trawl on the DNA sample from the semen on the letter had revealed nothing. Neither had the semen left in the girl. And they didn't match.

'Did you speak to DI MacFarlane?' she asked.

'Yes. He suspects the arsonist will strike again soon.'

'So we just wait and see?' she said.

'*They* wait and see. *We* worry about our own.'

She should keep her nose out of the East's affairs. That was fine by her. There was plenty of work here without bailing out the East. She changed the subject to the Glasgow case.

'Chrissy's tests confirm Dr Sissons' suspicions about the presence of thallium in the body.'

'What the hell's that?'

'Thallium salts are colourless, tasteless and odourless,' Rhona explained. 'A poisoner's dream.'

'Where the hell would he get thallium?'

'Rodenticides, pesticides, Chinese medicines, fireworks. He could also have sniffed it thinking it was cocaine. Wherever he got it, it was a potentially lethal dose.'

Bill wasn't convinced. 'Cocaine would be a bit upmarket for him.'

'Well, if there's cocaine contaminated with thallium out there, there'll be more like him soon.'

'Great.'

'I suggest you warn the drop-in centres to look out for tell-tale signs. I'll send you a standard description to pass round.'

'Thanks.'

'And Bill, I think the blisters on the wrists happened before death. If the victim was being fed thallium and getting his wrists burned, someone didn't like him very much.'

'He wasn't a dealer as far as we know. Maybe he owed his supplier money?'

'Suppliers don't normally kill their customers. It cuts the profit margin.'

'Maybe we should check back over the last year. He wasn't the first junkie to die of an overdose in that area,' Bill said thoughtfully.

'Just what I was thinking.'

'Mind you, there was no reason to think about poisoning in the other cases.'

'There is now. And Bill?' she caught him before he rang off. 'Personally I'd like to know who's behind the redevelopment plans for that area. Junkies have a bad habit of lowering the tone of the neighbourhood.'

* * *

When she finally got round to attacking her desk, the contents suggested she had been away for a week rather than a couple of days. The report from Chemistry lay on top. Rhona checked through it again. Most forensic laboratories felt confident in identifying the commonly found accelerants like petrol and kerosene on the basis of their chromatograms alone. Spenser had gone one step further. The Edinburgh sample report was conclusive. But then, Severino MacRae had known that by his nose.

Rhona pulled the brown envelope from her briefcase and emptied its contents on the desk. The photographs of the Princes Street building only served to confirm the conclusions. The burning pattern was obvious, the seat of the fire revealed as she'd suggested. She was momentarily embarrassed by the memory of that morning in the burned-out building, her determination to tell the man his job. Still, she had been right and no more insufferable than MacRae himself.

She had a quick look through the remaining photographs. The wide-angle lens had been used to photograph the building from the two opposite corners, showing the overall degree of fire damage and the locations of the various entrances and windows. The aerial photograph showed the force of the explosion and the trail of debris that sprayed the railings and beyond. The photographer had taken two shots, once right above the building, one nearer the front covering the debris, the railings and the gardens. The white tent was already up round the body. Rhona winced when she spotted the flash of blue among the roses behind the tent. So that was why MacRae had included this one. He couldn't resist the parting shot. Forensic Scientist being sick in the flowerbeds.

She checked the back in case he'd written a caption, but it was blank. It was his idea of a joke. She shoved the photographs to one side. Forty-six miles away, and MacRae was still irritating her.

Rhona opened her inbox. There was an email from Chemistry about their report, a couple from other forensic labs, a request from a forensic student to visit the lab. She opened each in turn, storing them in folders for later action.

She kept Liam's email for last. She took a breath then clicked it open, her heart thumping. The message was short and to the point. He would call when he knew what his movements were over the New Year. He signed it simply 'L'.

Disappointment and relief swept over her. Liam was as nervous as she was about meeting.

Rhona pulled her mind away from the subject of her son and got wired into the job she liked least, the paperwork. If she concentrated on her reports it would stop her thinking about Edinburgh and about Liam.

When she pushed open her front door three hours later, the flat smelt stuffy and unlived-in. She had stopped on her way up the stairs and thanked Mrs Harper for feeding the cat in her absence.

'My pleasure, dear. There's some post for you, I left it on the hall table, and your ansaphone's blinking.' Mrs Harper gave Rhona a knowing smile. She was one of Sean's many admirers, and she took her vicarious mothering seriously.

Rhona shuffled through the bills and circulars, wishing that Sean wrote letters the way he wrote music. The most she could hope for when he was away would be a postcard.

She went in search of some alcohol and found an unexpected bottle of white wine in the door of the fridge. She was the one who bought white wine. Sean didn't like it. She tried to remember when she'd bought it, and couldn't. She carried her filled glass to the hall and sat down to listen to the phone messages. When the tune began, Rhona thought the caller had the radio on too loud in the background. Then she realised the song by The Crazy World of Arthur Brown was the message.

The music stopped abruptly on 'I'll see you *burn*'. Only someone with a warped sense of humour and a liking for retro music would leave her a message like that. She fully expected it to be followed by some sarcastic remark from MacRae that included the word *lady*. But no. There was a short pause then Sean's enthusiastic voice. 'Hi Rhona. Got here okay. It's great. You can reach me on this number . . .'

Rhona wrote down the number. Chance appeared at her feet winding in and out of her legs, looking for food. Rhona went back to the kitchen, fed the cat and raided the fridge for something for herself. It was then she noticed the set table. Place-mat, knife, fork and wine glass. A fresh red rose in a tumbler of water.

Fear trickled down her spine. The strange message

on the ansaphone. Now this. She stood very still, listening to the silent flat. Maybe it was Mrs Harper? That was a distinct possibility, one she could check easily enough. But the song on the ansaphone?

She walked through the flat, checking every room for signs of an intruder. All the windows were tight closed. Nothing was disturbed. Everything looked just as Sean would have left it.

14

DETECTIVE CONSTABLE JANICE Clarke had wordlessly warned Rhona on entry. DI Wilson was not a happy man. Janice was Bill's equivalent of Chrissy. They might have been related, not in looks but in attitude. Janice handed her two cups. The right-hand one was hot, the other cold, the milk already congealing. Just the way Bill liked it. The old leather chair creaked round.

'So, what's wrong with your face?' she asked.

'Long time since I heard that one.' Bill broke his sour expression with a half-smile. 'There's been a call from our friends in the East asking about the possibility of contaminated cocaine.'

'Thallium?'

'Maybe. They've had two serious cases of suspected drug contamination in the last two weeks. Both critically ill in hospital. And something else. There was a house fire early this morning on an Edinburgh council estate. They found the body of an addict inside.'

'I'll take a bet all three addicts lived in a run-down area earmarked for redevelopment,' Rhona said.

Bill nodded. 'All from the same estate.'

It was too much of a coincidence. 'Who's the developer?'

'A well-known and respected company, with interests all over Scotland,' Bill raised his eyebrows, 'including council redevelopment in Glasgow.'

'I take it you pointed that out to your Edinburgh equivalent?'

'The company has its headquarters in Edinburgh.'

'He reminded you of that?'

'And the fact that the chairman of the company is a pillar of Edinburgh society.'

'Surely you're not going to let that stop you.'

Bill gave her a look that suggested pigs might fly.

'Janice and I are working on it.'

'Could you get me details on firms manufacturing fireworks?' she asked.

'What for?'

'Thallium is used in green-emitting fireworks. And Edinburgh, as we both know, is big on fireworks.'

'Before you go . . .' Bill betrayed his concern. 'I think you should know a body's been found in the hills near Arrochar.'

Rhona took a seat, her legs suddenly weak. The horror of her last case – a paedophile ring that murdered vulnerable youths – had ended with the disappearance of the main suspect, a man who called himself Simon.

'Initial examination suggests it could be him. Dr Sissons is doing a post-mortem.' He paused. 'I can get someone else to do the forensic work if you want?'

'I'd rather do it myself.'

'We haven't tracked down all the members of the

ring. If he survived your attack and the fire at the cottage, he had contacts that would help him.'

'I know.'

'Let's hope it's him, then.'

She nodded. 'I'm going to drive through to Edinburgh.'

'Thought you might,' he smiled. 'Best of luck.'

The City of Edinburgh Council had tidied up the housing scheme twice in the past ten years. It had been a waste of time. The half-hearted makeover couldn't cover the rot inside. The soul had already departed.

Residents of the more salubrious parts of Edinburgh would have given their eye teeth for the hundreds of parking spaces that lined the grid of houses. An attempt had been made to install a heart when it was first built, with a block that held a cinema, a church, a couple of shops and a bookie's. The cinema had turned into a bingo hall, the shops shut except the post office and one determined butcher, who had obviously been made of strong stuff, repainting his graffiti-covered walls regularly. Rhona could make out the sedimentary layers of expletives under the thin white paint.

If MacFarlane was surprised to see her he didn't show it. When he emerged from the burned-out building, Rhona fully expected MacRae to follow him. She had steeled herself for it. But MacFarlane was alone.

'I take it the body's gone?' she asked.

'An hour ago.'

'I'll call in at Pathology.'

'Suit yourself. You know the Doc. Not too keen on the West poking its nose in our affairs.'

'We've had similar cases. It might help. Is MacRae involved with this one?' The words were out before she could stop them.

MacFarlane's face was impassive. 'Sev's taking some leave.'

So Gillian had got what she wanted.

'Want to take a look inside?'

At least MacFarlane took her seriously, she thought, then felt bad. MacRae had taken her seriously. They just sparked off each other like a tinder box and dry paper. Together they could have started a fire in a swimming pool.

There wasn't much left inside the council flat. In a corner lay half a dozen cans and what looked like the remains of bedding. There was an old-fashioned stuffed armchair and blackened bits of kitchen table. Rhona stepped round the charred remains.

'Where did you find the body?'

'Over there.'

MacFarlane pointed at the far wall. The SOCOs had drawn the body outline halfway up the wall, as if the victim had been propped against it. The wall was heavily smoke-marked and soaking wet from the deluge of water, but here and there lurid purple wallpaper was still visible.

'Did you find the remains of any pictures?' Rhona said.

'Pictures?'

'That might have fallen off the wall.'

MacFarlane shook his head uncomprehendingly.

'I just wondered what these were for.'

The nails were six-inchers. They stuck out rigidly from the wall, three feet apart.

'Did you see the victim's hands?' Rhona asked. She dropped her forensic bag beside her and flipped it open.

'Hands?' Obviously MacFarlane wasn't sharing her thoughts. 'The body was badly burned. That's all I know.'

Rhona pointed to the wall near the nails. 'Did your forensic team sample the wall here?'

'I don't know. I'd have to check.'

Rhona rubbed a filter paper round each nail then dropped on the reagents. She showed MacFarlane the pink result. By the look on his face, MacFarlane was catching up.

'I think he was crucified before the place was set on fire.'

MacFarlane hitched a lift back with her. She suspected he wanted to talk, or maybe make sure Dr MacKenzie would give her house-room at the post-mortem. Mac-Farlane's excuse was that he was short of squad cars and wanted to leave two for the constables doing the rounds asking questions of the residents.

'I don't like my men in there without a getaway vehicle,' he said.

He wasn't joking.

Rhona swung out onto the main road, which had been traffic-calmed with crazy paving and big ugly bollards. A few struggling trees survived inside their mesh cages. Yet the housing scheme's setting couldn't have been better. Easy access to the ring road, a shopping mall nearby, a short car journey through Holyrood Park to Scotland's parliament building and the city centre. Private housing was already encroaching from the east, neat semis, toy houses in red brick with pseudo-Georgian entrances.

MacFarlane took his time. They were nearly at the Pathology Lab before he asked her why she'd come back.

She told him about her conversation with Bill Wilson, the contaminated cocaine and the burn marks on the Glasgow boy's wrists.

'So we go one better, and nail ours to the wall?' he said grimly.

'Edinburgh always has to go one better. It's traditional.'

MacFarlane looked thoughtful. A spate of drug-related deaths linked by fire. But nothing to do with the city centre fires, which were potentially more disastrous. Rhona asked who was dealing with them.

'Sev's off and Gallagher's still in hospital. So it's down to me.'

'So why was I sent away?'

No answer.

She pulled over on a double yellow line.

'It was MacRae, wasn't it?'

MacFarlane hesitated. 'Sev thought you'd be safer in Glasgow.' He looked uncomfortable.

'I would never have left if I'd known.'

'That's why he did it.'

They were causing a traffic jam on the narrow road. She indicated and drew out.

'What happens now?'

'We continue our enquiries and hope we're wrong about the timing.'

'You'll let the Hogmanay party go ahead?'

'We have no choice.'

You couldn't cancel the biggest New Year party in the world on the strength of a unsubstantiated threat. She changed tack.

'What made MacRae think I was in danger?'

'There was a letter after the fire at his house. It mentioned your name.'

A fleeting picture entered Rhona's brain. A single red rose. A place-setting. The song on the ansaphone.

'You okay?' MacFarlane looked worried.

'Of course I'm okay,' she said shortly. 'What about Amy?'

'Gillian took her up north to her mother's for a while.'

'So what's MacRae doing with his leave?'

'Drinking.'

The Pathology Unit loomed up in front of them. Rhona drew into a reserved space and switched off.

The pathologist's voice had a war-weary tone. Heat contraction of the skin of a corpse often produced splits which might be interpreted as tears or cuts inflicted during life, he told her. The distinction between burns inflicted during life and burns inflicted on an already dead body could be difficult, if not impossible, to detect at autopsy.

'So you don't think he was nailed to the wall?' Bluntness seemed Rhona's only instrument.

MacKenzie's pale blue eyes rolled upwards as if she had just committed an Edinburgh social gaffe. 'I didn't say that.'

Rhona sought refuge in MacFarlane's encouraging look.

'Dr MacLeod took samples from around the nails we found in the wall,' he said. 'If this body wasn't nailed to the wall, then someone else was.'

The pathologist turned his blue stare on MacFarlane.

'The hands could have been injured prior to death.' The tone was grudging, but the words were enough.

'Do we know how he died?' Rhona asked.

'Come and have a look.'

MacKenzie waved them over to the body. Rhona followed, with MacFarlane a foot behind.

'The thoracic and abdominal walls are partly burned away, but the viscera are largely intact and show no evidence of natural disease.' MacKenzie pointed at a basin. 'Our victim's last meal. The usual healthy diet, pie beans and chips. Oh, and there was vomit in the oesophagus. The larynx, trachea and bronchi contained a large amount of soot and the lungs and major blood vessels were bright red.'

MacKenzie moved further down the body with Rhona following. MacFarlane stayed where he was.

'As you can see, the testes and external genitalia are burned away, but the presence of a prostate and seminal vesicles confirm the body is male.'

'Age?' Rhona said.

'The medial epiphyses of the clavicles were almost completely fused, so twenty-one or more. The lack of atheroma in the coronary arteries, aorta and other major vessels suggest he was certainly under forty. A young adult male.'

'Death by smoke inhalation?'

MacKenzie nodded. 'Most likely.'

So whatever torture he'd been through didn't mean he'd escaped the terror of the fire.

'Any clue as to his identity?' she asked.

'The body is too badly charred for visual recognition. However, there were some surviving items that might provide a clue.'

The pathologist left the table and brought over a small metal tray for inspection. The smell in the room was oppressive. Barbecues were swiftly losing their appeal.

'Would it be possible to establish the presence of thallium in the body?' Rhona asked.

The pathologist was simultaneously evaluating the possibility of meeting her request and the reason for it.

'In a similar case in Glasgow, there was some evidence to suggest the boy had been poisoned with thallium,' she enlarged.

'Really? God forbid that we should be following in Glasgow's footsteps.'

The pathologist took them into a side room to examine the contents of the tray and left them to it. When the door clicked shut behind him, MacFarlane's sigh of relief matched her own. Rhona laid the tray on the work surface and perched on the stool beside it. MacFarlane seemed to be intent on sucking in air from the air conditioner that whined above them.

'Last time we met it was me being sick,' she teased.

'And me taking the mickey.'

They exchanged smiles.

'Shall we take a look at the victim's prized possessions?'

Two small earrings and a key with a metal tag lay on the tray.

'Probably a front-door key,' she suggested.

'Not a Yale.' He picked it up and turned it over in his hand. 'There's something scratched on the tag.'

The clumsily-etched word looked like 'Robbie'.

MacFarlane climbed into the passenger seat.

'Any luck on the semen in the girl?' he asked as she drove away.

'It didn't match the letter,' she told him.

'And we have no way of knowing if it was rape or not.'

She shook her head. 'I want to see the letter with my name in it.'

MacFarlane looked uneasy.

'Forensic has it.'

MacFarlane had been planning a visit to Forensic, but not with her in tow. He was uncomfortable about her being there at all. Rhona tried to look on the bright side. Hopefully the threatening letter had reached Forensic without a sojourn in MacRae's stale glove compartment.

15

MACRAE HADN'T MOVED from the flat in the last twenty-four hours. Jaz glared at the first-floor window then took off for the corner café with the dog at his heels. It had been a waste of time giving MacRae the drawing and telling him about Mary. MacRae hadn't done a bloody thing since he'd seen him in the pub, except go on a bender. Jaz bit into the pie the waitress brought him and took a slurp of tea. He was losing income arsing about outside MacRae's flat, waiting for him to come out and get on with the job.

Jaz broke a piece of the pie and dropped it under the table along with a handful of chips. It was expensive feeding Emps. Karen must have spent most of her earnings on the dog.

He spent the rest of the morning selling the *Big Issue* and deciding what to do next. He could take his drawing and description to the police station. Ask to speak to MacFarlane. He didn't hold out much hope there. He would be lucky to get past the Desk Sergeant. As far as the police were concerned, he was a low-life and always would be.

A woman was approaching the café and for a moment he thought it was the forensic scientist. When she got nearer he realised he was wrong, but it gave him an idea. If MacRae wouldn't do anything, maybe she would. Jaz shoved the remaining magazines in his bag and set off along Princes Street towards the West End.

When Rhona called Greg at work, he told her there was no problem about staying at the flat again. He wouldn't be back that night, so she would have the place to herself. She planned to call Chrissy and bring her up to date but decided not to mention the threatening letter that MacFarlane had allowed her to photocopy, against his better judgement.

At Greg's, she poured herself a glass of wine and ran a bath. She would have to seek out MacRae and persuade him to come back on the case, she decided. MacFarlane had been loyal enough not to confess how worried he was. MacRae might be the only hope of outmanoeuvring the arsonist before he struck again. Lying in the bath, Rhona reread the photocopied letter.

The contents showed a strong link between fire and sexual excitement. The author also hated women. Karen's genitalia had been burned before the fire started. The arsonist had moved on. Setting a building alight was no longer enough.

This was why MacRae hadn't wanted her around, she thought. Why he'd tried to get rid of her at their first meeting. Why he'd got MacFarlane to recall her to Glasgow.

She examined the text of the letter again. The words were all lower case except for an occasional capital letter. She wrote the letters in a sequence along the bottom of the page. They didn't make a word, but they did look familiar.

After she'd dried and dressed, she pulled out her laptop and opened the anonymous email. The letters were in a different order, but they were the same. I C H B U N R T E B T H. The more she stared at the characters, the more she realised it couldn't be a coincidence. She began by isolating the three vowels. She would assume there were at least two words, maybe three, each with a vowel. She made up 'burn', then concentrated on the other letters. Once she separated the word 'the', it was easy. BURN THE BITCH. The person sending the emails was the person writing the letters.

The sharpness of the buzzer interrupted her. The male voice on the intercom was a mixture of belligerence and apology. 'I have to talk to you about Mac-Rae.'

'You'd better come up.'

He stood in the hall taking in the polished French tiles, the glistening glass chandelier, the deep rug. Rhona wanted to tell him she felt the same when she saw Greg's flat for the first time, that her flat was a mess of cat hair and forensic journals. Instead she pointed the way through to the even more palatial sitting room.

The jacket that passed her was damp across the shoulders and the dark ponytail glistened with rain.

'Can I get you a coffee? Warm you up?'

She thought he was about to refuse then he relaxed and nodded, rubbing his hands together in front of the fire.

'Yeah. That would be great.'

When she came back from putting the kettle on, he was sitting on the couch with the dog sprawled at his feet.

'Some place.'

She smiled. 'Yes, but unfortunately not mine.'

'Oh.' He looked perturbed. 'I thought . . .'

'I live in Glasgow,' she explained. 'This is a friend's flat. He lets me stay when I come through.'

'Good friend.'

'Yes, he is.'

Rhona went back to the kitchen to make the coffee. Through the open door she observed his profile, almost feminine with the ponytail hanging over his shoulder. Rhona wondered if she had been wise to let him in, especially when Greg wasn't here. There were a lot of things lying about the place, things that could be slipped into his pocket, sold later for drugs or drink. Rhona chided herself as she poured the coffee. Just because Jaz was homeless didn't make him a criminal.

She brought through the coffee.

'The night after we talked about Karen, were you hanging about outside?'

Belligerence was back in his reply. 'I've been watching you and MacRae. I gave him a copy of this.'

He handed her a drawing. She examined it.

'This is very good.'

'I used to be an art student.' His voice was bitter. 'Before I screwed up.'

Rhona wanted to ask him what had gone wrong with his life, how he had ended up on the street. Instead she asked why the person in the drawing was important.

'I think he's Karen's murderer.'

'Why didn't you take the drawing to the police?'

His face darkened. 'Yeah, right.' He took the picture from her, stuffed it in his pocket and stood up.

'Thanks for the coffee.'

'Where are you going?'

'Not to the fuckin' police anyway.'

Rhona caught his arm. 'Don't leave yet. I'm sorry . . . I don't know your name?'

'Jaz,' he said relenting. 'My friends call me Jaz.'

'Well Jaz. I think it's time we talked properly, don't you?'

When Jaz left, Rhona went through to Greg's office, faxed the drawing to Chrissy and asked her to look through all the fire video footage they had. Some fire-raisers liked to watch the results of their exploits, so maybe there was a face in a crowd that fitted. She would check the Edinburgh footage herself.

Rhona sat down, suddenly tired. She knew she was only skirting the problem. At least when she had biological materials to work on she felt she was doing something constructive. The only person who seemed to have a handle on the arsonist was MacRae. And it seemed he had given up. She called DI MacFarlane and asked him for MacRae's address. He was silent for a moment. 'You're wasting your time. He's already made up his mind.'

'Then I'll have to change it for him.'

16

LOTHIAN ROAD WAS choked with traffic until she got
beyond Tollcross. MacFarlane had given her directions to MacRae's flat. Take a right at Tollcross and
head up the hill past Bruntsfield Links. Viewforth was
somewhere on the right. She missed the turning and
had to pull in and ask a *Big Issue* seller stationed outside
the Royal Bank of Scotland. He pointed her back the
way she'd come.

'Second on the left,' he informed her cheerily.

She bought a magazine in thanks.

MacRae's flat was on the top floor of the block. She
pressed the buzzer and waited. She was about to press
again when he answered gruffly.

'Yeah?'

'It's Rhona MacLeod. Can I come up?'

There was a heavy silence, then the stair door
opened. He was waiting at the door, towel round his
neck, hair wet. Behind him the room emitted a smell of
alcohol and shower gel.

'Sorry,' she said.

He looked her up and down. 'About what? My body?'

'I thought we'd got past that stage,' she shot back at
him.

'What stage?'

'The women-are-for-laying stage.'

'Never. Call me old-fashioned if you like.' He threw the towel to some hidden spot behind the door and waited, hands on hips.

'Can I come in?'

He stood back to let her past. 'Be my guest.'

He closed the door behind her.

'So, Dr Rhona MacLeod. What is it you want?'

'MacFarlane said you refused to help.'

'MacFarlane is right,' he said quietly.

The thought crossed Rhona's mind that she could walk away from this man, report her findings to Bill Wilson, take a few days off, visit Sean in Amsterdam. The scenario was an attractive one.

'We can help,' she said, determined.

His voice was low and angry. 'Take my advice, lady. Go back to Glasgow.' He reached for a T-shirt from the back of a chair.

'You never listen to anyone, do you?' she flung at him. 'No wonder your wife left you.'

He turned, his face furious.

'What did you say?'

Saying it once was stupid. Repeating it would be insane.

'I said, no wonder your wife left you.'

A nerve played the corner of his mouth. The scarring that crept over his shoulders looked blue. He was so close she could smell him. Soap and anger.

'For your information, Gillian left me because of this.'

He pointed to the scars.

'She didn't like to see it, or feel it. It reminded her of what I do.'

There was naked hurt in his eyes.

'Sean doesn't like what I do either.'

MacRae shrugged. 'Then we're two of a kind.'

'Except I don't give up.'

'You don't have a child.'

Rhona opened her mouth to tell him she did have a child, that she had tasted the same fear. Instead she said: 'MacFarlane said Gillian took Amy north.'

'As far away from me as possible.' He smiled grimly. 'Then she's safe.'

He turned away, dismissing her. 'I've told MacFarlane all I know.'

'Jaz gave you important information and you did nothing about it.'

He reached for a half-empty bottle of whisky and tipped some into a glass.

'I was busy.' He threw back the whisky.

'Then I'll have to deal with it alone.'

'Don't let me keep you.'

His door shut as she reached the bottom of the stairs. All the way down, she'd hoped he would call her back.

17

THE STREET WAS narrow, dipping down steeply and curving beneath the thoroughfare above. Edinburgh had a multitude of streets like this. Roads under roads. Layers of houses whose basements sat lightly on the past. Dig in your basement in the Old Town and you were likely to find a cobbled street, or the remnants of a medieval sewer. Ghost tour companies thrived on the warren of pathways and hovels that lurked beneath their more modern counterparts.

Rhona reached the address on the drawing and parked outside on a double yellow line. MacFarlane should be there within ten minutes. After waiting twenty minutes she locked the car, ran through the rain and ducked into the low entrance-way, hoping the squat door would be open. She was in luck. Someone had wedged it tight against the frame with a piece of wood, but it wasn't hard to free it and push her way in.

The building was in semi-darkness, the air musty. Rhona ran her hand along the wall, searching for a light switch. It gave a reassuring click but nothing happened. Whatever Mary Queen of Scots was using for light, it wasn't electricity. In front of her, a set of steps were splashed with green light from an overhead grating. She counted six before they twisted out of sight.

She had reached the bottom of the stairs when she heard the muffled sound of footsteps above her.

Instinct told her it wasn't MacFarlane.

The green light was cut off as a figure began its descent. Rhona pressed herself behind the curve of the staircase. Whoever was coming down would sense her soon, if he hadn't already. This room was larger than the one upstairs, although lower in height. There was nowhere to hide.

When he lunged at her Rhona was ready. Already lower than him, she brought her knee up as hard as she could, catching him full between the legs. He doubled up, swearing obscenely. Rhona launched herself upwards but a hand gripped her ankle, bringing her down heavily on the stone steps. Now it was her turn to swear.

'Rhona?' MacRae was lying on his side, knees to chin, his face as green as the stairwell light.

'What the hell are you doing here?'

'You asked me here, remember?' he choked.

'I didn't ask you to attack me.'

'Why didn't you call out?' He was dragging himself onto his knees, his expression curdling from agony to anger.

'Why didn't you?' she threw back.

'Christ, woman!'

'Don't "Christ, woman" me! I was here doing the job you refused to do, remember?'

'Move over,' he groaned, pulling himself onto the

step beside her, cradling his crotch. 'I've heard of ball breakers, but you take the prize.'

She caught his eye and started to laugh.

'No,' he pleaded painfully.

She waited while he regained his composure.

'What do we do now?'

'We wait for MacFarlane,' he said.

Without torches a search in the squat was useless. They had abandoned the attempt and were now sitting in the Saab. MacRae reached over and opened the glove compartment.

'You're not looking for a drink?'

'Too right I am.' MacRae extracted a can of Irn-Bru, opened it and drank it in a oner.

'What did you think of the letters?' he said.

'I'm pretty sure four are from the same person. I'm not a handwriting expert, but the tone and style are the same, plus the sexual innuendo. Your report to Mac-Farlane said the last four major fires have been deliberately started, probably by the same man?'

MacRae stared out of the window. There was no rain now, just a biting cold wind that seeped through the joints of the old Saab.

He nodded. 'A letter for every major fire.'

'Plus the warning to MacFarlane suggesting the next fire will be tonight,' Rhona paused, 'and the latest letter threatening you . . . and me.'

'MacFarlane showed you that?'

She nodded.

'Well I hope you like shit, because it looks like we're in it.'

'Deeper than you think.' Rhona handed him the photocopy. 'The capital letters make up the phrase at the bottom.'

'So what?' he shrugged. 'This is a nutcase. He likes to hide insults inside his other insults.'

'He likes to email them too.'

His careless tone had gone. 'The wanker's been emailing you?'

''I've had three anonymous emails, sent to the lab. They were just a string of jumbled capital letters. These letters.'

'And?'

'I didn't try to work out what they said . . . until this.'

'Is there anyone who might have it in for you?'

'I've testified in court lots of times. My evidence often helps the prosecution case.'

'But anything to do with fire?' he insisted.

Rhona shook her head. 'Sex crimes, murder . . .'

MacRae had slipped into thought. 'These emails . . . they started before you came to work with me?' They must have started about the same time as the Glasgow fires. She told him so.

MacRae looked puzzled. 'The city centre fires are different from the house fires,' he said. 'The house fires were lit to cover up something.'

'What?'

'You're the forensic expert.'

'The pathologist thought the dead girl in the Princes Street fire might have been raped.

'That doesn't fit.' MacRae shook his head. 'Fire's the sexual turn-on.'

'So?'

'The girl was in the wrong place at the wrong time. Somebody got to her first. If she was raped, you've got two crimes to solve.'

'Thanks very much.'

'Me, I'm only interested in this one.'

'We had no luck matching the DNA profile from the letter to the database.'

'The world and his brother know about DNA. When he sent that letter he was effectively saying, Fuck you! He knew we would try to match him and he knew we couldn't because he has no record.'

They had nothing on him. Nothing but his threats.

'Who is he?' she said.

MacRae was silent for a moment. 'He's fascinated by fire to the point that he shuts out everything else. It's a powerful act of creation. He wants it to go on growing. We kill it. So next time he has to make it bigger and more powerful. One we can't destroy.'

Silence settled over them. Outside, the wind moaned.

'How did you burn your back?'

MacRae didn't look surprised by her change of tack, as if he'd been expecting the question.

'I was seventeen. There was a deserted warehouse where me and my mates hung out. We would light a fire and sit round talking. Then one night I got lucky. This girl came with us. She and I left the fire and went into the shadows. That was when the explosion came. My pal Mikey was killed, his face blown away. The other two boys were badly burned. The girl was shielded by me.'

'What caused the explosion?'

'We had built our fire over an old chemical tank. The concrete floor expanded and had nowhere to go. It shattered, throwing lumps round us. The tank underneath was cracked. Whoosh!' He made a face. 'The most memorable sex I ever had.' He smiled cynically. 'So you see, he could be me.'

'MacFarlane was right. You do know him.'

'Not well enough.'

She was silent for a moment.

'Maybe we're wrong. Maybe the fires were lit for other reasons. Fraud, insurance? Maybe the letters are just a wind-up.'

'MacFarlane's found no evidence of fraud. We've had a letter for every fire,' he said. 'Either the letter-writer's lighting the fires, or he knows who is.'

'I wonder . . .' she said.

'What?'

'This person knows fire like you,' she hesitated. 'Could he be a fireman?'

'We've checked out all current personnel.'

'Okay. What about someone who used to be in the Brigade? Someone with a grudge against you.'

He shook his head.

'A long shot, but I'll think about it.'

They lapsed into silence until MacFarlane arrived five minutes later and they joined him in Queen Mary's *pied à terre*. MacFarlane gasped on his first deep breath inside the door. 'I hope the hospital authorities gave the Queen a bath. It smells like shit in here.'

He shouted for a light and a constable arrived with three heavy-duty torches. The trio of beams swept the desolate scene.

'Get your men to look for anything inflammable. Petrol cans, anything like that.' MacRae nodded at Rhona. 'Come on.'

At the bottom of the steps, torchlight revealed the room they had fought in, followed by a long, unevenly floored passageway with openings on either side.

Rhona sniffed. 'Can you smell methane?'

MacRae turned his torch on the roof. 'We must be near the main sewer. It runs the length of Princes Street.'

'Would that give someone access to all the buildings?'

'No, but it has benching either side, so you can walk through it. The Brigade uses it for training in sewer rescues. Pipes go up the buildings and vent onto their roofs to avoid a build-up of methane down here. Dangerous stuff.'

Rhona didn't need reminding. Methane's smell wasn't its only undesirable quality. Rhona was struggling to make sense of Jaz's suspicions. 'Why would the guy who attacked Mary want access to here?'

'Who said he did? Maybe he set Mary's hair alight because she smelt bad. We have no proof that he has anything to do with the fires at all.'

'But he wanted her out of the building. Jaz said so.'

'Jaz told us what Mary told him. Mary's an alkie.

Hallucination is her middle name. She thinks she's Mary Queen of Scots, for God's sake!' MacRae ended irritably.

What MacRae said was true. There was nothing down here but a bad smell.

Rhona left MacRae running his torch round the walls of the room while she headed down the narrow passage, flashing her torch into each opening. The floor was treacherously uneven. She caught her toe on a jagged edge of stone and only broke her fall by grabbing at the wall. Despite the light from the torch, her progress was slow. The rooms on either side varied in size. Some were little more than a hole in the wall, some opened onto larger areas. All were empty.

'Rhona?'

'Down here.'

MacRae's shadow advanced before him, thick and black. Rhona felt grateful for his presence.

'How far to the end?' he called in exasperation.

'About five yards. Then it peters out in a brick wall. Probably the foundations of a building.'

'So there's nothing?' MacRae was as disappointed as she was. His torch swept round the corner and onto her face.

'Watch it!' Rhona shouted, knowing it was too late. MacRae's strides were at least one-and-a-half hers. She had missed the hole, just off-centre in the passageway. MacRae didn't. He cursed as the torch hit the floor and went out.

'Thanks for the warning!'

'Are you okay?'

'Apart from the broken leg, you mean?'

'It can't be that bad.'

'How the hell would you know?' He removed his leg from the hole and stuck his head down instead. 'Hold on,' he said, 'I've found the source of the smell.'

When MacFarlane appeared minutes later he found them both on their knees.

'This hole opens into the main sewer,' MacRae informed him. 'Somebody's taken off the cover. Look, there it is against the wall. MacFarlane, check with Scottish Water. See if anyone's been down here recently.'

MacFarlane nodded. 'Where are you going?'

MacRae was already poised over the hole.

'To take a look.'

'Let's get a Scottish Water engineer down here first.' MacFarlane looked worried.

MacRae ignored him and handed Rhona his torch. 'I'll give you a shout when I'm down.'

He dropped through the hole.

Rhona held the torch above the hole hoping he could make it out in the darkness, then dropped it.

'I'm going to walk along a bit,' he shouted up. 'I won't be long.'

MacFarlane tried his mobile. 'I'll have to go up. I can't get a signal here.' Rhona waited until he was out of sight then climbed down the manhole after MacRae.

Fifteen metal rungs down, and her feet were on solid ground. To her right, dark water flowed through a brick tunnel. They should have waited for breathing apparatus, but she, like MacRae, was too impatient. She breathed in. Her throat was clear, her eyes didn't sting. There was methane, but at a manageable level.

MacRae's footsteps suggested he had gone to the left. Rhona swung her torch and headed in the opposite direction.

Not far along, another channel met the main sewer. She started to follow it. The roof here was lower and she had to keep her head well down, sweeping her torch in a wide arc in front of her, trying to ignore the excited squeaks of disturbed rats. Ten yards further, just as she was on the point of turning back, she spotted a series of long, thin blue lines on the curved brick wall.

Rhona dropped to her knees for a closer look.

Rhona reached up and caught MacRae's helping hand out of the manhole. MacFarlane was back. He looked relieved as she emerged. 'You shouldn't have gone down there without breathing apparatus,' Sev told her, for the benefit of MacFarlane.

'You did.'

He shrugged. 'Find anything interesting?'

'Something was dragged along one of the side sewers that run down to the Nor Loch,' she told him. 'I found fresh paint scrapings on the wall.'

MacRae looked thoughtful.

'Scottish Water don't know about this opening. It's not on their plan,'

MacFarlane said. 'I think we should find out what's been dragged along there,'

Rhona insisted. MacFarlane looked puzzled.

'What's so special about a scrape of paint?' Rhona looked at MacRae to see if he was thinking the same as her. He was.

'It's not the paint,' she told MacFarlane. 'It's where it came from.'

18

THE TRAIN WASN'T busy. Jaz would normally have hidden in the toilet and saved himself the fare, but with all the terrorist threats you had to have a ticket. It felt good to travel legally. He could sit and watch the countryside go by instead of keeping an eye out for an inspector.

Funding the train fare wasn't his only problem. He would have to work overtime next week to pay the rent. Finding Karen's killer was proving expensive, what with feeding Emps and the time he was spending off the job. But he didn't care. Karen should never have died.

Scotland threw itself past the window in a flurry of rain and the odd beautiful moment when the clouds parted and the sun shone through. They had passed the Highland boundary fault line and the hills rose, steeply wooded, on either side of the track.

Going north had been a split-second decision. He'd seen MacRae saying goodbye to his wife and kid in the station and jumped the train. He'd been thinking of bailing out of Edinburgh for a while anyway. Poking his nose into the attack on Mary had brought him too much interest from some quarters.

Jaz pressed his face to the glass. The warmer air in the compartment had steamed up the window. He wiped a patch and stared through, following the skyline. Mist hung in tendrils among the sharp pine trees. Jaz found himself remembering some of his favourite landscape paintings, the images that had set him on course to Art College in the first place. Soon, he promised himself, he would paint again.

He'd got on the train two carriages back from MacRae's wife and kid, then walked through. As he passed them the wee girl had reached out to pat the dog, but her mother pulled her back, telling her sharply that not all dogs were friendly.

'Your mum's right,' Jaz said. 'But this one is. Look.' He made Emps offer a paw and the girl had shaken it in delight. MacRae's wife had softened then and let her stroke the big head.

'My gran's got a dog called Bess,' she confided in him. 'We're going to see her.'

'That's nice,' he smiled back.

He'd considered sitting down next to them then thought better of it.

'I'd better keep going,' he said. 'Say goodbye, Emps.'

'Emps. That's a good name.'

He told her it was short for Emperor, then with an attempt at a smile at her mother he moved on.

Settled in the next carriage, he went over the other occupants of the train in his head. Most of the voices were Scottish although he'd spotted an American couple near the back of his carriage. There was no one suspicious-looking. No one except himself.

When he spotted Mrs MacRae gathering her luggage, Jaz got up and headed for the door. The American couple were already there, bags piled up in front of them.

Jaz accepted their offer of a ride to the village, in the hope that both the car that picked Amy up and the taxi would head in the same direction. They did. He was only minutes into a conversation about the beauties of Scotland, rain and all, when the car in front took a left turn. Jaz asked his hosts to let him off fifty yards further along.

'But there's nothing here,' the woman said looking round.

Jaz gestured in the direction of a distant barn.

'I can take a shortcut across the fields,' he explained. 'Give Emperor some exercise.'

It had been too easy finding them, Jaz told himself as he eased into position in the wet undergrowth within sight of the cottage. If he could find them, anyone could.

MacRae's wife appeared at the door of the cottage an hour later followed by another woman, obviously her mother. They had a short conversation which Jaz strained to catch. Whatever they were saying they didn't want the wee girl to hear. Then the two of them headed for the car parked in the drive and Jaz caught their final exchange.

'You'll have to go back some time, you know.'

MacRae's wife didn't look convinced.

'You can't keep them apart. Whatever Sev is, he loves his daughter.'

'I'm aware of that,' came the sharp reply. 'Can we change the subject?'

'I'll be back by teatime. You'll be alright here on your own?'

The response was short and tinged with suppressed fear.

'Of course.'

The old woman patted her daughter's arm. 'Keep Bess in the garden if Amy's out. She'll look after her.'

MacRae's wife tried a laugh. 'You're beginning to sound as paranoid as me,' she said.

Jaz shifted himself, easing the cramp in his right calf. The sodden shoulders of his parka were clamped to his skin like a neck brace. The rain was off for the moment and sunshine tentatively broke the pattern of grey. If Emps had been here he wouldn't have been so cold. Karen was right. Emps kept you warm.

The door opened and the wee girl came running out onto the grass. Behind her padded a big golden labrador. Jaz was glad he'd had the sense to leave Emps in the barn. All he needed was two dogs sniffing one another out.

The labrador paced the lawn. If it caught his scent, it made no move to come towards him, choosing instead to stay close to the girl. She was scuffling around under a big pine tree, at last securing what she was looking for. She threw the stick and it whizzed towards Jaz, landing three feet in front of his hiding place. He held his breath and lay perfectly still, planning what he would say when the dog discovered him.

The rheumy eyes found the stick and the greying muzzle sniffed at it. After what seemed a lifetime the dog lifted the stick and headed back. Jaz hoped that would be the end of it, but no. The stick came whizzing back. It flew over the fence to his left. Bess was making a valiant effort this time, running as fast as her fat stomach would allow. She stuck her nose through the fence and whined at the irretrievable stick.

'Bess!'

The white socks with the pink trim were on their way. He would give her another metre then stand up. Better to pretend he was looking for his dog than be caught lying in the undergrowth.

'Amy! Where are you?'

The socks stopped. The child reached down. Jaz caught a glimpse of dark hair as she selected a different stick. He could have sworn their eyes met, then she was up.

'I'm coming.'

'I told you not to leave the garden.'

Amy was indignant. 'I didn't leave the garden. I threw the stick as far as the fence. Bess couldn't find it. I had to get another one.'

The woman made an effort to sound normal.

'Granny'll be home soon. Come in and help me set the table for tea.'

Jaz watched as the door shut behind them.

Darkness was gathering. From the kitchen window, his shadow would be one of many. Jaz eased himself up and stood for a minute, letting the blood run into his cramped limbs. The smell of wood smoke from the cottage was making him think of food. He ignored the empty feeling in his stomach and tried to work out what to do.

The occupants of the cottage weren't planning on going anywhere tonight. He could take a chance and go and get Emps from the barn.

The barn was silent as he approached but as soon as he drew close he heard a low growl, which soon transformed into a welcoming whine. When he opened the barn door, Emps nearly knocked him over in his delight.

Inside it was warm and dry. Bales of hay, stacked at the back, emitted the smell of summer. Emps pranced about, pieces of straw flying from his coat.

'Good sleep, eh Emps?'

The dog licked his hand. It would be hard to leave the barn, but he had no choice. He'd already decided on their resting place for the night. The garage at the cottage might not have the warmth of the barn, but it would do.

Emperor bounded out the door ahead of him.

'Wait, Emps.'

There was a yelp, then silence. Jaz ran outside. The dog was nowhere to be seen.

'Emps! Come here, boy.'

There was a sudden movement behind him. Jaz swung round just as something hard and heavy smashed down on his head. He groaned, pain screaming through him.

The second blow hit him. With a soft grunt, Jaz slipped to the ground, unconscious.

19

THEY HAD ADJOURNED to MacRae's office. Rhona was surprised by its relative cleanliness, then remembered he had spent the last twenty-four hours holed up at home.

'With a bit of luck the rain will keep the punters away tonight,' MacRae suggested hopefully.

MacFarlane shook his head. 'The Met says to expect a clear night for the *Night Afore Fiesta*.'

'Just our luck.'

The sewer plan was spread on the desk; detailed entrances and underground walkways for sewer maintenance, a city beneath a city.

"We need to get a list of all those who have access to this information,' Rhona suggested.

MacFarlane nodded. 'We're doing that.'

Rhona looked at them both. 'It's a lot of time and man hours for a vague threat and a gut feeling.'

'The message from above is to take reasonable precautions. Nothing else.' MacFarlane looked apologetic.

Rhona could imagine the City Fathers' response. Edinburgh was set to make a lot of money from the next few days. The last thing they would want was the threat of arson keeping the crowds away. She felt sorry for MacFarlane. A hunch wasn't currency in this regime of balance sheets.

'The traffic stops at 5.30,' MacFarlane went on. 'We can do a full security check of the street before we let the crowds in.'

'And the sewer?' Rhona asked.

'Scottish Water's responsibility.'

'It would be difficult for an arsonist to get something set up while the shops are still trading,' MacRae said.

'Unless he has access to a basement,' Rhona reminded him.

MacFarlane was looking more worried by the minute. Clearing and searching Princes Street would be a major exercise, requiring time and manpower, neither of which he had. It would also attract interest. He voiced what they were all thinking.

'Maybe you were right.' He looked at MacRae. 'Maybe he wants us to concentrate on the Hogmanay celebrations while he goes elsewhere.'

MacRae looked grim. 'Well, we're about to find out.'

Rhona pressed the lab number. She would have to get back to Glasgow soon. It didn't take the numerous messages on her voice-mail from Chrissy to remind her where her real job was. Besides, officially Edinburgh didn't want her services. Bill Wilson had made that clear. She was here by her own choice.

'Dr MacLeod. I thought you were dead.'

'Thanks very much.'

'In fact, we were about to appoint a new Head of Department,' Chrissy went on.

'I get the point.'

'No you don't.' Chrissy's voice was serious. 'There's a murder case here you're supposed to be working on.'

'They've decided it was murder?'

'There were sufficient traces of thallium in the victim's body to cause death.'

'I take it you're to be the new Head of Department?' Rhona said laughing.

'Of course. Seriously though, when are you coming back?'

'Tomorrow,' Rhona said. 'Whatever happens.'

'Sounds ominous.'

'Tell Bill I asked Dr MacKenzie to look for thallium in the latest Edinburgh body. Find out if any traces were found.'

She rang off, promising to be back as soon as possible. Chrissy replied with a cynical 'Yeah'.

Neither man looked round when Rhona re-entered the room. 'There's nothing down there, Sev,' MacFarlane was saying. 'You checked the sewer yourself.'

'If you're going back down I want to go with you,' Rhona interrupted MacRae's glare.

'There's no need,' MacFarlane was firm. 'Scottish Water are checking.' He concentrated on MacRae. 'Go home for a while. Phone your kid.'

MacRae glanced at Rhona.

She pulled a face. 'We could both do with a shower.'

'Okay.' He seemed resigned. 'I'll see you back here in an hour.'

The call came through on MacFarlane's mobile as

she was about to leave. Rhona watched MacFarlane's face register puzzlement then concern. He waved her back from the door.

'That was Chemistry. They think the paint flakes were . . .'

She interrupted him. 'From a canister.'

His face was drawn. 'Of the type normally used for propane.'

Rhona tried to sound positive. 'Maybe it belonged to Scottish Water.'

MacFarlane wanted to believe her. 'I'll check.'

'Assuming nothing happens tonight, I'll have to show face in Glasgow tomorrow,' she told him.

'I understand.'

Traffic was thick round the sealed-off city centre. It took Rhona twenty minutes to get to Greg's flat. It was empty, although there were signs that Greg had come and gone. He'd opened a bottle of red wine and drunk half of it with a quick meal. Rhona had no qualms about pouring a glass to take into the shower.

She stripped off and dropped her clothes in a heap in the corner, stepped under the cascading water and began going over the list of events in her head.

Thallium poisoning in the Glasgow victim coupled with the fact that he had been tortured suggested a drugs war of some kind. If she was right and the Edinburgh victim had been crucified and then set alight, they only needed thallium to be detected in his system to link the two deaths. Neither death could yet be linked to the torched commercial property in Edinburgh, but instinct told her they were. She just didn't know how . . . yet. As for the threats to herself and MacRae . . .

Rhona turned off the shower and stepped out, the jigsaw incomplete.

When the front door opened she thought it was Greg coming back. She called 'Hi' from the kitchen and finished stuffing the dirty clothes into the washer-dryer. When she emerged, someone else stood in the hall.

20

JAZ OPENED HIS eyes. His head was throbbing so hard he couldn't think and his hands were pinioned at a 90 degree angle to the wall. The wire wound round his wrists was threatening to slice through his flesh like a cheese cutter. Jaz adjusted his stance in a vain effort to take the weight off his arms and tried to remember what had happened.

They'd been leaving the barn. He'd heard Emps yelp and he'd run outside, but the dog wasn't there. Then some bastard had hit him over the head.

He caught the smell of cigarette smoke as a figure emerged from the shadows; a man with hair cropped to the skull.

'Tommy!'

'Long time no see.'

Jaz couldn't believe his eyes. He hadn't seen Tommy since prison.

'What the fuck are you doing here?' Jaz said.

'Could say the same to you.' Tommy came closer as if to inspect his handiwork.

'Gonnae untie me, Tommy?' Tommy wasn't re-nowned for having a soft heart but it was worth a try. 'My shoulders are killing me.'

Tommy's smile would have curdled milk.

'Can't do that, mate. Not before you tell me what you're doing here. Orders, you know.'

Tommy Moffat had been thrown out of the army for not obeying orders. Doing what someone else told him was anathema to him. Jaz had spent two years with people like Tommy. It frightened him now to remember it. Even when his own brain was scrambled, the way Tommy treated folk had scared the hell out of him.

'You've been pissing off a few folk, Jaz.'

Tommy was sauntering round him, wearing the same vicious, sardonic look Jaz remembered only too well.

'Look, Tommy . . .'

'I heard you were working your passage back to Art College.'

'I am.'

Tommy was pulling something from his hip pocket. Jaz instinctively pressed himself against the wall but it wasn't a knife that emerged. It was a hammer.

'That's a pity,' Tommy fished in the other pocket. 'I havnae heard of a painter with nae hands.'

Jaz didn't have time to scream. The three-inch nail was through his right hand and into the barn wall with one hard blow. The second blow brought vomit to his mouth. Tommy lightly sidestepped the projectile.

'Now, a man with one good hand might still be able to paint.' Tommy kicked some straw over the offending mess. 'So, Jaz, want to keep one good hand?'

Jaz would have raised his head if he could. As it was

all his strength was in his body, lifting its weight off his arm and the crucified hand.

Tommy was selecting another nail. 'Now's the time to tell me why you're here, Jazzy boy.' He sighed. 'Otherwise it's byesy-bye to your painting career.'

'Jesus, Tommy.' The words escaped in a hiss of pain. 'Give us a chance.'

Tommy was looking at him, head on one side, enjoying himself.

'I'll tell you, right?'

He dragged a bale of hay nearer to Jaz.

'A wee warning, pal,' he said as he made himself comfortable. 'Make it good. I'm not here to listen to Jackanory.'

Jaz twisted his head round to look at his one good hand. Tommy was getting careless. Concentrating too much on his sadistic pleasures. The wire was looser now. Jaz worked on the wrist, turning it backwards and forwards. Every turn brought a stab of fire to his other hand. A dozen twists and his hand slid out. Letting his arm fall to his side was almost worse than holding it at ninety degrees to his body. Jaz buried his mouth in the collar of his parka. Now he had to pull the nail out.

Jaz sank to the ground and curled in a ball, the damaged hand clutched to his chest. After a few minutes he realised he was moaning Mammy, Mammy, Mammy. It struck him as weird since his Mammy had never been there when he needed her. After a while the pain was bearable and he could stand up. He dropped the parka on the floor and pulled off his top. It was clean at least. He wrapped his bad hand in it and pulled the parka back on.

By rights he should go, hit the road, jump on the train and disappear until things had cooled. But he wasn't going to. Jaz had never thought of himself as brave. Sticking a needle in his arm was as brave as he had ever got. And Robbie. Jaz tried not to play back the scene in his head that Tommy had described so vividly. Robbie had got in the way and Tommy had removed him. Jaz was getting in the way and Tommy was warning him. Jaz was the lucky one, but to convince Tommy he wasn't up north to spy on him, he'd had to say something about Amy.

The moon was a sliver of cream in a starred sky. Jaz tucked his bleeding hand under his left arm and headed for the cottage.

The wind felt like ice against his face. He used his teeth and his good hand to pull in the cord at the neck of the parka. He circled the garden. If Tommy jumped him now, he wouldn't stand a chance. A hammer wasn't Tommy's usual weapon. He usually preferred to pierce with something other than a nail.

The cottage sat in silence, the curtains drawn. Now he was here, Jaz had no idea what to do. If only Emps was with him. Tears sprung to his eyes. He didn't want to think what might have happened to the dog.

He made for the garage. Keeping low crossing the back garden, eyes on the light from the windows, he literally fell over the dog's dead body.

Bess lay on her side, eyes open, teeth bared in a

death-like grimace. Her head was pulled up and back, the red mark of Tommy's handiwork dividing her neck in two. Jaz slumped beside the warm body, knowing Tommy must have been here only minutes before. Then he noticed that the back door of the cottage stood open, light spilling out onto the grass.

21

'WHERE THE FUCK is she?'

'We talked about the paint then she left,' MacFarlane shouted back. 'She said she'd be here in an hour.'

Sev knew shouting at MacFarlane wasn't going to produce Rhona, but it made him feel better.

'Have you tried the friend's flat? Her mobile?'

'Yes and yes. The mobile's switched to the answering service.' MacFarlane shrugged his shoulders. 'Give her time. If she's having something to eat . . .'

Sev forced his attention back to the plan. 'She thinks there might be propane down there?'

'But where?' MacFarlane said. 'We've searched the length of the sewer. How could we miss gas canisters?'

'The channels that link the Princes Street sewer with the Nor Loch sewer, have they all been checked?'

'We can't check every drain in a couple of hours.' MacFarlane's voice was weary.

'This one meets the Princes Street sewer near where Rhona found the paint samples,' Sev stabbed at the paper, 'I'm going to take a look.' For once MacFarlane didn't argue.

The number of people swarming around the city

centre made Sev nervous. There were too many children. How can you arrange a family event, MacFarlane had said, then tell them not to bring the kids?

Sev looked up at the sky. Clear as a bell with a wee
thin moon. The Scottish weather had perversely
decided to go dry.

There were police about, some in uniform, some
not. MacFarlane had got an agreement to up the police
presence. That was all. If there had been a bomb alert,
they would have taken notice.

Sev headed for Mary's former squat. The punk with
the dog had been right about that connection. Come to
think of it, he hadn't seen Jaz since their meeting in the
pub. He made up his mind to ask MacFarlane if he was
still hanging around.

Mary Queen of Scots' palace had been cleared but it
still smelt bad. MacFarlane had organised a man from
Scottish Water to go down with Sev. He introduced
himself as Stewart and indicated a pile of gear for Sev
to put on; overalls, thigh waders, miner's head lamps
and breathing apparatus.

'Enough air for forty minutes,' he told Sev.

'I don't think . . .'

'Health and Safety,' the guy insisted.

Sev shut up and pulled on the gear. He'd trained
down here with the Brigade and knew the score.

Sev went first, waiting until Stewart reached the
bottom rung of the ladder before setting off along
the sewer. The sewer had been checked by sniffer
dogs but the variety of pungent smells that lingered
here would have put anyone or anything off the scent.

Fifty metres further on, Sev spotted the first of the connecting drains on the opposite wall. He waited for his companion to catch up, then jumped across.

He was exiting the last one when a series of bangs went off. Stewart threw himself against the wall.

MacFarlane buzzed his mobile.

'Sorry about the noise. A couple of silly buggers throwing bangers on the brazier outside the first aid tent.'

'It's good to know you're in control, MacFarlane.'

MacFarlane ignored the sarcasm. 'Any luck?'

'Nothing.'

'It's heaving up here, though why anyone wants to dance a Strip the Willow up and down George Street in the middle of winter defeats me.'

'I can hear a siren.'

'Not coming here,' MacFarlane assured him. 'There's a concert due to start in half an hour on the Ross bandstand. You coming up for the show?'

'Wouldn't miss it for the world. Any sign of Rhona?'

'Nope. I've sent a car round to check out the flat where she's staying.'

'And find out the home number of that assistant she's so pally with. Maybe she's spoken to her recently.'

Sev signalled to a relieved Stewart that they should go back up. There was nothing more they could do down here. The immediate vicinity of the Gardens was clear. MacFarlane had arranged a high police pre-

sence. There were men on the roofs and the Brigade
was on full alert.

When he reached the surface, Sev headed for a pub
on Rose Street, where the bartender poured his usual
without asking, while keeping one eye on the big screen
in the corner.

Sev downed the double whisky in a oner, enjoying
the kick. The one good thing about cutting down on
the drink, he decided, was enjoying its effect again. He
ordered another and had a look at what the rest of the
pub was watching.

The crowds for the *Afore Fiesta* event exceeded even
his expectations. A helicopter view was panning across
the Gardens and the length of Princes Street. The events
this year were designed to attract whole families. Sev was
glad Gillian had deserted him and gone north with Amy.
If she hadn't, Amy might have been out there now.

He pulled out his mobile and called his mother-in-
law. It rang four times then the ansaphone kicked in.
He resisted the temptation to curse into the mouth-
piece. Gillian would love that on her mother's ansaphone. Instead he left a message for Amy and rang off.
Wherever they were, they'd have to be back by Amy's
bedtime. He would call again later.

He concentrated on the big screen, watching the
crowd, looking for the face on the drawing. Every policeman out there had a copy of the sketch Jaz had done.

Sev ordered another drink. He went to throw it back
then decided to make it last. He had a long night ahead.

When the mobile drilled ten minutes later, he
thought it was Amy answering his message. It wasn't.

'Where the hell are you?' MacFarlane's voice was tense.

'Rose Street. Watching the telly.'

'I think you should get over here.'

22

THE WELL-DRESSED BLOND man looked embarrassed. Rhona told herself that intruders don't generally wear expensive Italian suits and stand in the hall looking mortified. The guy held out his hand.

'I'm sorry I startled you. Greg gave me a key.' He paused self consciously. 'We're seeing one another. He didn't tell you about me?'

'Of course he did.' Rhona assured him. 'You must be Justin.'

He looked relieved. 'Yes, I am.'

'Would you like to wait for Greg?'

He gave her a wide smile.

'Can I get you a coffee?'

'That would be great. Greg said he would be back about nine.'

When she came back with the coffee he'd settled himself on the settee. 'When Greg said you were staying, I must admit I was rather jealous.'

'I wouldn't worry about me,' she assured him. 'If there's one thing Greg's sure of it's his sexuality.'

He smiled. 'I hear you're a forensic scientist?'

'Yes.'

'Working on a case?'

'Always.'

Rhona wondered what age he was. Greg could certainly give him ten years. It was none of her business. Greg didn't mess in her sex life and she didn't mess in his. The secret of a long and happy friendship.

MacFarlane was in full flow when she reached the operations tent set up in the Gardens. It had taken half an hour to travel the short distance between Greg's flat and the end of Princes Street.

'Rhona!' MacRae grabbed her arm and led her in. 'We've been phoning everywhere for you.'

'Sorry.' Rhona was taken aback by MacRae's distracted appearance. 'I diverted my mobile while I was in the shower and Greg's ansaphone was on. What have I missed?'

MacFarlane pushed a piece of paper across the desk at her. MacRae was trying hard not to give her his own résumé as she read it. By the second paragraph she could see why. Right at the beginning, MacRae had planted the seed of doubt about Jaz. Everything on the paper suggested there were grounds for suspecting him.

'Well?'

She looked at MacRae. 'I don't believe it.'

'Why not?'

She hesitated, 'It doesn't feel right.'

'So speaks the true scientist,' MacRae pronounced.

MacFarlane took her side. 'Rhona's right. It's circumstantial.'

MacRae wasn't going to give up. 'He's been hanging about since the fire, sticking his nose in. He took the girl's dog, for God's sake. Psychological profiling of the arsonist suggests he will attempt to interject himself in the investigation because he feels safe enough to do so.'

MacRae took a breath before launching the next attack. 'Then you come up with the glad tidings that he served time with Robbie Stevens, the drug addict burned to death in the housing scheme arson attack. In fact they were cosier than that. They ended up inside together because they'd been running a nice little thieving business to feed their habits.'

'As far as we know Jaz has been clean since he got out,' MacFarlane said.

'Oh yeah? Then try this scenario for size. Jaz fancies the girl but she doesn't fancy him. He finds out where she's sleeping, rapes her then fires the place.'

'Okay,' MacFarlane came back, 'but you said the four fires in commercial property were lit by the same person.'

'It looks like it, but you can never be sure.' MacRae admitted grudgingly.

'You were sure,' Rhona said. 'And why link Jaz with Robbie Stevens' death? The arsonist is a professional. Why would he bother firing some poxy little flat in a housing scheme to get rid of a drug addict?'

MacRae glared at her. 'Maybe Jaz and Robbie were still working together. Maybe Robbie was messing him about. Maybe Jaz was working for someone else who wanted rid of Robbie. Who the fuck knows?'

Rhona was thinking back to her conversation with Jaz in the flat. The way he had sought her out, wanting her to put pressure on MacRae to get back on the case; wanting to find those responsible for Karen's death.

Why would he do that if he'd started the fire? Rhona didn't like thinking about the answer. Jaz could have given her a drawing of anyone, or of someone he didn't like. He could be diverting them from the real culprit . . . himself. But she had liked him. The dog trusted him.

'There's one way to find out if Jaz was involved,' she said.

'What?' MacRae came in.

'Bring him in, ask him to give a DNA sample. We can check it against the girl and the letter.'

They both looked at MacFarlane.

'There's one problem,' he said. 'Jaz and the dog have disappeared.'

'Since when?' MacRae asked.

'He was last seen on his pitch at Waverley Station yesterday morning,' MacFarlane said. 'The folk at the coffee bar and WH Smith's say he's regular as clockwork. He wasn't on his pitch today although a guard said he spotted him on the platform of a northbound train. We haven't been able to confirm that.'

'I saw Gillian and Amy off this morning,' MacRae said, looking worried.

The pieces were beginning to fit together, whether Rhona liked it or not. Jaz's preoccupation with getting MacRae back on the case. He'd been watching Gillian's house. He knew about the petrol bomb. It seemed so obvious. Jaz had tried to find out if she knew where Gillian and Amy were going. She had told him they were going north to stay with Amy's grandmother. They were going by train because Amy liked trains.

She'd spelt it out for him.

They were waiting for her to finish, MacRae's face already showing his worst fears had been confirmed.

'He's followed Gillian and Amy north,' she said.

23

THE BACK DOOR of the cottage swung open, exposing Jaz in a long streak of electric light. He pressed himself against the wall, his heart pounding.

The cottage was mocking in its silence. No long howl from Tommy, no sudden flash of steel at his face.

When he finally had the courage to go in, the hall was strangely welcoming, as if someone might emerge at any moment and say 'Hi'. In the kitchen three cups sat on the table, the teapot to hand. Beside the old-fashioned range Bess's basket lay waiting for her return.

Jaz trailed from room to room. They were all the same. Lived-in. Everything as it should be, except for the open front door and the blood-soaked body of the dead dog on the grass outside.

Jaz walked round the downstairs one more time then went back to the kitchen, lifted the blanket from Bess's basket and went outside.

He threw the blanket over Bess's body, silently cursing Tommy Moffat. The labrador was far too old to be a threat to anyone. She could bark, but that was about all. Which is probably why she died. Jaz had to stop himself picturing Emps lying somewhere be-

tween the cottage and the barn in exactly the same
state. Tommy Moffat was a heid-banger, a nasty,
twisted, creepy bastard. He would get him for this.

Jaz tucked his throbbing hand inside his coat and set
off to check the drive and the garage for the car. Both
were filled with nothing but shadows.

Where the fuck were they? Where was Tommy? Jaz
didn't have an answer. He decided that standing outside freezing wasn't making him think any better.

Back in the cottage, he filled the kettle and pulled it
over the hot ring to boil, then looked for the coffee. While
he clutched the cup and thawed out, he thought about
phoning the police. If they came and found the dead dog
and the open front door, they would look for the occupants. If the police got involved they'd find his fingerprints all over the house. They would come looking for
him. If Tommy had done something to the kid or the
women, suspicion would be bound to fall on him.

With any luck, Amy and her mum had gone out
before Tommy arrived. Tommy might have found the
place empty, got pissed off and killed the dog. Jaz was
warming to this version of events. Maybe Tommy
never came to the cottage in the first place. Maybe
someone else killed the dog. Jaz rinsed his cup at the
sink and put it back where he got it, his mind made up.

The phone in the hall had the call light flashing. He
pulled his cuff down to cover his finger and pressed the
play button. MacRae's voice was gruff and Jaz could
have sworn he heard a muffled curse before the message. MacRae wasn't pleased to find no one at home
and said he would call back later.

Jaz dialled 1471, wrote the number on the telephone pad, tore it off and stuck it in his pocket. He would look for Tommy first, then contact MacRae. Jaz wasn't sure who he was more frightened of Tommy Moffat, or MacRae when he found out his kid was missing.

Outside, the moon was filling the back garden with silver light. Jaz struggled over the fence, cursing as pain shot through his mangled right hand, and set off into the wood.

MacRae flung the phone on the desk. 'If that punk's gone anywhere near Amy, I'll kill him.'

'Hold on, Sev,' Rhona tried. 'Is there any reason why Amy and Gillian wouldn't be at the cottage? Could they have gone out somewhere?'

'Where, for Chrissake?'

'Visiting a neighbour?'

MacRae was making a concentrated effort not to shout at her.

'Amy talked about watching the Hogmanay celebrations.'

Rhona looked at him. 'Sky!'

'Gillian's mother doesn't have Sky.'

'So maybe they went somewhere that did?'

MacRae looked stricken. 'I don't know anyone up there. I don't know where to phone and find out.'

Rhona looked at MacFarlane and he nodded imperceptibly.

'We'll send a car to check the cottage,' he said to MacRae. 'Then we'll make some enquiries. It's a rural area. Probably everyone within a twenty-mile radius will know where Gillian and Amy are tonight.'

The café was half-empty. Rhona went to the counter and brought back two mugs of scaldingly hot tea. MacRae was sitting at the same table they'd used at their first meeting.

'Knew you'd want to be near the Ladies,' he said.

'After you drink this, you'll want to be near the Gents.'

They sat in silence. Rhona could hear the distant music, a fast reel that got faster by the minute. In a few minutes the dance would stop and the concert begin. Maybe MacRae had been right all along. Maybe it was a hoax and the Torch, as Sev had taken to calling him, never intended to target tonight or any other night in the celebrations. Maybe he just wanted them running around thinking he would.

A different kind of music was signalling the start of the concert. Different from the mad whirl of fiddle and bagpipe, this was a soaring sound. Hauntingly Celtic.

MacRae checked his mobile.

'MacFarlane will contact us as soon as he has word about Amy,' Rhona assured him.

'I think I'll head up there tomorrow.'

'Good idea.'

'Assuming all goes well tonight.'

'It will,' Rhona said with a certainty she wasn't sure she felt. 'I think you were right,' she answered the cynical look. 'I think he wanted to put the wind up us. That's all.'

'He succeeded.'

The ring of the mobile stopped whatever MacRae planned to say next. Rhona watched his relief as he listened to the message. He slipped the mobile back in his pocket.

'Gillian and Amy are at the hotel with the rest of the village, watching the concert on the big screen. Gillian says they're fine and she'll phone in the morning.'

He reached for the half bottle in his pocket and threw some into his tea. 'The local policeman says no one fitting Jaz's description has been seen in the village, but he'll keep a lookout.'

'Jaz isn't a killer.'

'Then where is he?' He wanted her to give him an explanation he could believe.

'Maybe he needed to disappear for a while. Maybe he was getting on someone's nerves, asking all those questions, poking his nose in,' she suggested. 'He may be involved in the drug fires, but I don't think he's the Torch.'

'Neither do I,' he conceded at last. 'It takes a special kind of hatred for that.'

An ugly thought struck Rhona.

'If there is some connection between him and Robbie Stevens . . .'. She met Sev's eye. Jaz was moving from being the villain to being the hunted in both their minds.

MacRae stood up. 'Fancy some fresh air?'

They cut up into George Street. The crowd had dispersed, the dance billed as 'the longest Strip the Willow in the world' was over. The big, old-fashioned clock that hung above the door of Ottakars showed eleven o'clock.

'I could walk you back to Greg's,' MacRae offered.

'Maybe we should hang around a bit longer?'

'MacFarlane will get in touch if we're needed.'

They walked in a comfortable silence. The air was sharp, the pavement sparkling with frost. The sound of the concert faded. They skirted Charlotte Square and went along Shandwick Place. Rhona wondered, not for the first time, what Severino MacRae would be like off the job. Then she wondered if he ever was off the job. He put the job before everything, like she did.

By the time they reached the flat, cars were filling the westbound carriageway with families heading home. Rhona could tell by the set of MacRae's shoulders he was relaxing. She felt the same. Above them Greg's windows were in darkness. She suddenly didn't want to walk into an empty flat. MacRae must have guessed what she was thinking.

'I could do with a coffee,' he said.

He was sitting with his back to her, watching the fire. Rhona sat the coffee on the table then on an impulse fetched the whisky decanter from the cabinet.

MacRae accepted the glass without comment and moved over so she could sit next to him on the sofa.

'One down. Two to go.' He lifted his glass.

'I don't think Greg'll be happy if we finish his whisky.'

'You know what I mean.' His voice softened.

He moved his face close to hers.

'We make a good team,' he said gently.

He watched her reaction, his eyes bright blue in the firelight. Time hung for a moment between them, then he ran his finger gently down her cheek.

'So what happens now?' he said.

The sound of the siren woke her. Rhona rolled over, searching for the light switch. The ambulance screamed past and the room dropped back into silence. She glanced at the clock. She hadn't heard Greg come in. For a moment she thought about visiting his room to check, then decided against it in case the boyfriend was curled up in bed beside him.

'Hey.' MacRae was standing at the door.

'Hey.'

'You couldn't point me in the direction of the shower?'

'Three doors down on the left,' she said.

'Thanks.' MacRae smiled wryly. 'And by the way, the couch was as comfortable as you said it would be.'

Turning him down had been harder than Rhona could ever have imagined. It was a classic scenario; those who get frightened together, end up in bed together. And she didn't want to go there.

He'd taken the rejection well. Maybe too well for her ego. When he reappeared she was in the kitchen, coffee at the ready. He sat opposite her and proceeded to take in the designer surroundings.

'Don't say a word,' she warned him.

'I wouldn't dream of it,' he answered sweetly. 'Where's the owner?'

'If he's not asleep next door then he's with his latest, who gave me a hell of a fright last night by appearing from nowhere. He's got a key, so it must be serious.'

They lapsed into silence, Rhona trying to keep her mind off what the morning might have been.

'So what happens now?' she said.

'We've had that conversation. You turned me down, remember?'

Rhona changed the subject. 'You said you were going north.'

MacRae's face darkened. 'I've decided against it. Gillian and I would only argue in front of Amy and I don't want that. Anyway, the Hogmanay celebrations aren't over yet.'

Two days still to go.

'I can hang around here if it helps?'

'Better get back to your own murder. Knowing the mean city there will be plenty of forensic work for you over the next couple of days.'

Glasgow at Hogmanay. A whole year's Friday and Saturday nights rolled into one. Sentimentality and violence walking hand in hand. A lethal combination.

They parted company at the door. MacRae didn't look back as he went down the stairs. He was trouble, in more ways than one.

It took an hour to pack and tidy up. She eventually knocked on Greg's bedroom door and glanced inside. The bed hadn't been slept in. He must have spent the night at Justin's. Rhona wondered if she should call him, then decided to leave a thank you note instead.

The journey back was uneventful. The clear cold skies clouded over as she neared Harthill, bringing thick sleet against the window.

A text message came in ten minutes later, making her heart skip a beat.

*Hillhead Underground 8? Lia*m

She texted back *Yes*.

24

THE MOTORBIKE WASN'T difficult to trace. The girl in the petrol station at the village was only too glad to talk about it. Jaz emerged with a can of Coke and a sandwich, some paracetamol, an invitation to a party and exactly what he wanted to know. The whereabouts of Tommy Moffat.

Tommy had arrived at the petrol station at about nine. Jaz imagined the girl's paroxysms of delight that someone with a cool motorbike was planning to spend Hogmanay in the village. He'd asked for somewhere to stay and she'd suggested her mum's Bed and Breakfast. Tommy had agreed and then asked her what he really wanted to know, where Skiach Lodge was. She had given him directions.

Jaz hadn't made quite the same impact. No motorbike and no cool gear, but she'd invited him to the party anyway. After all, tomorrow was Hogmanay.

Frost was forming on the road and now and then a sliver of frozen rain hit his face. Jaz passed a hotel bar loud with convivial voices. A kid pushed the door open and rushed outside, another kid following. They swung in a cold circle then dashed back in. Jaz almost followed them into the blast of warmth and good humour.

At the end of a string of houses, the road forked. Skiach Lodge was on the left hand fork.

As he passed the last street lamp, the way ahead grew murky. The pavement dwindled to a narrow track between the tar and the bordering trees. Jaz stumbled along, wondering if it was raining as hard in Edinburgh. MacRae would like that, he decided. It would put a damper on the whole proceedings. Jaz swung his thoughts away from MacRae and the woman forensic. He had his own job to do.

Skiach Lodge was well-hidden by trees, protected from the gaze of the casual passer-by. Jaz was over the wall and into the dense, wet undergrowth of wintering rhododendrons. He was soaked through and the bitter wind clawed at him. Whatever happened, he had to find shelter soon.

He made for the back entrance. A gate led through a high wall into ridges of frozen soil. Ahead, a kitchen window shone a welcome. Jaz kept hard against the wall and risked a look.

He had to admit the bastard looked at home. His feet were up on the fender, a can of lager at his mouth. Jaz wanted to crush the can down Tommy's throat. He clenched his teeth and listened.

Tommy was talking to somebody. Jaz couldn't see who it was but he knew it was female. Tommy was on his feet now, thrusting his tight-jeaned hips forward to show off the hard dick. The girl came into view. She was getting the message alright. She slipped between Tommy and the kitchen table. Tommy drained the last drop of his can and pulled down his zip.

Tommy was fully occupied. Jaz took the chance to get inside unnoticed.

He found himself in a narrow passageway. A door to the left lay ajar, revealing steps down to the basement. The sound of grunts and moans came from the kitchen. Jaz kept going down the passageway and found himself in a grand entrance hall with a sweeping staircase.

Behind him Tommy and his partner were reaching their climax. The girl must like living dangerously. On the last, long drawn out groan, a set of double doors on the opposite wall were pulled open. Jaz hid in the shadows as a man in a suit headed for the kitchen.

Tommy appeared minutes later, adjusting his zip, a smug grin on his face. There was a shouted greeting, then the double doors shut behind him. Jaz crept closer to listen.

By the time he left, Jaz was dry again. The basement steps had led to a boiler, on at full blast. He cleared a place behind it and settled down to dry out. After that he would check back at the cottage, see if Amy was back. Then he would look for Emps.

Judging by the conversation he'd tuned into, Tommy would soon be heading for the garage and his next shag. Just as well. With the information he'd overheard, Moffat had better get all the normal sex he could. Once Jaz made sure he was banged up inside, sex would take on a different hue.

The rain had stopped, and above him the sky was clear and midnight blue. Now that he had moonlight

Jaz found his way out of the grounds quickly. Five minutes along the main road he thought he heard a motorbike and threw himself into the ditch, soaking his feet again, but it was only a diesel van with a bad exhaust.

The hotel party had quietened down. There were only three vehicles left outside. Jaz took a chance and went in.

In the bar, Jaz ordered a pint and a hot pie and found a seat close to the fire. His injured hand was swollen and useless, and he had to rely on his teeth to open the paracetamol packet. He gulped down two tablets with his beer. He spotted Amy when she came out of the toilet behind her mum and turned away, relieved to see her unharmed but already thinking about what she would find when she got back to the cottage.

Jaz drained his pint and contemplated another. He had a look in his wallet. Not much chance of a Bed and Breakfast. He thought about asking if he could clear up the bar, wash all the glasses in exchange for bedding down beside the fire, but the barman didn't look the benevolent type. The last thing he wanted was to become an item for gossip. It would be better if Tommy thought he had left the area. Jaz shifted in the warm seat. Better hit the cold now before he got too comfortable.

He went to the bar and asked for another pie to take away. The barman put it in a bag for him along with the two remaining sausage rolls. He waved away payment and went back to the glasses. Jaz nodded his thanks and made for the door before he changed his mind and asked to stay.

Outside the cold was like a vice. Jaz pulled up his hood. Now that he knew Amy was alright, he would go straight to the barn. With any luck Emps would head back there looking for him . . . if he was alive. Jaz could only pray he was.

Even the piled hay in the barn couldn't keep the chill out of his bones. At dawn Jaz stood up and walked about, stamping the circulation back into his feet and throwing his good arm round his body. He would give it an hour, then try and hitch a lift back into town.

He fished the sausage rolls out of his pocket and wolfed them down, dreaming of a mug of hot tea.

The fields were covered with a layer of frost and an early sun was sending thin shivering rays across the empty furrows. Jaz suddenly remembered the significance of the day. Hogmanay. Tomorrow was a new year and a new start. Maybe for him, when he sorted things out. But not for Karen.

He heard the dog before he saw it; the sound of paws clipping the icy puddles that covered the churned mud round the barn. There was a strangled noise of excitement, then Emps was on him.

So there was a God, after all.

Jaz tried to hug the dog, but he yelped and leapt away.

'Whoa! What's up, Emps?'

The dog came back, twisting its back legs from side to side in a mockery of the missing tail.

Jaz gazed in horror at the mutilated and bleeding stump, while Emps licked the salty tears that ran down his face.

'I'll get him Emps. I promise. And when I get him I'll cut off his fuckin' dick and stick it down his fuckin' throat.'

25

BILL HAD BEEN true to his word. Rhona studied the contents of the forensic bags. If the body on the moor was that of the paedophile and murderer they'd been searching for for the last six months, it would lay her fears to rest. She could stop looking for him in the street, stop imagining she would wake up one night and find him standing at the foot of her bed.

Chrissy was watching her. 'I can deal with these,' she offered.

'I'd rather do it myself.'

Rhona pulled on her lab coat.

'But it's Hogmanay.'

'I'll be away by eight, I promise.'

Chrissy gave up. 'I've had a look at the fire video.'

'And?'

'The guy you talked about . . .'

'In the drawing?'

'No. Your fire investigator.'

'MacRae?' Rhona was puzzled.

'What does he look like?' Chrissy asked.

'He's about five eleven, dark hair, part Italian . . .'

'Does he wear a black leather jacket?' Chrissy asked.

'Yes, why?'

'Take a look at this.' Chrissy handed Rhona the remote.

He was standing on the edge of the crowd looking up. Rhona paused the video and stared. The resemblance was uncanny, but the video was of a Glasgow fire forty-six miles away from MacRae's territory.

'It can't be him,' Rhona said to convince herself.

'It looks like him then?'

Rhona nodded.

'Quite tasty.'

'He's badly scarred.' Rhona regretted the words as soon as they were out.

Chrissy looked interested. 'Really? Where?'

'Chrissy,' Rhona warned.

Chrissy raised her eyebrows.

'What makes you think it's not him?'

'He would have said if he'd been at the Glasgow fire.'

'Especially if he started it.'

'Don't be ridiculous.'

Chrissy ejected the video and replaced it with another and pressed rewind. She waited a moment then froze it.

'Take a look on the left.'

Rhona's heart missed a beat.

'Would you believe it?' Chrissy said. 'Old leather jacket's back again.'

The figure was further away from the camera this time making it more difficult to make out his features.

'I spotted him or someone who looks like him in three out of the last four.'

'There must be an explanation.'

'As to why MacRae keeps popping up in our fire videos?'

'It's not him,' Rhona was adamant. 'It's someone who looks like him, or,' she said with more certainty this time, 'someone who chooses to look like him.'

'Neat idea. A MacRae lookalike visiting fire scenes.'

'You didn't see anyone who looked like Jaz's drawing?'

Chrissy shook her head. 'What about the Edinburgh footage?'

Rhona went for her bag.

'That's funny.'

'What?'

'I put the video in the zipped pocket but now it's in the main part.'

'You took it out, watched it and put it back in a different pouch?' Chrissy suggested.

'I haven't had time to watch it.'

Rhona slipped in the Edinburgh footage. The fire that blazed on the screen was well established, already consuming the lower levels of the Princes Street building, spreading rapidly in a horizontal direction.

Since the building had been lying empty with few combustible linings and interior contents, the use of accelerants looked likely from observation alone, though the speed and action of the fire was not what Rhona was looking at.

She concentrated on the shots of the watching crowd. The perpetrator could often be standing within yards of the firefighters, watching them risk their lives dealing with their handiwork.

Rhona ran the footage four times.

'He's not there,' Chrissy said at last.

'No, he's not.'

The fire had started in the early hours of the morning when few people were about. The crowds were smaller than would be expected for such a spectacular blaze.

'The arsonist must have been disappointed by the turnout,' Rhona said. 'No wonder he threatened the New Year celebrations.'

'What?'

She explained about the letters, without mentioning her place in them.

Chrissy looked puzzled. 'You think the two spates of fire-raising are connected?'

'Yes. Though I have no real proof. I'm going to take a look through the most recent reports. There might be something I've missed.'

'Now?' Chrissy was incredulous. Four o'clock in the afternoon seemed a bad time to start wading through five detailed forensic reports. 'I take it Sean's not in town?'

'A gig in Amsterdam.'

'You should have stayed in Edinburgh with your tasty Italian,' was Chrissy's parting shot when she left at five.

Rhona hoped that was Chrissy's idea of a joke and she hadn't been reading her mind.

Rhona settled at her desk, resisting the temptation to try and get a hold of Bill Wilson and talk things through with him. If Bill had any sense he would be home with his family for Hogmanay. She selected one of the reports, thick with the minutiae of death, and set to work.

When her mobile alarm warned her it was quarter to eight, she had already trawled through three reports she had verified and signed some time in the last six months. The evidence suggested the fires had been started deliberately or were the result of extreme carelessness on the part of the victim, who was either a known or suspected member of the drug scene. There were no suspects for any of them.

She shelved the reports and locked up.

Outside, her breath met the air in a vaporised cloud. The security guard at the gate waved cheerio from the warmth of his box and shouted his good wishes for Hogmanay.

She decided to leave the car in the university car park. Hillhead underground station was only minutes away. To her left, the Gothic towers of the university loomed out of the darkness. The surrounding shrubbery was shrouded in shadow. The click of her footsteps on the frosty pavement seemed to echo her rapid heartbeat.

She was going to see her son for the first time in eighteen years. The tiny baby she had given up for adoption was a young man now. Would he look like her or Edward? What if he was like Edward in character? Then they might grow to hate one another. Rhona found herself slowing down. Maybe this wasn't a good idea after all.

Byres Road was busy, early revellers pouring in and out of the most popular bars.

A tall familiar figure stood outside the underground station, causing Rhona to stop in her tracks.

Three drunks wearing kilts and Scotland tops emerged, singing *Flower of Scotland* and she momentarily lost sight of him. Then he reappeared, threw her a half-smile and turned swiftly in at the underground entrance. A wave of revulsion swept over Rhona. It couldn't be him. He was dead. It was only a matter of time before it was confirmed. It had to be someone who looked like him. It was that horrible half-smile. That and her own private horror of ever seeing him again.

She pulled herself together. You can't see someone who's dead, she told herself. Not unless you believe in ghosts.

Her watch said ten past eight. The thought crept into her mind that Liam wasn't going to show. She waited for another twenty minutes then with a heavy heart sent a *Missed you. Please call* text message and went home.

Back in the empty flat she contemplated phoning Sean. She lifted the receiver then replaced it. If she spoke to him now he would know something was wrong and she couldn't bear to tell him that Liam hadn't turned up.

She wandered through the flat, talking to herself, hating the solitude she had once loved. Sharing her flat with Sean had destroyed her ability to be alone. She had never felt lonely in her home before him. Alone yes, lonely never.

She heard a noise and jumped, her nerves on edge, but it was only the cat come looking for food.

Once she'd fed it, she listened to the radio while making something for herself. Both Edinburgh and Glasgow were well into their New Year celebrations. Everything was going accordingly to plan. She imagined MacFarlane's relief . . . and Sev's.

'We make a good team,' he'd said.

The buzzer went at 11.30. She had switched on the television and poured a drink to toast the bells.

'Can I come up?'

Rhona pressed the door release and let him in, shocked by the pleasure that had rushed through her at the sound of his voice.

His eyes were heavily shadowed but there was no smell of alcohol on his breath. She led him through to the sitting room, saying nothing.

'All alone?'

She nodded.

'Where's the boyfriend?'

'Amsterdam.'

He was watching her face, reading the pain.

'What's up?' he said softly, intimately.

When she didn't answer, he took her in his arms and held her close.

'I hate fucking Hogmanay,' he said.

She breathed out against him. 'So do I.'

The phone rang in the hall.

'Leave it,' he told her.

26

BILL CALLED HER early to tell her about the car. Rhona listened, her head still stupid with sleep and too much whisky.

'I don't understand.'

'I tried to get you late last night, but you weren't answering. Chrissy came back to the lab to ask you to go for a drink. She saw your car go up in flames and thought you were in it. She tried to open the door.'

'My God! Is she alright?'

'Burned her hands but otherwise, yes, she's alright. She's in the Western Infirmary.'

'I'll get a taxi there right away. Oh, and Bill . . . where's my car?'

'They've taken it to the police garage. A team is checking it over.'

In the sitting-room the blanket and pillows she'd given Severino were folded at the end of the couch. An empty whisky bottle and two glasses stared reproachfully back at her from the table, a note beside them. He had gone for a walk to clear his head and would phone later.

Rhona was relieved not to have to face him.

The receptionist in Accident & Emergency directed

her to Ward Three. Chrissy was asleep when she went in. Rhona searched the pale face for burns. It was unmarked, but the hands . . .

'Oh Chrissy,' she whispered, distressed.

Chrissy opened her eyes.

'I thought you were asleep.'

'I have to pretend, or that Sister will take my temperature again.' She winced as she tried to pull herself up in bed.

'What's going on, Rhona?'

'I don't know.'

'If you ask me, someone's got it in for you.'

'It might have been an accident. We don't know yet.'

Chrissy wasn't convinced.

'Are you going to examine the car?'

Rhona nodded. 'I'm going there now.'

Chrissy was trying to get out of bed.

'Where do you think you're going?'

'With you.'

'Oh no you're not. You're staying here until they say you can leave.'

'But . . .'

Rhona held up her hand. 'No buts.'

'No evidence of a timing device?' Bill asked.

Rhona shook her head.

'But definitely arson?'

She nodded. 'The fire started in the passenger compartment. They identified two different sources of ignition.'

After she'd talked to the SOCOs and taken a look at

the car herself, she'd gone in search of Bill. The car was in a mess, but the quick use of a fire extinguisher by the security guard had confined the fire to the front two seats.

'Was there anything that might point to the identity of the arsonist?'

'There was a tin on the driver's seat with a photograph of me in it and an audio tape of the Stones singing *Jumping Jack Flash*.'

'I take it not belonging to you?'

She nodded. 'And someone left a song about fire on my ansaphone last week . . .'

Bill's voice grew serious.

'I don't like this, Rhona.'

Neither did she.

'Maybe the security cameras can throw some light on it. I've got someone ploughing through the footage now.' He looked at her, concerned. 'Is Sean about?'

'Amsterdam,' she told him.

He was obviously worried about her. 'I'll get a squad car to drop you home.'

She conceded that, at least.

'My advice is to stay home,' he told her. 'I'll let you know when we have anything.'

Rhona pressed the play button on the recorder. Mick Jagger's distinctive voice filled the room, the thump of bass guitar behind it.

'*Jumping Jack Flash*, the Rolling Stones, 1969 or '70,' Sev told her.

'I know.'

'So?'

'My car was set on fire last night after I left the lab. Whoever did it left a photo of me in the car, and that tape.'

There was a moment's silence as he digested that. Then she voiced her fear.

'It could mean he's planning to use propane.'

27

BILL WILSON HURRIED back to the police office. He'd promised his wife Margaret he would be back by three to serve the elderly relatives their Ne'erday dram, and he intended keeping his promise. The empty streets looked like a Sunday with a hangover. A few souls were wandering about looking for the remains of a party, but the rest were indoors continuing the celebrations or sleeping it off.

Janice had been one of the ones to draw the short straw and work Hogmanay. She'd taken the news well. She wasn't a big drinker anyway. When the team went for a pint after a shift, her limit seemed to be two glasses of wine.

Janice wasn't at her desk but there was a large yellow notelet on his. Some guy had phoned and said he knew Dr MacLeod and wanted to speak to the man in charge of the drug murders. He had refused to talk to anyone else.

Bill carried his over-milked coffee to his room and sat on his leather swivel chair to think.

'So you're back.'

Janice made it sound as if he was a kid skiving class. Bill waved the note at her.

'Don't know who it was,' she said. 'Sounded jumpy and would only speak to you. I could hear a dog whining in the background.'

'If he calls back, I want it traced.'

'We're short-staffed but I'll try. And, sir. The report on Meldrum Holdings is ready.'

Despite being down to three men and a dog, Janice had achieved the impossible. DI Wilson felt suitably chastened.

The report was ten pages long. Meldrum Holdings were wide-ranging in their interests, from construction to financial services to manufacturing. It would need a complicated flow chart to signal where the money came from and where it went. When regions had their own direct services it was easy enough to spot where the money went – down a black hole. Now that the private sector had been brought in for the construction and maintenance of public housing, things were a little less clear.

Meldrum Holdings looked as though they were doing a nice job of bulldozing run-down schemes. Now if they were doing a nice wee job of redeveloping them as well . . .

When he left at two, Bill was none the wiser. Linking anyone in Meldrum Holdings to arson in housing estates would be like coming up with the correct string of lottery numbers, and just about as pleasurable.

On his way home he took a detour. One of those things that happens on the Kingston Bridge, Bill convinced himself, trying to blot out the expression on

Margaret's face when he didn't arrive. He rehearsed his excuses. He was dreaming and ended up in the wrong lane and had to keep going to the next junction, before he could get off.

Minutes later the slip road he'd chosen deposited him in a desert of high-rise flats and creeping wasteland. The pub was on a corner, between the bookies and the post office-cum-general store.

No one in the pub looked at him but they all saw him. He went and sat at the bar.

'Happy New Year, Sarge,' said the balding, hollow-cheeked man next to him.

Wee Archie didn't believe in promotion. If he wasn't moving up in the world, then no one else was.

'Happy New Year, Archie.'

Bill nodded at the barman and Archie had his whisky and half pint replenished.

Archie had lived in this housing scheme all his life. He'd seen it begin good and end up bad. If anyone knew what was going on here, it was him.

It took two more shorts before Archie's brain went into play.

28

JAZ PUT DOWN the receiver and stepped out of the phone booth into the wind.

No trains, no boats, no planes out of Auchenblair on New Year's Day. He'd tried to hitch but nobody was driving anywhere other than round the corner and Jaz didn't fancy the hike to the main road for a lorry heading south. So he'd tried phoning. Except there was no MacRae and no MacFarlane and now no DI Wilson around. The lady scientist had been his last chance. He wasn't too happy about Emps either. The dog's nose was hot, and he kept whining. Worrying about Emps' pain made him forget his own.

The hills behind the village were white-topped and the sky hung heavy with snow. He decided to go to the hotel bar. There was no point holding on to cash for the train now. He would blow it on something to eat and a heat by the fire.

Amy jumped the two steps from the blue front door and landed right in front of him.

'What happened to Emperor?'

Emps was licking the wee girl's hand.

'He got his tail caught in a door.'

'You'll have to take him to the vet.'

'I will,' Jaz promised, 'as soon as I get back to Edinburgh.'

'Why don't you go now?' Amy looked horrified at the sight of the seeping stump.

'No transport until tomorrow,' he explained.

Mrs MacRae had appeared at the door.

Amy ran back up the steps. 'Mummy, Emps got hurt and he can't go to the vet until tomorrow. Granny could help him, couldn't she?'

Mrs MacRae was giving Jaz one of her 'Who the hell are you?' looks.

'It's okay, Amy,' Jaz was anxious to be away. 'Emps will be okay.'

Jaz made to walk on but Mrs MacRae had bent down to examine the dog's wound.

'What if Emperor dies like Bess?' Amy turned to Jaz. 'Bess hurt herself on a fence when we were out. She died.' Tears filled her eyes.

So that's what they'd told her about the dog.

'Amy, go inside and say goodbye to Jennie. Tell her we'll see her tomorrow at the party.'

'But Mummy . . .'

'Go.'

MacRae's wife turned to him.

'This dog needs a vet.'

'I'm stuck here until tomorrow,' Jaz began.

'If you come home with us, my mother will look at him for you.'

Arguing didn't look like an option. And Emps did need to see a vet. Anyway, getting close to MacRae's wife and kid had been the reason he came here in the first place.

'Okay.'

Bess's body had been removed from the front lawn. Jaz tried not to look for bloodstains as he followed Amy up the path. He would insist on waiting outside, he decided, his stomach jumping in fright at the sudden thought of MacRae turning up on New Year's Day and finding him sitting in his mother-in-law's kitchen. Christ! He would end up with more than a hole in his hand.

Amy was running ahead, throwing open the door and calling to her gran to come and see the poor dog.

Jaz stopped at the door.

'I'll wait here.'

'Nonsense,' Mrs MacRae said. 'You'll need to hold Emperor while we dress his wound.'

Emperor was asleep now, knocked out by the antibiotics he'd had pumped into him.

'You'd better leave Emps here so that I can keep an eye on him overnight.' Amy's gran topped up the mug of tea. 'Where are you staying?'

Jaz went through half a dozen scenarios in his head in quick succession then decided to opt for the truth, or nearly the truth.

'I expected to go back today,' he smiled ruefully, 'I forgot about the trains.'

'There's a room over the garage you can have for tonight.'

Mrs MacRae wasn't happy about the offer but a quick glance from her mother silenced her.

'It's not much, but it's warm and you can see Emperor first thing in the morning.'

'I don't want to put you to any trouble,' Jaz said.

'No trouble. The weather's closing in. You'd have problems going anywhere tonight.'

The four-paned kitchen window was thick with snow. Amy left her place by Emperor and ran over to the window in delight.

'Can I phone Dad and tell him?'

Jaz's heart sank. The first thing Amy would do was tell her father that Emperor was in the house. Then it would all be over. The police car would be here in minutes.

'Can I use your toilet?' Jaz asked quickly. He would have to leave Emps behind, but the dog was better off here, the state he was in.

'It's through the back,' MacRae's wife had the kitchen door open for him.

Amy was already dialling. Jaz listened from the hall. He could feel the wee girl's impatience as she waited for someone to pick up.

'Never mind Amy,' her mother was saying. 'Your dad'll be working. You can try again tomorrow.'

Jaz went into the bathroom and flushed the toilet. Maybe he would get a sleep in a bed tonight after all. As long as he was away sharp in the morning.

The room over the garage was used for storage, but the bed was comfortable and wonderfully warm. After showering he put his clothes back on and left his parka at the foot of the bed and climbed in.

When he left the kitchen, Emperor hadn't stirred from his deep sleep beside the range. The old woman had listened to the dog's heartbeat and pronounced his progress satisfactory. Nothing was said about his injuries or Bess's death. The old woman seemed to have accepted him at face value, but her daughter was a different matter.

Jaz had caught her looking at him during supper and he was sure she didn't believe a word of his story. He had a feeling she had decided keeping him there might be the best idea, at least until she'd spoken to her husband or the police.

He was awakened two hours later by the thump of snow sliding off the garage roof. He slipped out of bed and reached for his jacket, deciding to check on Emperor.

The kitchen was in darkness apart from a small lamp near the Aga. Jaz bent over the dog, relieved to see the blanket rise and fall with gentle regularity.

'How's he doing?' Amy's gran was standing at the door in her dressing gown.

'Okay, I think.'

'Let's have a look.'

She lifted the heavy eyelids. 'The sedative should wear off soon. He'll be up and about by morning.'

'I want to thank you.'

'No need. It's my job.'

'But you usually get paid.'

'I'm retired. I like to keep my hand in.' She fetched two mugs from the cupboard. 'Emperor is very fond of you. Have you had him since he was a puppy?'

Jaz decided on the truth. 'He belonged to a friend who died.'

'I'm sorry.'

She lifted the boiling kettle and made a pot of tea.

'My daughter doesn't trust you.' She took a seat at the table. 'She wanted to phone the police after you went to bed.'

'What?' Jaz was on his feet.

The old woman waved him back to his seat. 'I told her not to,' she smiled. 'She still listens to me now and again.' She sipped her tea. 'I told her anyone who cared about their dog as much as you do couldn't be all bad.'

'Thanks. I'll be out of your way in the morning.'

She glanced at the window.

'You might be stuck with us a little longer than that. Snow has a habit of slowing the world down, sometimes for the better.'

Sitting in that kitchen drinking tea, watching the snow fall outside, was like being in a different universe. If the old woman wanted him to tell her his life story, the truth about Karen, why he was here, she was going the right way about it.

'I know who killed your dog.'

'Was it you who covered Bess with a blanket?'

He nodded and she waited for him to go on.

'A bloke called Tommy Moffat. He's a . . . well, he's a nutcase.'

'Why did he kill Bess?'

'Because he wanted to. Because he felt like it,' he said angrily. 'Who knows? Maybe she just barked and annoyed him.'

'Where is this Tommy Moffat now?'

'He's gone,' Jaz said, hoping that was true.

'Did he have anything to do with Emperor's tail and your hand?'

Jaz nodded.

'Can I take a look at it?'

He held it out.

'The wound's deep and quite inflamed. Would you let me dress it for you and give you a shot of anti-biotics?'

Jaz hesitated then nodded.

She poured hot water into a basin and carefully cleaned and dressed the wound. Then she pulled up his sleeve, exposing the old needle tracks.

She said nothing as she slid the needle into his arm.

'This might make you feel sleepy.'

'What if the police . . . ?'

'There will be no police here tonight.'

Jaz went back to his room and got into bed. The world outside was dark and silent, wrapped in a white cocoon. For the first time in forty-eight hours, Jaz felt safe.

WEE ARCHIE WAS a one-syllable man. Talking to him was a case of twenty questions. Bill Wilson was conscious he had reached nineteen and didn't have his answer yet.

One more question and Archie had had enough. He might be a drinker but he always went home for his mid-day meal. A happily married man, was Archie, and he wasn't going to miss his New Year lunch. When they got outside, he threw his parting shot as Bill got in the car.

'After our boy died, Marge was all for joining them. Somebody has to clean the place up,' he said angrily. 'Your lot aren't doing anything about it.'

If Archie's veiled suggestions were to be believed, clearing out drug pushers from the estate was a joint effort. Big business working with a local enterprise group. It was what the government would call a private-public partnership. The clean residents get rid of the junkies while big business makes a killing on the building and land deals. Bill wondered if the local vigilantes realised they would be the next to go.

On the way home, Bill phoned the hospital to check

on Chrissy. The ward sister said Chrissy was asleep
and sounded pleased about that. She would be dis-
charged in the morning. The sister didn't say 'Thank
God', but Bill could hear it in the tone of her voice.
Chrissy was not in the model patients' league.

He called Rhona's home number.

A sleepy Irish voice answered.

'Sean?'

'Hi Bill. Sorry, I'm half asleep.'

'Is Rhona there?'

'No. She doesn't even know I'm back. There was a
cancellation so I jumped a plane. She's been here
recently though. Looks like the remains of last night's
celebrations.'

Bill filled him in about the car fire.

'God, I had no idea this was all going on.' He
scrabbled about in the background. 'An urgent fax
arrived half an hour ago, something about coffee cups.
Do you want me to read it?'

The fax was two pages long. One was technical
gibberish to both of them. The second stated a match
between DNA residue on one of the cups submitted
and the semen residue on the letter.

'Have you tried her mobile?' Bill said.

'It's sitting in the recharger. I'm going to try Mrs
Harper downstairs. She might have spoken to Rhona
or seen her leave.'

When Sean rang off, Bill sat in his car trying to figure
out what the hell coffee cups had to do with anything. It
took five minutes for Sean to call back.

'Mrs Harper saw her leave with a dark-haired man in

a leather jacket about lunchtime,' Sean told him. 'She doesn't know if there was a car.'

'I'll go round by the hospital and check with Chrissy. See if she knows anything about the cups or this guy.'

Bill headed for the Infirmary. One thing was certain, if anyone knew the whole story it would be Chrissy. How much she would be prepared to reveal was a different matter. Chrissy took loyalty very seriously.

The ward sister threw him a look of relief when he arrived.

'She's up and about,' she said. 'Try the television room.'

Chrissy was in there trying to organise a game of cards with the other residents, who just wanted to watch an hour-long episode of *Eastenders*.

'DI Wilson. You've come to rescue me.'

She took him to the quiet room.

'The cup came from Greg's flat. Rhona took it from there after the boy with the dog turned up. MacRae put the wind up her about him,' she said. 'It's funny though, she told me the cup tested clean.'

'She had more than one cup tested.'

'Didn't know about that,' Chrissy looked puzzled. 'Why don't you ask Rhona?'

'We don't know where she is,' Bill told her. 'Her neighbour saw her go off with a dark-haired guy in a leather jacket about lunchtime.'

'What?' Chrissy sounded alarmed. 'There was a guy like that in the videos hanging about every fire. No clear facial image. Just the dark hair and the leather jacket. I told her it looked like MacRae.'

'I'll contact MacFarlane,' Bill reassured her. 'Chances are Rhona's in Edinburgh with them.'

'If the cup tested positive . . . then the boy with the dog must have sent the letter.'

'Yes,' said Bill, rising to leave.

Chrissy got up too. 'I'm coming with you.'

'You're not allowed out until tomorrow,' Bill tried.

'They'll be glad to see the tail-end of me.'

30

'JAZ DIDN'T HAVE anything to do with Karen's death.'

MacRae didn't turn his head from the snowy windscreen. He was waiting for her to prove what she said was true.

'When he came to the flat, I kept his coffee cup.'

He took his eyes off the road. 'What?'

'Careful!' The stretch of road at Harthill was renowned for its bad weather accidents.

The highest point between Glasgow and Edinburgh was the very place to come off the road in a snowstorm.

MacRae slowed down. 'Why?'

'I was worried he might have stolen something, so when he left I bagged the cup. When nothing was missing I forgot about it. Then you got suspicious about him so I analysed it. The DNA pattern didn't match either the letter or the semen in Karen.'

'I still don't trust him.'

'You don't trust anyone.'

MacRae grunted and swung left into Harthill Service Station.

'I want to phone Amy.'

★   ★   ★

Rhona waited for MacRae to return. She hadn't been completely honest with him. She'd removed three cups from Greg's flat. After Jaz left, she'd sat his cup by the sink. When MacRae threw suspicion on Jaz, she decided to test the cup. But there were three beside the sink by then and they all looked the same. One result was back.

'The line's down.' MacRae looked worried. 'Heavy snow.'

'Mobile?'

'No chance. They're surrounded by hills.'

'Amy'll be pleased.'

'What?'

'The snow.'

They looked out at the thickening cover.

'We'd better get moving,' she suggested.

Rhona was back in the car when she remembered. 'Shit!'

'What's up?'

'I've left my mobile and Greg's keys behind.'

MacRae didn't look round. 'No problem. I can get you in anywhere.'

Mary Queen of Scots' squat was littered with a fresh covering of empty lager cans. Either the Queen had taken up residence again or someone else had.

When they got to the manhole it was back in place.

'It's fucking padlocked,' MacRae looked at her in frustration.

'What about a car jack?'

*   *   *

The sewer was warm and damp. Rhona wondered why Mary Queen of Scots and her entourage hadn't made their home down here, away from the police and the cold. MacRae must have been reading her mind.

'Most people don't know this place exists.' He stopped and used the torch to check the map. 'I marked each of the side tunnels I checked out.' He pointed at the opposite wall. 'I think we're about level with the toilets at the western end of the Gardens.'

While they were walking their footsteps had played back at them, jumping across the tunnel walls, making them sound like an advancing army. Now they were standing still the echo that rang behind did not belong to them. Rhona was sure of it. She looked at MacRae and mouthed 'Keep talking'.

'I vote we head back,' she suggested loudly. 'We shouldn't be down here without the proper equipment anyway.'

The footsteps had stopped. If someone from Scottish Water was down there they would have made their presence known by now.

'Good idea,' MacRae shouted as Rhona took off.

The cobbled ledge rang beneath her feet. MacRae's breath rasped as he pounded along behind her. A distant thump was followed by the sound of splashing water. Disturbed silt propelled noxious gases into the air. Rhona coughed as they hit the back of her throat and flooded her eyes with water.

She upped her pace, praying she wouldn't miss her footing in the darkness and fall off the ledge. She swerved instinctively as the tunnel curved right but

MacRae didn't react so quickly. There was a crunch then a stream of curses as he collided with the wall.

Rhona's beam of light caught a foot as it slipped into a right-hand tunnel. She jumped across the channel and looked down the side sewer. Nothing. It sounded as though her quarry had gone to ground or else found a way out.

Rhona, head well down, entered the side tunnel, hearing MacRae cross, gasping for breath, behind her.

Ahead, a dark shape blocked the tunnel. She stepped closer and the smell of death hit her like an intervening wall. Bending down, she examined the body. A week of heat and damp had decomposed it beyond all recognition.

Somewhere in the distance, she heard feet clamber up metal steps. A gush of noise and fresh air signalled an escape into the Gardens.

MacRae was coming towards her, bent double.

'Christ, something smells bad.'

He peered past her.

'Anyone we know?'

'I'd say the guy in the drawing. Hair colour and clothes are the same and he's wearing a nose ring.'

'No wonder the police couldn't find him. Did you see who we were chasing?'

'I saw a man's shoe in the torchlight. Brown . . . black . . . I'm not sure.'

'You're shivering.'

'I'm fine,' she lied.

'Let's get out of here. There's an exit fifty yards further along.'

★   ★   ★

Rhona took a gulp of hot coffee, but it did little to bring warmth back to her chilled bones. She'd insisted on going back down the sewer with Dr Mackenzie for the *in situ* examination. For once MacKenzie hadn't argued. Maybe being the one to find a body had its compensations.

She then spent half an hour with MacRae viewing the surveillance tapes of Princes Street on the night of the fire. Three men were caught on camera passing the building.

'The one on the left could be our decomposing body,' MacRae suggested.

'Maybe. But it would need computer enhancement to prove it. What about the other two?'

'Never seen them before in my life. They're there, then they disappear,' MacRae said. 'But that doesn't mean they went into the building. They might just have turned up into George Street.'

'We can check a DNA sample from the sewer body against the semen in Karen's body.'

'He's dead, she's dead,' MacRae said. 'What's the point?'

'Then we'll check it against the letter.'

MacRae shrugged. They were no nearer the fire-raiser now than they'd ever been. They'd found a body in a sewer. Even if he was the rapist, it didn't mean he had anything to do with the fire. Whoever had run from them in the sewer might have.

MacRae fished in his pocket and handed her an envelope. 'MacFarlane asked me to give you this.'

Rhona tore it open. She read the faxed forensic report on the remaining cups with growing alarm.

MacRae hadn't trusted Jaz from the outset. Did Jaz give them the drawing already knowing the guy was dead? Jaz had been watching Greg's apartment and MacRae's family. Jaz drank coffee in Greg's flat. Now they had matched a DNA trace on the semen in the letter with the cup taken from Greg's. Which must mean Jaz sent the letter.'

She grabbed MacRae's arm.

'What the hell's wrong?'

'We have to get inside Greg's apartment.'

31

GREG'S FRONT DOOR swung open.

It had taken just ten seconds for MacRae to defeat the fancy security system.

'You've done this before?'

'Don't tell MacFarlane.'

The flat was clean and empty. There were fresh flowers in a vase on the hall table and a neat pile of unopened mail by the phone.

The bedroom wardrobe revealed a partially cleared rail and no shoes. Rhona was convinced Greg hadn't been there since she spoke to him that first night.

'What are we looking for?'

Rhona was skimming through the telephone book. She found the number and dialled. A man's voice answered.

She tried to sound casual. 'Is Greg there?'

'No,' the voice sounded amused. 'Should he be?' Whoever Justin was he'd changed his voice since their last meeting.

'I believe we met in Greg's flat a few days ago,' Rhona tried. 'You arrived just as I was leaving.'

The voice was puzzled but anxious to help. During the ensuing conversation Rhona learned that Justin

Roberts was not the man who let himself into Greg's flat and sat calmly on the sofa.

By the time she hung up, MacRae had rediscovered the drinks cabinet and was helping himself.

'I need a drink,' he said as if she might argue. He sat down where the pseudo Justin Roberts had sat, feet up, giving her the once-over. That was what had been odd, Rhona realised. She had never been sized up by a gay man before.

'So your friend's gone to Rome. What's the problem?'

A niggling doubt was turning into a terrible realisation.

'I've been stupid.'

'What the hell are you talking about?'

'I gave him a name and an identity.'

MacRae looked lost.

'The second time I stayed . . . there was a guy came into the flat. I assumed it was Greg's boyfriend Justin Roberts.'

MacRae was catching on, fast.

'And it wasn't?'

She shook her head. Everything was adding up. 'I think he's the man we're looking for.'

The drill of the phone interrupted her explanation. The ansaphone cut in and started its bland message. Then a voice Rhona recognised ordered her to pick up.

'Yes?'

There was a short silence, then:

'I want you to know I can see you both quite clearly.'

Rhona looked round, mentally stripping the room, searching for the camera.

'Don't bother. You won't find it.'

'Bast . . .'

Rhona covered MacRae's expletive with her hand. She spoke quietly into the receiver.

'What do you want?'

'We're going to play a little game, you and I. If you win, MacRae's child will live. If you lose, both the building you are in and the granny's cottage will be destroyed by fire.'

Rhona forced her voice to remain calm. The arsonist was power-assertive. Confronting him would only make matters worse. Beside her MacRae's breath was coming in gasps, his skin grey.

'Tell me what to do.'

She listened to his orders, sick at the thought of the consequences of his action. An explosion here would seriously undermine the building, break gas pipes. The arsonist would get his show alright. Bigger and louder than any pyrotechnic display in Princes Street Gardens.

'We have to clear the building first,' she insisted.

'No! he said harshly. 'You have exactly twenty minutes. You will go alone. MacRae will remain in my line of sight. Is that understood?'

'Yes.'

Rhona touched MacRae's arm. 'There's still time. Try and call MacFarlane,' she whispered.

The basement was empty apart from some packing cases lining the walls. But if she had been sent to look, there had to be something to find. It just wouldn't be obvious.

Rhona walked up and down, stamping to check the sound. Nothing. She headed diagonally towards the opposite wall. This time the sound was different. She was a foot from the corner. Four packing cases stood between her and the wall. She dragged them back.

A narrow set of steps led to a darkened room below street level. At the bottom a sewer vent pipe climbed the wall.

MacRae's voice echoed in her head. 'Every building has a six-inch-diameter pipe leading into the sewer. They don't all have a way in.'

Rhona wouldn't believe that. Couldn't.

She dropped to her knees on the rough concrete floor and began to crawl about, exploring the surface with her hands.

The metal ring of the manhole cover jabbed her shin. She grabbed it and pulled, in a paroxysm of effort. Sewer gas escaped from the black hole, making her gag. She braced herself and dropped inside.

Propane was denser than air. If the gas was already on it would have gathered below. He would set the timer to spark ignition ten minutes later.

She stood trying to get her bearings. Running alongside, the muted flow of water was barely audible. As her eyes became accustomed to the dark, she made out a door on her left and reached for the handle.

Inside was a pair of overalls, an assortment of tools and a torch. As she switched on the torch, she caught the scent of gas.

Now was the time to run. Her heart was racing. How long did she have? If he had been lying to her, then death was imminent. If he was telling the truth, she had five minutes to find the propane and stop it igniting.

In her head time rushed past, yet in the claustrophobic atmosphere of the tunnel it stood still. Breathing as shallowly as possible, she followed the sickening hiss of the gas.

The canisters stood side by side, hidden behind an archway that led from one sewer into the next. Attached was the trigger device. Simple and effective. A spark in a gas-filled area. A memory of the carnage of an IRA terrorist bomb in the height of the Troubles flooded Rhona's head. Forensic bags full of samples that had occupied her days and filled her nights with tortured images of the dead. This explosion would wreak the same havoc.

As in the moments before death she thought of those she cared about. Liam, Sean . . . Severino waiting above, his child in the hands of a madman.

She pulled off her jacket, immersed it in the dark water then walked towards the device.

Sev stood in the same moment of time. In his mind his arms were about Amy, sheltering her from the fire that would rage round her. The scars on his back burned with the memory of his own pain and the pain that would be hers. He wept silently for what he had done to his daughter. He found himself praying. God, let there be angels. God, let Amy's guardian angel protect her. Please God, protect Rhona.

He had turned on the mobile in his pocket and

pressed what he thought was the key for MacFarlane. He'd whispered his message and hoped it was heard.

All his fears about this arsonist had come true. He had focused on the woman, given her a task that could not be fulfilled. He would gloat over her failure. Rhona's death in that fire, his own death, Amy's death, reduced to a snuff movie.

Severino could feel the eyes of the camera on him. Taste the watcher's excitement. He understood it. He had tasted it himself. Fire. The ultimate cleanser. The ultimate life force. The ultimate orgasm.

She forced the small black box under the water, jamming it below the side ledge. Air bubbled to the surface and dissipated. She got off her knees and walked back to the canisters, turning the valves until the hissing stopped.

She stumbled towards the steps, waves of nausea sweeping over her. Her body moved into shock, her limbs shaking with fear, relief and cold.

Sirens announced the imminent arrival of fire engines. She heard voices from the basement; MacFarlane's, then MacRae's, both edged with fear.

'Rhona! Thank Christ!'

Severino caught her as she stumbled up the steps and gathered her in his arms.

She looked up at him.

'Amy?' she said.

32

ABOVE HIM THE skylight was shrouded in white cloud. Jaz reached over and flicked on the bedside lamp. This time he had been asleep. Well and truly asleep.

The room was chilly, the radiator cold. He reached for his jacket. He would check on Emps. Make sure he was alright.

Outside, a single line of footprints led to the cottage. Someone had arrived here recently. But who?

Jaz crept forward, conscious of the crunch of his feet in the snow. The front door was off the latch. He slipped into the hall and stood listening.

Someone was weeping, a small pitiful sound like a child. Amy?

He pushed open the kitchen door. Amy sat in the chair beside the Aga, a teddy bear clasped in her arms, her face streaked with tears.

'Amy. What's wrong?' His eyes darted to the empty dog basket. 'Where's Emps?'

Tommy stepped into view. 'Thought I told you to get lost.'

Jaz looked at Amy's terrified face. 'Amy, come here.'

Amy tried to get up, but Tommy caught her arm and wrenched her back, holding the knife to her neck.

'Amy's not going anywhere, Jazzy-boy, and neither are you.'

Jaz stood still. The most important thing was to get Tommy away from Amy. If he could get him outside, confuse him in the dark, she might have a chance.

Jaz sprang through the open door, ran the length of the hall and dived into the open air, slamming the door behind him. Tommy was seconds after, promising to slit Jaz's fucking throat from ear to ear.

The hedge round the house was at least three feet thick. He could hide in there and wait until Tommy came by.

Tommy was outside now, sweeping the beam of a torch across the front garden. On the third swing, the beam hovered above Jaz then descended, exposing his hiding place and blinding his eyes.

Tommy laughed, a horrible sound. But he was so intent on mocking his prey he hadn't spotted Emperor crawling belly-down towards him across the snow.

As the dog cannoned into Tommy, knocking him to the ground, Amy came running out of the cottage. Jaz grabbed her and made a dash for the front door, meeting the edge of Tommy's knife on the way.

Emps started barking as lights sprang from the trees and half a dozen armed policemen came running across the snow towards the cottage.

33

RHONA WALKED ROUND the lab, touching the equipment which structured her life.

She had stopped the arsonist blowing up the Edinburgh building. Amy was safe. Safe and sound and as far away from her father as Gillian could manage. But they hadn't found the pyromaniac . . . yet.

Outside, January light touched the dripping skeleton branches of trees. Kelvingrove Park had survived the New Year celebrations. As had she. A new year had begun, for Glasgow and for her. Sean had returned. Unexpected and – she toyed with the idea – almost unwelcome.

Fear of death was erotic. She and Severino had tasted that fear together. It was worth everything in that moment . . . but when fear subsided?

Her mobile drilled a sharp note. She glanced at the screen, expecting Sean's name.

It was Liam.

She pressed the green key and waited, holding her breath.

His voice sounded improbably young. She conjured a vision of him in her head, as she had done a thousand times before.

'Can I come and see you?'

'I'd like that.'

He stumbled. 'I'm sorry . . .'

She stopped him. 'It doesn't matter.'

'I was scared.'

Relief swept over her. So that was why he hadn't turned up.

'So was I.'

There was a silence.

'I'll be there in half an hour,' he said.

She whispered 'Okay' and hung up.

She concentrated on the details of the case while she waited for Liam to arrive.

The body in the sewer was the guy in Jaz's drawing. His name was Joe MacMurdo. He was known to the Glasgow force as a small-time drug dealer. MacMurdo's DNA had matched the semen found in Karen. It looked like Karen had been raped by MacMurdo then left to die in the fire. After all, who cares about a homeless girl without a family? But Jaz had cared enough to put his own life in danger, she reminded herself.

Soon all the pieces would come together. The process had already begun. DI Wilson had passed details of Meldrum Holdings to the Procurator Fiscal. With Jaz's statement on what he had overheard between Tommy and the Financial Director of Meldrum Holdings, they thought they had a case of intimidation and murder associated with the company. Bill Wilson suspected the Finance Director for Meldrum Holdings would be the fall guy. Already the big guns behind the company were marshalling their lawyers, pleading ignorance of any crooked dealing.

Tommy Moffat was in the frame for MacMurdo's murder and being involved in the rape. If Tommy thought they had enough on him, he might squeal about Meldrum Holdings in the hope of a reduced sentence.

They had already established that he had been cutting the drugs with anything he could find, including the white stuff his wee brother brought home from the fireworks factory. Tommy had it both ways: he made money from dealing, then picked up his hit money as the addicts died off and left the schemes empty for Meldrum Holdings to develop.

The arsonist was the enigma. Severino had tried to persuade her to have a police guard until they picked him up, but that seemed too melodramatic for Rhona. Security was tight in the lab already. Having a policeman stand around all day getting bored was overkill.

She glanced at the clock. Where was Chrissy? She'd only gone to drop off a forensic bag at Chemistry. She should have been back by now.

She checked the window. Liam should be arriving any moment. Sure enough, a tall, blond figure was coming across the car park. She watched the long-legged stride. Saw him hesitate then approach the gate guard. They both looked up at her window. Rhona stepped back, her heart hammering, her mouth dry.

She was terrified to meet her own child. Frightened of what she would see in his eyes.

The lab phone rang. She didn't move. If she met Liam, things would never be the same again, for either of them. Sweat broke out on her brow as the phone continued to ring. She steeled herself and picked up.

'Dr MacLeod?'

'Yes?'

'I have a young man in reception called Liam Hope. Says he's here to see you.'

She asked the security guard to send him up, her voice sounding like someone else. She should have gone down to meet him, but she couldn't trust her legs to carry her.

She was facing the door, waiting for Liam's silhouette to appear in the small pane of glass. The movement behind her caused her to turn, thinking Chrissy had returned unnoticed.

Severino stood behind her, dressed in a white lab coat, a visitor badge pinned to his lapel. He smiled. She opened her mouth to ask how he had got in, then realised it wasn't Sev, merely a caricature of him.

The man from Greg's apartment wasn't smiling this time, and he wasn't embarrassed. The blond hair had been dyed black, the glasses discarded.

'How the hell . . . ?

She didn't get to finish. He caught her arm and twisted it up her back. The pain was excruciating.

She thrust her free hand backwards, hoping to hit him in the crotch. He laughed, pushing her elbow even higher. Her mouth filled with bile as nausea swept over her.

'Do that again and I'll break your arm.'

She responded through clenched teeth, thinking all the time of Liam's imminent arrival.

'What do you want?'

He stiffened, hearing the footsteps in the corridor.

'Please God, no,' she whispered.

Then she heard the knock at the door and saw the tall silhouette behind the glass.

'Who is it?' he spat in her ear.

'I don't know,' she lied.

'Tell them you're busy.'

The knock came again.

'Sorry, I'm busy.' Her voice sounded cold and remote. 'Can you come back later?'

Rhona willed Liam to walk away, but he wasn't giving up this time.

There was a moment's silence then, 'Rhona?' He pressed his face against the glass. 'Please. It's me, Liam.'

The door began to open.

A rush of fear and love swamped Rhona.

'No!' she cried as the cold metal of a gun met her ribs.

Her son's face was startled.

Liam looked down at the gun then up at her face.

'Get inside, now!'

Liam did as he was told.

'Shut the door and lock it.' The man looked Liam up and down. 'Who are you?'

'Dr MacLeod's son.'

There was a moment's silence.

'Now that's one thing I didn't know about Dr MacLeod.'

Even the cynical voice reminded her of Sev.

Rhona edged her body between the gun and Liam. Chrissy would appear any minute. She just had to stay calm and keep him talking.

'Why are you here?' she tried.

'I made you a promise. I came to keep it.'

'What's he talking about?' Liam asked.

Rhona threw Liam a look, willing him to stay calm.

'You're very like MacRae,' she suggested.

A flash of anger crossed his face.

'That bastard ruined my life.'

'How did he do that?'

'They threw me out of the Brigade because of him.'

He waved them towards the sample cupboard at the back of the lab and pushed them inside.

Rhona grabbed Liam's hand, squeezing it tightly. His pulse beat swiftly in the nape of his neck, but his face was resolved. He wasn't going to panic. Yet.

The door snapped shut behind them and the key turned.

'What did he mean, what he promised?'

The mix of letters in those emails rearranged themselves in Rhona's head.

BURN THE BITCH. That was his promise.

'Security will be here soon,' she told Liam, wishing she believed it herself.

A new sprinkler system had been installed the previous year. If it worked they had a chance, provided the smoke didn't get them first.

She heard him moving about the lab, piling stuff

against the cupboard door. Then the crackle as the paper caught.

Smoke began to drift under the door.

'The sprinklers will come on,' she told Liam.

But they didn't.

The smoke was thickening. Where the hell was the alarm and the sprinklers? Liam's face was grey with fear. She pulled off her lab coat and thrust it at him.

'Cover your mouth with this.'

At the back was a panel that led to the riser, a shaft that ran up through the building. It housed the network and power cables and more recently the sprinkler pipes when they did up the lab. It also had a metal ladder. But the panel needed a maintenance key to open it. Liam was watching her, his eyes bloodshot and streaming above the lab coat. She looked wildly about her for something to force the lock.

'Here. Try this.'

He thrust a Swiss army knife into her hand. He had flicked open a blade and she inserted it into the lock. It really needed a round key, but it might work. She was praying out loud as she felt the blade turn. There was a resistance then a sudden click. Tears streamed down her face as the panel dropped forward.

Air rushed down the shaft, escaping through into the lab, feeding the fire even more.

'Can you climb?'

Liam looked up.

'I think so.'

'There's an opening into the room above. Look for a

panel on the left of the shaft. You'll have to force it open.'

'What about you?'

'I'll follow,' she promised.

She watched his feet disappear. What the hell had happened to the smoke alarms and all the fancy computer-controlled equipment they'd installed last year?

She had brought Liam here. If her son died it would be her fault.

She began to climb.

Liam had reached the panel. The shaft was full of smoke and she couldn't see him, but she could hear him battering the wall.

It was too late. The fumes had seeped into every part of her. Her brain, her stomach, her lungs. She couldn't fight for breath any more.

Then she heard the alarm go off, a glorious shrieking sound, as smoke escaped with Liam into the next level.

Liam was out. That was all she cared about.

She closed her eyes and let go.

'Rhona!'

Liam's voice was a thousand miles away, but his hand held hers and he was pulling her free.

34

JAZ STUDIED THE headstone.

**In Memory of
Karen Carlyle
18th August 1989–28th December 2004
Aged 15 yrs
Love
Jaz and Emperor**

At least there had been someone at her funeral. Rhona came. But not Liam. He had left to work in Africa for a year. She pretended she was alright about that, but Jaz knew by her eyes that she wasn't. DI MacFarlane was there, and DI Wilson.

And MacRae, looking like shit. Glancing all the time at Rhona as if he wanted to say something, and couldn't. MacRae had told him Amy had wanted to come but her mother wouldn't let her. Jaz didn't blame the mother for that. A funeral wasn't the place for a wee girl.

It had taken a while to find out who Karen was, but MacFarlane promised he would do it, and he had.

Emps put his cold nose in Jaz's hand.

'Okay, boy. Let's go.'

He set off across the frosted grass, Emps running by his side. Karen's death had made him even more determined not to screw up this time. He owed it to her. He had started evening classes at college, was painting again. He planned to paint Karen the way he remembered her. In Rose Street, playing the penny whistle. That way, she would always be alive.

'I didn't sleep with him.'

Sean's eyes held hers. 'It doesn't matter.'

'Then what does?' she said sharply.

He ran his fingers through his hair. He didn't want to argue when the outcome was inevitable. He took her hand and stroked the palm with his thumb.

'I'm not asking you to go,' she said defensively.

He lifted her hand and kissed it, sending a shiver through her body.

'You met someone in Amsterdam.' If that were true, it would make it easier.

He shook his head. 'This isn't about me.'

'You need space to decide . . .' The words *who you want* were left unsaid. 'I'll be in my old room at the club . . . if you need me.'

He let her hand fall. It felt cold without him.

'You'll come and hear me on Friday?'

She nodded. She wanted to kiss him, but didn't.

She'd felt frightened as he left. Frightened to be alone. It lasted until the door closed behind him. Then she felt relief.

She stood in the empty flat. Sean's suitcase gone from the hall, the saxophone from the corner of the bedroom.

So that was it.

She tested her feelings, recognising the hole that Sean's departure had left inside her.

She had told him Sev had stayed at the flat on Hogmanay and held her in his arms as the bells tolled in the New Year, because in those moments they both needed someone. That was all, she'd insisted, and almost meant it. Sean had read between the lines.

The cat came and wrapped itself round her legs in a flurry of cupboard love.

'Just you and me again.'

She picked Chance up and carried him into the kitchen. The grass in the convent garden below the window was frosted icing. Two nuns were strolling around, their footprints criss-crossing the white topping. If only her world was like theirs: calm, peaceful and orderly.

Since the fire in the laboratory, she had lost all the men in her life. Liam had promised to write, but he was going somewhere remote. A school on the Nigeria-Cameroon border. She wouldn't hear from him very often. She wondered if she ever would.

That last night they'd sat in a bar in Byres Road, where the surrounding noise made conversation easier. He was interested in her work and worried for her safety. She found herself liking this young man she had loved from a distance for so long.

Watching his face as he spoke, she thought she

detected both herself and Edward in him. She didn't regret either resemblance, because Liam was his own man. She asked if he would like to know who his father was.

'Not if you don't want to tell me.'

She told him everything. How much she had loved Edward, how wrong she had been to give her son up.

'I've thought about you every day of my life.' She looked down, not wanting him to see the tears in her eyes.

He was silent for a moment, giving her time.

'I had a happy childhood. But there were things about me I didn't understand . . .' He paused, trying to put his thoughts into words. 'I liked being alone.' He gave a half smile. 'Mum and Dad thought I was lonely.'

'And were you?'

He shook his head. 'No. But when they told me about the adoption, I understood why I was different.'

They had begun to talk of other things. His trip to Africa, his university course, her work.

She suspected that, like her, he needed to go away and think about this. He had met her once. Maybe that was all he needed or wanted. When they parted he turned and waved, and she took a mental image of her son to hold close to her in case she never saw him again.

Severino too had come to see her, blaming himself for her ordeal. She'd had a hunch about the arsonist and he didn't act on it quickly enough.

Tim Redpath had served with the fire service for ten

years. He had been dedicated to the work. Some said, consumed by it. Fire became more important than anything else in his life. Like me, Severino said. He was suspected of starting some of the fires he attended and had been dismissed from the service. His life fell apart. When he started buying drugs, Tommy Moffat had seen the potential in Tim's obsession.

'And the connection with Greg?'

'Once he established where you were staying, he did a bit of detective work,' he paused. 'If I had been thinking more and drinking less . . .' Sev's voice tailed off. 'I'm sorry.'

'For what?'

He looked at the suitcase waiting in the hall.

'For fucking up your life.'

'I managed that all by myself.'

He met her eyes.

'Do you think, you and I . . .'

She ran it over in her head, not for the first time.

'No.'

'I had to ask.'

When they kissed, his breath was sweet.

'Irn-Bru.' He smiled wryly.

She drew away.

'What about Gillian?'

'Moving to Auchenblair permanently. There's a nice steady guy there. Runs the local hotel. He's always had a soft spot for Gillian. Amy's going to the village school.'

'I'm sorry.'

'You're not the only one who can mess up.' He stroked her face. 'What will you do now?'

'Go back to work.'

'We're alike, you and I.'

'That would be the problem.'

Rhona listened to the silence, then walked from room to room reclaiming her home. Sean was right. She needed time and space. If they got back together it would be on different terms. They would each have to learn to commit.

She felt a strange peace envelop her. She had found Liam. The arsonist was caught. And she knew at last that her nemesis was dead. The forensic tests on the remains found in the hills were complete. Weakened by loss of blood, he had died of exposure. The paedophile who called himself Simon would never again trawl the internet for vulnerable young men. She need never search for him in a crowd again.

The convent bells began to toll for evening prayer. Rhona carried the cat into the sitting-room, switched on the stereo and sat down in front of the fire as the saxophone's notes filled the air.

Alone, Rhona listened to it play its song of love.

LIN ANDERSON

Deadly Code

HODDER

ACKNOWLEDGEMENTS

Thanks to Mairi Leach and Talitha and Ross
MacKenzie for help with Gaelic phrases, and to
the staff of Raasay House Outdoor Centre for
great food and hospitality on my various visits.
Hamish Haswell-Smith's *Scottish Islands*
was most useful for information on safe
harbours in Raasay.

Raasay is a real island but all of the characters
in *Deadly Code* are fictitious, as are some of
the more specific locations.

To Detective Inspector Bill Mitchell

THE VOICES WERE there again. Chitter chatter, chitter chatter. The two men were bad enough, whispering confidences, offering advice. She could just about cope with them.

But not the woman. It was the woman's voice she hated most. Screeching away at her.

Esther's stupid. Esther's stupid.

The wind met her abruptly at the Underground entrance, snatching the voice from her head. She imagined the woman being dragged away screaming, and smiled.

'It's a pound.' She was startled back into reality.

'Sorry. Right.'

She walked back from the unmoving turnstile and slipped a pound coin under the glass partition.

Her right hand shook as she tried to pluck the ticket from the curved metal tray. The guy waited, his chin raised in mock patience, as she fumbled.

Her hands didn't work any more. They didn't do what she told them.

She walked stiffly to the turnstile. As the slot sucked in the ticket, the woman's voice was back, nipping her brain.

When the train emerged from the tunnel, the roar momentarily drowned the voice. She looked down at the track and imagined being enveloped in a thick black silence.

Then the woman was back, calling her *a stupid bitch, a stupid fucking bitch.*

Esther stumbled forward, tipping her centre of gravity towards the edge.

I

A BODY IN water is prey to all manner of hazards: rocks, fish, boats in too much of a hurry to notice the soft thump of swollen flesh against a bow. This body – or more precisely, bit of a body – was no exception.

The left foot had been severed from the leg ten centimetres below the patella. Both fibula and tibia bones were divided at the same place. All the toes were intact, although the nails had disintegrated or been eaten off during the foot's time in the water.

Dr Rhona MacLeod stepped back from the examination table and eased the mask from her face, letting in the tang of the sea and the smell of watered death.

'Well?' The pathologist, Dr Sissons, raised an eyebrow.

DI Bill Wilson stood opposite. He raised an eyebrow to match, making sure Sissons didn't see, then winked at Rhona.

Chrissy McInsh, Rhona's young assistant, stepped back, her face growing pale. This week her hair was bright auburn. The contrast made her face even paler. Mortuary assistants grew used to the smell of corrupt flesh. Forensic assistants didn't get exposed to it often enough to become immune.

'I'd say the foot's been in the water between three and four weeks,' Rhona said.

Sissons nodded in agreement.

'A fisherman caught it in Raasay Sound,' said Bill.

'So the crime scene is a fishing boat?' Rhona smiled. 'I pity the crime scene manager on that one.'

'Tempers are running high on Skye. A boat went down there a month ago,' Bill said. 'They haven't found the bodies of the crew yet. Locals blame an MOD submarine. Chances are, the foot belongs to one of the missing men.'

'It wouldn't be the first time a submarine has snagged a net and sunk a boat.'

Bill nodded. 'Then again, it could be someone trying to get rid of a body.'

'Judging by the size, it's male.' Sissons glanced at Rhona. 'Dr MacLeod will confirm that with DNA sampling.'

'How did it get separated from the body?' Bill asked.

'Difficult to be certain,' Sissons said, 'after this amount of time in the water.'

Rhona contemplated the grey mass of soggy flesh. The limb had been cut off just below the knee, but by what? Most Glasgow villains liked to dispatch their victims with a knife, although hatchets, axes, machetes, meat cleavers and samurai swords were also popular. Glasgow was knifing capital of the UK, the Western Isles of Scotland were not.

'I'll take samples from the cut-off point,' she suggested. 'There might be microscopic fragments of metal left in the wound.'

There was a gagging sound. Chrissy was making for the door.

'Out on the town last night,' Rhona explained. 'Stomach's a little fragile.'

'I have to go,' Sissons said. 'I'll leave the rest to Dr MacLeod.'

'A call-out?' Rhona asked when he had left.

'A body. Fortunately not in my division.'

'The rest of this one could turn up.'

'Then again, it might not.'

The rugged west of Scotland, including the islands, had thousands of miles of coastline, mostly uninhabited. Depending on weather and tides, the rest of the body could end up anywhere, or never be found.

'We could DNA-test the families of the missing fishermen,' Rhona suggested.

'No authorisation to do that yet.'

'The MOD won't like the publicity.'

'There won't be any if they can help it.'

After Bill left, Rhona carefully examined the wound and succeeded in retrieving what could be particles of metal and some fibres. She bagged the metal for delivery to Chemistry and set about making slides of the fibres.

It was while she was extracting the samples that she noticed a possible area of pigmented or tattooed skin above the ankle bone.

Putrefaction had rendered the mark indistinct but if she removed the loose epidermis, it would be clearer on the underlying dermis. If her hunch was right and it was the remains of a tattoo, it might help identify the owner.

An hour later there was a shuffle outside and the door squeaked open.

'Finished with Long John Silver yet?'

Chrissy was holding her nose.

'Almost. How's the stomach?'

'Fine. I came to remind you of the time.'

Rhona glanced at the big clock above the door, already knowing she was running at least two hours behind. Trust the foot to arrive on this particular afternoon.

The phone rang when she was pulling on her coat.

'How's it going?'

'Hey, Bill.' Rhona managed a smile despite her hurry.

Married with two teenage kids, DI Bill Wilson represented the father-figure Rhona had lost when her own father died two years before. Her adoptive parents had a marriage made in heaven. Her dad had outlived her mother by only a couple of years.

Bill Wilson filled the gap left by her father in her life. They also worked well together. Attuned to each other's thought processes, their combined brains had solved a number of difficult cases.

Rhona waited, sensing Bill's sombre mood.

'I've had a meeting with the Super. The Ministry of Defence want the discovery of the foot kept low profile until we find out who it belongs to.'

Rhona wasn't surprised.

'If it helps, I've dug out what might be tiny fragments

of metal and rope. I also identified a faint mark above the ankle bone that just might be a tattoo. If we manage to enhance the image digitally, it could identify the owner.'

'Good.'

Rhona caught sight of the clock again. 'Sorry Bill I have to go. I have an early flight to LA and I haven't done my homework yet.'

'Business class, I hope?'

'Paid for by our transatlantic cousins.'

Rhona took a last look round the lab, then slipped her laptop into its case and slung it over her shoulder.

The disappearance of fishing boats was not uncommon in the waters off the west coast of Scotland. The MOD had to practise submarine manoeuvres somewhere and where better than Raasay Sound? If the MOD thought they were responsible for this death, it would go some way to explaining the secrecy. Get in before the press. Stop uncomfortable questions being asked in parliament. Anyway, if the rest of the body didn't turn up, some poor woman would be burying a foot in place of her fisherman husband.

Rhona pulled the lab door shut and headed for the stairs. Old George was on duty in reception, strains of the 'Grand Ole Opry' escaping from his earphones.

'Hey, Doc.'

She was halfway to the front door when he called her back.

'This was handed in for you. Something about your trip.'

Rhona took the white envelope and turned it over. It

had the travel agent's address on the back. God, she had said she would pick up the final bits of paper this afternoon and the work on the tattoo had put it right out of her head.

'Thanks, George. Wouldn't have got far without this.'

He smiled and pointed to the CD, giving Rhona the thumbs up. The image of a severed foot was replaced with something much worse: a long night shift with only George's choice of country music for company.

She took a left into University Avenue and headed for Byres Road. Early May in Scotland could bring four seasons in one day, or one hour. This evening it was spring-like with a sharp wind that sent threatening clouds rushing across the sky.

Rhona took a deep breath of the crisp air. After the stuffiness of the lab it tasted good. She loved this part of Glasgow. The gothic university campus standing dominant on the hill, watching over the city. At its southern foot, the green of Kelvingrove Park. Northwards, the university gardens, criss-crossed by downward paths ending in the grounds of the Western Infirmary.

Rhona had been a student here. On graduation, she'd had to go south for work, but she'd eventually succeeded in coming back to her favourite city.

She took a right into University Gardens, passing the Maths building. Further along, the Gregory Building housed her GUARD colleagues (Glasgow University Archaeological Research Division). The GUARD team was responsible for analysing stomach contents of victims, and more generally entomological and botanical evidence.

Expertise was a team effort now. Gone were the days when a single renowned forensic expert entered the witness box and gave his opinion, though those eminent fathers of forensics, Professor Glaister in Glasgow and Sir Sydney Smith in Edinburgh, had paved the way for the work she did now.

Rhona quickened her step. In about twelve hours she would be boarding a plane for Los Angeles and she had done next to nothing to prepare for either her departure or the paper she was to deliver.

The Underground entrance was littered with spent tickets making small pirouettes in the wind that rushed to fill the two tunnels. This was one subway tourists could not get lost on. Opposite directions took you to the same places if you stayed on long enough. It was like travelling a Mobius strip. You started and ended in the same spot, having apparently flipped across to the other side of the track on the way.

As Rhona waited on the narrow central platform, a mixed group of Glasgow's nouveau-cool appeared at the top of the stairs, all giggles and expensive aftershave. They clattered down the steps, hearing the rumble from the tunnel, anticipating a train.

The young woman arrived seconds later. She stood next to Rhona, mouth moving silently, shoulders hunched. She was high on something.

Drugs – Glasgow's curse.

Rhona tried not to stare at the pale face, the clouded eyes, the mouth plucking silent words. How old was she? Eighteen, nineteen? Did her mother know she was like this?

Rhona thought of her own teenage son, Liam, doing voluntary work in some village in Nigeria that didn't even exist on a map.

As the train emerged from the tunnel, the girl stumbled and for a screaming moment Rhona thought she might fall in front of it. Then the orange door hissed open and the girl was inside and curled against the glass in a corner seat.

Rhona sat opposite, irritated by her need to categorise her, examine her like a piece of forensic evidence. It was both the *raison d'être* and the curse of her profession. Everyone in the world was a potential victim. Everyone was some mother's child.

The young woman had stopped her silent mouthings and was staring sideways through the glass. She reached up and pushed a strand of damp blonde hair behind her left ear, exposing a beauty spot in the shape of a small and perfect heart. Without the hunched shoulders and haunted eyes, she could be a pre-Raphaelite painting. She turned in Rhona's direction. For a moment their eyes met and then she was up and heading for the door as the train drew into the next station, but not before Rhona saw the mixture of torment and tears on her face.

The big bay window shone with light. Sean was already home. The familiar knot arrived in Rhona's stomach. Ever since they had got back together she had been like this. Wanting to arrive home to an empty flat. Seeking the luxury of being alone again.

Then she would see him and the knot would dissolve. She couldn't explain it, even to herself.

She had always enjoyed living alone. When a day went badly she could go home and shut the door. Her work brought her into contact with so much horror, there had to be somewhere she switched off. Somewhere she didn't have to talk. Her cat, Chance, was there if she needed to unburden her soul and he never talked back, apart from an occasional purr.

When Sean entered her life, he had disturbed its equilibrium. His blue eyes and Irish charm had invoked a passion she feared she could not control. Worse, did not want to control.

Then Sean moved out. Her decision, of course.

The parting hadn't lasted long. One night, after a difficult day, she found herself outside the jazz club again. She sat in the shadows listening to Sean play his saxophone. When he played the tune he wrote for her, she realised he knew she was there, waiting.

Rhona stood the briefcase on the hall floor and hung up her coat. Chance came running to greet her, wrapping her legs in a cocoon of warm fur.

'In the kitchen,' Sean called.

Rhona hesitated for a moment before she went in. 'You're late.'

'Sorry. I was late leaving. We had a leg, or I should say a foot, in last thing.'

'A leg?'

Rhona made a face and chose not to explain. Sean handed her a glass of red wine, at exactly the right temperature.

'Château de France '94,' he said. 'Good.'

Rhona listened as he related the story of the acquisition of the wine.

'So what's the celebration?'

'Your trip, of course. Not every day my lady gets an all-expensespaid trip to LA, where she is *the* guest speaker.'

'*A* guest speaker,' Rhona corrected him. 'It's not that important.'

But he knew it was. They raised their glasses.

'What's for dinner?' she said, anchoring her thoughts in the here and now.

'Leg of lamb,' Sean said. 'Not a good choice.'

Rhona laughed.

He played the audition tape as they sat in front of the fire finishing the wine, anticipating sex.

Rhona had known there was something Sean wanted to tell her. It was in his greeting, the choice of wine, the nice meal.

So this was it.

'What do you think?' he said.

The voice was a mixture of woman and girl. Sexy and childlike at the same time. A powerful combination.

Rhona tried not to put a face to the voice. Instead she asked, 'Who is she?'

'Her name's Esther. She came to the club today and asked to audition. We gave her a shot.'

'She's good.' It was an understatement.

'Yeah.' Sean was pleased, as if he were responsible for the wonderful sound.

'Have you met her before?' Rhona was trying to keep the edge from her voice.

He shook his head. 'She turned up out of the blue. Said she'd stopped performing for a while, but was keen to get back.'

Rhona examined her glass, thinking they had been here before. She knew from the moment they met that Sean liked women. He was honest about it. Monogamy had not been his strong point – until now. Or so he said.

He put his glass down. 'What's wrong?'

'Nothing.'

The sultry voice flowed between them, pushing them apart. Sean stood up and switched it off.

'More wine?'

Rhona shook her head. Sean refilled his own glass. She got up. 'I'd better pack.'

He caught her arm. 'I hired her to sing, Rhona, not to fuck.'

'I never said that.'

'But you thought it, didn't you?'

His mouth came down hard on hers and she felt the familiar surge of desire. Sometimes she thought of Sean as a drug, his presence bringing waves of pleasure that drowned out everything else.

The window was open. Cool night air rippled over their warm naked bodies. Her shiver was as much from desire as it was from the chill.

Sean was good at this. He played her body in a way that no one else could. Sometimes gentle, sometimes so hard she thought she would break and shatter into tiny pieces. Tonight his tongue was a whisper across her skin, every cell vibrating in response. Her blood beat in anticipation.

He slipped his hands beneath and lifted her. The entrance was as smooth as silk, as sweet as honey.

She shuddered on the cusp of orgasm and he retreated.

'Not yet,' he whispered into her hair.

She rose at three o'clock. Sean breathed silently, his head dark against the pillow. As she got up, the thought crossed her mind that during her absence the new singer might fill the place she had just vacated.

Sex was food to Sean. As necessary to life as playing his saxophone. And what about her?

She was no innocent either. An image of Severino MacRae crossed her mind. When they were thrown together during an arson case, the Chief Fire Investigator's attitude had driven her first to distraction, then into a sexual dance that had been as compelling as the investigation itself.

At times like those, she thought she might break Sean's spell over her by having sex with someone else. It didn't matter what she thought. Her body's response to Sean was something she could not control.

The sitting room was in darkness, the big wooden shutters open to reveal the night sky over Glasgow;

the biggest, some would say the friendliest city in Scotland.

But it was also the most violent, with a knife and drugs culture that walked hand in hand. A tally of a hundred drug-related deaths a year wasn't unusual.

The haunted face she had looked into on the Underground suggested the girl could have a place in the next statistics.

And she, Rhona, had said nothing, done nothing, even when she imagined in that split second that the girl might jump.

What happened to the words *Are you alright? Can I help?*

You can't help everyone, Sean had said when she told him the story over dinner. And he was right.

In her job, she couldn't prevent death. She could only help the dead explain how or why they had died.

At first the black words on the white screen danced in front of Rhona's eyes, but gradually she was sucked into the comfort of ideas begun, explored, formulated, proved. This was the time she liked to write: in the dark, the peace, the streets below empty of people. This was the time she thought best. Even as a student she had gone to bed struggling with some scientific problem, only to waken in the middle of the night having solved it mysteriously in her sleep. Two hours later the paper was complete. She checked the acknowledgments. Some of these people would be at the conference. The thought filled her with both pleasure and fear. The perfect mixture.

By the time Sean appeared naked at the sitting room door, she was packed and ready to leave.

'Is it that time already?'

'I've called a taxi. It'll be here in a minute.'

'Come here.'

He slipped his hands under her coat and ran them up her spine. His body was bed-warm against hers. She breathed in the smell of his skin.

'You'll phone?' he said.

'Of course.'

They parted at the front door with a kiss, the tip of Sean's tongue a reminder of what had happened between them earlier.

Glasgow was as quiet as the grave.

She watched the empty streets roll past. In the cold light of dawn, nothing seemed to matter. Death or life was inconsequential. Rhona felt herself relax, the taste of guilt at her sense of release from Sean sharp in her mouth.

Two hours and three cups of coffee later, she was still sitting in the airport lounge. Her flight had been delayed initially by twenty minutes, then by an hour.

Rhona took vengeance on her empty polystyrene cup. 'And another thing,' she muttered to herself. 'How many cups of airport coffee can a person swallow before they die of poisoning?'

'I believe four is the maximum.'

'What?'

'A person can only drink four of those before . . .' The man to her right sliced across his throat with his finger. 'There was an article in last month's *Scientific American* by someone who travels a lot.'

A smile was beyond Rhona.

'As long as that's the last delay,' she said.

As if on cue, the departure board sprang to life.

'Did that just change to 10.30?' Rhona looked at her neighbour in despair. He nodded equally despairingly.

'God,' she said. 'I'd be quicker swimming.'

'The Atlantic, perhaps, but then there is the great American land mass to cross before you reach California.' He paused. 'Of course, you could go in the other direction but that would involve travelling to Edinburgh first. And I gather people from Glasgow are not keen on Edinburgh?'

He had succeeded. She smiled. He held out his hand. He introduced himself. 'Andre Frith.'

'Dr Andre Frith? The University of California?'

He nodded. 'I recognised you from your picture.' He waved the pre-conference blurb. 'I came over to propose we have a coffee together.' He looked at the crushed coffee cup. 'But maybe not.'

'What about something to eat instead?' Rhona suggested.

2

SPIKE WAS OUT the door before the girl serving knew he had ever been in. Two boys waiting for hot pies saw him pocket the packet of potato scones from the counter but said nothing.

Spike didn't run. Outside the baker's, the street was busy with school kids eating fast food and dropping the papers at their feet. Spike joined them for a bit, then strolled across the road. No point in being about when the bell went for the end of lunchtime. Folk might wonder why he wasn't back in school with the rest of them. He resisted the warm smell of potato coming from his pocket even though he was hungry. He had plans for the tattie scones.

When he reached the tenement block, he walked straight past the front entrance and nipped in through the back railings in case the woman on the first floor spotted him. He ducked under half-a-dozen grey nappies flapping on a line. Nothing there worth nicking.

When he reached the third floor, he heard the peevish whine of the baby. He didn't like hearing it cry. It reminded him of his wee brother Calum. Next door was flapping open, caught in the stair's sucking breeze. The baby's whine was louder now.

'Christ. Pick it up. Pick the kid up.'

He ignored the bad smell that drifted out the neighbours' door and turned the key in his own. He was halfway in when the baby emitted a high-pitched cry. It was no use. He would have to make sure it was alright. He almost gagged at the smell of stale piss as he made his way to the living room. The baby had stopped whining now and was weeping, a lost sound that expected no answer. Spike pushed open the living room door. It ground its way over broken glass.

He looked about angrily. Where the fuck was she this time? *She* was on the settee, junked out of her mind. And beside her, head slumped back, mouth hanging open, was the kid's father. Spike swept the baby up from the floor and took it to the bathroom.

He ran the dirty wee hand under the tap and dried it on his shirt. The cut was only a nick, and couldn't have hurt much – it had probably been more shock than pain that had brought on the crying. Spike brushed at the knees of his dirty trousers, sending fragments of glass down the toilet pan.

'Okay. Now what do we do?' he asked his patient.

Some snot escaped the child's nose, ran down his face and met the remains of a tear. Spike pulled a bit of toilet paper off the roll and wiped the mess away.

'Come on,' he said. 'We're leaving.'

He was sharing his dinner with his new best friend when he heard the front door open. He had fried the tattie scones and heated some beans. The baby was sitting surrounded by cushions, wee hands waving in the air in anticipation of the next mashed spoonful.

Spike shovelled another one in and handed it a mug of milk. He looked up as Esther came into the kitchen.

'We've got a visitor,' he said.

'So I see.'

She tried to smile, but he knew by the shadows round her eyes.

'It's bad, isn't it?' he said.

'No!'

He jumped at the sharpness of her tone and she looked sorry.

'It's okay. Honestly. It was bad in the Underground but it's quieter now.'

'I made some food,' he said. 'Yours is in the grill.'

They were drinking mugs of tea when the baby's mother banged on the door.

'Did you take the wean?'

'What do you care?'

'Fucking wee smart-arse.'

She pushed past Spike and pulled the child up by his arm. He let out a squeal of rage as the biscuit he was eating flew to the floor.

'Don't feed my wean. I've told you before.'

'You feed it then.'

She kicked the door as she went out.

Esther was pale and frightened.

'They were both out of their minds on the settee,' he explained. 'The place smelt like a pisshole.'

Esther looked worried. 'She'll tell the social about you. She knows you're a runaway.'

'Then we'll move,' he said. 'I'm fed up listening to them shagging anyway.'

'Spike.'

'What?'

He could feel his face shift into worry.

'You might not be able to stay here any more.'

'You want me out?'

'No.' She shook her head. 'It's just . . . if the singing doesn't work out . . . there won't be any money.'

'There's none now.'

He fetched the pot and poured more tea. He felt sixteen going on sixty.

Esther took the mug and nursed it, her mind someplace else.

Spike wondered about going to a doctor, asking about the voices. When he'd tried to persuade Esther to make an appointment, she'd looked so frightened. He couldn't bear it when she looked at him like that.

'Spike?' She smiled. 'Thanks.'

'What for?'

She leaned forward and touched his head with her lips. 'For everything.' She got up. 'I'd better get ready. Don't want to be late.'

'I'll walk you down.'

She looked as if she might argue, then thought better of it. While she got ready he cleared the dishes and washed up. In his whole life, this was the first place he had been happy. Esther made him happy.

'Right. How do I look?'

She'd changed and put up her hair, revealing the heart-shaped mole. Her eyes were black-rimmed, lashes thick with mascara. She stretched her red mouth into a smile.

'For the punters, right?'

He prayed that the voices would leave her alone for tonight.

'Right,' he said. 'Let's go.'

He liked walking with her. In the dark she could be his girlfriend. In the dark he wasn't sixteen. She put her arm through his. The streets were filling up with punters, blokes set on a night out.

They passed the Fantasy Bar. Four guys got out of a taxi and hung about the steps before they went in. Spike hated them, hated the way they were men before they were human.

'Heh, I'm not there yet,' she said, tugging him on.

The jazz club was busy, a trail of people edging its way in the door.

'I'll see you later,' she said and squeezed his arm.

'I could come in.'

The doorman gave him a look that suggested otherwise.

'I'll be back for you.'

Esther nodded, trying to hide her nervousness.

After she disappeared Spike stood for a while, ignoring the doorman's bugger-off look.

He tried to imagine Esther on stage, the red lips trembling with sound. He thought about looking for a back entrance, finding a way in, hiding, watching her sing.

The doorman had had enough.

'Get lost, son.'

Spike gave him the finger and walked on.

3

RHONA MADE HERSELF look down. Below her, the west coast of Scotland peeped through a curtain of grey cloud, each island a jigsaw piece of green and purple against the charcoal water.

'Shit.'

'Pardon me?'

'I'm sorry. I hate flying. It's unnatural.'

'But you're a scientist. You know . . .'

'. . . that the laws of physics dictate this thing will stay in the air. I know, but I still hate looking down.'

'Why don't you pull the blind and pretend we're in a train instead.'

'Good idea. Just don't mention any train crashes.'

The plane was busy. Beyond the curtains of business class, Rhona could hear a wall of voices and the clatter of a trolley. In here life was quiet, well ordered, peaceful and spacious. On her left Andre Frith was reading some papers, on her right a small flat screen begged her to switch on and enjoy the inflight movie. All expenses paid was the way to travel.

Her DNA research had brought her here. For the last couple of years she had been involved in a think-tank to see how DNA studies and certain other branches of genetic research might aid crime investigators in the future. The next step was to match the DNA characteristics of bacteria and virus samples to one another so that they could determine if two individuals were in the same environment, or in close enough contact with one another to pass micro-organisms back and forth. Challenging, but not insurmountable. Such research was welcomed by the university. It brought money in the form of grants. It also brought prestige and invitations to conferences in exotic places.

Her companion turned and gave her one of those American smiles, all white teeth, golden tan and crinkly blue eyes. Rhona was suddenly reminded of Harrison Ford.

'You didn't mention why you were in Scotland,' she said.

'Didn't I? I was in Scotland because . . . well, Scotland is beautiful.'

'So you were a tourist?'

'Yes and no. I had a little business to deal with first, then I took a look at your west coast. I'm afraid, like so many Americans, I was searching for my roots.

'Your family was Scottish?'

'My great-great-great-grandmother came from Raasay. She was one of the MacLeods cleared from there in the 1800s.'

'So we're related?'

He laughed. 'Looks like it.'

'And did you find what you were looking for?'

He looked sad. 'I found a pile of stones.'

'I'm sorry.'

'Don't be. It was enough.'

He pulled a photograph from his pocket. It showed two women seated on stiff-backed chairs, a man standing behind them. The sepia colours made the women look ugly and severe.

He pointed at the one on the right. 'My grandmother,' he said. 'Scary, isn't she?'

'Yes, she is.'

'She was born in the Red River Valley, which is where her mother ended up. According to family legend, my great-great-grandmother spoke only Gaelic until the day she died. She had made up her mind she was coming back, you see.' He smiled. 'A determined lady.'

'But she didn't.'

'No. But I did.'

The prospect of the LA Conference didn't seem so daunting, now she was on speaking terms with at least one of the contributors.

Andre Frith was to deliver a paper on 'The New Weapons of Ethnic Cleansing'. At least sixteen countries, Rhona knew, had bioweapon programs, including Syria, North Korea and China. Russia, Andre reminded her, had already developed a new generation of untreatable diseases which were resistant to antibiotics.

'And on that positive note, here come the pre-dinner drinks,' he announced. 'Champagne, madam?'

Rhona nodded her acceptance. Talking shop with a handsome biochemist over a glass or two of cham-

pagne could make her forget there was nothing between her and the Atlantic except fresh air and the laws
of physics.

Rhona rolled across the king-size empty bed and
looked at the clock. No wonder Santa Monica was
going strong. It might be two in the morning on her
internal clock but it was late afternoon here. It would be
easier if she got up, went and found a place to eat, then
slept when everybody else did.

As she stood in the shower, water pounding on her
head, she thanked God she had time to put her brain
back together before she had to address the conference.

Andre had left her at the airport, promising to call on
Sunday and take her for a short drive. Rhona had no
idea what this might mean in American terms. Probably nothing under seventy miles.

On her way to the hotel she chatted with her taxi
driver. He told her he lived in the desert and it took him
two hours to get home. He had to leave the city at eight
o'clock to avoid the rush hour.

Catching a five-minute ride to work, or even walking
for twenty minutes, began to look like heaven in
comparison. Rhona made a mental note to remind
Chrissy how lucky she was; how lucky they both were.

She momentarily forgot the time difference and
phoned Chrissy, who was initially disgruntled to be
woken up. 'So, you're trying to say it's hell over there?'
She didn't sound convinced.

Rhona took in the spacious air-conditioned room;
the blue sky outside, the sun shining through the

window, the smell of fresh coffee and fruit just delivered by the management.

'Not hell, just hectic,' she said.

'So where is this Andre taking you tomorrow?'

'To meet some more MacLeods.'

'You've got family over there?'

'I'm meeting the Californian branch of the Clan MacLeod.'

'They'll be nutcases.'

'Thanks.'

'Nothing personal,' Chrissy said. 'But chances are they'll be the Jacobite brigade.'

Rhona chose to ignore that remark. Instead she asked Chrissy a favour, which was followed by silence.

'Never heard of them, but I'll check for you. What were they called again?'

'ReGene.' Rhona spelt it out for her.

'Sounds like an advert for Lee Cooper.'

'The card was here when I arrived. A Dr Lynne Franklin wants to arrange a meeting.'

'Looks like you're in demand.'

'I'd like to know a bit about the company before I agree to speak to her.'

'She probably thinks you've got a DNA vaccine up your sleeve, ready for worldwide distribution.'

Rhona resisted a retort. With Chrissy always wanting the last word, they could be there all night.

'By the way,' Chrissy said, 'I'm going to the jazz club tonight. See how Sean's getting on without you.'

'Oh.'

'Danny says the band's new singer is very hot.'

Danny was the latest in Chrissy's long string of boyfriends.

'I thought I'd better view the competition.' Chrissy paused. '*My* competition, I mean.'

No answer could adequately express what Rhona felt at that moment, so she didn't voice one.

'I'll email when I've done the background on Re-Gene,' Chrissy went on. 'Oh, DI Wilson says thanks for the report on the foot. He'll talk to you when you get back.'

Rhona rang off quickly before Chrissy could fire more ammunition at her. Chrissy believed in being up-front about everything, including Sean. Making a meal of Rhona's jealous streak was Chrissy's way of telling her not to worry. It rarely worked.

Rhona opened the suitcase and found something to wear that suited another climate – and another planet, she thought, as she emerged from the cool elegance of the marble reception area into the late afternoon sunshine of Third Street, Santa Monica.

A guy with long hair and a longer coat stood on the corner, money rising and falling from his flicked hand with monotonous regularity. He had the look of a Jesus who had just ejected the money lenders from the temple and now wasn't sure what to do with their small change.

Rhona tossed a coin into the embroidered hat at his feet. If he spotted her contribution to his welfare he didn't acknowledge it.

The pedestrian precinct of Third Street was already teeming with people, hanging out and being cool, and

that was only the beggars. An alcoholic told the truth
on his cardboard sign: *Okay, I won't lie, I need a drink,
please give.* Honesty seemed to be paying off.

Rhona took her time, reading restaurant menus
posted in glass cases on the sidewalk, trying not to
be intimidated by the waiters and waitresses, all definite members of the beautiful people's club.

'Madam, you like Italian?'

This one was particularly handsome and sexy. It was
obvious why he was told to hang about the entrance.

Rhona succumbed and shortly afterwards found
herself sitting in an alcove, sipping cool white wine
and wiping up deliciously fragrant olive oil with freshly
baked bread. Okay, so you could do this in Glasgow,
but it wasn't quite the same. Rhona felt guilty at the
thought. While she waited for the main course, she
took another look at the message on the back of the
ReGene card.

*Looking forward to your paper. Could we meet some
time while you're here? Dr Lynne Franklin.*

It told Rhona nothing except that ReGene had a
fancy address in Los Angeles and a second address in
the Bahamas. Whatever the company did, it made
money at it. Rhona slipped the card back into her
wallet and concentrated on the arrival of the main
course.

Noticing her Scottish accent, the waiter hung
around and gave her his family history, including
the low-down on his Italian relatives who ran a Glasgow restaurant. By the end of the meal, he had asked
whether she was dating anyone. It was while she was

saying (somewhat reluctantly) she was, that a girl came in. She was tall, much taller than Rhona, with the blonde good looks of a Beach Boys album cover. Rollerblades made her even taller, so that after her perfectly performed halt she stood six inches above Rhona's waiter, who she had obviously come to see.

Trying not to think of a Steve Martin film, Rhona removed herself from the middle of the ensuing confrontation and took her check to the counter to pay. The equally handsome man on the till gave her a perfect smile and wished her a good day.

On the Santa Monica promenade, things weren't any better. Replicas of the restaurant girl whizzed past on rollerblades. Male rollerbladers looked like Rambo in very small shorts.

Santa Monica didn't look like Glasgow but according to Andre the two places had one thing in common. You could buy anything on this promenade, including drugs and sex, provided you had the money.

She glanced at her watch.

It would be four in the morning in Glasgow. Sean would probably be back from his gig at the club.

Rhona pulled out her mobile and pressed the familiar number, imagining the signal waving its way around the world. It rang out half-a-dozen times before she hung up.

When she got back to the hotel there was a message waiting for her at reception. Andre would be round at ten o'clock the next morning to take her to the MacLeod tent at a Highland games.

Rhona tried to imagine what Chrissy would say about that. It didn't bear repeating, even in her head.

Before she went to bed, she set up her computer and checked her email. Nothing.

No phone calls from home, no emails. It was true, living in hotel rooms made you disappear.

Rhona didn't notice the gold-edged envelope until she climbed into bed. Lying on the bedside table, it looked too smart for an advertising leaflet.

In that, she was wrong. It was an advertising leaflet. A really classy one. The embossed card inside suggested that, alone in Santa Monica, Dr MacLeod might like some intelligent and charming male company for dinner and seeing the sights. No prices quoted. Obviously if you had to ask the price, you couldn't afford the man.

Rhona tucked the card back in the envelope, but not before she'd noted the name and phone number on the back. Jason, it seemed, was the one on special offer.

Rhona switched off the light, wishing she had someone to share the joke with.

Professional woman, alone in Santa Monica on business, seeks charming intelligent man to share dinner and . . .

4

CHRISSY WAS WAITING outside the jazz club for Danny when the girl and boy arrived.

'I'm a friend of Sean's. I'm singing here tonight.'

The doorman waved the girl past, but stopped the boy.

Chrissy didn't blame him. No way was the guy twenty-one. She wondered if the girl was his big sister and he just wanted to hear her sing. She thought about pleading his case, saying she would keep an eye on him.

Then the bouncer told him to get lost. The boy didn't argue, just gave him the finger and walked away.

Danny showed up minutes later and swept Chrissy inside. The basement room was throbbing with music.

'Drink?' Danny mouthed.

All the tables were taken so she waited for him near the bar. The club was a popular haunt with university staff, especially forensics and pathology. It was close to work and stayed open late. If you were called out to an incident in the middle of the night, you could come here afterwards and drown your sorrows. There were two mortuary technicians she recognised at a table doing exactly that.

Danny handed her a Bacardi Breezer and slipped an arm round her waist.

At the end of his solo number, Sean spotted her and smiled over.

At least half a dozen women, including the two mortuary technicians, turned to look enviously at her. Sean was working his usual magic.

When the young woman came on stage, the place went quiet. Sean took her hand and brought her forward. She wore a red sequinned dress that hugged her slim body. Her hair was swept up at the back, exposing a heart-shaped mole on her cheek. The mix of intensity and vulnerability reminded Chrissy of old footage of Janis Joplin.

'Ladies and gentlemen, I'd like you to meet Esther Dickson.'

The charcoal eyes darted about the audience, as frightened as a roe deer caught in the headlights of a car.

Sean played the intro.

She hesitated and missed her entrance.

Sean played the opening again.

This time she came in right on cue.

The background chatter faded as the low sensual voice filled the room. Chrissy felt a shiver run down her spine. She was good, really good. The audience was hanging on every note. Esther was more confident now. She knew she had them in the palm of her hand.

At the end of the song, the audience clapped wildly and shouted for more. Chrissy looked at Danny. He was loving it.

'Watch out Rhona.'

'What?' Danny pulled his eyes from the stage.

'I said, watch out Rhona. This one only needs to sing to get a guy off.'

Danny grinned like a man with a hard-on. 'Yeah, baby.'

Esther sang three songs. The whole audience was sexed out. She left the stage before they finished clapping.

Danny gave Chrissy a kiss with a promise in it and went to the bar for a refill. Chrissy followed the singer to the Ladies. She found her leaning over the basin, running cold water through her hands.

'You're very good,' Chrissy said.

'Thanks.' The voice was flat, as though the life had drained away with the songs.

Chrissy examined Esther's reflection in the mirror. She had seen this female before somewhere. But where?

'Are you singing anywhere else?'

Esther looked at her sharply.

'What the fuck do you care?'

Chrissy rummaged in her bag. She *had* seen her before. She was sure of it. 'It's cool,' she made a show of renewing her lipstick, 'I just thought I'd heard you before.'

Esther shrugged and touched up her own mask of eye-shadow and lipstick. 'Couldn't have. I just moved here.'

'With your brother?'

'My brother?'

'The young guy outside.'

'Spike's not my brother. He's a mate.'

The girl had stopped being defensive. Whatever Chrissy said now had to keep things that way. She didn't get the chance.

'Shut the fuck up!' The girl hissed at the mirror.

'What?'

Esther ignored her and headed for a cubicle, slamming the door in Chrissy's face. From inside came the sound of muttering. Chrissy knocked. 'Are you okay?'

The girl didn't reply, at least not to Chrissy. The muttering went on, then the sound of retching and the thump of something hitting the floor. Chrissy banged on the door.

'Hey, are you alright in there?'

'Fuck off and leave me alone.'

It took Chrissy five minutes to find Scan. The band was taking a break and he had gone outside for some air. When she brought him back to the toilet, the cubicle was empty.

'She was on something.'

'You don't know that,' Sean said firmly.

The thought crossed Chrissy's mind that he knew more about Esther than he was letting on.

'She was swearing at the mirror.'

A half-smile played Sean's lips. 'Maybe she was swearing at you.'

Chrissy wasn't giving up. 'I've seen her someplace before.'

Sean looked mildly irritated. 'I'm only interested in where she is at this moment. We have a second half to do.'

Chrissy gazed past Sean.

Esther had appeared at the door. 'Is there a problem?' she said truculently.

'Not with me,' Chrissy shot back.

'Could you give us a minute?' Sean said quietly.

'Fine.' Sean *did* know more about Esther Dickson than he was letting on. Chrissy headed for the bar and a stiff drink.

Esther was back on stage ten minutes later. She seemed calm, dreamy even. An addict after a fix?

Chrissy stood with Danny's arm about her and listened to Esther's haunting voice. Sean had given her the girl's version of events on his way to the stage. He might be convinced, but she wasn't.

In the shadows near the bar she spotted the boy with the spiky hair, who had somehow sneaked in. He wore the same expression as Danny. Whatever substance the girl had in her voice should be powdered and marketed.

But magic voice or not, the story of a migraine attack just didn't make it with Chrissy.

She was sure she'd seen Esther before. And she had the feeling the girl was bad news. Bad news Rhona needed to know about.

5

THINGS WERE QUIET now. He could tell by her eyes.
Spike took Esther's hand and slipped it through his
arm.

'Chips?'

'Yeah.' She waved the money Sean had given her.
'Let's make it a fish supper.'

The all-night café was empty apart from a few
stragglers who needed the sustenance in order to get
home.

She sat down and handed him the plastic menu with
a flourish. 'No expense spared.'

After the feast he said, 'You were great.'

When she asked how he knew, he told her he'd
climbed in a toilet window.

She laughed. 'Did anyone see you?'

She laughed even more when he said, 'Only the guy
wanking off in the cubicle I landed in. And he wasn't
going to tell anybody.'

'And I thought I was singing in a respectable jazz
club.'

'Wanking is respectable,' he told her, 'unless you've
been brought up . . .' he came to a halt, a shadow
crossing his face.

She reached out and took his hand.

'Like you?'

'Like me.'

He went quiet.

'Heh?' She squeezed his hand. 'We're doing fine.'

She was always positive when the voices weren't there. He suspected something in her past had made her ill like this but Esther never spoke about it and he didn't ask. He didn't want to talk about his either.

They had met in Safeways. She was shopping, he was there to steal something to eat. She spotted him slipping a tin of corned beef in his pocket and made him put it in her trolley. When they got to the counter, she paid for it.

Outside she asked him where he was staying and he took too long to lie, so she took him home. In his head he made her the big sister he never had. It didn't always work.

'Okay,' she said. 'Let's go home.'

Spike stood up, happy. He loved it when she spoke like that, as if they would be together forever. He had played out the scenario a million times in his head. It didn't matter that he was only fourteen. He could look after Esther, hold her when she was frightened, even maybe . . .

He shut down his brain at that point. He hated himself for even thinking about making a move on her. He would never do that. Never.

Her voice punctured his thoughts.

'Sean was great. Even when I almost blew it in the toilet.'

'What?'

'Someone came in when . . . when things were bad. She told Sean I was taking stuff.'

'Jesus.'

She smiled at his worried face. 'It's okay. I told him I had a migraine and was sick. He believed me.'

He hated when the voices came and he wasn't with her. Sometimes he felt they were waiting for him to go away, just so they could torment her.

They were passing a block of red sandstone tenements. On the ground floor, plants filled a window box and trailed down in a burst of flowers. Their scent hung heavy in the night air.

'Maybe we could move,' she said suddenly, 'get a better flat.'

She grabbed his arm in excitement. 'Sean says he can run me six weeks, maybe more. With that sort of money I could put down a deposit on a decent place. Sean says once the word is out I'll get more gigs.'

Spike fought back the fear that slid up his throat. Now she was back singing, she might not need him any more.

She touched his arm.

'You'll come with me, won't you Spike?' Her voice was small and lonely again.

His fear subsided.

'Of course I will.'

Then he thought about the baby.

'We'll tell the social about the baby,' she said, reading his mind.

The child was half-starved. It would be totally starved if Spike wasn't there to feed it.

'She was going to shop you anyway.'

Esther was right. The mother was always threatening to tell the authorities about him. It was only a matter of time. And the baby wasn't his responsibility.

'Okay.' He tried a smile. 'Okay.'

She was happy now. They had a plan, a plan for the future.

Above them, the street lamps sent soft lights to reflect their images in the puddles. Spike saw them there together, arm and arm.

Nothing or nobody would get them, he decided. He would see to that.

When they reached the tenement block, the stairwell was in darkness. He took her hand and they negotiated the broken bottles that littered the entrance. He felt in his pocket for his lighter.

'Some bastard's smashed the lights.'

He went up the left hand side, sliding his arm along the wall, encouraging the small blue flame to light up the next step.

When they reached their landing, Spike produced the key.

'Spike.' Esther pointed at the broken lock.

'What the fuck!'

He made a move to go in, but she caught his arm.

'No.' Her face was terrified in the flare of the lighter.

Whoever was inside had heard them. Footsteps came towards the door. Esther ran for the stairs. Spike flipped the lighter shut and followed. They stumbled their way down. They were one level below when they heard the door open. Spike held Esther against him. He could feel the thump of her heart.

'There's nobody there,' a man's voice called.

Esther gave a whimper. As the door swung shut, Spike took a quick look. A thickset figure was framed in the doorway.

Esther's eyes were wide with fear.

'Who was it?'

She was shaking, her words rattling through her teeth. Spike suddenly realised she thought the intruder had come looking for her.

'We have to get away from here,' she pleaded.

He took off his jacket and put it round her. 'It's okay. I think it was the Flintstone guy from next door,' he lied. 'He probably came to give me a kicking for taking the baby again.'

Relief flooded her face. 'Are you sure?'

He nodded. 'We'll come back tomorrow. He'll have given up by then.'

Spike ran it over in his mind. His own fear of discovery had started just after he met Esther. Bags, the *Big Issue* seller, had shown him a photo. It didn't look like him and even Bags didn't recognise him from it. In the photo his hair was short and neat. In the photo, he was fourteen.

'Looks like a computer nerd,' Spike had said, trying to sound casual. 'Who's looking for him?'

'A Yank. Gave me a twenty to keep a lookout.'

'Easy shit.'

'Yeah. Wish he was looking for me.'

Bags had a phone number to call. He waved it in front of Spike like another twenty.

'So if you see the nerd?'

'Sure.'

If an American was looking for him, it had to be something to do with his father. A cold knot formed in Spike's chest.

He'd been even more careful after that. If it hadn't been for Esther he would have left Glasgow, gone to London. They would never find him there.

They bedded down in the park under a tree, Esther curled against him, he holding his body a celibate inch away. Eventually she slept and he listened to the soft sound of her breathing.

She had told him once that the voices were there in her sleep, weaving their way into her dreams. He imagined people attached to these disembodied voices and routinely killed them to set her free, but they always came back to haunt her, especially when she was nervous or frightened.

The voices were sent to punish her. That's what she believed. Punish her for what?

Spike had no idea who the guy in their flat had been, but it wasn't their neighbour. He had been convinced it was somebody looking for him, but Esther thought the man had come for her and it had frightened the wits out of her.

Who was Esther afraid of? Some old boyfriend who'd been bad to her? Spike hated the thought of someone hurting Esther. He hated the thought of someone else being with her.

Spike felt his cock harden and immediately pulled back from the warmth of Esther's body.

He spat his distaste for himself into the grass.

'Heh.' She was awake and watching.

He jumped up and walked towards the bushes, afraid she would see his erection.

When he re-emerged, she was ready to go.

They went back to the café.

Esther was listless and Spike sensed she had entered that other world. The world of voices that told her she was shite, a nothing who didn't deserve to live.

'Esther?'

She didn't respond.

'Esther! Look at me.'

She lifted her head.

'We'll find somewhere else to stay. Don't worry.'

She gave him a small smile.

When he met her after her rehearsal, she was transformed. There was no rush to find a place, she told him excitedly.

'Sean says we can stay at his while his girlfriend's in California. That'll give us time to find somewhere decent.'

It didn't sound right to Spike. Why would this Sean guy offer Esther a room while his girlfriend was away?

'I don't think that's a good idea. He'll ask about me.'

'I told him you were my young cousin from up north. He doesn't mind.'

He doesn't mind. He doesn't mind. The words blew Spike's brain. Sean might not mind but Spike fucking well did.

'We don't need Sean. I'll find us somewhere.'

But she wasn't listening.

'Please, Spike. Sean gave me the key. We could at least take a look.'

A big black cat met them in the hall. Esther bent down and rubbed its head.

'Sean says it's called Chance.'

The cat made off and Esther followed.

Spike hung back, hating being in someone else's place. He took in the thick rugs, the polished wooden floor.

This was crazy. They couldn't stay here.

'Spike. Come and see this.'

He found her in a kitchen, standing at the window.

'It looks like a convent at the back.'

He joined her at the window and looked down on a trim lawn and neat flower beds. In the middle of the grass stood the Virgin Mary.

The whole thing was madness. They shouldn't be here. Already the space between them and the real world was diminishing. At the flat they were themselves, separate. They didn't have to discuss who they were, where they had come from. Here there would be questions and they would have to have answers.

'You don't want to be here, do you?' Esther was looking at him sadly.

'It's better if I don't stay with you.'

He knew how afraid she was of being alone with the voices.

'No. We'll find somewhere else.'

She made for the door, decided. Spike felt mean. You couldn't blame her for wanting this. To be warm, comfortable, clean, safe.

'So where's our room then?' he forced himself to say.

Her face lit up.

'You'll hardly see Sean. Anyway, he's not the nosy type.'

Yeah, thought Spike, but what about when the girlfriend comes home?

He almost chickened out when he saw the double bed. He forced himself not to imagine them there, his arms about her.

'We could share the bed,' she suggested, her voice light.

'It's alright. I'll just sleep on the couch.'

She opened another door and Spike caught a glimpse of mirrored tiles.

'A bathroom . . . with a shower!' Esther was like a kid on Christmas morning.

He smiled. 'I bet there's hot water too.'

She turned on the shower and began pulling off her clothes.

'I'll go and get our stuff,' he mumbled awkwardly.

'Sean says we can borrow his van tomorrow.'

'I'll just pick up some clothes and some CDs.'

'Okay, but be careful.'

Outside, the sun was blinking through the clouds. The pavement was lined with trees, big spreading sycamores waving their long pendulous May flowers. He was in the same city as before, but it was hard to believe it.

The American would never look for him in this part of Glasgow. Christ, even Bags wouldn't look for him here. He smiled, thinking about Bags' face if he knew Spike was holed up in a posh flat in the West End.

He tried to convince himself. All he had to do was lay low. Eventually, whoever was looking for him would get fed up, think he was dead too.

If only his father hadn't made him post the letters the day before it happened. He had insisted Spike take them to the post office. Mrs MacMurdo, the postmistress, read the American address. He knew she had, although she never mentioned it.

Nobody said things on the island but they knew everything. Not everything, he reminded himself. He shoved his hands in his pockets to stop himself looking at them. The marks were getting worse. Esther would notice them soon. He would have to think up something to tell her.

Maybe it was thinking about home that made him remember the baby. The nearer he got to the old flat, the more worried he became. It was like coming home after school to find his baby brother Calum alone and crying in the house while his mother walked the cliffs and his father worked in his laboratory.

He started to run.

When he reached his landing, he found the baby sitting outside the door in a buggy. Beneath a silly pom-pom hat, tear lines streaked the dirty wee face. It was hungrily chewing on an old nappy.

Inside, the Flintstones were at it, bump bump bump. If he wasn't shagging her, he was thumping her. Or a mixture of both.

'Hey, mate. Time for some food.'

Spike lifted the buggy down the stairs.

6

RHONA TRIED THE tuner on the car radio again.

'Is there nothing but country and western?' she said.

'What's wrong with country and western?'

Rhona couldn't tell if Andre was joking or not. Interpreting the nuances of American speech was tricky. Surely there was news, national or international, out there somewhere?

At last she found a station worth listening to; a deep and sincere voice, pity about what he was saying: *Friends and listeners. Send in your donation now and when the financial crash comes, as come it will, God will look favourably on one who lives by his laws.*

Rhona stole a look at Andre.

'Hallelujah!' he said.

'You don't believe all that?'

'My parents were Baptists, and their parents before them. Of course I'm a believer.'

The sincere voice had been replaced by a good old-fashioned hymn. Andre joined in with gusto. Rhona thought there was a smirk on his face but she couldn't be sure, so she kept her mouth shut and concentrated on the scenery.

*   *   *

Clan tents scattered the lawns and nestled round the lake of the big colonial-style mansion. A couple strolled past arm-in-arm, the young woman in a crinoline with a tartan sash, her beau in full Jacobite regalia, complete with giant claymore. Rhona tried not to stare.

'How come I'm the one who's Scottish here and I'm the only one who doesn't look it?'

'Sshh,' Andre said. 'These people are real Scots. They'd probably say you're the mongrel.'

'But that's ridiculous. I was born in Scotland.'

'Doesn't mean a thing. Were your great-great-great-grandparents Scottish?'

'Scottish and Irish.'

'See! You're a mongrel.'

Two young plaided men stopped arguing in Gaelic to nod at Andre, then stood aside to let him enter the MacLeod tent. Rhona followed. One of them said something that sounded suggestive as she passed. She decided by the laughter that followed her that it was.

Now she was sitting on a rattan rocking-chair with a glass in her hand. Beside her, a matron in a long kilt was stitching a clan sampler. The elderly man refilling her glass with malt whisky had been introduced as the Clan Chief this side of the Atlantic. He was suggesting that, as a visiting MacLeod, she might like to take part in the judging of the Highland dancing.

'I'm sorry. I don't know much about Highland dancing.'

The Chief this side of the Water gave her a disappointed look.

'I'm sorry to hear you folks don't keep up the traditions over there. We sure do here.'

Rhona retreated to her whisky, realising her accent wasn't enough. Around here you had to *do* Scottish as well as *be* Scottish.

The Chief over the Water abandoned her and, taking Andre by the arm, urged him to a far corner of the tent for some real Scottish conversation. At least, from where Rhona was sitting it looked passionate. Andre looked as though he was disagreeing, but as the Chief's expression became more determined, Andre seemed to concede. Whatever the Chief was asking him to do, Rhona didn't think it was judging the Highland dancing.

'Would you excuse me a moment?' Andre was beside her looking slightly embarrassed. 'I have to go speak to someone. Will you be

okay here for a bit?'

'I'll maybe take a wander outside,' she said.

'Of course. I'll see you back here in half-an-hour?'

Rhona nodded. She would be glad to be alone. She had a feeling Andre was only taking her to the bits of the games he wanted her to see.

The heat outside the tent hit her like a wall. They were inland, away from the ocean's breeze. Broiling hot California. Beside the lake a small boy practised his pipes, sending *Scotland the Brave* across the silted water.

'Bizarre.'

'Sorry. What did you say?' It was the young Jacobite from the door of the tent. He gave her a delicious smile.

'I'm sorry. I said, it's bizarre.'

'Who's bizarre?' The smile drooped under his white cockade.

'Not you,' she laughed. 'This.' She swept her arm in an inclusive gesture. 'Any Highland games I've been to usually resulted in a fight to get into the beer tent out of the wind and the rain.'

As he walked alongside her, Rhona couldn't help imagining what Chrissy would say: something like, *And how long is your sword then*?

'You guys go to Highland gatherings back in Scotland?' her young Jacobite was asking enthusiastically.

'I've been to one or two.' Although the Cowal Games in Millport had never been like this.

The tent on their left sported a large symbol over the entrance.

'What's in there?'

'Come and see,' he said, taking her by the hand. Being led into a dark space by a tall handsome Jacobite with a big sword. This was a story Chrissy would love.

Inside it was relatively cool. Rhona stood for a moment waiting for her eyes to adjust to the change of light.

'*Alba gu brath.*' Her Highlander's voice was a heady mixture of American and Gaelic. He was standing in reverence in front of a flag. At first it looked like the Saltire, a simple white cross on a blue background. But there was a difference. In the centre of this cross was a small crest, like a coat of arms, with the word ReAlba. Below the flag was a map of Scotland, delicately etched like something out of an ancient book. This map was old, God knows how old, and protected from the air by a glass case. At the foot was an inscription, written in brown ink in tight, swirling but firm-handed letters. Rhona's Gaelic was rusty. Her Jacobite came to the rescue:

'*For the Men of the West. So that they should know from whence they came.*'

'Right.' It sounded heavy stuff. Definitely not a tent to be found at the Cowal Games.

'And ReAlba?'

'I thought you came here with Andre?' he said sharply.

'I did.'

He was looking at her suspiciously now. The friendly chat was turning decidedly cool. Rhona went on regardless.

'ReAlba. Let me guess. Some Scottish organisation?'

'Rhona! There you are.'

Andre's voice had a distinctly petulant tone about it. No more flashing smile and crinkled eyes. He took her arm and firmly escorted her towards the door of the tent, but not before she had pocketed a couple of the leaflets from the table in front of the Men of the West's map.

Outside the tent, the smile was back, crinkles and all.

'What the hell is ReAlba?' Rhona demanded.

'I'll tell you in the car.'

'You'll tell me in the car?'

This afternoon was beginning to resemble a *Monty Python* episode. 'You can tell me while I have a beer,' she informed him.

She removed her arm from his grip and walked towards the beer tent, where Scotch pies were being sold in large numbers. Rhona asked for one. Surely a Scotch pie would be the same regardless of which side of the Atlantic it was on.

Rhona waited until they were sitting in the shade of an old tree.

She had drunk her beer, eaten her pie and read the leaflet. Then she presented it to Andre.

Andre gave it a cursory glance, shrugged and handed it back.

'You can't believe this,' she said. 'You're a scientist, for God's sake.'

Andre's voice was quietly firm: 'You're a scientist and you can't accept the laws of physics.'

'Planes do fall out of the sky.'

'There are an estimated twenty million people of Scots descent in the States,' he said. 'That's four times the number that live in Scotland. Why shouldn't they have an opinion about their homeland?'

'It isn't their home.'

'People in Chinatown call China home.'

'This stuff,' Rhona flapped the leaflet in his face, 'is racist rubbish. The Declaration of Arbroath did not say Scotland was for whites.'

'Can we talk about this on our way back?'

People were looking round at them. Obviously a Scottish voice raised in anger was causing some interest. Rhona suddenly heard herself. Coming to another person's country and telling them what to do. It happened enough in Scotland, and she didn't like it then.

'It's the racist bit I can't take,' she said. 'Celts and Gaels are white, therefore America should be white. It says the Declaration of Independence was written for white people and black people cause all the problems here.' She paused for breath. 'And they make out the Western Isles of Scotland to be some mythical land of the Gael, which should have a no-entry policy for anyone who isn't one.'

Andre was silent.

Rhona backed off, for the moment. 'Okay. I'm on my high horse, as Sean would say.'

'Sean?'

She hadn't mentioned Sean since they met. There hadn't been any reason to.

'Husband?'

'Boyfriend.'

'Pity.' Andre made a wry face.

Rhona wondered if it mattered. Instinct told her it did.

'You ready?'

Rhona nodded and picked up her things. She hadn't totally avoided thinking about Andre as a man. An intelligent, attractive, charming man. She had just assumed he was attached. That moment's look when he asked about Sean suggested he wasn't, but would like to be.

Andre asked her to dinner when he dropped her at the hotel. Rhona hesitated. Saying no would be churlish and Andre's company would be better than eating alone, surrounded by the beautiful people on Third Street.

'Look,' he said. 'If it puts your mind at rest, I am not a member of ReAlba.'

'But the Jacobite warrior said . . .'

'However, my father was, and his father before him.'

'Oh.'

'Rhona. My family was burned out after the Forty-Five rebellion. The tiny island they called home had one hundred and twenty-six pipers at the battle of Culloden.' Andre smiled. 'I know, swords might have proved more useful. When the Jacobites lost, the island paid dearly for supporting the cause. My family stuck it for a while, then left with the arrival of the sheep. I am an American but it doesn't stop me remembering *why* I am an American.'

It was a pretty speech. Rhona wondered briefly if he had used it before.

'Okay,' she said. 'You win. I'll be ready at eight.'

Rhona watched the car drive away. Andre. An expert in genetic weapons who just might be a racist. An interesting combination. If she ran this past Chrissy she knew what she would say. 'So what? You've made a career out of dead bodies. That doesn't mean you have murderous thoughts.'

The hotel room didn't feel so cool and chic on her return. It just felt big and empty. There was something wrong about coming in from the heat to the cool, instead of the other way round. It made inside feel less safe, somehow.

Rhona wondered briefly if she should phone the flat and speak to Sean. It would be nice to hear a voice from home. She glanced at her watch. Okay, so Sean would still be in bed. Probably alone, but why tempt fate?

Rhona had been in this state of mind before about Sean, too often for her own good. Some of the time it had been warranted, most of the time it had not (or so Chrissy said).

Rhona decided against the phone call. She would check her email instead.

7

TWO MESSAGES AWAITED her. Neither from Sean. He refused to go electronic. Recording a message for the ansaphone was, he declared, his limit.

There was one from Chrissy, entitled *jazz and things*. The second looked like a conference memo for tomorrow. Rhona double-clicked and viewed a confirmation of her schedule, while trying not to acknowledge the sudden flutter of apprehension in the pit of her stomach.

Now for Chrissy's message.

The *things* part came first and the tone was decidedly nippy. Chrissy had gone into the lab to do some overtime but had been unable to process the tests, because the samples were gone. She had checked the mortuary but the foot was also absent. Dr Sissons had been unavailable. There was no evidence of a break-in at the lab and nothing on the security cameras. Chrissy had phoned and reported the foot and samples missing to DI Wilson, who told her he would get back to her.

Rhona could almost hear the irritation at this point.

On a positive note, Chrissy had taken the digital image to the computing department. They had done some work on it and the result was in the attacheded file.

Mention of the jazz club was short. Sean's new singer was good, very good. Unfortunately she had the look of heroin chic.

Another woman reading Chrissy's email would have assumed the new singer was skinny, white, with big charcoal eyes. Definitely not Sean's type.

Rhona knew Chrissy was telling her something else.

Heroin chic. Translation – the new singer was at worst a junkie, at best liked partying.

What the hell was Sean playing at?

Okay, so the club was popular with her colleagues. But not everyone in the law and order establishment appreciated their Chief Forensic's relationship with an ex-con, good musician or not.

Sean was a working partner in the jazz club. If this Esther girl was using or supplying on the premises, Sean could be held responsible.

Rhona decided she needed a drink. Propped up on the bar was an invitation to try a cocktail. Room service would be delighted to mix it for her. Something with at least two different types of alcohol sounded good to Rhona. She dialled room service and headed for the shower.

The pounding needles on her head didn't help. She would have to speak to Sean. Find out what he had to say. She turned her attention to the missing samples.

Every sample bag was strictly monitored. Every movement had to be logged. If the samples went missing from her lab, then it was ultimately her responsibility.

And, according to Chrissy, the foot was no longer in

the mortuary. Rhona could not imagine the eminent Doctor Sissons countenancing anything underhand. But if the MOD was involved . . .

Rhona cut her shower short and pulled on a bathrobe.

The hum of the air conditioner had strengthened, making the air cold and almost drowning the background sound of the television. The bedroom had suddenly turned from empty silence to electronic overload. Rhona stared at the shifting television screen she'd switched on for company.

It was then she noticed the man's shadow.

He was in the alcove that housed the desk with her laptop, bent over the computer screen.

Two thoughts raced through Rhona's mind in quick succession. One, she had nothing to defend herself with. And two, she should have kept the chain on the door.

It was too late. Her visitor had heard her.

Rhona stepped back a little, trying to judge how far the bathroom and a lockable door might be while her eyes noted the plain black jacket and grey trousers and hoped her instinct was right and it was room service come to make her cocktail.

It was.

Her intruder's body language moved swiftly from surprise through discomfort to formality.

'You ordered a cocktail, ma'am?' The young man stood to attention and indicated the shaker on the desk beside her computer. 'A Manhattan?'

'Great.'

Rhona hastily retreated to the bathroom to try and regain her dignity.

When she reappeared a few minutes later, the television had been turned down and the room had returned to a comfortable temperature.

'Your drink, ma'am,' said the young man holding out a little silver tray with a stemmed glass of pale golden liquid.

He waited while she tasted it.

The liquid was cold and sharp against her throat. Rhona resisted the desire to cough and smiled instead.

'Good,' she said.

He looked relieved. Rhona wondered how many customers complained just for the hell of it. She thought about trying to engage him in conversation, then decided against it. She had already tried that with various members of hotel staff. It hadn't worked. Polite and helpful, real conversation was not considered part of the job.

The waiter was replacing the bottles in the drink cabinet, tidying up. Behind him, the computer screen was flashing Chrissy's downloaded file. Rhona went over for a look.

The screen held six images, three above and three below. In the top left-hand corner was the photograph she had taken with the digital camera of the area above the decomposing ankle. From left to right, what was little more than a smudge began to take shape and change colour. By the third image it had become a definite pattern.

Maybe a letter?

The pattern was complex, but the middle part might be a letter. Rhona sat down at the desk for a closer look.

If it was a letter it was one of those old-fashioned ones, all curves and sweeping lines. Real writing.

It wasn't crystal clear, but if the computer guys had achieved this from that photograph of spongy grey flesh then she would have to stop slagging them off for sitting in front of a computer all day.

Rhona was suddenly aware of the waiter standing behind her, staring over her shoulder at the screen.

She turned to a face full of pleasant blandness.

'What do you think?' she said.

'Looks kinda Celtic.'

'Yes.'

He topped up her Manhattan from the cocktail shaker and headed for the door, before she could ask him anything else.

'Have a nice day, ma'am.'

Reality LA-style had returned.

The door clicked shut behind him. Rhona put the chain on this time and turned back to the screen. The guys in the Computing Department had done her proud. The smudge was now a distinguishing mark. A mark that might help them find the owner of the foot.

An hour later Rhona was sitting in LA's most popular restaurant on Main Street, Santa Monica, trying to keep her attention on what Andre was saying. She had made two phone calls after the waiter left.

DI Bill Wilson had told her that the investigation had been taken out of his hands, and by implication hers.

Rhona was not amused.

'You know where the samples are?'

He hesitated for a second. 'No.'

She had worked with Bill Wilson for years. If he was lying to her, he must have a very good reason.

'What the hell is going on, Bill?'

'Just concentrate on your conference. We'll talk when you get back.'

The second phone call was worse. The answering machine wasn't on so Rhona let the phone ring out, determined to waken Sean. But it wasn't Sean who answered. It was a young female voice.

Rhona was past the niceties. 'Who the hell are you?'

She could tell the girl was taken aback by her attitude. Rhona didn't care.

'I'm Esther, the new singer with Sean's band.'

'And what the fuck are you doing in my flat?'

Rhona listened in silence while the girl stumbled through some lame excuse about staying for a few days until she got her own place sorted out, then the phone was commandeered by Sean.

'It's true,' he said.

'Like hell it is.'

'Esther was in a squat. It got raided. She had nowhere else to go.'

'You had no right to let her stay in *my* flat.'

Sean went silent. Somewhere in the background Rhona heard the girl say she would pack and go. A door closed then Sean was back on.

'She's ill. It would better if she stayed here for a few days.'

'Is she on something?'

Silence, then: 'Chrissy's been in touch, I take it?'

Sean's voice was dry. A bad sign. Sean never lost his temper, even when she was trying to goad him into an argument. But the quiet tone showed how upset he was.

'Well, is she?' she repeated.

'She says not.'

'Christ, Sean. This could lose me my job.'

'What are you talking about?'

'If she's taking stuff, she's dealing in it or doing something else to pay for it . . .'

'And mixing with undesirables doesn't look good on your cv.'

Sean had told Rhona about his conviction for possession as soon as things got serious between them. Rhona had dismissed it then. It was ten years ago, she'd said, it's past, forgotten. But at the same time Rhona knew there would be someone out there who would love to know that information about her. So she told Bill Wilson. He'd said there was no big deal. It was on record that most cabinet ministers had smoked dope in their student days and marched with CND. Either that or they were gay. He told her to forget it. That's what she'd done. Until now.

'Maybe you'd rather I moved out too?' Sean was saying.

'Maybe I would.'

The words were out before she could stop them.

'We'll talk when you get back.'

His voice was low and sad and it made her feel like shit. Plus she was pissed-off with people telling her they would talk about it later, in the car, when she got back.

By the time Andre arrived she had finished all the Manhattan mix in the shaker. It hadn't made her feel any better. She just wanted to get her paper delivered and get home where she belonged.

Or maybe she didn't want to go home at all?

If Andre sensed her mood, he said nothing about it. He was all charm and good fun. Even now, when she wasn't listening to him.

His offer of more wine finally registered. Rhona nodded an okay and tried to concentrate.

Across from her the door was opening and two more beautiful people were ushered in. The woman wore a long muted gold evening dress which perfectly matched her tan. Her companion was younger than her and very attentive.

'Someone's brought dessert with them,' Rhona said cynically.

'What?'

Andre turned for a better look.

'Andre!'

The woman was over in an instant. On closer inspection, Rhona had to admit she was the equal of her companion in the looks stakes.

'And you, I believe, are Dr MacLeod,' she held out her hand to Rhona. 'Dr Lynne Franklin.'

'ReGene?'

'That's right.' Dr Franklin waved her companion over.

'I'm so looking forward to your paper tomorrow. I hoped we might get an opportunity to talk together afterwards.'

'Why don't you join us?' Rhona suggested. 'We could talk now.'

Andre looked less than enthusiastic. Rhona didn't care. Dr Franklin fluttered for a bit, then agreed.

'That would be great,' she said, 'if Andre doesn't mind?'

Andre minded but he didn't have any choice.

The companion, who turned out to be called Jason, sat next to Rhona.

'What do you think?' Lynne Franklin smiled across the table at Rhona.

'I think it's a great offer.' Rhona tried to imagine Sean playing saxophone in a Bahamas beach club. Then she remembered what he was likely to be doing right that minute.

'You don't have to commit yourself in any way at the moment,' Lynne Franklin was saying, obviously spotting the change in Rhona's expression. 'But I'd sure like you to think about it.'

By the time Lynne Franklin and her escort left, Rhona was thinking about it. Lynne Franklin had put two provisional offers on the table. One, that Rhona come and work for ReGene in their Bahamas division or, alternatively, ReGene fund her current research in Glasgow.

Rhona tried not to indulge in dreams about what the university would do with that money. The earlier Manhattans coupled with the wine at dinner weren't doing much for her common sense.

Before she left, Dr Franklin kissed Andre on the cheek and said she would see him soon. Andre nodded, although Rhona had a feeling he was glad to see her go.

'You didn't mention you knew Dr Franklin.'

'Neither did you.'

'I don't,' Rhona said. 'She left her card at the hotel. Said she wanted to meet me. She isn't another one of your real Scots I hope?'

Andre looked uncomfortable.

Rhona felt bad. Andre had treated her with kindness and hospitality and she was treating him like shit.

'Sorry,' she said. 'Cynicism is part of the Scottish psyche.'

Andre smiled. 'The part I like best.'

Rhona picked up her bag to avoid meeting his eyes.

'You want to get back to the hotel?' he said.

She nodded.

The drive to the hotel was studiously quiet. Sitting in the back, the driver separated from them by a smoked shield, Rhona felt exposed and vulnerable. The revelation that Sean had moved Esther into her flat as soon as she was out of the country had thrown her. She felt used.

Her privacy was something she treasured. It kept her sane. Letting Sean McGuire into her life and into her home had compromised that. And now his actions were threatening her professional life too.

When they drew up outside the hotel, Andre got out of the cab with her.

'I'd better go up,' she said.

'Yeah. Big day tomorrow.'

'Thanks for a great evening.'

'Sure.'

Rhona stood at the entrance, willing herself to turn away and go in. She didn't. Andre paid the fare. As he walked towards her, Rhona knew the smallest sign of rejection would be enough.

They crossed the hotel lobby in silence. The lift was open and empty. Standing inside, Andre beside her, Rhona wondered if this was how it was for Sean. The anticipation of someone new, anticipating how different it would be. She thought of the girl's voice on the phone. She imagined this Esther spread-eagled across her bed, the muscles on Sean's back flexing as he drove himself into her.

The elevator opened.

She sensed Andre's eagerness as she fumbled with the keycard.

'Here, let me.'

He took the card and slipped it in the slot and pushed open the door.

He stepped into the darkness and used the card in the power slot. The lights came on and the air conditioner hummed into action.

She shivered.

'Want me to turn it off?'

'Yes.'

He was watching her, waiting for her to decide what

would happen next. Whatever it was he would go along with it.

He broke the silence. 'I'd settle for a drink.'

She wanted to be the one to decide and was irritated by his retreat.

'If you don't want to . . .' she said sharply.

'Oh, I want to alright.'

He pulled her towards him.

'The question is, do you?'

'I asked you up.'

'No you didn't.'

Andre led her to the sofa and pushed her gently down.

'My guess is something bad happened tonight and you're thousands of miles from home. I also think one night stands are not really your scene. Not that the sex wouldn't be great.'

'Thanks.'

Andre headed for the bar.

'Maybe another drink isn't such a good idea,' Rhona said.

'We have already agreed not to seduce one another. So another drink won't matter.'

'That's true.' The way he looked at her at that moment made Rhona wish it wasn't.

'I'm mixing a drink,' he said, 'because you're going to need one when I tell you the real reason I wanted to come up here tonight.'

'So it was nothing to do with sex?'

'Not unless sex and dismembered limbs go together.'

8

THE BABY MUNCHED contentedly on a pancake and jam. Mary in the café had waved away Spike's offer of money.

'It's on the house,' she said. 'And Tesco has a toilet with a changing mat and free nappies.'

Spike looked down at his charge's damp trousers. He'd grown used to changing Calum. When his mother got bad, he was the only one who would. He thanked Mary and she winked at him.

'You're taking him back home?'

Spike nodded. 'Half an hour.'

She smiled and went off to the next table.

Spike wiped the dribbling mouth and wondered what the fuck he was doing. If Ma Flintstone realised her son was missing, she would go mad. He would just clean him up and then take him back.

Tesco was busy. He had to stand in a queue for the family toilet. One of the women waiting gave him a funny look, but he just ignored her. Once inside, he laid the baby on the mat and pulled down the wet trousers.

The disposable nappy had gone lumpy, overwhelmed by the amount of urine it had to deal with. Spike threw it in the bin, stood the child in warm soapy water in the sink and washed his thin wee bum.

Then he laid him on the mat and dried him with a paper towel. His tiny penis was red raw with nappy rash.

Spike looked about for cream. There was a tube on the ledge above the sink that someone had left. He squeezed some and rubbed it over the angry skin. The baby was whimpering now, despite his attempts to be gentle.

He turned him over.

In the strong overhead light, the bruising round the back passage was obvious. Spike almost sobbed as he pressed the nappy shut. The bastard. The fucking bastard.

He put the child's trousers back on and lifted him against his shoulder, holding him tightly. The whimpering stopped. On his way out he pinched a bar of chocolate and stuffed it in his pocket.

'Fuck them both,' he told the kid when he'd turned the corner. He pulled off the paper and handed him the chocolate, which the child grabbed and gnawed at ravenously.

Spike opened the telephone booth and squashed inside. He sat the baby on the ledge while he dialled. Esther answered.

'I'll pick you up after the rehearsal,' he said.

'Okay.'

'Esther. We're not going back to Sean's.'

She was silent for a moment. 'Where are we going?'

'I'll tell you when I see you,' he said and rang off.

Now he was for it, he told the baby. Now they would really be looking for him and he didn't fucking care.

The child grinned back at him, drooling chocolate.

9

THE BUZZ OF a morning call woke Rhona. She had left the curtains open and the early sun flooded the room with light. For a moment she had no idea where she was, then she remembered and glanced at the other three quarters of the king-size bed. Empty and unrumpled.

Rhona didn't know whether to be glad or sad.

Reaching for her mobile, she checked her voice mail for a message from Andre. Nothing. She pulled out her diary and rang the mobile number he'd given her. The hum of the phone was immediately replaced by an American drawl. *Could the caller please leave a message . . .*

As she stepped out of the shower, room service arrived with breakfast. Tucked beside the coffee pot was another card from Lynne Franklin wishing her well for the conference. Unfortunately, an urgent business matter had come up and she couldn't be there to hear Rhona's paper. However, she would certainly be in touch about funding on Rhona's return to Scotland.

So she was hot property?

Rhona poured her coffee and allowed herself a

moment's pleasure at the thought of announcing this at the next meeting of the university finance committee, then she put it firmly out of her head.

Like Andre's revelation, it would have to be put on hold until she got back to Glasgow.

The black limousine wound its way effortlessly through the Santa Monica traffic. If car horns were honking at their assertive progress, the noise didn't penetrate the peaceful interior.

When reception had rung to tell her the car was there, Rhona had assumed it was the standard cab organised to take her to the conference. How wrong she was.

Rhona examined the luxurious interior, glad the smoked-glass windows allowed her to look out but not the general public to look in. She could imagine what Chrissy would have to say about her new-found status. *Fur coat and no knickers!* In Glasgow that would be an insult, here it was probably true of everyone who rode in this limo, Rhona decided. Somehow the common sense and grey solidity of Glasgow belonged to another world.

Rhona sat back in the soft leather seat and tried not to be irritated by Lynne Franklin's obvious attempts to buy her. Whatever Andre had revealed last night, he could not be drawn on her. ReGene, he assured her, was a legitimate company. Lynne was in a position to offer Rhona funding. She should consider the offer.

Rhona had been seconds away from asking Andre if

there was something between him and Lynne Franklin, but the look on his face had been enough to stop her.

Outside her cool cocoon, the freeway traffic was snaking in eight lanes above the hot dusty sprawl of LA. With confidence, the limo crossed the freeway taking its rightful place in the fast lane, sweeping all protesters aside. Rhona tried not to think about an armed driver in a spurned car taking umbrage at such arrogance.

The internal phone rang five minutes later. The driver's eyes in the rear mirror signalled that it must be for her. Rhona picked it up.

'Rhona?'

'Andre. I thought you said . . .'

'Listen, Rhona. Tell the driver to turn round and take you back to the hotel.'

'What?'

'Tell him to get off the freeway and go back the coast road.'

'But what about the conference?'

'Postponed.'

'Postponed? But . . .'

The tone of Andre's voice shut her up. 'A bomb went off just before nine,' he said.

'Oh my God.'

'They've cleared the building and cancelled today's proceedings. It's chaos down here. Once you get caught up in it you'll never get out. Give the driver the phone.'

Rhona handed the phone over and watched his impassive face as he took Andre's directions. He handed the phone back.

'I'll meet you back at the hotel,' Andre said.

'Are you alright?' Rhona asked.

'Sure. I'll see you later.'

Rhona put the phone down. The comfortable interior of the limousine didn't seem so safe anymore. A car
moved alongside, sitting window to window with them.
The backseat passenger turned to look at her car. The
tartan regalia was gone, the hair tied back in a neat
ponytail, but the eyes of the Jacobite warrior were the
same uncompromising blue.

The crowd of protesters spilled round the corner of her
hotel and onto Third Street. The driver must have
spotted the placards before Rhona because he was
already making a left swerve in front of the oncoming
traffic and trying to head back up Santa Monica
Boulevard. The power of the limo was of little use
in the sudden rush to move in the other direction. The
driver turned to Rhona.

'You'd better get out.'

'What?'

He had stopped trying to merge into the stubborn
stream of traffic that led from the demonstration and
had pulled onto the pavement instead.

'You'll be safer out of the car, ma'am.'

Vehicle after vehicle had stopped at the sight of the
protesters and was turning away, trying to escape up
the boulevard or down the side streets. They weren't
having any luck either.

'Those people,' he gestured behind them, 'are Pro-
Lifers and they know this car.'

He was right.

A girl with long red hair was already pointing in their direction and screaming with delight. A boy joined her, the words *Genetic Pigs* jumping above his head as he ran.

The driver's expression was no longer impassive.

'Please, ma'am.'

'What about you?'

'They don't care about me,' he told her. 'It's delegates they're after.' He sprung the door for her and the noise and heat flooded in.

'Are you sure?'

He nodded and moved into drive. As the limo jumped forward, a placard flew against the far side.

'Go!'

She did. The bookshop was six steps away across the sidewalk. Rhona made it in two. About twenty protesters were running through the stationary traffic, ignoring the honking horns, jumping over bonnets. They reached the driver's side as Rhona flung open the door of the shop. The girl at the counter was already on the 911 call.

The protesters couldn't see the driver, but they knew he was there. The big engine was purring away, ready to go, given half a chance. It wasn't going to get it.

Two protesters jumped on the roof, two on the bonnet. A girl arrived with a plastic container and passed it to a guy on the bonnet. Red stuff flew at the windscreen, slithering down, a mess of entrails and blood. They were wrenching at the door handles now, but the limo didn't like unwelcome visitors and it sure as hell wasn't going to open against its will. The windscreen wipers flew at the blood, whipping it back in the faces of the protesters before someone snapped them off and flung them into the crowd.

Now they were hammering at the windows. Rhona stood in the middle of the bookstore crowd and watched in fascination as the limo began to rock to and fro.

Then they heard loudspeakers and the noise of police helicopters. Some of the crowd looked up, shouting abuse at the sky. A line of riot police was moving towards the protesters from the direction of Rhona's hotel.

But the driver wasn't waiting for the police.

The sidewalk was clear of pedestrians and the limo took it, moving from zero to forty in seconds. The bodies on the roof were the first to go. The girl on the bonnet hung on longer but the limo was on its way.

Rhona almost cheered with relief.

'Hey!' The girl on the counter was talking to her. 'Someone might have seen you come in.' She pointed to the back of the shop. 'There's a fire escape over there.'

Rhona thanked her and pushed her way through the gaping crowd, opened the fire door and looked out. Everything was quiet. She exited and headed for the daylight at the end of the dark alleyway.

Genetic pigs. Jesus. The whole thing was ridiculous. Rhona was used to stalkers and criminals who blamed her for putting them away, but she had never before been targeted by people who advocated life over death.

10

CHRISSY HELD DI Wilson's gaze, her sharp eyes un-wavering.

They could say what they liked about Glasgow hard men, Glasgow hard women were much worse.

'Okay. Okay,' he conceded. 'As far as I know the MOD have the foot and the samples.'

'Why?'

'That, I don't know.'

It looked like the truth, but Chrissy wasn't one to give in easily.

'A number of people have come forward to be tested in case the body is a missing relative.' Chrissy waited. 'Dr MacLeod instructed me to test their DNA.'

Still no answer.

'I've been told to wait,' she said. 'Why?'

Bill shook his head. 'Orders from above.'

That was just the answer to really piss Chrissy off.

'Who is this missing body?' she asked.

'I don't know.'

'Must be somebody special to have the MOD pinching his foot.'

Silence.

'Christ, Bill. You know how Rhona hates the cloak and dagger stuff.'

'Look, Chrissy, I don't know any more than you about it.'

Chrissy could tell she was wasting her time. Bill Wilson had the look of man turned mule.

'Never mind,' she said. 'Rhona touches down at two o'clock. You can tell her that yourself.'

The lab phone ended the conversation, not that it was going anywhere anyway. Chrissy lifted the receiver sharply and briskly interrogated the caller, her flushed face paling and then reddening again as she listened.

'Seems whoever this guy is, he's anxious to get back on dry land,' she said.

'What?'

'Your office.' She held out the receiver. 'A Skye woman out walking her dog on Rigg beach found a hand in a rock pool.'

As the plane made its last sweep over Ayrshire, Rhona forced herself to view Scotland from above. After the vastness of California, the smallness of her homeland seemed a pleasure.

Wee houses, wee roads, wee fields. Wee, solid, dependable. And cold. Already her fellow passengers were pulling on jumpers and jackets. Rhona joined them. She never thought she would be pleased to be cold again.

She closed her eyes as they touched down and said a silent prayer to whatever deity was listening. When she pulled her briefcase from the rack it still held the undelivered academic paper. Not wholly undelivered. Locked in secrecy in a small hotel in the Californian mountains, she and the other delegates had talked to one another behind closed doors. The Californian state authorities were not anxious for another demonstration of the size of the one against the World Trade Organisation in Seattle. The US might be happy to talk all things genetic, including genetic bombs and cloning, they just didn't want to do it in public anymore.

Rhona thought about the flat and bed then decided against it. *Who's been sleeping in my bed?* was the phrase that made up her mind.

A driver was waiting for her in the arrivals lounge, a big sign with *Dr MacLeod* on it in front of his chest.

Rhona had told Chrissy she would touch down at two o'clock. A good following wind had landed them early. She found her mobile at the bottom of her bag and rang the lab. Even the sound of the ring made her feel at home.

'Chrissy?' she said. 'I'm on my way.'

'Hey, you're early. There'll be no one there to pick you up yet.'

'There is.'

'Old George on the door was organising it. He's missed you.'

'Nice to know someone has.'

Rhona asked the driver to take a run past the jazz club. It wasn't exactly on the way and he didn't look that keen, but Rhona insisted. If Esther was still singing the blues, that meant Sean was still screwing her.

If he ever was, a small voice suggested. Rhona ignored it.

The club was in darkness. Not the darkness of two o'clock in the afternoon. The darkness of *Closed Until Further Notice.*

'Stop the car,' she told the driver.

'But . . .'

'I said stop the car.'

They pulled in behind what was definitely a CID car. Across the entrance hung the familiar yellow tape signalling an incident. Rhona ignored the protestations of the driver and dipped under the tape. Just inside the door, the constable on duty recognised her and looked embarrassed. Before he could answer her questions, a face appeared at the top of the stairs. It was the last face Rhona wanted to see.

'Dr MacLeod. Nice to have you back.' Detective Sergeant Dominic O'Brien was lying of course, although you would never have guessed it from the smooth smile and bright eyes.

'What's going on here?' Rhona asked, already knowing the answer. If O'Brien was here, drugs was the word.

'A drugs bust,' he said, the smile never leaving his face. 'Seems the owner of this little establishment's been partying a bit too hard.'

He waited for Rhona to say something. She didn't, so he went on. 'We got a tip-off that drugs were being dealt on the premises. We followed it up and found a young woman out of her mind in the toilets, along with a quantity of amphetamine powder and ecstasy tablets.'

Rhona willed her face immobile. O'Brien was disappointed. Heavy news like that shouldn't go unmarked.

'So,' he paused, saving the best bit for the end, 'We brought Mr Sean McGuire in for questioning and found our man has more talents than playing the saxophone.'

Our man.

Bastard. Ever since Rhona had turned down O'Brien's drunken prick at a police ball he'd been anxious to show her just the sort of a man she'd missed out on.

Rhona kept her face impassive to piss him off.

It worked. O'Brien was running out of sarcasm. 'The place is shut until further notice,' he said.

'The girl?' Rhona said.

'What?'

'What happened to the girl?'

'Aw,' Sergeant O'Brien was losing interest, 'they took her to the local psycho ward.'

Rhona got back in the car. She was so busy seething at this latest development, she missed the fact they were on the wrong road. When she did, she banged on the glass partition and demanded to know what the hell was going on. The driver didn't answer.

They were coming up West George Street. For a moment Rhona thought she was being taken to Strathclyde Police Headquarters in Pitt Street, but the car didn't take a left. It kept on up the hill to Blythswood Square, where it drew up outside number five. Rhona recognised the rounded arch. The building wasn't open to the public but people came to view the Charles Rennie Mackintosh door.

The driver never got a chance to press the brass doorbell. The door was opened immediately by a man in a formal black suit and tie. He ushered her inside. The hall was panelled in polished wood, the floor a chessboard black and white marble. She followed him through a set of double doors into a room lit by long windows that looked out over the green of the central square. A suave man in his mid-fifties stood beside an imposing fireplace. His hair was iron grey, his eyes intelligent and appraising.

He came towards her, hand outstretched. 'Dr MacLeod,' he said, 'Thank you for coming.'

'I didn't come by choice. I came because the driver brought me here.'

'I apologise for that. It was necessary to speak with you as soon as you got back from America.'

'Who are you?'

'My name is Andrew Phillips. I'm with the Ministry of Defence.'

He headed for the drinks cabinet.

'Can I offer you a drink? Whisky?'

He poured some into a cut-crystal glass and gave it to her.

'We've called you here . . .'

'Is that the Royal We?'

He smiled, but she caught the irritation in his eyes.

'The MOD has an interest in a case you've been working on.'

He looked at her as if she might comment.

Rhona decided to let her brain work and keep her mouth shut. The suit would have to do all the talking.

'The foot you sampled?' He took a mouthful of his own whisky. 'We have reason to believe it may have come from someone . . .'

'Dr Fitzgerald MacAulay.'

She never expected him to be thrown. A raised eyebrow perhaps, nothing more. How wrong she was. Even people like him had hearts, because she could see the pulse from his beating rather quickly below his right eye.

The polished voice became more clipped. 'I must ask you, Dr MacLeod, what it is you know about Dr MacAulay?'

It was too late to backtrack now. She tried to look nonchalant.

'His name came up at the conference in relation to genetic engineering,' she paused, choosing her words carefully. 'Rumour has it he came to this country, gave up his work and disappeared.' She was running out of ideas. 'It was a poor attempt at a joke after that,' she apologised.

Phillips looked mollified, but only slightly.

'A Dr MacAulay did come here from America some years ago to work for us.'

She finished his sentence again. 'At Porton Down.'

'Yes. However, Dr MacAulay left our employ soon after arriving . . . through ill health.' His lip curled in distaste. 'We lost touch with him for a variety of reasons.'

'Incompetence being one of them?'

The polite mask was slipping. Behind it was something rather different.

'Look,' she explained, 'I've just arrived back from Los Angeles. My head feels as though I've been travelling the wrong way round the world for twelve hours so I probably have jet lag. Could you just tell me why I'm here?'

She had to sit down. Her legs felt like water. She made for the nearest chair.

'Dr MacLeod.'

Her name, Rhona decided, seemed to be acquiring a threadbare status. Either that, or she was going deaf. Phillips' mouth was moving but she had no idea what he was saying.

She wondered for a moment if this was a dream. She decided she didn't care anyway. In fact, she felt positively relaxed about it all, even when she felt the cold splash of whisky on her legs and heard the crystal smash on the fancy marble floor.

II

SPIKE HAD BEEN at the corner when he spotted the police car and ambulance parked outside the jazz club.

The ambulance could be for anybody, he told himself. One of the old cleaning women had probably had a heart attack. Or with a bit of luck, that bastard of a doorman that hadn't let him in to watch Esther sing. But the ambulance wasn't there for either of them. Spike knew it wasn't.

He pushed the sleeping baby towards the club, ignoring the drumming of his heart and the sick feeling in the pit of his stomach.

Two medics were emerging from the entrance. Between them Esther stumbled forward, her face confused and distraught. One of the medics was telling her to get in the back of the ambulance, everything would be alright, she mustn't worry.

A howl of fear jammed itself in Spike's throat and he stopped dead, even though the ambulance doors were swinging shut and Esther was disappearing inside.

A lorry thundered past, waking up the baby. It started yelling. Spike shushed it, his brain trying desperately to engage, to think of something that would stop the ambulance taking Esther away, knowing it was already too late. The van doors were shut by the time Spike's voice escaped his clenched throat.

'Esther!'

He started to run and the baby's cries suddenly changed to glee, as the buggy jumped the cracks in the pavement, bouncing up and down. The ambulance was forcing its way into the line of traffic, light flashing.

Fuck!

The man coming out of the entrance jumped back to avoid the buggy, landing heavily on the toes of the policeman who was just behind him. Spike remembered this guy, smiling down at him from the stage, the cat that got the cream, introducing Esther like he was responsible for her great voice. Well, the bold Sean McGuire didn't look so happy now.

'What the hell's going on?' The policeman forgot his crushed toes and followed Sean's intent stare.

Spike didn't like the interest he was getting. He bent over the baby, who had returned to crying, pulled the sobbing bundle from the pram and held it close, shielding his face with the coloured hat. He desperately wanted to ask what had happened. Whatever it was, it looked like McGuire was getting the blame. Spike tried not to be too glad about that. With McGuire lifted, he had little chance of finding out where they'd taken Esther. He watched in silence as McGuire was directed into the back of the police car.

As luck would have it, the doorman came out as Spike was persuading the baby back into the buggy.

'Heh!'

A good doorman never forgets a face, especially a troublemaker's face. The doorman remembered Spike.

'What do you want, son?'

'Where have they taken Esther?'

The doorman looked at the baby. You could guess what he was thinking. The wean must be the lassie's. The boy was its minder. She went singing to earn the money for dope.

'Try the local psycho ward, son,' he shrugged, 'that's where they all end up.'

Spike didn't answer, knowing if Esther was headed for the mental hospital he would have to get her out fast, before they pumped her full of sedatives and sectioned her.

12

'ARE YOU SURE your stomach can stand it? I wouldn't want you passing out again.'

'I'm fine,' Rhona said firmly. 'Let's take a look.'

'What, now?' Chrissy looked puzzled.

'Why not?'

'Well I thought . . .'

Chrissy short of words was a sight to behold.

'You thought what?' Rhona knew what she was going to say, but she would let her say it all the same.

Chrissy said: 'I thought you would want to talk to Sean first.'

'Sean can wait.'

Rhona didn't want to think about Sean at this moment, or what had happened at the club. She would have to deal with that later.

After she'd recovered from her faint, Phillips had told her that the investigation surrounding the foot was being taken over by the MOD and she was not to discuss the matter any further. Rhona reminded him that this was Scotland and under Scottish law, the Procurator Fiscal for the area decided whether a crime had been committed and instructed the police to investigate. Phillips quoted the Prevention of Terrorism Act 2005.

Rhona shut up at this point. Whoever the foot belonged to, it looked like a potential embarrassment to the MOD.

She arrived at the lab full of righteous indignation which Chrissy fuelled even further with the story of the removed foot and samples.

'Bill says he can do nothing. Sissons won't talk about it and I wasn't allowed to process DNA samples from the possible relatives.'

'The foot didn't come from a fisherman.'

'But I thought if the MOD was worried about a submarine . . .'

'I suspect that's not the issue any more. They're worried about something else.'

'Who do they think it is?'

Rhona shook her head. 'Phillips started quoting the Antiterrorism Act.'

'Bloody hell.'

They both considered the implication of that.

Chrissy's face took on a wry look.

'They don't know we have the hand.'

The vision of Phillips' face when he heard that she had the hand before he did almost made up for Rhona's irritation. She reached for her lab coat and pulled it on over her travel suit and whisky-splashed legs.

'You smell like a drunk,' Chrissy told her.

'Always the kind word.'

The two women looked at one another, silently acknowledging their pleasure at seeing each other.

'Okay, you'd better show me where you hid it.'

Chrissy, Rhona had to admit, had been pretty devious. In fact Chrissy and Bill Wilson were looking like the perfect criminal team.

They always said when the good went bad, they were very good at it.

The hand was stashed in a back room behind the main lab. Chrissy had pinched (or borrowed) a wee fridge from somewhere and the hand was resting on the middle shelf. Rhona pulled on her gloves and took it out, trying not to think of disintegrating boiled chicken.

'We can get it down to pathology as soon as we've sampled,' Chrissy said with a worried face.

'Of course.'

It was just as well she had known nothing of the hand when she was interviewed (or interrogated) by the smarmy Phillips. It was enough that she revealed she'd heard of Dr MacAulay. That in itself had taken some explaining.

Fainting and breaking his crystal glass had helped, although she wasn't totally convinced Phillips hadn't put some truth drug in her drink.

One thing was sure, Rhona hadn't mentioned Andre's name.

A body decomposes in air twice as quickly as it does in water. The left hand had been in water about the same length of time as the foot. The information from Bill was that the woman had thrown a stick for her dog and it had not returned with it. Instead it had stood among the rocks and barked until she came for a look.

It could have been worse. The dog might have

retrieved the hand, tossing the decomposing tissues in the air. This way it was still in one piece.

'How long before the MOD finds out?'

'Bill thinks you've got twenty-four hours. They established a crime scene. Appointed a crime scene manager. Went through the usual procedures. The hand wasn't necessarily linked to the foot, but people on Skye are angry about the missing fishermen. They think bits of their bodies are floating about. The local constabulary contacted Bill directly.'

Twenty-four hours was long enough for her to process the hand. If it had grabbed at something before the body hit the water, there could be fragments below the nails. Rope, fibre, wood splinters, paint from the rails, polish from a deck; maybe hair or skin from an assailant.

During her time in California, Rhona had learned that the disappearance of Dr Fitzgerald MacAulay was a thorn in the side of both the American and British governments. Saying his name during her interview with Phillips had been foolish. But better to come out with the truth. Wasn't that what Scots were good at. Saying it as it was and watching the fallout?

Phillips' reaction had convinced her that she was right. They were looking for MacAulay. The foot might not be his. But they were going to make sure.

There was no way that Rhona would be able to prove the hand was MacAulay's since she would not be allowed access to his DNA profile, even if the MOD had one.

Fingerprints might be the answer, although it would

take time to remove the fragile flakes of skin from the tips of the digits and stabilise them sufficiently to allow prints to be taken. But what if there was a record somewhere on the hand's owner?

It was worth a try.

Rigg beach was on the east coast of Skye, looking over Raasay Sound. It seemed likely the hand and foot belonged together.

Three hours later, Rhona had the nylon membrane with the invisible blotted DNA ready for incubation overnight.

The dissolving nails had revealed a hair, definitely human. It might belong to an assailant. She almost whooped for joy when she found both microscopic fragments of metal and some fibres.

The samples of metal fragments from the foot had been removed from the lab before they were properly examined. Her slides of the rope fibres found on it had also been removed. Even if she took a DNA sample from the hand, she couldn't compare it to the foot. So whatever she did now wouldn't confirm that they belonged to the same person. But at least she could try and find out how the hand had become separated from the body.

The fibres could be from a fisherman's net. Then again, they could be from a rope used to tie a body to the sea bed. Trawl nets were mostly high density polyethylene.

Her examination revealed that the fibres from the wound weren't from fishing net. They were manila, a natural fibre still used for mooring and anchor lines.

You had to whip or tape the ends to keep them from unravelling. Manila had a minimum of stretch and was very strong, but it also shrank when wet and rotted. As a tied body decomposed, could the action of the sea and a rope be enough to break it up? Rhona recorded her results then got cleaned up and headed for her laptop, trying to ignore her brain's desire to shut down for a twelve-hour sleep.

The Caledonian MacBrayne website told her what she wanted to know. A ferry left Sconser on Skye for Raasay every hour Monday to Saturday. It took fifteen minutes to cross Raasay Sound.

If the body had worked its way free from a sunken boat, then the propeller of the ferry or a yacht could have mangled it and sent the bits on their separate ways.

Some research on a propeller company website gave her the information she needed. A propeller of a ferry or similar sized fishing boat would likely be a mix of bronze and nickel. Bronze was an alloy of copper and tin. It was strong, durable and easily workable, hot or cold.

If the tiny particles were of a similar mix, that would suggest a propeller had cut up the body, and not a machete or samurai sword. Chemical analysis would confirm the constituents of the metal, but it wouldn't tell whether someone had been murdered. A propeller was a better weapon than a machete, with its knife-like blades rotating four thousand times per minute.

The fisherman trawled a foot instead of fish. The Rigg woman got a hand instead of her dog's stick.

According to Chrissy, the local police were on the lookout for a torso. The torso could provide a lot more information.

Spotting decomposing bodies washed up on idyllic beaches was not exactly what the Scottish Tourist Board had in mind for its visitors. The sooner the remainder of the body was retrieved, the better.

The call came through from Dr Sissons as Rhona was abandoning the lab for her beckoning bed.

On the way upstairs to his office, she made up her mind to say as little as possible. It didn't matter now if the hand's location was common knowledge.

But Dr Sissons didn't want to talk about the hand. It took five minutes of prevarication; he was even forced to ask her about the LA conference; then he got round to it.

He gave her an envelope.

'What's this?'

He waited while she opened it and scanned the contents. Someone had informed the appropriate authorities that she was in a relationship with a suspected drug dealer. There had also been a complaint from the MOD regarding the mishandling of a specimen. She was required to take some leave until both matters have been resolved.

She should have known it. O'Brien had been oozing self-satisfaction from the moment he'd spotted her at the door of the jazz club.

Her relationship with the jazz club had already been leaked to the press, Dr Sissons told her.

O'Brien had been quick off the mark. Revenge for her turning down his sexual advances.

'I'm sure this will be cleared up quickly. I, for one, have the utmost faith in your professionalism, Dr MacLeod.'

It was unusual to have Sissons on her side.

'Thanks. How long?' Rhona asked, already knowing the answer.

'As long as it takes.'

It was a revelation to see the usually unflappable Sissons looking both uncomfortable and embarrassed.

The kitchen was filled with the half-light of a dwindling day. Some attempt had been made to clear up; the area round the sink was neatly stacked with unwashed dishes.

Rhona pulled open the fridge and took out the statutory bottle of white kept for emergencies.

There was a message flashing on the ansaphone. Sean's voice was calm. He would be back by ten. They would talk then.

Rhona took the wine bottle and glass to the bedroom. The room was the same as she'd left it what seemed like a century before. The saxophone was in the corner on its stand. Rhona picked up a shirt and hung it over the back of the chair. Below it lay a piece of paper.

She unfolded it. It was a songsheet. The music had been scribbled by hand.

Below were words, scored out and rewritten many times.

There's something inside me
A feeling so strong
No shadow can darken
It's here I belong
Dark clouds may gather
Rain start to fall
But I'll be here

When words try to hurt me
Lost dreams fill my mind
A vision of darkness
I left far behind . . .

It was titled *Esther's Song.*

Rhona took a mouthful of wine then stripped and slid between the sheets, trying not to think who might have been there during her absence.

But the bed smelt only of Sean. Rhona pulled the duvet close. Cocooned in its feathers, she drifted off and dreamed she was drowning in a shoal of rotting flesh.

13

THE HOSPITAL WAS a half dozen buildings spread out among the trees and busy car parks.

An old guy with slack lips shuffled across the road to meet Spike and stare into the buggy without speaking.

Spike had stopped at the chippie and bought the baby a sausage. It was holding on to it, gnawing the end intermittently with the concentration of the half-starved.

Spike pushed the pram past the guy and headed for the sign showing the various wards. The guard on the gate had told him ward sixteen was the most likely. Anyone brought in on an emergency would end up there until the doctor on duty had seen them.

'She a relative of yours, son?'

Spike nodded. 'My sister,' he rehearsed, knowing a ward doctor would not be so easily fooled.

Ward sixteen was a four-storey affair with an automatic door. Just inside, a pretend conservatory contained three people smoking like it was their last fag; the floor at their feet was littered with dog-ends. Nobody looked up as Spike walked past.

He took the lift to the third floor. A charge nurse asked his name and tickled the child under the chin.

Spike took a chance that they had extracted Esther's name from her and added his own to the front. The charge nurse smiled and took him down the corridor.

Esther was in a single room, lying staring up at the ceiling. Spike left the baby at the door and went in.

'Hey.'

'Hey.' She lifted her head and swung her feet over the side of the bed.

Spike went over and put his arms about her, breathing in the softness of her hair.

'You okay?'

She nodded. Her eyes were heavy, but they were focusing on him and not on the voices.

'We've got to get you out of here.'

The kid was gurgling from the corridor. Spike pulled the pram inside and Esther smiled at the mad hat and the half-eaten sausage.

'I'm sorry,' she said.

'What for?'

Spike couldn't look at her. Instead he pulled her jacket out of the cupboard and helped her put it on.

'I'm going to tell them the baby's yours. Okay?'

She looked puzzled.

'We're going to walk him round the grounds for ten minutes, then I've told them I'll bring you back.'

She seemed scared, so he explained.

'There's a taxi rank on the main road. We'll get one to the bus station. We'll go away for a couple of days, until this blows over.'

'What about the baby?'

'He's coming with us.'

She was frightened again.

'Spike, we can't take him,' she whispered.

He told her what he'd found.

'I'm not leaving him with those bastards.'

The charge nurse made him sign a form and put an address on it. The doctor would be round at six and he had to have Esther back by then. Spike agreed to everything.

They walked past the conservatory with no plants. The three residents were still at it, their pile of dog-ends the only thing growing
in there.

Esther pushed the pram.

'I've stashed some gear at the bus station in a locker,' Spike said.

Esther nodded and bounced the buggy over a crack in the pavement. The pom-pom on his coloured hat bobbed wildly as the little boy gurgled with pleasure.

Spike stared out as Glasgow dropped behind them and the scrubby verges got greener. The bus was half-full. A woman across from him was talking quietly in Gaelic to her husband. Spike tried not to listen, but her words dropped into his ears like the soft rush of water on the shore.

A sudden pain gripped his chest. Christ, he must be mad heading north. What the hell was he thinking of? He looked round, sure that Esther would hear the pounding of his heart, but she was asleep and dreaming, her eyes moving behind the grey sockets. He took her hand and she gave a little sigh and dropped her head on his shoulder.

Spike didn't like looking at his hands. Didn't like thinking what they had done. Didn't like the way they reminded him of what he was. He slid his hand from Esther's.

Outside the dark was stealing the day. Spike wiped a dribble from the baby's chin, then slipped his hand in his pocket.

14

THE SHORELINE WAS long, a million years of seashells ground into soft white sand. The right foot, helped by the wash of a western wind, sailed in with the tide and came to rest halfway up the beach. A crab, scuttling eastwards, found the jagged opening above the ankle bone and crawled inside.

Rhona looked down. In the dark it was difficult to see, but there was definitely one of them on her right breast. The body was white, elliptical; like a small hard insect shell. She screamed and flicked at it, sending it scuttling into the darkness. It was then she spotted the others, a myriad of them, like eyes in a black night. She stood up and tried to run towards the daylight, but rotting arms snaked her legs, tripping her up, landing her face down in soft white swollen flesh.

The alarm dragged her mind towards the day. At the same time the buzzer sounded, three short insistent drones. Rhona sat up, examining her right breast, knowing there was nothing there but checking all the same.

She killed the alarm and pulled on her dressing gown. There was no need to hurry, whoever was at the buzzer was not giving up. Already the button was marking the next three-beat bar.

Rhona snatched the handset off its cradle.

'Alright, alright.'

Bill's voice was half drowned by other voices.

'Are you going to let me in?'

When she opened the door, his face was grey in the watery light of the stairwell.

'Press vultures are out in force.'

Rhona stood back and let him in. In the few minutes she had waited for him to climb the stairs, she had forced her brain into wakefulness and realised how alone she was. Sean had not come home, at ten o'clock or any other time.

'Where's Sean?' Bill said.

'You tell me.'

Bill Wilson looked old, like a newspaper caught in the rain.

'Bloody hell,' he said.

They were in the sitting room. Rhona sat down, legs drifting from under her.

'Should I be worried?'

Bill was still standing. A bad sign.

'There was a phone call from the hospital,' he said. 'The girl picked up in the drugs raid was removed last night by someone claiming to be her brother.'

The mugs of coffee sat between them on the kitchen table. Bill's had grown a white skin waiting for him to drink it.

Rhona already knew it wasn't Sean who had removed Esther from the hospital. That had been easy enough to establish. Where the hell was he now, if he had been released from custody at eight o'clock?

'I'm sorry, Rhona.'

'About what?' Rhona looked at the weary face marked with the strain of the previous night's events.

'Your job.'

She shrugged. 'Standing up for colleagues against the MOD is not in Dr Sissons' rule book. He tried all the same.' She looked across the table. 'What about Sean?'

'O'Brien says he got an anonymous tip off. He had no option but to check it out. A female operative found the girl ga-ga in the toilets. A quantity of amphetamine powder and ecstasy tablets were found in there with her.'

'That doesn't mean Sean was supplying.'

'No. But it looks like it.'

Rhona studied her coffee. 'Esther could be a witness.'

Bill nodded. 'And she's gone.'

He pulled the morning newspaper from the inside pocket of his coat and spread it out on the table for her to read. The London-owned Scottish tabloid was having fun, running the line of Scots junkies living off the UK treasury; but this time with the help of a government servant's live-in lover. Forensic science was having a bad morning.

She paused. 'O'Brien could be lying.'

'Why would he lie?'

'Hell hath no fury like a man scorned?'

Bill knew the story. 'O'Brien's a fool. But he's not bent.'

Bill was right. If there had been stuff at the club, O'Brien wasn't the one that put it there. He just enjoyed finding it.

By the time Bill left, he had gently warned her not to show any more interest in the drugs bust or in the dismembered body, for both their sakes. His Super had been adamant.

'Sleep off your jet lag,' he added. 'Leave it to me.'

Rhona watched from the landing as he nodded up to her before opening the main door to a gaggle of questions.

Between them, she and Bill Wilson had put many men behind bars. It only needed one of them to decide to get even.

The dose of caffeine had woken Rhona up. She ignored the bed and sat down at her laptop. Chrissy would know all about her fall from grace by now. A Miss Angry letter was bound to be winging its way through cyberspace.

There were two messages in the inbox. The first subject heading was the name of a jazz song. Rhona double-clicked and opened it up.

Sorry I didn't come home last night. I wanted to avoid the Evening Post *blokes parked on your doorstep. I'm going to ask around, see if I can find out who planted the stuff and why.*

Esther's gone from the hospital. She'll be with Spike.
She's ill, Rhona. If you can find her, get her to a doctor.

You were right. This electronic stuff's not so bad after all.
I'm sorry,

Sean.

'If you can find her, get her to a doctor.'

The spare room was tidy. Nothing left of its recent occupant except a faint smell of perfume.

Rhona let her mind work through everything that had happened in the last twenty-four hours.

Below, the convent garden reminded her she had survived another winter. The trees were bright with fresh leaves and sometime during her sojourn in LA the borders had become a splash of colour.

Sean wouldn't come back, at least not until he could prove he had nothing to do with the drugs at the club; staying out of it didn't seem an option, despite Bill's advice.

Rhona went back to the computer.

Chrissy's email was short and steeped in anger. She promised to keep Rhona informed about what was happening at the lab. She would call round soon.

Rhona poured another cup of coffee and dropped onto the sofa. Okay. There was plenty she could do. There was another article to write, requested by an American biomedical journal. And she would have to speak to Lynne Franklin, although whether ReGene would wish to recruit a suspected drug-dealer's girlfriend was another matter.

And there was Andre.

According to Andre, Dr Fitzgerald MacAulay had moved to Britain in the 1980s, working at Porton Down.

'At what?' Rhona had asked him.

'At the time, most countries viewed biological weapons as limited to nonspecific targeting,' Andre said.

'And they wanted something more efficient?'

He nodded. 'MacAulay was good. Better than good. He was already thinking gene-specific viruses. He just didn't know how to do it . . . then.'

'And now?'

Andre did not have to spell it out to her. How FBI crime labs, like their British counterparts, had routinely stumbled on genetic markers specific to blacks, whites, Hispanics and Native Americans; there was a genetic marker present in the DNA of Palestinian Arabs distinguishing them from Israeli Jews.

'And MacAulay?' she said.

'He disappeared at what was essentially the peak of his career . . . and the peak of his interest to the British government.'

Rhona could hardly believe it, 'And no one knew where he went?'

'They thought the Soviet Union at first, but that was never a possibility. MacAulay was as right-wing as they come. Believed in American Capitalism and the right to bear arms.'

'No wonder Mrs Thatcher wanted him here.'

Rhona was avoiding asking Andre how he knew all this and why the interest anyway? But Andre didn't need the question.

'Dr Fitzgerald MacAulay was my father.'

Rhona still remembered her reaction. The open mouth, the puzzled face and then the stupid remark, *but your name is Frith.*

'My mother's name. They never married.'

Andre went on, ignoring the look on her face. 'A letter was posted in Raasay. It said he was coming back to the States. He never arrived. I came to look for him. No one in Raasay knew him. They said the only Americans were the tourists.' He paused. 'Maybe he was a tourist. Maybe he visited the island like me and posted the letter from there.'

Rhona still couldn't see the connection with the foot she'd examined.

'There's one way I would know if the foot belonged to my father.

He had a tattoo on his ankle. The sign that showed he belonged to

the clan.'

Rhona's heart went cold. 'The clan?'

'The Clan of the Men of the West.'

'ReAlba.'

The wise move then would have been to tell Andre the truth. The foot did have a tattoo, in fact she'd just received the digital image of it. But she didn't. Instead she told him the foot she'd examined had been badly decomposed. There was no obvious tattoo. Then she suggested Andre contact the British government and tell them what he had told her.

Even now, Rhona wasn't sure why she hadn't told Andre about the tattoo. Okay, so she never discussed cases outside the lab, but the police wanted to identify the foot. If it was his father, Andre had a right to know.

Maybe the real reason she didn't tell him was because she didn't trust him.

Rhona repacked her case before she went to bed, piling the dirty washing on the kitchen floor. *The Rough Guide to Scotland* offered her various possibilities. Raasay House was an outdoor centre, which also did bed and breakfast. There was the Raasay Hotel, or there was Mrs MacMurdo at the Post Office.

15

ESTHER WAS SMILING. The baby smiled back at her, making Spike wonder at the power of a full stomach. The pinched look was gone from his wee face. The stolen fleecy jacket bunched up around his red cheeks as Esther threw the wee one up and caught him again.

Their laughter was a better tonic than the oxygen-filled air and the dark serrated edge of the Cuillin over the water behind them.

Spike had spent the morning scouring the shops for what they needed, leaving Esther to drink tea and eat scones in a tourist café.

Now he was ready, the backpack stuffed with nappies and baby food. He had already decided not to hitch a lift to the dinghy. Once they were out of the more touristy places, people would ask questions.

'Ready?'

'Of course we're ready.' Esther met the baby nose to nose and kissed him.

Spike lifted him into the carrier and slipped it onto his back.

'Let's go, then.'

They took the coast road out of town, keeping the sea on their left. Now that they were here, the apprehension that had invaded Spike on the bus had gone. Whatever happened, he would rather it happened here.

After a mile he cut inland, letting the water drop behind them. Esther climbed quietly behind him. Every so often Spike stopped and turned, but Esther's eyes were clear and bright.

They reached the dinghy two hours later. Spike had felt the baby fall asleep, the weight of the backpack suddenly changing. He stopped when they reached the headland, eased the straps from his shoulders and laid the baby like a papoose on the grass.

'Wait here,' he told Esther.

The pebble beach was hidden beneath a thick over-hang of broom but Spike knew the dinghy's where-abouts by the single standing stone. Spring sunshine had forced the broom into flower and as Spike pushed his way through, the heady scent of coconut filled his nostrils.

The sailing dinghy was where he had left it, pulled into a shallow cave under the overhang. Standing in the entrance, Spike waited for the nausea of remembering, but there was nothing but the scent of salt water.

At the back of the cave, the bundle of clothes had dried in stiff folds. Spike shook them out and laid them on the ground.

The tins of food stood undisturbed. He pulled his army knife from his pocket and sliced the circle of the lid. He didn't want to light a fire until they were at the blackhouse. Esther would have to dine on cold beans and corned-beef.

When he emerged, Esther had the baby bare-arsed on the grass, its wee legs kicking for the sky. Spike handed her a plastic plate with the sliced beef and cold beans.

'A picnic,' she said.

She propped the baby up against her legs and fed it a mashed mouthful before she started to eat.

'Duncan,' she said.

'What?'

'I'm going to call him Duncan.'

She swooped the spoon down from a great height.

'Duncan. Duncan.'

His wee mouth spread like a hatchling's.

Spike pointed across the water. 'That mountain is called Dun Caan.'

Esther laughed. 'See. I knew that was his name.'

Spike had never heard the baby's real name. '*It* was his name. *It* or *the wean*. Something to put outside the door when the Flintstones were humping or shooting up.

The thing, that's what his father had called Calum. *The thing*, as if Calum had no heart and no soul.

Spike got up and lifted the empty plates. A splutter of water seeped from the ground nearby, trying to find its way to the open sea. He rinsed the plates, wiped them with moss and shoved them in the backpack.

The sky above them was clear but that could change very quickly.

'Time for a sail,' he called to Esther. 'Hope you don't get seasick.'

16

GLASGOW DROPPED BEHIND her like a cloud. Rhona slipped a CD in the drive and let the music envelop her escape. She took the Loch Lomond road at a steady pace, the beauty of the loch reminding her there was more to life than overtaking.

Sean had not called by the time she left and she had no idea where he was. She hadn't spoken to Chrissy either. Chrissy didn't need to be implicated in any of this, if things turned out for the worse.

Rhona tapped out the swift fiddle music on the steering wheel, then indulged in a bout of nostalgia as Duncan Chisholm's strings slowed to match the ripples of the wind on the loch.

This was what the American diaspora craved. A sense of belonging to a past time and place. A landscape that created the soul and played it in bittersweet tunes your whole life long.

The further north she went the more the essence of the city fell away from her. She was going home. A home that no longer held her and hers. A home long forsaken but still there, its contours etched deep in her heart. Loch Lomond gave way to Glen Falloch, Crianlarich and then Rannoch Moor.

Today the sun was shining on Glencoe. It was not a place full of the sorrow of its tragic history but a place of tourists seeking the hot blood of highland conflict to make sense of their present.

Rhona stopped at the visitor centre and, as she drank a coffee, tried to imagine what Andre the American had made of it all.

Despite her cynicism, the atmosphere of Glencoe moved in on her like the Campbells on the MacDonalds. She was glad to leave the Valley of Weeping and descend towards Fort William, which was full of early tourists and rural weekenders eager for retail therapy. Forty-seven miles later, she skirted Morar sands and emerged in Mallaig. The ferry was in port, cars unloading in a steady stream onto the quay. Rhona headed for the Coffee Pot, an attempt to bring café society to downtown Mallaig.

Seven sailings a day, the girl who brought her order told her. Mallaig to Armadale, the scenic route to Skye. Rhona knew that already but she didn't want to spoil the girl's enthusiasm for talking to tourists, so she thanked her with a smile. Before she left the café she tried the mobile, which worked perfectly. She hadn't expected a connection. Chrissy answered almost immediately.

'Where are you? I've been phoning the flat all day.'

Rhona wasn't willing to say, even to Chrissy.

'I couldn't stay in the flat.'

Silence.

'Sissons is walking about with a bad smell under his nose,' Chrissy said.

'More dead bodies than he can handle?'

'Just another foot, washed up on a nice clean white beach in the inner Hebrides.'

'I'm off the case, Chrissy.'

'Like hell you are.'

There was a noise that meant someone had come into the lab. Chrissy obviously didn't want to speak in their presence. 'Thanks, that will be fine,' she said, and hung up.

Rhona wished she could have asked about the results of the tests on the hand. Wished she knew whether the hand and foot were a match. Wished Sean had not fucked-up so badly. Wished she was back in her lab.

The Small Isles peeped at her out of the mist halfway across the Sound of Sleat. Rum, Canna, Eigg and Muck. Hard-to-forget names in a hard-to-forget landscape. Over the sea to Skye. If only she had a pound for every time that song in memory of Bonnie Prince Charlie had been sung, she could retire.

As the ferry docked at Armadale pier, Rhona had to admit why she had come the scenic route. If she had gone further north and crossed by the bridge, she would have had to make a conscious decision to go to the south of the island to look at the cottage. It was better this way. Driving past, knowing she could stop if she wanted to.

She had not set foot on the island since her father's funeral. Even now, two years later, she sometimes had to stop herself from dialling the number. After all, dead men don't answer the phone.

Rhona pulled off the road and found the path that skirted the hill and led down to the beach. She had intended to rush past the cottage, head for Broadford and stay the night there. Now it didn't seem so difficult to see it. Maybe she could stay nearby after all.

The path to the beach was well trodden and the front door of the house and the boat shed had been painted a bright saltire blue. Rhona was suddenly glad she had agreed to rent the cottage to Sabhal Mor Ostaig, the Gaelic college, for one of its teachers. Whoever had moved in was taking care of the place.

A young man came out of the boat shed, whistling. He didn't see Rhona at first and stopped to gaze over the water to Knoydart. Rhona followed his gaze.

'The view from Arainn Chalium Chille across to Knoydart has been described as the most stirring in the world,' he said, acknowledging her presence. 'That's what they told me when I applied for the job at the college.' His voice was low but definitely North Atlantic. 'To be truthful, it was probably why I took it.'

Rhona did a quick calculation and came up with Cape Breton. The Gaelic College had strong links with a similar establishment in Cape Breton. Exchanges were commonplace.

'I always thought the view from the cottage was even better than the view from the college.'

'You know the cottage?' He looked round at it affectionately.

'I know it well. I lived here once.'

'Then you'd better come inside and have a coffee.'

*   *   ★

The last time Rhona had stepped through the doorway, she had been clearing the cottage of her father's things. It had taken her a year after his death to do that. She had carted everything to Glasgow, given his clothes to a charity shop and stacked her shelves with his books.

Now the shelves in the living room were filled with books again. Rhona ran an eye over the Gaelic titles.

The young man brought her a mug of coffee from the kitchen and waved her to a seat beside the newly lit fire. He had made the room his own, but the old comfort was still there.

'I'm Norman MacLeod,' he told her, 'from St Ann's Bay, Cape Breton Island.'

'Rhona MacLeod, sometime Skye, now Glasgow.'

They shook hands, laughing at the coincidence of their shared name.

'How long have you been here?'

'Since September.'

They talked about the Gaelic College and the resurgence in the language and culture of the Gaels. Her host was almost evangelical in his enthusiasm for the language

As she left, he recommended a new B&B five miles further on. Rhona had already made up her mind to head for Broadford, but let him go back to his desk to collect the leaflet anyway.

She turned back when she reached the car. Norman MacLeod had followed her progress and was giving her a last wave as she climbed in and drove off.

When she reached Broadford, Rhona drove straight through and headed on to catch the ferry at Sconser.

She phoned the Raasay Post Office from the ferry terminal and asked if there was a room free. Mrs MacMurdo sounded surprised and delighted to get a visitor so early in the season.

The crossing took fifteen minutes. Rhona left her car and went up on deck to take in the view. Raasay House, *Taigh Mor an teilean*, 'The Big House on the Island', stood in the southwest corner, May sunshine washing its gracious facade with a golden light. On the slope of lush green grass that led to Raasay Sound, distant figures ran about as if in a game.

Andre had reminded her of its story. When the Raasay MacLeods chose to support the Jacobite cause, government troops burned down all homes on the island, including Raasay House, then set about raping the women and murdering the men.

'It didn't stop the local people smuggling Prince Charles Edward Stuart onto the island and off again in his search for a way back to France.'

'Americans have a romantic view of Scottish history,' she had retorted.

'And you don't?'

It was hard not to, once you were here.

Rhona waited in the car for her turn to drive up the ramp. She'd returned to the islands every time a major change happened in her life. Maybe that was part of the reason she was here now.

Instead of turning left for the village, she pulled into the ferry car park and fished out a card.

She texted Dr Lynne Franklin that, if the offer of a job still stood, she was open to discussion.

17

THEY HAD BEEN lucky to get this far unnoticed.

Spike looked up at the towering cliffs and tried to remember exactly where he had landed the dinghy the last time he had been here. He had escaped for a weekend's fishing. Anything to get away from the rising tide of his father's frustration and anger. Calum was ill again. While his mother walked the floor with his baby brother, his father cursed the genes that had given him such a sickly child.

The sun was sinking rapidly now and a snare of panic caught at Spike. He ignored it and pulled the rope towards him, curving the dinghy into the wind. The pebbled strip of shore hung under the cliffs. When he felt the bump as the rudder scraped bottom, he slipped over the side into the water thick with seaweed, so brutally cold he gasped.

Esther looked wan but she rallied as he began to pull ashore. She laid Duncan in the stern and plopped over the side to help him. The cliffs cut out the dying rays of the sun and Spike saw, despite her encouraging smile, that her lips were blue.

They pulled the dinghy as far under the cliffs as they could, then Esther lifted up the silent child and kissed his startled face. Spike hoisted the bags on his back, conscious of how far they still had to go before they could light a fire and get warm. His hands and arms were aching, a dull rheumatic pain that set his teeth on edge. He looked down at his hands, but they were mere shadows in the fading light.

Spike made Esther climb the steep path in front of him, worried she would slip and fall. She was bending to balance the weight of the baby, placing her feet carefully on the uneven surface. When they reached the top, they both fell into the heather and breathed in great gulps of air.

It took more than half-an-hour of walking through the twisted heather stems before they reached the corrie. Whoever wrote songs about marching through heather, thought Spike, had never tried to walk in the stuff.

Behind him Esther was humming a tune. It had worked like a lullaby, because Duncan was asleep, his face squashed sideways to her back.

They had been climbing since the cliff edge. Head down to negotiate the dull brown knots of heather, Esther had been unaware of what was unfolding around her. Spike waited for her to catch up so that he might watch her when she raised her eyes and took in where she was.

The first time he had found this spot, Spike had been almost blinded by anger and fear. He had left the house before he did something stupid. Before he smashed everything in that room. Before he hit the man he called father.

Then he reached this place.

The setting sun was throwing its last rays at the loch,

staining the surface red. Spike watched Esther's delight blossom, knowing how she felt.

A sudden lightness filled his heart, stirring him on.

'Come on,' he said. 'Come and see your new home.'

The blackhouse was surrounded by early grass, a green patch in a sea of brown heather. Once it had been a croft, with a family and animals and crops grown in the runrig system that still rippled the hill behind. Now only the left-hand section was wind and waterproof. Spike had made it that way on his various visits, and he'd brought food and bedding and fishing gear. At first it had been fun, like camping out. Then it became more serious.

He ignored the familiar fear that dogged his memory and went inside. The fire was set in the hearth, although the kindling looked damp. He substituted some windswept heather and drier sticks from the bunch in the corner.

When he lit it, the flames shot up in a wild crackle. He boxed the heather in with peats and went looking for Esther. She was sitting outside, watching the last light on the loch as if it would never return.

'You okay?'

'Yes,' she said and he knew she meant it.

Whatever happened now, he didn't want it to happen anywhere else.

They stripped off and hung their wet clothes over a line strung between the beams near the fire. Spike pulled out dry clothes from the backpack but Esther chose to wrap a blanket round herself instead. Duncan was already asleep on a bundle of heather, having gorged himself on two tins of baby food. Spike suddenly realised he hadn't heard him whinge once since he'd given him to Esther to look after. Having a mother was obviously a novelty he was enjoying.

Spike re-stacked the peats and told Esther he was going outside for more heather for the beds. She nodded, not taking her eyes from the glow of the fire.

Sometime in the recent past someone had made attempts at resurrecting the blackhouse, maybe as a bothy for walkers or climbers. They had returfed a section of roof, but winter gales had partially wrecked their efforts. Still, there was enough covered space for a pile of driftwood, peat and heather.

The loch had descended into blackness, a dark crater under the navy sky. A curlew called to him across the water, a long cry that echoed around the walls of the natural amphitheatre. Spike stopped to listen, hearing his own cry in the bird's lonely call.

He filled an old creel, killing time before he had to go back into the cottage. He sat down on a rock, glad he couldn't see his hands in the darkness. The marks were getting more noticeable. Like Lady Macbeth, he couldn't rub them off. He laughed suddenly and the echo threw itself back at him, a mocking hyena.

'Spike.'

Esther was standing in the doorway, firelight shaping the blanket round her shoulders. He could see her clearly but she glanced about, seeing nothing in the sudden blackness.

'Coming,' he said, and lifted the creel.

*   *   *

She woke with a cry. Spike was still awake, but the haunting quality of the cry threw him into a panic. Esther's mouth was moving quickly, babbling, answering some voice he couldn't hear. Her eyes were blank, viewing another place.

'Hey. It's alright.' He crawled towards her.

She turned, registering his presence.

'They were there again,' she said, her voice small like a child's.

Spike put his arms about her, wishing he could squeeze the horror from her body. She shuddered and pressed her face against his chest.

'Spike.'

'What?'

'Don't leave me.'

'Never,' he said, and meant it.

She breathed out against him, a deep sighing breath. When her face tipped up to look at him trustingly, Spike bent and placed his lips gently on hers.

When she fell asleep, he slipped his arm from under her head and stood up. In the faint light from the fire, Spike examined the body that had stupidly entered hers. His father had been right. He was an abomination. An abomination that should not be allowed to live and must never reproduce.

He crumpled to the floor in front of the dying fire. In the corner, the baby whimpered and a small fist waved in the air.

Spike buried his head in his hands and wept.

18

RHONA SPREAD THE newspaper open on the bed. The article was front page news.

> *Police confirmed today that forensic tests on the human body parts caught in a fisherman's nets in Raasay Sound and on two beaches on Skye, belong to a Polish fisherman reported missing from a factory ship. A spokesman for the MOD, who have a presence in the area, said this confirmed the truth of their denial that a British submarine had been involved in a fishing incident in Raasay Sound.*

The photograph of Phillips next to the article showed him to be perfectly relaxed about the MOD's version of the truth. For a brief moment Rhona contemplated the notion that Phillips might be speaking in good faith. After all, she had told no one officially about the ReAlba tattoo, not even Bill Wilson.

No. The reaction of Phillips to her announcement of the name MacAulay had been too strong a signal that the Ministry of Defence had another agenda. One she was not party to.

Mrs MacMurdo had already delivered tea and a morning paper, fresh from the ferry, and told her breakfast would be ready in fifteen minutes.

The plate was large and well stocked. No acres of empty white porcelain around a slither of bacon for Mrs MacMurdo's guests. Rhona ignored the calorie and cholesterol count and tucked in. If she was planning walking detective work, she would need it. Besides, fresh highland air made you remember your appetite.

Mrs MacMurdo left her to demolish her traditional Scottish breakfast and reappeared with a fresh pot of tea directly Rhona placed her knife and fork side by side on her plate.

'I'll be busy now with the Post Office,' she said, lifting the plate and encouraging Rhona to have more toast. 'I never lock the door, so you can come and go as you please.'

Rhona thanked her and said something about a walk. Mrs MacMurdo nodded and asked her where on Skye she was from. Rhona wasn't surprised. She hadn't lived on Skye since she was five and her father only returned there after he retired, but the closer she got to home the more she suspected her voice echoed its origins. Once her parentage was examined and established, Mrs MacMurdo wished her a fine day and left.

Back in her room, Rhona mused over her life story as known by Mrs MacMurdo. Her father had been that nice man from Driesh Cottage, who died two years ago. He had only one daughter, she was in the Forensic Service in Glasgow.

'Aye, your father was keen on the walking and fishing,' Mrs MacMurdo had told her. 'We've missed seeing him around here.' She paused. 'Still, it's nice to finally meet that daughter he talked about so much.'

Rhona tried not to think about the number of times she had planned to come and stay with her father for some fishing and walking and had failed to do so, usually because of work.

'You'll be glad you weren't here last week,' Mrs MacMurdo went on. 'The place was swarming with police from the mainland trying to find the rest of that poor soul's body.'

She pointed at the newspaper on the chair beside Rhona. 'Now they're saying it was a Polish fisherman from one of those big factory ships.' Mrs MacMurdo did not look convinced. 'Of course, with all those tests you do, I'm sure you know more than the likes of me.'

Her landlady didn't wait for a reply but hurried off to answer the bell from one of her Post Office customers.

Rhona was inclined to agree. Unless there was an active branch of ReAlba in Poland, the foot had not belonged to a Polish factory fisherman. It might suit the MOD to support such a story, but Rhona wasn't in the business of making up identities for dead people. And neither, normally, was DI Wilson.

One thing was certain. If Dr Fitzgerald MacAulay had been part of the life of this island or one nearby, Mrs MacMurdo would be the woman to know about it.

Before she set off on her walk, Rhona checked her computer for emails. There was one from Chrissy, outlining what the official position was on the body parts and did Rhona want her to drop the tattoo bombshell?

An email from Sean had been sent from some downtown Cybercafé. Word on the street was that the jazz club, Sean, and by association, Rhona, had been set up. He asked if Rhona knew anything about a Joe Maley who was rumoured to be running a west coast drugs business.

Jesus. Joe Maley. Sentenced to five years . . . Rhona counted up . . . approximately three years ago. That was one prison release either Bill Wilson had missed or else had chosen not to tell her about.

And Maley certainly harboured a grudge big enough to set the heather on fire. It was she who had stood in court and provided the evidence that put him away. A forensic examiner finding particles of cocaine on the money his club was laundering didn't help his case. No one believed his innocent plea. His expensive lawyer wasn't expensive enough. Maley's fancy eating place on Byres Road disappeared and he went on the prison payroll.

But how could Joe Maley know that by trying to stitch her up he was playing into the hands of the MOD?

The conspiracy theory was taking over, Rhona decided. She was like that girl on the Glasgow Underground, muttering away to herself, obsessed with being watched. Paranoia on legs.

Rhona switched off the computer and lifted her jacket. What she needed was a good dose of West Highland air to clear her brain.

Early sunshine was shifting the mist and across the water the black topped Cuillin rose like a mirage. Rhona felt unexpectedly happy to be out of the city and on the islands once again, despite the circumstances.

She left the house, shutting the door carefully behind her. Mrs MacMurdo waved out of the Post Office window and Rhona was left in no doubt that the current customer was learning who the latest Bed and Breakfast guest was.

Rhona left the village and followed the path that ran north through woods. After a while she passed an ancient broch with part of the walls and galleries still standing. Inside, there was nothing but time and the sky above. People had lived, loved and died on this island for centuries. Now there were only scattered desolate ruins as a reminder of their lives.

When she reached the southern slopes of Dun Caan, she sat beside a lochan and ate the sandwiches Mrs MacMurdo had given her. It seemed ridiculous to be eating again only two hours after a breakfast fit for two men.

Rhona didn't care.

She lay back against a hillock and closed her eyes.

The sun was warm on her face but a cool wind skimmed the surface of the loch. Somewhere in the far distance a boat chugged through the water. Rhona sat up, thinking it must be the ferry ploughing between Raasay and Skye but it was east of her, moving up the Inner Sound towards the deserted shielings of Screapadal. She pulled out her binoculars and had a look. A woman lay on the deck taking in the sun and a man stood on the bow pointing his binoculars in her direction. Rhona waved in case he had spotted her, then watched the yacht mooch past, keeping close to the cliff as if looking for somewhere to anchor.

Beyond the boat, dark clouds were slowly creeping in from the east. Climbing Dun Caan, she decided, would have to wait for another day.

By the time she reached the tar road, the rain was sweeping in and the waterproof jacket was sending drips down her trouser legs and into her boots. When the jeep drew alongside, Rhona accepted the lift without pausing to gaze up from under her hood. Halfway in, she realised who her Prince Charming was. Norman MacLeod gave her a North Atlantic grin and turned the windscreen wipers to a higher speed.

'The Post Office?' he said.

'Thanks.'

'No problem. I'm headed for the ferry anyway. Were you climbing Dun Caan?'

'Halfway.'

'You didn't say you were coming to Raasay.' His voice had taken on a semi-petulant tone that irritated Rhona slightly. What business was it of his?

'I just took a notion,' she lied.

She glanced sideways, watching him construct a thought before putting it into words.

'You'd better watch Mrs MacMurdo,' he said with a laugh. 'She's a bit of a gossip. I bet she knows your life history by now.'

'Probably. Why are you over here yourself?'

He hadn't expected the question, or at least not its directness.

'Oh, I have one or two friends on the island,' he said in Gaelic. 'I come over from time to time to practise my

Gaelic on them.' He laughed. 'They tell me I've got a terrible accent.'

Fortunately the Post Office appeared from the sheeting rain before Rhona had to voice an opinion on his accent. She certainly didn't want to have to admit to the fact that his Gaelic sounded pretty good.

'So, are you planning to stay around for a few days?' Rhona opened the jeep door. 'Probably.' God she sounded cagey. It was difficult not to. 'It depends on the weather,' she added. If in doubt, rely on the weather.

'Yes it can be unpredictable,' he said with humourless understatement.

They observed the downpour together.

'Thanks again for the lift.'

Mrs MacMurdo was waiting in the hall.

'You'll be wanting something hot,' she said firmly. 'Come through to the kitchen when you've changed. I'll put the kettle on.'

Kitchens like Mrs MacMurdo's deserve to be savoured like good food, Rhona decided. The big solid fuel range beamed out comfort. Mrs MacMurdo waved her into a seat and placed a mug of hot tea on the edge of the range beside her. She refilled her own mug and sat herself down opposite Rhona.

'I see you got a lift from the Gaelic teacher from the college,' she said crisply.

'It was lucky he came along. I would have been even more drenched.'

Rhona could sense her landlady had something to say about Norman MacLeod. Whether she would

choose to say it was another matter. Rhona decided to
clear the air herself.

'I just met Norman yesterday. I dropped into Dad's
cottage on the way here.'

Mrs MacMurdo said nothing but chose to stir
purposefully at a bubbling pot.

'I've made some stew for tea. I hope that will be
alright?'

'Great.'

'Oh, and there was a phone call while you were out.
It was a man. American. Wouldn't leave his name. Just
asked if there was a Rhona MacLeod staying here.'

The word *American* had a disapproving ring to it. If
it wasn't Norman MacLeod, Mrs MacMurdo seemed
to be saying, then who was it?

Rhona was wondering the same thing.

After eating, Rhona went up to her room. Tucked
under the eaves, the window alcove housed a small
desk and chair. She had already set up her laptop there.

Watching the soft swell of the water through the
Narrows, it was difficult to imagine anything bad happening here. Peace seemed part of the place. Yet the
reason most tourists visited these islands was because of
their violent history. Every landmark told a horrific tale of
clan killing clan. It made Rhona think of ReAlba and the
Men of the West, caught in the past, ready to wipe out
anyone who wasn't one of their clan. But why use swords
when they could manipulate the codes of life itself?

Rhona began work on her paper, trying to ignore all
other thoughts. The house sank into silence and she

decided Mrs MacMurdo must have gone to bed. She made up her mind that she would speak to her landlady tomorrow about Dr Fitzgerald MacAulay.

Andre said he'd had no luck with his enquiries, but although island people were friendly to strangers, they liked their privacy. To Mrs MacMurdo, Rhona was one of them. Maybe she would confide in Rhona what she would not tell an inquisitive American tourist.

The nightmare that wakened her was the same one. Always the same one. The warmth and comfort of the bedclothes changing into the heavy wet cloying chill of water thick with debris. This time the water was filled with weeds, long tentacles curling round her legs and pulling her down until her lungs ached to burst.

Rhona's eyes flew open. A yellow moon split the darkness and danced its beams through the window. Her hammering heart began to slow. She took three long deep breaths. A clock on the mantelpiece ticked a steady beat and she willed her heart to match.

This was stupid. Ever since she had got involved in this case she had dreamt of drowning. Having recurrent nightmares about the way her forensic victims might have died wasn't the way to stay sane.

Rhona got up and pulled on her dressing gown. Beneath her window, the path left the back door of the Post Office and went eastwards. Mrs MacMurdo had already told her there was a nice walk in that direction. Maybe tomorrow, she promised herself, turning back to her warm bed.

The soft knock on the back door brought her to the

window again. Rhona craned her neck trying to see who was standing on the step. The figure was male and not very tall. His face was turned from her, but she had a feeling he was a young man. The knock was louder this time, its echo drifting up the narrow stair.

Rhona waited, silently wondering if she should go and open the door, but the third knock brought movement. She heard Mrs MacMurdo's bedroom door open and the swish of her slippers on the polished floor. Then the back door creaked open.

The surprised gasp sent Rhona to her own door and onto the landing. There was such delight in her landlady's voice; the visitor was someone she was pleased to see, whatever the hour. She ushered him inside. Rhona chanced a view, but the hall light was dim and the young man was quickly taken into the kitchen and the door shut behind him.

Rhona got into bed and tried to go back to sleep. After all, it was none of her business who was visiting her landlady in the middle of the night.

She was finally dozing off when there was a tap at her own door. In the stair light, Mrs MacMurdo looked both embarrassed and concerned.

'I'm sorry to bother you at this late hour, Dr MacLeod, but I wonder if you can help? There's a boy here who used to live on the island. He's camping up by the loch with a friend and she's been taken ill. We need a car to fetch her down.'

A teenage boy walked up and down in front of the range, distraught. As Rhona entered, he shifted his look to Mrs MacMurdo, as if he wasn't sure about this latest development.

'It's alright, Donald. Dr MacLeod will help.'

'I thought if I brought her to the island, she would get peace. It did get better for a while, but now it's worse. She keeps hearing things. Things that really scare her.'

'Where is she?' Rhona asked.

He turned to Mrs MacMurdo. 'She's up near the loch in the ruins of the blackhouse.'

'We should get the police,' Rhona suggested.

'No,' Mrs MacMurdo said firmly. 'Constable Johnstone is on Skye. 'It's better if we bring the lassie here. Then we'll decide.'

As they drove away, Rhona could see the boy's hands were shaking. When he saw her looking at them he quickly shoved them in his pockets, but not before she noticed their dry, wrinkled surface. Rhona took a quick look at his face. The skin there was as papery as on his hands. There was something wrong with this young man, something more than worry.

'Donald?'

He didn't answer, his eyes staring straight ahead.

'Donald?'

He realised she was speaking to him and turned to face her.

'Sorry. No one calls me that any more. Not since I left the island. My name's Spike now. Just call me Spike.'

19

THE MOON HAD disappeared behind thick cloud. Rhona, following the boy's instructions, took a left onto a gravel road just wide enough for the car. Her headlights danced across a mixture of young birch trees and thick heather, the wheels following ruts trailed by some jeep through the mud left by the heavy rain. The boy said nothing, his face wooden with fear.

'What's your friend's name?'

He looked round at her suspiciously.

'Her name's Helen.'

Rhona's brain slowed down, stopped putting two and two together to get five. Spike. There were probably hundreds of guys called Spike. It went with the territory. Gelled hair, combat jacket, jeans. Choose a name that fitted the image. Anything but Donald. They were half-an-hour on the forestry track before he told her to stop. She got out of the car and set off on the sheep trail that the forestry track had become.

'Not that way!' he shouted at her. 'It takes you over the cliff.'

Rhona stopped, glad his eyes were keener than hers.

'You stay with the car,' he told her. 'I'll get Helen.'

'But what if you need help?'

'I'll manage.'

Rhona nodded. The boy looked a hundred per cent more at home out here than she felt. She got back in the car and turned off the headlights. If she flattened the battery, they wouldn't be going anywhere.

As her eyes grew accustomed to the dark, Rhona could make out the line of the cliffs and the grey swell of water beyond. Mainland lights twinkled in the distance and here and there a single pinpoint suggested someone on another island. She rolled down the window and night air swept in, bringing the tangy softness of the sea and a fine whisper of coming rain.

She switched on the roof light to look at her watch. Spike had been gone an hour. He'd told her it would take that at least. She settled back in her seat and pulled up the hood on her jacket. The fine smirr of rain was thickening, pattering the windscreen.

Rhona was already contemplating what she would do if Spike didn't reappear. She would have to sit here until it was light. Going back alone in this downpour was not an option.

A figure suddenly emerged like a ghost in front of her, hood pulled up, a large lump under his jacket. Rhona switched on the headlights to guide him and a wail like a child's cry rose into the air. Spike threw open the car door and slid inside, his face grey with worry.

'She's gone. She's fucking gone.'

He unzipped the jacket and a baby's face peeped out solemnly at her. 'No matter how ill she was, Esther wouldn't have left him alone.'

'Esther?' Rhona said in a small voice.

Spike stared at her in the realisation that the name meant something to Rhona, something important.

'Who the fuck are you?' he said.

They wedged the baby on the back seat behind one of Rhona's bags. Rhona didn't tell Spike how concerned she was about finding her way back in the rain. He was worried enough.

'I have to stay at the blackhouse in case Esther comes back. When it's light, I'll be able to look properly.'

Rhona didn't mention police or search parties. Things were bad enough. Spike hadn't told her why he was so anxious about the police knowing he was here. Rhona had her suspicions. She hadn't mentioned the raid on the club and neither had he. They had established that he and Esther had stayed at her flat, that was all.

'I didn't want to stay there, it was Esther,' he'd told her defiantly. 'And she wasn't shagging Sean, if that's what you're thinking.'

Rhona didn't admit what she was thinking and she didn't tell him that Sean was in trouble and so was she.

'Don't worry. I'll take good care of the baby.'

Spike didn't look back as he strode off into the rain, even when little Duncan let out a cry of anguish at his disappearance.

Rhona was trying to reverse the car when she heard the boat. The soft swish of rain had been joined by the steady putt of an outboard motor. She killed the lights and sat in silence, wondering if what she had heard was the hammering of her own heart. The baby had gone silent and when she looked round his eyes were like saucers. 'Sshh,' she told the startled face. 'I'll be back in a minute.'

The door opened with a squeak and she stood behind it in the pelting rain, calculating how far she was from the cliff edge and whether an incoming boat could see her. If she couldn't see them chances were they couldn't see her. Rhona silently closed the door and moved towards the cliff edge.

The track had narrowed to the width of a sheep and the heather on either side was thick and tall. It pulled at her legs as she passed, springing back with a thudding wet sound that seemed momentous in the silence.

The engine spluttered to a halt and now there was only the slap of waves against the rocks below. Rhona sat down and edged her way forward. Spike was right, the sheep track did go down at what looked like a forty-five degree angle. It would be madness to try and descend. She would just have to watch whatever was going on from here.

The crunch of gravel signalled an exit from the boat and then she heard the scrape of a keel being pulled on shore. No voices, just a grunt of effort, then silence.

If the people below were intent on coming up the cliff track then she was sitting right in their path. But there wasn't a sound. No footsteps, no voices, nothing. The occupants of the boat were either creeping up the hill in complete silence or they had disappeared into a cave.

The rain had lessened to a steady drizzle and the

moon was trying a reappearance. Rhona pulled herself back from the edge and retraced her steps to the car. Now was the time to leave, while there was a glimmer of light and before the baby started crying. Whoever was creeping about the shoreline in the middle of the night was unlikely to be thrilled by her presence at the proceedings.

She was climbing into the car when she heard the howl. It reverberated as if it had hit a circular wall and was replaying again and again. The silence below the cliff changed to shouts and she heard the loose rattle of scree as someone started to scramble up the hillside path.

Rhona threw the gears into reverse, trying to turn the wheel free of the heather. The howl echoed in her mind. She tried not to imagine who or what had made that terrible cry.

She reversed one more time, tearing roots from the bank to scatter across her path. Now she was facing the right way. All she had to do was retrace her route, but without Spike's directions. Rhona put her foot down and the car jumped forward. Behind her, two dark figures pulled themselves over the cliff edge.

As she dipped into the village the sky was striped with the promise of morning. Rhona felt suddenly tired, as though she had manually dragged the car through the heather. In the back, sandwiched between a bag and a coat, the baby slept the sleep of the innocent.

As she drew up outside the Post Office, Mrs Mac-Murdo appeared at the door. If her landlady was surprised to find her latest guest was a baby she didn't show it. Mrs MacMurdo was obviously made of stern stuff. She took one look at the sleeping bundle, opened the door, picked the baby up and carried it inside.

'There'll be time enough for explanations once you dry off,' she told Rhona, who hadn't noticed how wet and cold she was until she stepped out of the car. She stumbled up the front step, her legs feeling as if they were stuck in the accelerator-brake position. Her eyes were smarting from peering through the rain and mud-splattered windshield, and she didn't want to think about what had happened to the underside of her car during its numerous forays into uncharted heather.

The kitchen was heavenly, warm and dry. Rhona kicked off her shoes at the door. Mrs MacMurdo had put a tartan blanket into a wood basket and was carefully placing the sleeping baby inside.

'Poor wee thing,' she said to the oblivious infant. She ushered Rhona into the chair beside the stove and produced a bottle of Talisker from the cupboard.

'Not that I approve of strong drink. But at times such as these, as my husband used to say.'

Mrs MacMurdo did not partake of a glass herself, but poured another nip for Rhona as soon as she finished the first.

'Right,' she said, seeing Rhona relax. 'Where's . . .'

'Spike?' Rhona finished for her.

'Spike? So that's what the boy's calling himself. His father wouldn't have liked that much.'

'His girlfriend had disappeared from the blackhouse when he got there. Spike brought the baby to me and went back to wait for Esther. If the girl is ill and lost in the hills,' Rhona added, 'we'll have to call in the police.'

But Mrs MacMurdo wasn't listening. She was looking across at the sleeping child. 'Donald didn't say anything about a baby.'

Rhona was puzzled by that too. Sean hadn't mentioned Esther having a baby either.

'It can't be Donald's child,' Mrs MacMurdo said.

'Why?'

'Donald left the island two months ago, just before his sixteenth birthday.'

'Spike's only sixteen?'

An image flashed across Rhona's mind: the trembling, spotted hands, the white, drawn face.

Mrs MacMurdo met her look.

'Aye. I was thinking the same thing myself. Whatever happened in that time has made Donald MacAulay into a man. And not a well or happy one, at that.'

Rhona was silent, weighing up just how much of the story she should reveal. Her own best interests would be served if Esther gave herself up to the police; then they could question her and maybe find out the truth about the jazz club. Then she could go back to work.

Mrs MacMurdo spoke before Rhona could answer.

'I think it's time you told me the real reason you came to the island, Dr MacLeod.'

20

THE FEAR THAT thumped his stomach had turned to nausea.

Spike turned from the wind and vomited into the heather. The rain whipped the mess away, spreading it in a semi-circle round him. He grabbed a bunch of moss and wiped roughly at his mouth.

Christ. What if she had gone into the loch?

He imagined Esther waking up, calling for him, leaving in a panic, walking on and on until the brown water lapped her body and the cold seeped into her soul.

He wanted to scream her name. *Esther, Esther.* He could feel the words rise in his throat, then they escaped, resounding across the moorland in an anguished cry.

When he reached the blackhouse he hurried inside, praying she was back, but the fire was almost dead, the bed empty. Spike sat down and covered his face. He always knew this would happen. Knew Esther would leave him. He thought he could hold on to her, look after her. And it was his fault. He had driven her away.

Spike left the blackhouse and went down to the water's edge.

Ahead of him, the wall of rock was a looming shadow over the dark loch. Spike suddenly hated its grey vastness; the black water, the solemn emptiness. He should never have brought Esther here. He should never have entrusted her to this place. He picked up a stone and hurled it at the smooth water, breaking it into a hundred swelling circles, knowing all the time that he was to blame.

If he hadn't had sex with her, she would still be here. His father was right. Always right.

'You are an abomination before God!' he screamed and the mountain returned his call.

ABOMINATION. ABOMINATION.

It was dawn before Spike crawled back indoors and lay on Esther's bed, looking for her scent in the heather and the blanket. In his grief he didn't see the note lying near the pillow. He didn't find it until two hours later, when he opened his eyes to a world without Esther.

Spike almost wept with joy. Esther was alive. Esther had not run away from him. Esther had not drowned herself. Esther was alive. He scanned the note again. They must have taken her when he was at the Post Office. When he came back and she wasn't there, he'd lost the plot, snatching the baby and taking him to that woman in the car.

He hadn't looked about. He hadn't seen the note.

And all the time he'd been lying sleeping, they were waiting at the cave with Esther.

Spike grabbed some stuff and threw it in the back-pack, then scattered the remains of the fire. As he left the blackhouse, he consoled himself with the thought that at least Duncan was okay with Mrs MacMurdo. All he had to do was give the bastards what they wanted, then they would let Esther go. He would get her the best of help. For that he needed money. And if the gear was that important to them, the bastards would pay.

When he reached the cliff, Spike looked about for any sign that Esther had been there. There was nothing, only a squashed cigarette packet stuck in a clump of heather. Spike shoved it in his pocket, going over the scenario that must have played out here after he'd left.

The track was a mass of churned mud and heather. What had happened to the woman to make her speed off like that?

Spike allowed himself a small hope that Esther had escaped in the car, then dismissed it. Luck had never been on his side. It was unlikely to be different this time.

The cave below smelt of damp tobacco smoke and the remains of a fire. Spike walked round, checking for any remnants of occupation. If he was right, the bastards had brought Esther here to bargain with him and something had sent them up the cliff path. The woman had taken fright and got out fast.

Spike tried not to think about Esther and how she must have felt when he didn't turn up. He dragged his mind back to how the bastards had got there. There was only one way. By boat. And that meant there was another boat out there. A bigger one. And he would find it.

Spike went looking for his dinghy, relieved to find it still sitting in the shadows. He threw in his backpack and wrapped himself round the bow, using his anger to power the pull. The dinghy jerked free of the shingle and slid forward less than a metre.

He tried again, knowing that if it didn't move, there was something wrong. The keel slithered another couple of inches then sunk deep into the shingle. Spike grabbed his backpack and flung it to the stern, then felt his way round the wet wood.

The gash was clean and about thirty centimetres long, tucked under the front bench, deep into the keel. Whatever they had used had hacked a long split in the wood, leaving it to swallow stones and sand.

Spike stood up, trying to stay calm, trying to think. The water was flat and grey, the light wind coming from the west. If they were operating from a boat, they would have to anchor somewhere round the island.

He went over the possibilities. Not Churchton Bay, not if they wanted to lie low. Oskaig Point further up the west coast? Spike tested the wind on his face. It was okay just now, but it was definitely on the rise. If it came strong from the north or the west, Oskaig would be the place to go. Either that, or north of the island at Eilean Fladday.

But he didn't have a fucking boat, he reminded himself, all the time knowing where he could get one.

He had worked so hard to blank out that last night on the island. Blanking it out had saved his sanity. But now its images were sweeping in again like the vicious seventh wave on a shore. Spike let them wash over him and this time he didn't look at his shaking hands. Whatever had happened that night was in the past, he told himself firmly. He couldn't change things. There was only one thing that mattered now. Esther.

He walked up and down, trying to make up his mind. Even if he did decide to use his father's boat, he had to get to it first. He looked up at the cliff and along the shoreline. The beach petered out after a hundred yards, meeting an abrupt headland on either side. There was no way round the coast. If he was going for the boat, he had to go home and through the tunnel. His mind went cold at the thought. When he'd spoken to Mrs MacMurdo the night before, she hadn't mentioned his father, only said she still had a key to the cottage if he wanted to go there. She must have realised by the look of horror on his face that it was the last place he wanted to go.

Spike started the climb back up the cliff face. The wind was fresh now and hitting him hard. After the heat of anger in the cave, his body temperature was dropping, the parka hardly cutting the force of the wind. When he reached the top, he stopped to get his breath. As he turned to go, he spotted the big yacht. It was down near Rubha na' Leac, slipping southwest towards the Narrows of Raasay.

GOD KNOWS WHERE Mrs MacMurdo had found the highchair. It looked like a museum piece. The baby had obviously been changed and fed. He waved a rattle happily in Rhona's direction as she opened the kitchen door.

'You'll be hungry,' Mrs MacMurdo said. 'I've cooked some breakfast. Once you've eaten we'll sort out what to do next.'

Sorting out seemed to be something Mrs Mac-Murdo was good at. 'This body the police are looking for,' she continued, sitting down opposite Rhona. 'Who do you think it belongs to?'

'I don't think it belongs to a Polish fisherman.'

Mrs MacMurdo poured the tea. 'I was worried at first it might be Mr MacLeod, Donald's father . . .'

'Donald's father?'

'Until I got the postcard.'

'I'm sorry, I don't understand.'

Mrs MacMurdo fetched a card from behind the tea caddy. 'This came about a week ago, from America.' She showed Rhona. It was a picture of a Highland gathering, California style, with Highland dancing being done in the shade of a weeping willow under a clear blue sky.

'Donald's father was very keen on all things Scottish.' Mrs MacMurdo sounded faintly embarrassed by this. 'He always said he wanted to live in the old country, as he put it,' she paused. 'When he came to live in the cottage, we didn't know he was married. Then his wife arrived with the boy. Donald. They kept very much to themselves. Donald was sent to the local primary school, but other children weren't allowed to visit the house. There was a second baby, Calum, but he died. After that his poor wife lost her wits. They found her body at the foot of the cliffs near Brochel.'

'What about Spike?'

'He used to come to the Post Office for things. He never said much, but I liked the boy.'

'When did he leave the island?'

'The last time I saw him was when he came to post a letter to America for his father two months ago. I never saw either of them again until Donald appeared at my door.'

'Did you tell the police?'

Mrs MacMurdo looked disapprovingly at Rhona.

'Constable Johnstone checked the cottage, but Donald and his father often went away. It wasn't unusual.'

She handed Rhona the postcard to read. On the back was a brief message about arriving safely and enjoying the Californian sun. There was a phone number and a request for Mrs MacMurdo to let him know when Donald came back to the cottage. *Donald went to stay with an aunt on the mainland. We*

*had an argument before he left. I want to make sure that
he's okay.*

'Did you phone?'

Mrs MacMurdo nodded. 'Last night when you were
out. A woman answered. She thanked me and said she
would pass the message on to Donald's father.'

'Do you know if Spike's father was a member of a
group called ReAlba?'

'ReAlba?' Mrs MacMurdo looked startled.

'It's a racist organisation with Scottish links. Something to do with a clan calling themselves the Men of
the West.'

'Sounds like some daft American nonsense to me.'
Mrs MacMurdo rose to pull the kettle onto the hot
plate. 'Why do you want to know?'

'There was a tattoo on the foot found in the fishing
net, just above the ankle. This is a copy.'

The edges of the printout were damp from the
pocket of her coat but the swirling Celtic image was
clear enough. Mrs MacMurdo looked at it closely.
Rhona had the strong impression she was at war with
herself over this one.

'You've seen it before?'

'No,' Mrs MacMurdo said firmly. 'No I haven't.'
She lifted the baby from the highchair. 'I'll have to
open the Post Office.'

'Do you think Spike might have taken Esther to his
home?' The thought had just occurred to Rhona.

Mrs MacMurdo looked concerned. 'I don't think so,
but it might be worth taking a look.' She fished in a
drawer and handed Rhona a key. 'It's a bit out of the

way. You can drive as far as Brochel then you have to walk from there.' She fetched a map. 'It's better to go by boat, but if you've got a good head for heights, a path goes down the escarpment here.' She pointed to a spot south of the cleared shielings of Screapadal.

Rhona took the map. 'I'll try and phone when I get there.'

Mrs MacMurdo nodded and propped Duncan over her shoulder. 'I'd rather we didn't get the police in until we have to,' she said quietly. 'Not until I've spoken to Donald properly . . . in case he's in some sort of trouble.' She smiled apologetically at Rhona. 'Constable Johnstone is not a local man, you understand.'

Rhona understood perfectly.

She repacked her small rucksack, trying not to think of steep paths down escarpments. If only she could believe her own lies about not being bothered by heights.

She checked her mobile and found a text message from Lynne Franklin suggesting if she was free she should come stateside for a week and visit ReGene properly. If she liked the company, they could talk business.

> And bring the boyfriend.
> Plenty opportunities in California
> for a good jazz musician. Lynne.

Rhona sat down on the bed. Did Lynne Franklin know she was currently on leave, and why? If she was in Scotland, and reading the newspapers . . .

Even contemplating joining ReGene made Rhona

guilty enough to phone the lab. But it wasn't Chrissy who answered. The call went through to the switchboard and she got George instead.

'George, can you put me through to Chrissy?' she asked. 'The direct line doesn't seem to be working.'

'I'll put you straight through to Pathology, Dr MacLeod.'

'Pathology? Why?'

But George was gone and in his place was the beep of the Pathology phone.

'Dr MacLeod.' The normally bland voice was tinged with annoyance. 'So good of you to get in touch.'

'What?' Sissons was making no sense.

'We have been trying to get hold of you for the last twenty-four hours. You don't answer your phone or email.'

'I'm on leave.'

'Paid leave, Dr MacLeod, which means you continue to make yourself available to the Forensic Services department.'

The guy was an anal-retentive, pathological pathologist.

'Pardon?' Dr Sissons said, hearing Rhona's mutterings.

'Nothing. What's all the urgency about?'

Dr Sissons cleared his throat. 'The police have evidence to suggest that the substances found at the club were brought in by an outside party.'

'So I'm no longer a threat to the integrity of the department?'

'If you recall, I never suggested you were.'

That was true.

'There has been another incident. Another piece of what might be our body has been located . . .'

'Where?' said Rhona, knowing it had only been a matter of time.

'A small island off Raasay. Eilean Fladday, I think it's called. Do you know it?'

He had pronounced it wrongly but, 'Yes,' Rhona said.

'The area is under the Northern Constabulary, but they have requested our presence in view of the possibility that it is part of our body.'

So it was *our* missing body now, when only a couple of days ago she had been told to stay away from anything to do with the case. Rhona wondered if Dr Sissons had cleared this latest development with Phillips, but she decided not to ask.

'Do you think you could get up there?' he said as if it was the ends of the earth.

'How soon?' Rhona said, knowing she could get within sight of the island in a matter of an hour. Whether the causeway that linked it to Raasay was above water depended on the state of the tides.

'Apparently they've put it in the cold store of the local fish farm so it should be alright until you get to it.'

'Has a pathologist seen it?'

'No. The Procurator Fiscal wants it sent here, but I thought it would be better if you saw it *in situ*.'

'How did you know where I was?'

'A calculated guess. After all you are from that area; and no, your assistant did not inform me.'

Rhona hated the self-satisfaction in his voice. 'Chrissy didn't know. And in answer to your question, I can be there in four hours.'

'That long?'

'Yes, that long,' she lied. 'Who do I speak to when I get there?'

'A Constable Johnstone, I believe.'

Rhona rang off. There was only one road to the north of the island. She would stop off on her way there and take a look at Spike's house.

Before she left, she checked her email. There were three messages from Chrissy all saying the same thing.

Sissons is going mad looking for you. The foot and hand match. They've found something else and they want YOU to look at it! I haven't mentioned IT yet. How many years do you get for withholding evidence?

Rhona waved at Mrs MacMurdo as she got in the car. The child was sitting inside the Post Office in an ancient pram. Rhona wondered what story Mrs Mac-Murdo was telling her regulars about how she had acquired the baby.

Although she already knew she had her forensic bag with her, Rhona checked in the boot of the car before she drove away. And *she* had called Dr Sissons an anal-retentive?

Dun Caan rose like a truncated Fujiama, the lower slopes hidden in a trail of mist moving in from the east.

The road was deserted except for herself and a jeep. At first Rhona thought it must be a local who would want to overtake but when she slowed down, it slowed down too, disappearing behind a curve in the road. She didn't see it again until she dropped down towards Brochel and caught her first glimpse of the fairy-tale castle atop the sheer outcrop of rock.

The jeep didn't follow her down to the shore but instead continued north towards Arnish. Rhona was relieved. She would rather she didn't have company.

The mist was skirting the shore, a grey-white line dividing land and sea. Rhona put on her walking boots and took her waterproof from the back seat. If the path was too steep or the mist got too bad she would simply turn back for the car, she told herself firmly. But the mist kept to the shoreline. As she left the beach and walked towards the woodland, Rhona began to relax, allowing herself a moment of pleasure over her reinstatement. If the police had decided the drugs were brought into the club from outside, that might mean Sean was in the clear. When she got back to the Post Office, she would call him. She would return to Glasgow tomorrow and complete her report to include the tattoo.

The only problem left was Spike and Esther.

If she was right and the men who climbed the cliff the night before had something to do with Spike, she didn't have the heart to tell Mrs MacMurdo. Not yet, anyway. The police might believe that the drugs had been brought into the club from outside but that didn't mean Spike and Esther had nothing to do with it.

The castle had disappeared behind her and Rhona was now in thick woodland. Once or twice she heard red deer moving through the undergrowth, but caught no sight of the sleek dark bodies that shared the woods with her.

The ruined shielings appeared through the mist on the other side of the trees; broken skeletons of stone, as dismembered as the body she sought to fit together.

Rhona stopped, remembering Andre's face when he told her of the scattered stones, all that was left of his origins. It would be hard to stand in this place and not feel the pull of the past. This is what organisations like ReAlba played on, these strings of memory and hurt and loss and . . . maybe even revenge?

Beyond the deserted village, the path grew weak, skirting the long stretch of Druim an Aonaich like a faint snail's trail across the hillside.

'There is nothing marked on the map, but there is a path. Keep walking until you see the large stone. You can't miss it. It is tall, maybe ten feet, but it has a round hole in the centre, eye height. They say if you look through the hole you will see the pirate ship of Iain Garbh sailing back to Brochel Castle with his holds filled with gold,' Mrs MacMurdo had laughed. 'Fools' stories about fools' gold. Good for the tourists.'

The reddish stone rose above the low mist that began to circle Rhona. She suppressed the impulse to look through the stone's eye and searched instead for the path that cut down towards the sea.

'The path makes an abrupt turn, disappearing through some whin. Most people don't realise it's there.'

If it hadn't been for Mrs MacMurdo's directions, Rhona would have assumed it had dwindled to its natural end. She pushed back the whin, breathing in the yellow coconut smell. On the other side the path narrowed. The mist here was thin, its creeping presence broken by each outcrop of rock.

The water was calm between Raasay and Apor Crossan, the long split of Loch Torridon in the distance. It was little wonder Spike's father chose such a place to hide from the world.

She stopped halfway down and peered over the edge, clinging to the rockface on her right. The cliff bulged, hiding whatever was below. Rhona hesitated, nervous that if she went on and the mist thickened, this was her only way back. But she was so close, she couldn't go back now.

The cottage sat on a narrow stretch of grass. A stream ran past, tumbling down the last ten feet of cliff to plunge into a sea without a shore. Already the gathering mist was enveloping the cottage so that Rhona could not make out its exact length. The front door faced the sea, opening onto a porch. Inside, she could see the usual wellie boots and assorted outdoor gear hanging on a set of pegs.

The emptiness of the house echoed round her as she let herself in and walked through the hall to the kitchen with its black range and tiny window facing the Sound. It made Rhona think of Spike and the lonely edge in his voice as he'd told her how he never wanted to stay in her poncy flat. She remembered how angry she had been when she discovered Sean had taken in Spike and

Esther. How she didn't want them in her home, using her things.

Now she was the intruder in Spike's home.

She walked from the kitchen into the living room. A pile of peat ash lay in the fireplace. A door in the opposite wall opened into a bedroom which had obviously belonged to a boy. On a shelf above the bed, a row of Star Wars figures stood in combat mode beside some well-thumbed story books. The room was neat and tidy and completely unlived in. Spike had not been here. No one had been in the cottage for a long time.

Back in the sitting room, a narrow staircase beside the fireplace led to another bedroom with a single bed and a child's cot. From a small dressing table, a dark-haired woman smiled out at her, one arm round a boy of about twelve, the other holding a baby upright on her knee. Rhona glanced round the meagre little room. Wherever Spike's father slept, she didn't think it was in here.

An open skylight let in waves of damp air. Rhona climbed onto a chair to shut it, thinking of the rain that was never far away, but the catch was broken and the window only flapped back against the roof.

She stuck her head out to check on the mist, hoping the rising wind meant it had cleared. The sky was thick with rain clouds but the mist had dispersed and she could now see all round the cottage, the rock wall behind and the sea beyond. It would be a good time to look for the cave that held the boathouse. Everything had to be brought in by boat, Mrs MacMurdo had said. Even the peat for the fire.

Looking back up the steep path, Rhona wasn't surprised.

She made one last attempt at fastening the skylight but the catch was snapped in two. She wondered if there was something she could use to tie the window shut. If the rain came in, it would soak everything in the room.

If the rain came in?

Rhona jumped down and felt around the floor. There had been a downpour the previous night. The rug was chilly to the touch but bone dry. That meant the catch had been broken recently. She climbed back up and examined the frame, looking for the telltale signs she should have seen the first time. The left side of the frame had a dent in it the size of a thumb print. Someone had jemmied the window open.

The wind was humming along the roof now, throwing her hair in her face. As Rhona climbed down, the draught played with the bedroom door, slamming it shut. The front door joined in, playing the same tune. Rhona stood tense and still, listening hard. The cottage descended back into silence. She started down the stair. The room below was as empty as before.

If someone had broken the catch to get in, they hadn't been interested in any of the rooms she'd visited, which only left the boathouse.

'You can get to the boathouse through a tunnel under the store room. The cottage was built there because of all the caves. There's supposed to be a subterranean tunnel all the way from the loch to the sea

but that's probably just an old wives' tale,' Mrs Mac-
Murdo had told her.

The store room was off the kitchen and Rhona had
to duck under a low lintel to avoid banging her head.
The room smelled of earth and damp and animals but
looked just as empty and undisturbed as all the others.
The trapdoor was in the corner. Here the straw was
brushed back and the dust held the criss-cross of
footprints, new or old, Rhona couldn't tell. She pulled
at the ring and the sound and smell of the sea rushed in
as the trapdoor rose.

Rhona peered down. Steps curved away into the
darkness. She stumbled against the wall twice, scraping
her hand on the rough sandstone. Rhona thought
about the torch in the boot of the car and cursed
herself for her second stupidity of the day. She should
have treated this visit to the cottage like a forensic job
and come better prepared. There might be a torch in
the kitchen but she didn't feel like going back now. If
the tunnel led to the boathouse and the boathouse had
access to the open sea, there had to be daylight at the
end of it.

If she had nursed any notion that Spike's missing
father had been Dr Fitzgerald MacAulay, it had eva-
porated. Mrs MacMurdo had declared she'd never
heard of a scientist called Dr Fitzgerald MacAulay and
when asked about Spike's father had informed Rhona
that she thought he was a writer. It had sounded like a
guess. Well-off people who came to the islands to get
away from it all were either there to play at crofting,
Mrs MacMurdo said, or else they were writers. Rhona

had the strong impression she was not fond of either group.

But if Spike's father was a writer, he must have taken all evidence of it back with him to America. She hadn't even found a bedroom that might have been his, let alone a study to work in.

Sudden daylight stunned Rhona's eyes into temporary blindness. The tunnel had taken a final abrupt turn and deposited her in a cave the size of a small theatre. The walls rose high to an arched roof whose distant details Rhona couldn't make out. At her feet was a narrow jetty with a couple of metal rings sunk into the stone. The cave could have given shelter to at least two boats, but the water that lapped the jetty's edge was empty.

Rhona sat down on a ledge, surprised by her own disappointment. She had no idea what she had expected to find. Certainly not this nothingness. She picked up a pebble and threw it aimlessly across the water, anticipating a crack as it hit the opposite wall. Seconds later she heard a dull thud like an echo at the bottom of a well.

She got up and walked along the jetty, her eye following the shadow of the opposite wall. If there was an opening over there, she couldn't see it. She went back to her original position and felt about for another pebble.

This attempt brought it ricochetting back at her. Another disappeared into the opening, making a dull echoing sound as it hit some far wall.

The place was a mass of caves, that's what Mrs

MacMurdo had said. Big ones, small ones. The hole in the wall was most likely a dead end, Rhona told herself.

She was focusing on the opposite side, convincing herself she could see a metal ring much like the ones on the jetty, when she heard the distant sound of an engine.

22

THE DOOR BUZZER sounded as irritated as Chrissy felt. If Sean was there, he wasn't answering. When a voice shouted at her in the middle of the third long buzz it caught Chrissy by surprise.

'It's Chrissy, Mrs Harper. I'm sorry to bother you, I was looking for Sean. Do you know if he's in?'

'Oh he's in alright,' Mrs Harper wasn't amused. 'He's been playing music since early morning.'

'Could I come up and knock on the door?'

'You can come up, but it won't do any good. He won't answer.'

By the time she reached the second floor, the offending music was hitting Chrissy loud and strong. Trad Jazz wasn't easy on the ear at nine o'clock on a Monday morning. Mrs Harper was waiting for Chrissy on the landing with her *I told you so* face on. Chrissy banged on Rhona's door.

'I've done that already,' Mrs Harper told her.

Chrissy flapped the letterbox instead.

'I've tried that too.'

Chrissy pushed the letterbox open and tried to peer in.

'What's that smell?' Mrs Harper said, wrinkling her

nose in disgust, imagining a kitchen filling up with rotting food and unwashed dishes.

But it wasn't that kind of smell.

A seed of panic took root in Chrissy's stomach. She turned to Mrs Harper, trying to keep her voice steady.

'Have you got a key?'

'Of course I have, but only to water the plants when they're both away.'

'Please get it.'

Mrs Harper looked aghast.

'We can't just barge in if Sean's there.'

'If Sean's in there, he's either gone fucking deaf or something's rendered him unconscious.'

Mrs Harper flushed and her hand fluttered to her throat.

'Please could you just go and get the key?' Chrissy insisted.

Rhona's hall was empty and cold. The smell was distinctive, sweet and sickly. Chrissy regretted having sworn, but Mrs Harper had already forgiven the outburst and was nodding her encouragement.

Chrissy tried the bedroom first, praying Sean was dead drunk and fast asleep, but the bed was empty, the covers tossed to the floor. The place was a pigsty. Chrissy abandoned the bedroom and opened the living room door. The stink made her gag.

'What's wrong?' Mrs Harper quavered anxiously from down the hall.

Chrissy knew whatever lay dead inside had been that way for a while. She went in and shut the door behind her. The last thing she wanted was Mrs Harper coming in and seeing the source of that smell.

The body was behind the sofa. Sun beating through the glass had accelerated decomposition, separating fur from flesh. The cat's head had been severed from its body.

Chrissy almost sobbed with relief, hating herself for being pleased. Pleased it was the bloody cat and not Sean. Feeling like shite because it was Rhona's cat. Her poor defenceless bloody cat.

'Chrissy!' Mrs Harper called.

'It's alright,' Chrissy called back. 'Rhona's cat's dead, that's all.'

That's all! 'Could you phone for the police, Mrs Harper? Ask for DI Wilson and tell him there's been a break-in at Dr MacLeod's flat.'

Mrs Harper bustled off. Chrissy ranged through the flat, almost sobbing with fury. In the spare bedroom, the fact that the mess was the result of a break-in was more obvious. The contents of drawers had been tipped onto the floor. On one wall, a faint yellow arc. It smelt of piss.

Chrissy sat in the hall and waited for the police car to arrive. She heard its siren moan outside. Too late to do any good. She had made Mrs Harper retreat to her nice civilised flat to have a stiff sherry and worry about what the world was coming to.

'What the fuck?' Bill said as he pushed open the front door and the smell hit him.

'Some bastard's broke in and killed Rhona's cat.'

Chrissy bit her bottom lip as Bill went through to the living room. She heard him swear again. This time he could have taught even her a thing or two about cursing.

They had moved to the café-bar down the street to get away from the stink. Bill was waiting for his coffee to congeal the way he liked it. Chrissy was already half-way down a glass of something stronger.

'And what is Rhona doing on Raasay?'

Chrissy hadn't seen Bill Wilson this mad for a long time.

'First of all, I didn't know she had gone there until she spoke to Dr Sissons. And remember, she does come from Skye. Maybe she just went home for a visit.' Chrissy knew it wouldn't wash. By the look on Bill's face, it didn't.

Chrissy gave in. 'She went because of the tattoo.'

'Tattoo?' Bill looked exasperated.

'Rhona told you she thought there was a faint mark on the foot, just above the ankle? She took a photograph and gave the image to the computing department. They did their enhancing thing on it and came up with this.'

She handed Bill a copy of the printout.

Bill stared at it. 'Why wasn't I told about this before?'

'If you remember,' Chrissy said angrily, 'Rhona was taken off the case. Sissons didn't want to hear anything she said. The MOD told her to stay clear and then declared the foot belonged to a Polish fisherman, for God's sake. Even you told Rhona to keep out of it.'

'Looks like she didn't take my advice,' Bill said quietly. 'And Rhona thinks the tattoo means membership of this group called ReAlba?'

Chrissy nodded. 'Rhona met them at a highland games in California. She said their literature was racist. They were calling for a genetic war against non-whites,' she paused. 'And remember the riots in LA? Rhona thought the protesters were against genetic engineering but later she realised some people were protesting against G-bombs, this century's equivalent of nuclear weapons.'

Bill looked puzzled so Chrissy explained. 'You target the people who have genes you don't like. Black skin, yellow skin. Blue eyes. The virus only kills people with that particular strand in their DNA.'

Chrissy watched as the implications dawned on Bill.

'But how has that, or the racist crap, got anything to do with body parts being washed up on the west coast of Scotland?'

'That's what Rhona wanted to find out,' Chrissy said.

Bill looked thoughtful. 'They're sending an RAF helicopter to pick up the latest body part and bring it south.'

Chrissy raised her eyebrows. 'Important treatment for a factory-ship worker.'

'Exactly what I was thinking.'

They both fell silent.

'You don't think the break-in is anything to do with this ReAlba lot, do you?' Chrissy asked.

Bill shook his head. 'No, I think it's closer to home than that.' He paused. 'Joe Maley's out.'

The name hung between them like a foul miasma, worse than the dead cat. Joe Maley, Glasgow's answer to the Godfather, minus the good looks.

'You warned Rhona?' Chrissy said, knowing by his face he hadn't.

'I was planning to tell her next time I saw her.'

It was difficult to get angrier than she already felt, but Chrissy managed. 'You know how that bastard hates Rhona.'

Bill didn't answer. Instead he pulled a photo from his pocket.

'Recognise her?'

The photo was crap. God knows how many pockets it had lived in. But Chrissy knew the pale face and big eyes even if she couldn't hear the voice.

'It's the singer Sean hired. The one I found ga-ga in the toilets. The one O'Brien packed off to the mental ward.'

'Maley's looking for her.'

'Why?'

'She was his girlfriend before he was sent down.'

'So that's where I saw her before. In the courtroom.'

Chrissy didn't like the scenario that was forming in her mind. 'If Maley thought Rhona's boyfriend was screwing his girl . . .'

'Bingo.'

'Maybe it was Maley that took Esther from the hospital,' Chrissy suggested.

Bill shook his head. 'A woman who works at the bus

station says she definitely saw this girl get on a coach going north. She was with a youth and a baby.'

'You think Esther has a baby?'

'If she has, it's not Maley's,' Bill said. 'He's been inside too long.'

'God, I hope he doesn't think it's Sean's.'

'Maley doesn't need an excuse. He's a psychopath. And if he's back on speed . . .'

Bill didn't have to finish. Chrissy had seen speed freaks close up. She had one in her own family. Her brother Joseph had relied on her for his drink money, then discovered speed made him run faster and longer. She had watched him descend from a wheedling pain in the neck to a jumpy paranoid whose anger exploded at the least provocation. When he disappeared to London, she hadn't mourned his going.

Maley pumped up on speed would be as unpredictable and vicious as they come.

'Where did Esther go?'

'The bus was heading for Skye.'

'Great,' said Chrissy.

23

RHONA WILLED THE approaching boat to chug straight on past. She had no desire to be found in the cave by anyone who might be using Spike's father's mooring and have to think up an explanation as to why she was there.

Unless it was Spike?

The engine noise had reached the entrance. Now it was suddenly all around her, echoing off the cavern walls. The engine spluttered to a halt, leaving only the sound of water lapping the stone edge at her feet and the distant cries of gulls.

Rhona resisted the temptation to call Spike's name and waited as the boat swung silently round the corner, blocking the entrance and cutting the light.

It was in far enough now for her to see the shadow of the occupant. Too tall for Spike. The man swore as his head hit a dip in the roof, knocking the boat sideways and sending waves to break over her feet.

Rhona was poised, ready to run back up the tunnel. If she was quick enough, she could bolt the trapdoor before any pursuer reached it.

The man looked up from rubbing his head and caught sight of her. It took her a moment to register

who he was, because he was the last person she
expected to see. By the surprised expression on his
face he felt the same way about her.

'Rhona. What the hell are you doing here?'

'I could ask you the same thing.'

Andre Frith was dressed in oilskins. His face, red-
dened by the force of the wind and weather, no longer
wore the charm of Santa Monica. She suspected he
was seriously annoyed at her presence but working
hard to cover it.

He manoeuvred the boat alongside and threw her a
rope. She slipped it through a metal ring and knotted it,
then stood back to let him step ashore.

Rhona found a bottle of whisky in a cupboard beside
the fireplace in the sitting room. She poured two
glasses of the pale golden liquid and handed one to
Andre.

He grimaced slightly, missing his usual ice and soda.

Rhona ignored his distaste. If he was so keen to be
Scottish, let him drink whisky the way it should be
drunk.

She threw back her own dram and immediately
poured another, waiting for Andre to say something,
determined not to be the first to explain her presence.

Andre looked as if he was carefully planning what he
was about to say. He would reveal the minimum.
Alternatively he would tell her a pack of lies. She would
have to decide which.

'Look . . .' he began.

Rhona hated that word. Sean always said it when he

was trying to get round her, or persuade her to his way of thinking.

Andre's face suddenly cleared as though he had made up his mind to come clean.

'I came here to look for MacAulay.'

'MacAulay?' She thought about that. 'You think the man who lived in this cottage was Dr Fitzgerald MacAulay?'

When he answered, his voice was certain.

'I know he was.'

'How?'

'Come with me.'

He led her through to the kitchen. The black range sat in a deep alcove which would once have housed a low peat fire with a cooking pot suspended above.

The stone lintel was well worn. Hundreds of hands had touched it over time. In the centre of the long single stone was a carved symbol. A symbol she recognised.

ReAlba . . . the Men of the West.

'The symbol's all over the place once you start looking. There's one outside too.'

He opened the front door.

This time the ancient stone symbol was broken by the wind and the weather, but Andre was right. She hadn't noticed it when she walked in, but once you knew what you were looking for . . .

'Why was he here?'

'To work.'

A feeling of dread crept over her. 'On what?'

A gust of wind slammed against them. The Inner Sound seethed, the heavy swell cresting in white foam.

'We'd better get inside,' Andre said.

He bolted the door against the strength of the wind.

'I have to get back to the car,' Rhona said, suddenly remembering about Eilean Fladday.

'You'd better wait until the storm blows over.' Andre suggested, 'then I could take you round to Brochel in the boat and you could pick up your car.'

'How do you know where my car is?'

Andre smiled. 'Where else would you park it? And no. I haven't been following you. I didn't even know you were on the island.' He laughed. 'You must have seen the look on my face when you loomed up in the cave.'

He had looked stunned. But by what? Not by the fact that she was on the island. She suspected he already knew that. No, Andre was only surprised to have found her in the boathouse.

Rain beat at the tiny windows of the sitting room. A blast of wind moaned across the roof, sending peat ash to scatter at their feet. It would be difficult enough driving between Brochel and Arnish without the walk up the steep path to the castle.

He read her thoughts. 'At least you could sit in the cabin of the boat and stay dry.'

She wavered.

'Why don't I see if I can boil a kettle and we can have something hot to drink while we wait for the squall to die down. It's getting pretty chilly in here.'

She nodded, letting him wander through to the kitchen to try and turn on the calor gas and boil some

water, while she contemplated just how much Andre
knew.

He had been quick to show her the ReAlba symbols
but he hadn't mentioned how he'd got into the cottage
in the first place to find them. Rhona's mind flew to the
skylight catch in the upstairs bedroom. Had Andre
been the one to break it?

Andre arrived five minutes later with two mugs of
coffee.

'The granules were solid in the jar, but it smells
alright.'

It smelt better than alright. The chill rose from her
wet feet and sent a shiver through Rhona, making her
teeth chitter.

'Hey, you're frozen.' Andre sounded concerned.

'I'll survive.'

'Maybe I should light the fire?'

Rhona suddenly had an image of Andre keeping her
there. Persuading her to wait until the rain lessened.
Making her coffee, lighting the fire. All classic delaying
tactics.

'The coffee will warm me up. Then I really will have
to go.'

He nodded. He was giving up, for the moment.

Rhona nursed the mug, enjoying its warmth. She
would have tipped some whisky into its blackness, if
she didn't have to drive to Arnish and examine a body
part which might or might not belong to Fitzgerald
MacAulay.

'You said you thought your father was working
here?'

'Yes.'

'Where?' She took in the small sitting room, the low ceiling, the tiny windows that hardly let in any light.

'Not in the cottage. Somewhere else on the island.' He paused. 'I thought at first it might be below in the caves. After all he could bring it in by boat.'

'Bring in what?'

Andre shrugged. 'Everything he needed for his laboratory.'

'A laboratory?' she said, disbelievingly. Yet it made sense. If MacAulay wanted peace to work away from the American and British governments, he could do a disappearing trick and end up here as a writer with a wife and children. Then he could work undisturbed. She remembered what Mrs MacMurdo had said about no children being allowed near the cottage. Spike's isolation.

Andre looked at her curiously. 'What?'

In that split second Rhona decided not to mention Spike. Even if Andre had been asking around and had found out MacAulay was living here with a family, that didn't mean he knew that Spike was on the island now.

'I just thought of the things he might have been working on.'

'Yes.' Andre's face clouded. 'That's my biggest worry.'

Half an hour later, the squall was over and a ridiculously blue sky filled the small window. They rinsed their mugs and stood them on the draining board, suddenly conscious of their intruder status.

Rhona made sure the front door was locked before she followed Andre to the trapdoor and the steps to the boathouse. It made her feel slightly better about prying in Spike's house. If only she could speak to Spike properly, she was sure she could find out if Andre was telling her the truth.

Rhona sat in the cabin while Andre guided the boat out of the cavern. She realised why he had gone past the entrance, then had reappeared. The opening was guarded by two stone pillars.

'You can't enter from the north,' Andre explained. 'There's too much rock near the surface. You have to go past the pillars and come in from the south.'

Rhona was silent, wondering just how Andre knew about the rocks and how often he had been in the cave.

'Before you ask, I know about the passage because of the maps sitting above your head.'

It sounded like a truce.

'Okay,' she said. 'Mrs MacMurdo from the Post Office gave me a key to the cottage.'

'Mrs MacMurdo gave you a key!' Andre laughed. 'That's a lot more than I got when I visited the Post Office. I suppose it helps if you're local.'

He was giving her the chance to tell him why she had come to the island.

'You were right,' she said. 'There was a tattoo.'

He waited for her to continue.

'It was above the ankle. I wasn't sure what it was, so I removed a layer and came up with a digital image.'

'I see.'

He looked upset. Rhona realised what the news might mean to him personally.

'You should know that, a week ago, Mrs MacMurdo received a postcard from the man who used to live in the cottage. The postcard came from America.'

'What?'

There was no mistaking his honest surprise this time.

'So the foot may belong to someone else,' she said.

'But I thought . . .' He stopped. 'So MacAulay's still alive?'

'You can't be sure MacAulay was the one living in the cottage. Mrs MacMurdo says the man's name was MacLeod. He was a writer. He had a wife and . . .'

Andre waited for her to go on. She didn't.

'And children.' He finished the sentence for her. 'He had a wife and children, Rhona. The wife killed herself after the youngest child died. There was another boy, Donald, around fifteen years of age.' He paused. 'That's who you came looking for, Rhona, wasn't it?'

24

THE WALK ALONG the cliffs left Spike tired, cold, and sick with worry for Esther. He realised all the time he had been staying with her in Glasgow, he had been putting her in danger. Now it had happened. The bastards had her and it was his fault. Why the fuck had he come back here?

He buried his hands in his pockets and concentrated on the path, picking his way through a mix of rough scree and sea pinks that clung bravely to the salty rock ledges.

The sea pounded on the shore in a grey-white foam, sending its drumming echo up the cliff face. The wind was coming from the northwest, biting into his skin every time he looked up from the path. To his left, the mountain rose like an ancient volcano.

Spike thought of the cottage and the loch and what had happened there. What he had done to Esther. He drew his hands from his pockets and examined them carefully in the clear morning light. Dark-spotted like a lizard, the skin shrivelled and old, they told Spike what he already knew. That it didn't matter what happened to him now.

It took him two hours to get there. When he emerged

through the hole in the ancient rock, the sun split the clouds and its long rays dropped on the cottage. Spike suddenly remembered his mother. He had tried to help her, but she didn't want him, because he wasn't hers. He was something else, something she didn't want to discuss, or even look at. Something amoral, something evil. An abomination before God.

He shook his head, throwing the image at the sky, and descended the last few yards to the cottage, his mind a blank.

The gargoyle symbol of his abomination sneered at him from above the door. He ignored it and went round the side, pulling himself onto the roof via the water barrel. The tiles were damp and slippery from the rain. He held onto the ridge and crept sideways like a crab.

He had planned to smash it, but when he got there the skylight was open. Spike eased the glass back and dropped into his mother's bedroom, hoping that whoever had arrived before him wasn't still there.

He stood like a statue, only his eyes moving over the familiar pieces of furniture. The room was as unloving as it had been when he left, the cot like an empty coffin in the corner. After five minutes of silence, Spike decided the cottage was empty.

He made his way through the sitting room without looking round. Who had been here after he'd left that night? His mother's bedroom hadn't been soaked by the heavy rain, which could only mean the broken catch on the skylight was recent. Spike wondered if Mrs MacMurdo had sent the lady doctor to look for him when he hadn't turned up at the Post Office, then he remembered Mrs MacMurdo had a key.

The only other person who might have come after him was Maley.

The corner of the store room had been cleared, which meant the bastards knew about the trapdoor. But his father had never brought anyone to the cottage. No one except Mrs MacMurdo had ever been in the place. Any meetings his father had with Maley's scum had been far away from here. His father arranged for the drugs to be brought in by sea. He stored them until Maley's men arrived from the mainland to collect them. That was the arrangement. What Maley did with them afterwards didn't matter to his father. He had organised the money to fund his work.

And his work was all he fucking cared about.

Spike threw back the trapdoor and stared down into the darkness. The smell of damp and salt poured out. Damp and salt and . . . the stink of human sweat.

He didn't have a chance to step back before two hands gripped his ankles and jerked him downwards, smashing his head against the rock wall and knocking him unconscious.

'Tell us where it fucking well is.'

Maley was speaking in a singy-songy voice, mimicking Spike's West Highland accent. Spike didn't answer. Instead his eyes darted round Maley and his two heavies to the deck of the boat, looking for some sign that Esther was here.

A nod from Maley and a fist came straight at Spike.

He flinched, expecting another smack, but this time the hand stopped short of hitting him and squeezed his jaw together, pushing his unwilling tongue out between his teeth.

'Well.' Maley's voice had transformed into a sneer. 'The teuchter's got a fucking tongue after all.'

Spike didn't care about the sneer. He didn't care about the taste of blood in his mouth or the trickle of urine that ran down his leg. He just wanted to know that Esther was okay.

'He's pissing himself.'

They were laughing, like three weird sisters cackling together about what they would do next.

Maley opened a box at his feet, laying the lid back so that Spike could see the array of sharp instruments.

Spike didn't want Maley to see his fear, so he concentrated on the shadow of Dun Caan, rising like a black fortress above the island.

'Right,' said Maley. 'Let's ring the bastard.'

Maley grabbed Spike's tongue and yanked it forward.

'Not too far back. We want you to be able to speak, don't we?' Spike screamed as something pierced the side of his tongue sending a burning blast of pain up his jaw. In his head he was shouting *Jesus, Jesus, Jesus* . . . while his mouth ran bloody dribble over his tongue, round a metal ring and onto a chain that now linked him to Maley.

'They say a man's best friend is his dog, and you just became my wee pet mongrel.' Maley waved the chain in Spike's face. 'And you know how they train dogs, teuchter? They pull on the lead every time it doesn't do what it's fucking well told.'

Maley smiled and ran the chain through his hand in agonising jerks until his face was within spitting distance of Spike.

'We have been in every fucking cave on this fucking island, except the fucking right one. Your nutcase of an old man hid the stuff somewhere and you know where it is. So you are going to take us there. Understand?'

The boat was on the move, the beat of the engine drumming the side of Spike's head. His tongue throbbed and the back of his throat ached with the effort of keeping his tongue outside his mouth.

When his smarting eyes followed the chain to its end, he found a padlock wrapped twice round the deck rail. Even if he managed to free his hands and feet, the only way he was going anywhere was with a key.

And he wasn't going anywhere without Esther.

The trouble was, he wasn't even sure Esther was on the boat. He had come to momentarily as Maley's men dragged him down the tunnel and dropped him into the motor launch tied up in the boathouse. Then they must have hit him again, because the next thing he remembered was Maley screaming at him and pushing the ring through his tongue.

Spike looked about him, recognising the power and style of the boat that was slipping its way along the familiar coastline. This boat was money and plenty of it. If Maley was making this amount from dealing, he was doing better than alright.

But this wasn't Maley's boat, Spike knew that. This boat belonged to someone more powerful than Maley. Maley might be looking for the last drugs delivery but he wasn't the one financing the search. That someone had to be one of the racist American bastards his father was always mouthing on about.

All the time his father had been spouting racist crap about white Celtic supremacy and the return of the true Gaels to the west coast, Spike had tuned out. He had got used to the quasi-religious rantings, the obsession with all things Celtic, the hatred of Blacks, Jews, and anyone who couldn't trace their descent from some mythical 'Men of the West'. It was like fucking *Highlander* gone mad.

Trouble was, until that last night in the boat, Spike hadn't realised how serious it all was.

Maley might think it was all about the drugs, but he was wrong. The drugs just helped with the financing.

Spike almost laughed. Because Maley, stupid bastard that he was, had no idea what an important cargo he was really carrying.

Salt lay stiff on Spike's face, cracking his lips. He would have given anything to lie face down in dark Loch na Mhna and fill his burning mouth with her cool peat waters.

He closed his eyes and thought of Esther standing by the loch, the baby in her arms, her face full of the beauty of the place; and he vowed that he would give up everything, including himself, to make sure she was alright.

The cloud cover had thinned and a pale sun blinked down from the clear northern sky. In this swell it would take them a couple of hours to get to the cave. Ten minutes after that, Maley would know Spike had lied to him.

But if he was right, Maley would never reach the cave. At least not in two hours. Maley would have to hole up somewhere within the next half hour. He might have the use of a fancy boat, but Maley sure as hell did not know west highland weather.

Spike watched as the horizon began to change; blue to grey and slowly to black, while a northwesterly wind danced across his parched lips, chafing the dried skin, making it beg for the rain that would follow soon enough.

25

THE SALMON CAGES filled the sea loch like the grid map of an American city, platforms serving as sidewalks. Rhona stopped the car on the brow of the hill, resentful at this incursion of industrial fishing on the free waters of the loch, yet knowing that anything that filled the empty village houses with residents other than holiday home owners was a bonus.

She had left Andre at Brochel. They had parted badly. She would not tell him where she was going or why, and this time he could not follow her. Wherever his vehicle was, it wasn't at Brochel and Rhona did not look back as she climbed the hill from the castle and met the Arnish turn-off.

The two-kilometre road to Arnish was rough and narrow, but still a tribute to the postman who had built it himself after the council had refused to help his community. Twenty-two years of pick, shovel and wheelbarrow. By the time it was finished, the other families had gone, leaving Calum, the road builder, alone in his village.

Smoke drifted from a cluster of chimneys and Rhona could smell the sweet scent of peat. As she reached the foot of the hill, she spotted the police Land Rover outside a large metal shed, and decided she'd found the temporary mortuary.

Constable Johnstone must have been listening for the car, because he emerged from the shed before Rhona could pull on the hand brake.

Mrs MacMurdo was right. Johnstone was not local. He looked like a man who had joined the Northern Constabulary for a quiet life and had been seriously disappointed by recent events on his patch. He also had the look of a man with someone on his back. Phillips, perhaps?

'Dr MacLeod?' The constable held out his hand as Rhona opened the boot and pulled out her forensic bag. 'We wondered where you'd gone. Someone reported seeing your car parked at Brochel.'

If Constable Johnstone expected her to enlighten him, he was wrong. Rhona simply smiled and waited to be shown inside.

'They're sending an RAF helicopter to take the sample south,' he informed her as he opened the door. 'It should be here in an hour, which doesn't leave you much time.'

'And who exactly are *they*?' Rhona said, already seeing Phillips' name on an MOD document.

Johnstone didn't answer.

'Well whoever *they* are, they'll just have to wait until I finish,' Rhona told him.

Somehow there was relief in being back in the world of the dead. Bodies, or bits of bodies, didn't give you grief, at least not personal grief. They just lay there, waiting to be understood.

Latex gloves on, Rhona lifted the right hand gently from the metal tray. The fingertips were gone, but the shape and size of the hand was consistent with her notes from the previous sample.

The fish farm worker who found it reported seeing something waving at him from below the water, *like a drowning man,* he'd told her in Gaelic, with a nervous smile. When he'd knelt down, he could clearly see the arm, the fingers caught in the net. He was afraid, he told Rhona, that the salmon might have been feeding on it.

Rhona thanked him and asked what the Sassenach restaurants that bought his salmon would think if they knew what the fish had been eating.

Constable Johnstone was the only one who didn't laugh.

The forearm was badly decomposed. Rhona bent close, trying to ignore the smell. Fish odour and dead human were not a sweet combination.

Above her, the metal roof had started to drum with the sound of pelting rain. The wind was scouring the building, looking for every opening in the structure. It was colder than Strathclyde mortuary.

Constable Johnstone was right when he had warned her about the deteriorating weather. Rhona was suddenly sorry for the man. The Ministry of Defence on his back, bad weather, and a stubborn female in his face. So much for a quiet life.

Rhona contemplated the piece of rotting flesh that might or might not have been MacAulay. Sampling a body was more than an incident, it was a story. A story of a life, or at least the end of a life. Calculated guesses about the end of that life were the best she or anyone else could do.

She didn't like to think about the implications if it was MacAulay. If Andre was right and his father was working on some biogenetic project here on Raasay . . .

Whoever it was, Rhona decided, it was not her responsibility. She would send her report on the tattoo to Glasgow with the body part and let Sissons sort it out.

Rhona concentrated on what sampling could be done, determined not to be put off by the constant reappearance of Constable Johnstone at the door, wanting her to hurry up.

By the time she'd finished, the wind was trying to lift the roof off the metal shed. One look from the policeman as he re-entered told Rhona what she already suspected. The helicopter would be going nowhere until the wind dropped. It seemed Phillips and the MOD would have to wait for their body part.

'All finished,' Rhona said. 'The samples are tagged and I've rewrapped the limb. I'm assuming it's going to Glasgow?'

The constable nodded.

'I've enclosed some notes for my assistant there.'

Constable Johnstone hesitated. 'There was a message from a DI Wilson, telling us you would be going back with the sample,' he shouted above the din on the roof.

'Really?'

Summoned here, summoned there, by some man or

other. Rhona was beginning to feel like a beck-and-call girl.

'The only place I'm going,' she said firmly, 'is Mrs MacMurdo's, where I intend to have a hot bath and a large whisky. And, Constable Johnstone, if anyone else phones, you can tell them that.'

The sky had closed like a dark lid over the island. Climbing from Arnish, Rhona almost wished she had taken up the offer of a spell in one of the cottages until the wind died down.

On the brow of the hill the car threatened to take off like Chitty Chitty Bang Bang, then she dipped towards Brochel and the tyres gripped the road again. Below her, the castle rose on its pinnacle of sheer rock above a frenzied sea.

She was almost at Holoman Island on the west coast when she saw the yacht. It was battling its way northwards to Oskaig, dipping in and out of the waves like some mad fairground ride. Rhona watched, horrified and fascinated at the same time, until a squall of rain drove against her window, scattering the image in a thousand drops.

By the time she reached Oskaig, Rhona couldn't see a yard in front of her, never mind a hundred yards away. With any luck, she told herself, the yacht had tucked in south of Oskaig Point and was riding out the storm.

The Post Office was in darkness when she pulled up outside, creating morbid thoughts of electricity pylons down and no hot water for baths. The big front door was shut firmly against the wind and after knocking a couple of times, Rhona headed round the back.

The back door was open. A paraffin lamp sat on the kitchen table. The room was warm, soft waves of heat rippling from the solid fuel range despite the no electricity situation.

Mrs MacMurdo's note was brief.

Gone next door with the baby. Mrs MacKenzie wanted some company. The water's hot enough for a bath. Tea in the slow oven.

Rhona checked the various doors in the big range and found the slow oven and the rich casserole of venison and potatoes. She would have sold her soul for a glass of Sean's red wine to go with it, but wine did not feature in Mrs MacMurdo's cookbook. Whisky, however, was a different matter. There was a glass and a bottle of malt on the table next to the note.

Rhona half-filled the glass with the smoky brown liquid, lifted the lamp and headed upstairs to run her bath. Her body ached from dropping down trapdoors and creeping along tunnels. She was annoyed and frustrated, and not just about her work.

She turned on the taps and watched the hot brown water fill the tub, reminding herself of what her father had taught her. Always remember to take pleasure in the small things of life. Hot water, good food and good whisky.

She would soak in the tub and drink her dram. Then she would sit in the warmth of the kitchen and eat. Then she would try and phone Sean. When the power came on again, she would email Chrissy and tell her she would be back to work tomorrow.

But what about Spike and Esther and the baby?

She would explain everything to Bill Wilson. He would help. If Esther was mentally ill, she needed help, and Bill could organise that for her. If Spike turned up, which he would, she would talk to him. Tell him about Andre. Spike could decide for himself.

Rhona slipped into the peaty water, letting the softness climb her thighs and settle on her hips and breasts.

Lamplight and warm whisky lulled her into relaxation. She leaned her head back, half-closing her eyes, listening to the wind skim the rooftop and prowl at the windows, knowing that this house had braved a thousand such storms.

She must have dozed off, because it was the scratching that woke her up. Mrs MacMurdo had warned her about the mice. *Ever since the cat died, they've been a problem.* But the scratching seemed too far away for her to care. Rhona shut her eyes again, allowing the lantern light to filter through her lashes. Somewhere deep in her brain she worried about Spike and Esther but she was too tired to do anything about it.

The water was cooling, sending little shivers up her thighs and she knew she would have to get out soon. She had hung the towel and her bathrobe behind the door and the thought of climbing out and padding naked across the floor did not appeal.

Rhona moved the water in small waves and in its wash she felt momentarily warm again.

The squeaking had reached the bathroom door and

Rhona heard the sound of tiny claws as they slithered across the wooden floorboards. It was time Mrs Mac-Murdo got another cat. She smiled, missing Chance, her own black panther. Suddenly, Rhona was home-sick. Homesick for her city flat, for the hum of the traffic outside, for Chance miaowing and threading between her legs. But most of all, Rhona was homesick and hungry for Sean.

She stood up and the draught from the window wrapped her wet body in its chill embrace. Shivering, she reached for the towel and her bathrobe. Below, the back door snapped open and closed and Rhona heard the bolt slide shut against the storm.

Mrs MacMurdo was home.

Rhona lifted the lamp and opened the bathroom door, looking forward to sitting in the heat of the kitchen, eating her meal and talking to Mrs MacMur-do.

With a bit of luck, Spike might have been in touch already.

Rhona saw him from the top of the stairs. Maley looked up and gave her that smile, the one Rhona remembered from the dock as the judge passed sentence.

'Dr MacLeod. Just the woman I've been looking for.'

SPIKE BENT HIS head, securing it between his knees. The boat was climbing again, riding the crest. Whoever was in charge below deck knew what they were doing, he had to give them that. It wasn't bloody Maley, anyway. Spike had watched him spew his lot up over the side. But at least vomiting had taken Maley's mind off the fun of torture.

They had put Spike in a store room near the wheel-house as the storm hit. Maley had taken great delight in leading him there by the chain, tugging it every five seconds and shouting 'Fucking hurry up, mongrel.' Then Maley had wrapped the chain round a metal pipe and relocked the padlock, as if there was anywhere Spike could go.

Once Maley had disappeared, Spike slid the chain down the pipe and jammed himself between some containers and the wall. When the swell started, he concentrated, reminding his stomach that it had survived such storms before.

When he was wee, his teacher had told him a Gaelic poem that described every possible wave. She'd read it out to the class and Spike had marvelled at the way the language had a word for the shape of every rise and every fall, every crest and trough, every curl and every colour.

He watched through the porthole as the poem unfolded before his eyes and knew that, despite everything, he was actually praying.

This time the boat hadn't climbed so high, nor fallen so far. Spike lifted his head and looked out of the porthole. The yacht must be coming into the lee of Oskaig Point and the swell was lessening.

Then he heard the grind of the wire through the winch and the scrape and judder of the anchor as it caught on the bottom.

The bigger of the two guys arrived shortly afterwards, his face halfway between green and red, smelling of the booze he'd hit to line his stomach.

Spike stood so that the bastard wouldn't have the pleasure of jerking him up.

'Right, mongrel. The boss wants a wee chat.'

Esther was sitting on a long seat under the window, her eyes empty, her hands lifeless in her lap. A wash of emotion swept over Spike as they pushed him through the door. He wanted to go to her, put his arms around her like he'd done in the hospital, tell her it was going to be alright.

'Esther!' Her name forced its way past the swollen tongue and out of the shattered mouth.

Esther looked blankly at him.

'Hey, baby,' Maley said. 'See, I've brought you back your wee pet.'

Maley was standing beside Esther and he began

stroking her hair, running his hand down the side of her head and onto her shoulder, curving her chin, slipping underneath it and down inside the shirt.

'Fuck you, you bastard!'

Spike lurched forward, the words snarling from his throat. He was within a foot of Esther when the big guy jerked back the chain. The ring sliced at his tongue, and his mouth filled with the hot saltiness of blood. He dropped to his knees on the floor. Then he screwed himself round, trying to look at Esther, as if looking at her would protect her. But Esther was gazing at Maley, her lips parted, waiting for the kiss that was on its way.

Spike stopped fighting and let the real pain seep in. Now he knew the truth. Esther wasn't a prisoner. Esther knew Maley. Esther knew Maley very well indeed.

Maley turned and sneered at Spike, then tipped up Esther's chin and stuck his tongue in her mouth.

Spike rolled over and placed his face against the cool metal wall. His mouth pounded where the ring had torn the flesh. What difference would it make if he pulled it right out? At least he'd lose the bastard chain. Spike tried not to think what Maley would do when he found the chain off, or where he would sink the ring in next.

It didn't fucking matter, anyway. Maley didn't need him anymore. Lying on the floor of the cabin with a heel in his crotch, Spike had told Maley what he wanted to know, because it didn't matter anymore. And all the time Esther had looked through him like he wasn't there.

Spike winced, remembering how he'd told Maley that Doctor MacLeod was the woman on the cliff top without realising that Maley knew her. He'd shut up as soon as he saw the hate in Maley's eyes, but Maley had pulled down Spike's pants and told the big guy to bring another ring and they would attach the teuchter's fucking tongue to his balls if he didn't tell him where the MacLeod woman was right now.

So Spike told him, even though he realised Maley would go after her.

The wind had dropped and the sharp splatter of the rain was less insistent against the porthole. Sometime in his misery, Spike had heard them lower the dinghy and realised someone had gone ashore. Then he heard the distant beat of helicopter blades and knew the coastguard was searching for battered boats in the wake of the storm. If the swell was down and Maley had gone ashore, he could slip overboard. He just needed rid of the bastard ring.

Spike felt his way to the end of the chain. His mouth was wet, a constant dribble of blood and saliva dripping from his chin like a baby.

Spike pried his right shoe off and stretched down to wrinkle his sock over his ankle. He stuffed the wet sock in his mouth, his eyes smarting as the salt water found his tongue, then he wound the chain tightly round his other foot and pulled.

The normally clear water was clouded with shattered shells, shifting sand and seaweed being driven remorselessly towards shore.

Spike could make out the shadow of the anchor chain, and for a moment he imagined twisting his leg in it until the water found his nose and lungs and filled them completely.

Then his feet kicked upwards and his head broke the surface.

It had been easy to get out of the store room. No one had thought for a moment that he would pull out the chain. He'd forced himself to stumble for the open door as soon as he got free. At first his feet refused to obey and he'd skittered about the deck like a drunk, grabbing at anything within reach just to stay upright, then the fresh air hit him and he filled his lungs.

As he stumbled past the main cabin he heard the men swearing and laughing. He tried not to look in, knowing if they spotted him now, he wouldn't have time to swim away before they dropped a dinghy and fetched him back. The two heavies were at the table drinking, but the seat beside the window was empty.

Esther was gone.

Spike tipped head-first over the railing and the waves closed above him. The wind was blowing from the northeast and would carry him steadily south. If he could keep his head above water and swim with the current, he would be driven ashore before the Narrows of Raasay.

After he pulled the ring out, he'd lain, the sock still gripped between his teeth, his body rattling against the floor, trying to concentrate on what he would do next.

He knew that going for Esther would be a waste of time. From the look on her face in the cabin, she had already made up her mind who she wanted to be with and it wasn't him. Spike forced away the image of her blank face and thought about the baby and Mrs MacMurdo and Dr MacLeod.

The expression on Maley's face when Spike said the woman's name kept coming back to him. The bastard had asked him to describe her, tell him where she was staying on the island, all the time grinding his boot into Spike's crotch, and Spike had blabbed, opening his mouth and letting it all run out like bloody diarrhoea.

'So that's why the bitch wasn't at the flat,' Maley grinned down at him. 'You've just made me a fucking happy man.'

The sky and water were one, a restless grey. Spike concentrated on the shoreline; one arm movement, then another, ignoring the chill that had captured his body and was moving in on his soul.

If he could get to shore, he could get to the Post Office. He could try and warn the doctor about Maley. He could tell Mrs MacMurdo everything, even about his father. He wanted to tell her about his father, before it was too late.

It seemed to Spike that warm blood had found its way back through his arms and legs, then his chest. His head was buzzing with warmth and laughter, the bubbling laughter of Esther and the baby that day in the sunshine, before they sailed back to the island.

Spike stopped fighting the waves and lay unmoving, letting the image and the scent and the warm memory wash over him.

27

THE MOUSE RAN across Rhona's foot, squeaking and scrabbling to get away, its fear matching her own. She forced herself to stay put and plan her next step, knowing Maley was in no hurry. The door was bolted. There was nowhere for her to go.

Maley was grinning up at her, the glassy eyes of the Cheshire Cat, with her as the mouse.

'What do you want, Maley?'

'What do I want?' Maley repeated with slow relish. 'Why, Dr MacLeod, I want you.'

He had one foot on the bottom stair, his arm resting on the banister.

'Don't be stupid, Joe,' Rhona said. 'If you touch me, they'll get you and you'll be back inside.'

He shook his head. 'That's where you're wrong, Dr MacLeod. By the time they find what's left of you, I'll be far, far away.'

'This is an island, Joe. A one-stop island with a ferry when the weather's good enough. You can't go anywhere without the whole island knowing about it.'

Maley was loving this. His ego was working overtime. He would tell her the whole story just so he could watch her squirm.

'I've got friends. Friends that helped get me out of jail and friends that will help keep me out. That operation you fucked up? Well it's right back on track. Our American cousins saw to that.'

His hand was sliding up the banister. Rhona could smell him now. Booze and salt and the acrid smell of male sweat. If she turned to run, he would be right behind her. Before she could open a door he would have her on the floor. But he wasn't moving on her yet.

Somewhere behind her on the landing, the trapped mouse scratched frantically at a closed door.

'Sounds like you need a cat around here,' Maley was grinning. 'Oh I forgot, you *had* a cat, didn't you, Dr MacLeod. A big black cat.'

Rhona froze. Jesus. He had been in the flat. Joe Maley had been in her flat.

'What . . .'

'Now, now, Dr MacLeod. I just went to pick up what was mine. And she wasn't there. And that made me angry.'

She? Who the hell was he talking about?

Maley licked his lips. 'Didn't you know? While you were away in California, your bastard of a boyfriend was screwing my wee girl.'

His wee girl?

Rhona's brain had the answer before she sent it to search. Esther. He was talking about Esther. So the police were right. Esther was a plant in the club.

Christ. Sean was a stupid bastard, following his prick instead of his head.

'I don't know what you're talking about,' she said, keeping her face calm.

'That's funny, neither did your cat when I asked it,' he said smugly. 'Fucking pissed me off that did.'

Rhona tried to ignore the images that were flooding her mind. If she could just keep him talking, maybe Mrs MacMurdo would come back.

She wasn't reacting enough and Maley was getting bored. She was the mouse that didn't squeal and squirm.

He started up the stairs.

Rhona slid one foot nearer the banister, her hand still gripping the lamp. The light from the lamp played across his face, making his teeth and eyes glint. When he was three stairs from her, she swung it at him. It flew past his head and hit the hall floor, and then there was just the two of them and the darkness.

His hand was gripping her throat, forcing her head up and back; his knees were on her arms, pinning them close to the floor. Rhona let her body go limp and kept her eyes shut, like a subdued animal. Maley was breathing into her face. A drop of his spittle hit her cheek.

If he was planning to strangle her, there was nothing she could do about it.

But Maley wasn't ready to do that, yet.

Her bathrobe had fallen open in the struggle. Maley was taking in the view, his breath getting faster. He used his knees and free hand to move her arms under her body and slipped his own body lower than her crotch.

Every nerve in Rhona's body told her to writhe and jerk and yell and fight, but sense told her the opposite. Maley was bigger than her, Maley was stronger than her, but Maley wasn't smarter than her. What brain he had was in his cock.

Rhona waited till he was busy with his zip, then she rolled, pushing away hard from the floor beneath her, unbalancing him.

His grip loosened on her neck as he tried to right himself and she swung back and rolled again, this time throwing him hard against the wall. One hand free, Rhona grabbed at his open crotch, her nails finding flesh. Maley gave a howl and slapped her hard across the face, but the swipe knocked him sideways. She squeezed tighter, digging in her nails; like a nutcracker on a nut.

Maley was yelping like a kicked dog, throwing his fist wildly at her face, smacking the floor as she turned her head. All the energy Rhona had stored as he prowled her limp body was in her next move. She screwed her hand round, twisting the nutcracker.

Now Maley was howling in her ear, a long howl of *bitch.* But his hands were off her, cradling his crotch.

Rhona let go and rolled away.

Her feet found the top stair and she launched herself down two at a time.

'You'll pay for that, bitch!'

Rhona dived for the open kitchen door. She slammed it shut and put all her weight against it, knowing without a lock she had no chance.

Maley flung himself at the door. Her feet slithered

forwards and met the table leg. The next time he would be through. She glanced wildly round for something to defend herself with and spotted the knife rack.

Maley suddenly released his pressure. She heard him step back and knew he was planning a run at it.

Rhona dived for a knife as headlights hit the window and a vehicle screeched up outside.

The answer to her prayer.

Maley didn't wait to find out who it was.

Rhona heard the back door bang and knew Maley was gone.

The whisky bottle stood half empty between them on the table. When Mrs MacMurdo came back from putting the baby to bed, she poured another for Rhona without asking. Andre waved his offer away.

'I have to go,' he said.

'Go where?' Rhona forced her hand flat on the table to stop it trembling.

He hesitated and Rhona knew he didn't want to say anything in front of anyone else.

'I'm going to bed,' Mrs MacMurdo said. 'Constable Johnstone will be here in the morning and we can clear this all up. Whoever the intruder was, he can't get off the island until the weather improves.'

Rhona smiled her thanks as Mrs MacMurdo closed the door behind her. God knows what the poor woman thought was going on. Ever since Rhona had arrived in her house, her life had been turned upside down. Rhona was damned sure she wasn't going to tell her to add attempted rape and murder to the list.

Andre reached out and covered Rhona's trembling hand.

'Hey, are you alright?'

Rhona nodded.

'Look the best thing you can do is go home,' Andre was saying. 'Leave me to sort this out.'

'No,' she said. 'Whatever is going on here, I'm part of it now,' she paused. 'And if I'm part of it, maybe it's time you told me the truth.'

Andre was silent for a moment.

'Maybe it is.'

He reached for his inside pocket. The light from the lamp caught the black holster tucked under his left arm and he smiled apologetically as he flipped open the leather wallet and showed her an FBI badge.

'I'm sorry,' he said.

'So you should be.' Rhona stood up. 'All that shite about MacAulay being your father and the sob story about your Scottish roots.' She began to walk up and down, trying to control her anger. It was obvious now. Too obvious.

She turned on him. 'That's why you spoke to me in the airport. That's why you took me to the highland games, to dinner.' She stopped, remembering the embarrassment in the hotel room.

Andre came towards her but she took a step away from him.

'There were reasons why we did not want to alert the authorities over here,' he said. 'I had to find out if the foot belonged to MacAulay. I had to find out what you knew.'

Rhona glared at him. 'So where does Maley come into this?'

'Maley was running a drug syndicate using the west coast islands to bring the stuff in. We knew there was American money involved and the profit was financing something. We just didn't know what. Then we received a letter, posted here, from MacAulay. In it he made threats, threats that involved the work he said he was doing. Threats that we thought he might be able to back up. So I came looking for him. The rest you know.'

He was watching her, watching to see if she was buying the story. Everything Rhona knew up to now fitted what he said. If he was lying he was making a good job of it.

'That's why you went looking for Spike,' she said accusingly. 'Not because he might be your long-lost brother. You thought he would know something.'

Andre wasn't denying it.

'You thought the same, Rhona,' he said quietly.

He was right. She hadn't gone to the cottage to help Spike or Esther. She had gone to find out who Spike's father was.

Andre was looking at the postcard sitting on the shelf above the range. The postcard supposedly from MacAulay.

Rhona sat back down, suddenly tired of it all. MacAulay, Spike, Maley. Especially Maley. The way he'd looked up at her from the hall. Pleased . . . pleased because he knew he would find her there.

'No one knew I was staying here,' she said puzzled.

No one, not Chrissy, not DI Wilson, not Sean. She'd even led Sissons to believe it would take her four hours to get to Eilean Fladday.

'No one knew except you and Spike.' Rhona suddenly realised the horror of what that meant.

'Maley has Spike,' she said.

28

THAT'S WHY THE two men couldn't see him, Spike decided, they were part of his dream. A dream he didn't want to wake up from.

Water began playing with his feet, rippling up, washing back, bringing them back to life. Now it was his hands, and the sudden cloying cold of wet sand between his fingers. The next wave brought a shiver with it, sliding up his spine, running like an ache through his limbs.

He was coming back to reality.

Spike tried to drift back, stay in that other place; a place somewhere between death and life, where he had been floating without thought or pain; warm, comfortable and safe.

He muffled a cry as the men's words drifted towards him. He couldn't make out what they were saying but he could hear their American accents.

Suddenly Spike didn't want them to know he lay there on the shore; didn't want them to know he was alive at all.

The seaweed was thick along the beach, huge swathes that slithered beneath his feet like brown snakes.

Clouds of small black flies hovered above the mounds, dancing away as he walked through.

After the men left he had sat tucked below the rock, shivering in his wet clothes, until his legs stopped shaking long enough to carry him up the bank. Then he'd cut inland, not wanting to follow the road in case the men were somewhere between him and the village.

Now he was in woods, sheltered at least from the wind that drove in from the sea. As he walked, his shivering became a pattern. A gentle ripple that built up and up until the violent juddering of his teeth and bones brought him to a standstill. His body would descend into a strange calm that made him want to lie down and sleep forever before the cycle began again.

When the shadows of the chapel rose out of the gloom of the ancient burial ground, Spike's confused mind told him that he had already died and there was no point in going on; still he kept walking, shouting *Fuck* at the darkness to keep himself awake.

The baby was crying. Spike could hear it, a long wail that churned his stomach. The hill dipped steeply to the back garden and suddenly he was slipping and sliding towards the gate. He pulled himself up and stumbled down the path, his mouth alive with the snapping of his teeth against one another. If Maley had hurt Duncan, he would kill him.

Spike launched himself at the door and it spilled open, then his face was on cold linoleum and the taste of warmth and whisky was on his swollen tongue.

RHONA STOOD AT the door as the car headed off into the darkness. Andre wouldn't stay, despite Mrs MacMurdo's protestations when she came down to heat milk for the fractious baby.

He had something he had to do, he said.

To Rhona, at the door, he was less cautious. There was a yacht at anchor off Oskaig Point. He wanted to check in case it had something to do with Maley. If he drove further up the hill, he might get a decent enough signal to contact the coastguard. Rhona wanted to go with him and didn't want him to go at the same time.

'Will you be okay?'

'Of course,' she said, not really meaning it.

He turned, then stopped and pulled the gun from the holster.

'Can you use this?'

She was annoyed at him for seeing how scared she was.

'This isn't America.'

'You don't have to use it, just have it.'

'No,' she said firmly.

He reluctantly slipped the gun back into the holster.

'What about the lab?'

'We'll find the lab,' he said. 'Get some sleep, then

we'll take a look at the boathouse again. Maybe the other cave you found leads to it.'

He touched her arm briefly, then turned and made for the car. As he drove away, his headlamps were the only lights to be seen. The storm had knocked out the power, except for houses with their own generator and, of course, Maley's yacht.

Rhona built up the range with thick black peats and pulled the kettle onto the hot plate, knowing she would have to drink something hot or else she would never feel warm again.

Delayed shock was sending shudders up her spine and through her arms. She managed to pour the boiled water into the teapot, then sat down in front of the open firebox, nursing the hot sweet tea, grateful that at least now she knew the truth about Andre.

And knowing the truth meant she could trust him.

The baby gave a wail as if he was having a nightmare, then there were footsteps and whimpers as Mrs MacMurdo went to nurse him back to sleep.

The peat was well caught now and waves of heat flowed about her, calming her shivering limbs. She thought over what Maley had said about the flat and tried to convince herself that he had been lying in order to frighten her. Lying, at least, about the cat.

Esther was another matter.

If Esther was Maley's girl and he'd found out she was with Sean . . . a shiver of fear swept through her. Sean had been the one to warn her that Maley was out. But did Sean know what he was doing when he befriended Maley's girlfriend?

Rhona was half asleep when she heard the slamming of the back gate and the stumbled footsteps outside. Her first fearful thought was Maley, then she heard the Gaelic voice screaming obscenities and knew it was Spike, even before the back door flew open and the boy fell in.

Spike mumbled an apology at Mrs MacMurdo for swearing but she pretended not to notice, handing him a mug of something hot and urging him to drink.

The first swig made him grimace with pain and Mrs MacMurdo held open his mouth to look at the mess inside.

'Who did this to you, Donald?' She moved his head sideways to look at the bruising where Maley's boot had landed.

Spike spoke slowly and carefully. 'I came to warn you.'

'I know,' Rhona said.

'Warn her about what?' Mrs MacMurdo said, catching sight of the look that passed between them. 'I think it's time I phoned your father, Donald. This whole thing is getting out of hand.'

Spike's eyes filled with fear.

'What do you mean, phone my father?'

Spike took and read the postcard Rhona handed him.

'I phoned the number two days ago,' Mrs MacMurdo told him. 'A woman said she would tell your father that you were here.'

Spike was silent.

'Your father didn't write that postcard, did he Spike?' Rhona said.

Spike looked up at her, his thin frame lost in the weight of blankets Mrs MacMurdo had draped round him.

'It's alright, Donald, you can tell us the truth.' Mrs MacMurdo's soft voice seemed to soothe Spike and he looked sadly at her as if he were about to tell her something that would make her feel bad about him and he didn't want that. He turned to Rhona.

'My father made me go with him that night. He told me he needed help. I hadn't seen him for days. Then he came home, all pleased with himself and said he was ready.'

'Ready for what?' Rhona asked.

He shook his head. 'I don't know.'

Rhona nodded at him to go on.

'We took the boat out at about midnight. He wouldn't say where we were going. We headed south, keeping close to the coast.' Spike hesitated, seeing Mrs MacMurdo's stern expression. 'I thought we were going to collect a . . . a delivery from one of the caves below Druim an Aonaich.'

'Is that where your father hid the drugs?' Rhona said.

Spike nodded. 'Then he stopped the boat.' His voice was breaking into pieces. 'He said I was a mistake, an experiment that had gone wrong. An abomination.'

Behind Rhona, a Gaelic curse crossed Mrs Mac-Murdo's lips.

'Then he came at me,' Spike said, 'and . . . I killed him.'

30

THE YACHT HAD gone. Rhona scanned north to Holoman Bay but it too was empty.

'Looks like Maley's left.'

Spike disagreed. 'Maley won't leave without the drugs.'

Rhona suspected he was right.

She pulled away from the side of the narrow road
and headed towards Brochel. They had taken the
turning down towards Holoman Island, just to make
sure the yacht hadn't moved along the coast when the
storm died down. With no sign of it yet, the chances
were it had crossed to Skye.

After she persuaded Spike to go upstairs and get
some sleep, Rhona told Mrs MacMurdo the truth
about their American visitor.

'That explains why he was nosing about here last
month, asking all those questions. He showed me that
symbol.'

'ReAlba?'

Mrs MacMurdo nodded. 'Then you turned up and
showed me the same thing and . . . I'm afraid I lied and
said I'd never seen it before. I'm sorry.'

Rhona patted her arm. 'It doesn't matter. The main
thing is, we have Spike back.'

'And Esther?'

'He says she's gone back to Maley,' Rhona said.

'What about the bairn?'

Rhona shook her head. She didn't know. That was one part of the story Maley hadn't told her.

'I'll take care of the baby,' Mrs MacMurdo said firmly, 'at least until we know.' She looked at Rhona. 'What will happen to Donald?'

Spike's confession had been genuine, Rhona was sure of that. Whether he was right and it was his fault that his father was dead, was another matter. They'd struggled and his father had gone overboard. When he didn't reappear Spike had panicked, diving in himself, searching madly under and around the boat, but there was no sign of a body. He had stayed until daylight, submerging again and again until he gave up, exhausted.

'If his father attacked him and Spike tried to defend himself, he doesn't have anything to worry about,' Rhona said, hoping it was true.

Spike was staring through the windscreen, deep in thought. Rhona noticed his wrinkled skin was so thin, it was almost translucent.

'Spike?'

He turned.

'There's an American I think you should meet.' Rhona carried on talking despite his evident desperation. 'His name is Andre Frith. He knew your father.'

'No fucking way,' Spike said. 'I'll take you to the lab, then I'm off. That's what we agreed.'

Rhona knew if she persisted he would be out the car and away and she would never see him again.

'You're right, that's what we agreed,' Rhona said quietly, knowing she had already betrayed him.

When the mail had left the island that morning, it carried with it enough DNA from the sleeping boy to establish whether the body parts they'd found were his father's. By tomorrow morning, Chrissy would have the sample along with the entire story.

All Rhona had to do now was keep Spike with her until she found out the truth.

Spike lapsed into silence until they were minutes from Brochel, then he told Rhona to turn down a dirt track and made her hide the car among some trees.

The wind had dropped and the stillness had brought the mist creeping in from the sea again, drifting about them in long milky strands. Spike walked on ahead and Rhona concentrated on keeping his back in view. When she dropped too far behind, Spike stopped and waited, and Rhona was absurdly grateful each time his slight figure loomed out of the mist in front of her.

'It would have been easier by boat,' he said on the third occasion this happened.

'Does the lab have a direct link to the sea?'

'Of course,' Spike said. 'That's how my father brought in what he needed.'

'And what did he need?'

Droplets of moisture hung from his hair making Rhona want to reach out and sweep them away.

'You know what my father was.'

She had stopped to catch her breath and Spike seemed in no hurry to move on. Rhona wondered briefly if he was lost, but quickly dismissed the thought. Everything she'd seen suggested Spike could move about this island like a deer, the landscape as familiar as a scent.

'ReAlba was his life,' he said bitterly. 'He would talk of the Coming, how soon it would be. How the Men of the West would triumph.'

'What did he mean?'

'How the fuck should I know?' His face was twisted and bitter. 'All I know is that it didn't include anyone who wasn't a direct descendant of the clan.'

He stood up.

'The next bit's hard,' he said. 'But there's a tunnel from the loch over there.'

Rhona glanced in the direction of his pointing hand. If there was a loch ahead, she certainly hadn't spotted it.

'It's in a corrie,' he told her, 'You'll see it in a minute. *Loch na Minha* – Loch of the Woman.'

The loch was peat-coloured, an oval mirror reflecting the hill that surrounded it.

They walked past the blackhouse where, Spike told her, he'd stayed with Esther. He wouldn't go inside but Rhona did, smelling the sweet heather beds and the fragrant scent of a peat fire. A bright splash of colour caught her eye. Outside again, she handed Spike the woollen baby hat she'd retrieved from the corner. He thrust it into his pocket without speaking.

With each step they seemed to be moving further and further from the sea as they traversed the lochside to the steeper wall of the corrie.

'We have to climb from here.' Spike must have seen her worried look, because he added, 'There's a crevasse, big enough to scramble up. After that, it's easy.'

Easy? Rhona had heard that word before.

Spike took her hand and led her to a break in the rockface and she saw that he was right. The fissure was three feet wide. It climbed in giant stepping-stones up the face of the rock. Spike went first and pulled her up after him.

At the top, the corrie wall was dotted with caves like a forgotten shore. Spike led Rhona to an opening, then stooped and disappeared into the darkness.

Rhona had lost all sense of direction. The tunnel wound like a snake through the hill, at times branching off in more than one direction, but Spike was always waiting for her at the crossroads.

'Legend says the loch was once salt water. A waterhorse came through this tunnel from the sea and devoured a young girl. Her father, mad with grief, hunted the monster and tried to kill it, but when he found it, it was made of jelly.'

Spike stood back to let Rhona pass through the metal door.

The tunnel had reached its end.

Rhona heard the switch and from semi-darkness her eyes were blasted into light; light that sprang like the sun from the metal tables and glass cabinets arranged neatly under the arched stone roof.

Rhona had heard about such structures, had even crawled down Maeshowe's long low tunnel in Orkney and emerged in its great amphitheatre, but nothing had prepared her for this.

'It amused my father to use an ancient burial chamber to manipulate life,' Spike told her.

Their eyes were becoming accustomed to the light, and the gleaming emptiness told them the truth. They had found the lab, but whatever MacAulay had been working on was gone.

'The bastards have taken it.'

'Who has taken it, Spike? Who knew about the lab?'

He sat down heavily, leaning his arms on a lab table. Rhona could read in his face what the last twenty-four hours had been for the boy. And he was a boy, despite the pinched face of an old man.

She went over and rested her arm about his shoulders.

'Do you know what your father was planning?'

He looked past her, at the wall.

The map sat behind a perspex screen. Orange, yellow brown and black shadings identified the racial predominance of each of the American states. Black, Chinese, Puerto Rican, Asian, Jew. White superiority under threat.

To the right a smaller map, a group of islands, jewels in the western sea. Skye, Raasay; their racial story in coloured detail; Gael and incomer.

'Spike, was your father going to do something here?'

'I thought if he was dead, it would all end,' he said. 'But it hasn't, has it?'

'Is there any way out of here except by the tunnel?'

He nodded at a duplicate metal door on the other side of the domed structure.

'There's a cave where the boat comes in.'

Rhona pulled him to his feet.

'Go and see if we still have a boat.'

Spike opened the door and Rhona heard the low boom of crashing waves.

'I won't be long,' he shouted.

But Rhona was already too busy to hear. There was an office area at the back of the dome, cut off from the lab by a glass screen. The quickest way to find out what MacAulay had been working on would be to check his records. Much as she disliked the character Spike called father, there was no doubt the man was a meticulous scientist. If he had been playing genetic wargames, the information could still be here somewhere.

She lifted a pile of files from a cabinet and made for the desk. The wall in front of her was a patchwork of newspaper cuttings and extracts from scientific articles that made her skin crawl. They were grouped in chronological order, covering the last five years. The most recent was a UK cutting about a call for American public health officials to prepare for the possibility of a terrorist attack using biological weapons.

Genetic modification by those with access to sophisti-cated laboratory facilities could lead to the development of

GM pathogens with enhanced resistance to antibiotics or, in theory, genetically targeted to affect selected ethnic groups.

It looked as though the columnist had been reading MacAulay's mail.

The rest of the articles were in a similar vein. Right-wing bombers in the US, the Japanese poison gas episode, the nail bomb in London.

The man revelled in disasters.

Rhona opened the first file. Lists of names, some with amounts of money beside them under the headings 'Donation' or 'Prepayment'. Some were for a couple of hundred dollars, others were in the thousands. There was no mention of what the money was for.

The next two files were the same. Lists of people or lists of equipment. No mention of ReAlba, no mention of what had been going on here.

Rhona went back to the cabinet and pushed her way through the files, scrabbling with sheets of paper that were no more unusual than her own office paperwork.

She needed the lab-books. They would tell her what the hell had been going on.

It was no use. There was a mountain of things to figure out here and it wasn't her responsibility to do it. What she had to do was tell the authorities where the lab was and get off the island and go home. Even Phillips would be her friend when she told him what she'd found.

Rhona left the glass enclosure.

The insistent booming noise in the lab had intensified. It made her feel giddy. She began to feel as if she was on a fairground ride that would not stop. As she reached out and steadied herself against a metal table, her eyes were drawn upwards. The domed ceiling shivered with echoes.

Boom. Boom. Boom.

She staggered to a sink, the sharp acid taste of vomit in her throat.

Boom. Boom. Boom.

The noise was no longer outside her. It was inside her brain.

She clasped the table edge, her balance going. Her body felt light, so light. If she let go, she knew she would float.

Spike's voice broke the spell.

'Hey, are you alright?'

He had closed the seaward door and the deep resonant sound was gone. Rhona pulled her eyes from the ceiling and found she was holding tightly to the table edge.

"That noise. It was inside my head,' she said slowly, trying to understand. 'I thought I was floating upwards,' Rhona could hardly believe what she was saying.

'I'm sorry, I should have closed the door,' Spike explained. 'The mound is built like an acoustic theatre. It manipulates sound, especially low continuous sound like chanting or . . .'

'The sound of the sea,' she finished for him. 'It was weird, like . . .'

'Like a religious experience?' Spike gave a grim

laugh. 'My father knew the right fucking place to play God.'

The engine hummed into life. Spike untied the rope and manoeuvred them out of the cave, towards daylight. When they were well away from the cliff, Rhona tried her mobile, but there was no signal. If she wanted to make a call, she would probably have to get to a land line.

'The nearest is at Brochel, if the line isn't down from the storm,' Spike told her.

So they headed north, with Druim an Aonaich hanging over them, cutting the sun. Spike stayed parallel to the coast, keeping clear of the choppy waters at the cliff edge. Even then, they could feel the great pull of the undertow, as wave fought wave, to and from the rockface. When they reached Screapadal, Spike pointed towards the ruins of the village.

'That's where I fought with my father. I thought he would swim ashore and walk back to the cottage but he didn't.'

Rhona stared, thinking Spike must be wrong, that in the dark and horror of it all he must have forgotten where he had been.

'Are you sure it was here?'

Spike looked at her and Rhona knew for sure he was telling her the truth. Which could mean only one thing.

'Spike, the foot was trawled up in Raasay Sound on the other side of the island,' she said. 'The first hand was found on Rigg Beach on Skye.'

'What?'

'The other hand was found in a salmon cage in Loch Arnish,' Rhona said. 'How could your father's body get to the other side of the island from here?'

Rhona watched him trying to work it out. Even with tides and prevailing winds . . .

Spike shook his head. 'I don't understand.'

'I think I do,' Rhona said slowly. 'Your father didn't drown. Well, not here anyway.'

She could feel the possibility of that scenario sink in.

'Which means you weren't responsible for his death,' she said gently.

They sat in silence, the plop of the water as it broke against the bow the only sound between them.

The big yacht came creeping into view over Spike's shoulder. The sails were full of wind but it was the high-powered engine that was speeding the boat across the Inner Sound towards them from the direction of Applecross on the mainland. Chances were, it contained tourists cruising their way around the Western Isles.

Spike was following her gaze, turning to get a better view.

'Fuck!' He grabbed at the wheel, turning it full circle so that Rhona was thrown hard against the metal rail.

'What is it?' she shouted, knowing the answer before he said it.

'Maley.'

Spike's voice was faint above the noise of the forced engine. The dinghy rose, fighting the swell and the sudden change in direction. For a moment the stern hung in space, then it dropped, the propeller churned water and they were heading back the way they had come.

The big yacht cut the distance between them with the speed of a bullet.

31

THE ROOM WAS white, brightened by the light from the porthole above her. Rhona tried to sit up, but the movement of her head brought a sharp stab of pain and with it the memory of what had happened to Spike.

The yacht bearing down on them, the worry as Spike sailed too close to the cliff edge. The frantic search for the opening, knowing the big yacht couldn't follow them into the cave. She had watched him struggle to keep the tiller steady, his eyes searching for the shadow that spelled the hidden opening to the lab.

Then they saw it, the outcrop that split the surface of the water with four, maybe five jagged points, just north of the opening. On the way out they had sailed due east, then turned, avoiding the outcrop. Now they were being washed through it, the submerged rock slicing the hull.

All she remembered after that was her own scream and the cold sea closing above her.

The pain in Rhona's head had dropped to a dull throb. She threw back the covers and swung her legs out of bed, grabbing the white bathrobe that lay on a nearby chair and staggering to the wash-basin, knowing that throwing cold water in her face wouldn't change anything.

The fact was, Spike was probably dead because of her. If she had waited and let Andre come with them or brought in the police, instead of thinking she could do it all by herself, he would be alive now.

Rhona lay back down, legs quivering with exhaustion and distress. She had to believe Spike had either made it to shore or was somewhere on this yacht. Either way, she would find him.

The yacht was moving again, the engine vibrating like a drill. She closed her aching eyes and wished herself a hundred miles away, sitting at her kitchen window watching the sun set on the gardens of the convent. Anywhere but here. Anywhere but now.

When the door opened, she was lying curled on top of the bed. A thickset man smiled down at her, a smile that roamed like a hand over her body. Rhona swung herself upright to show him she still had the strength to hurt him if he dared come near.

He laughed contemptuously, then threw her some dry clothes.

The cabin was luxurious and empty. The man showed her inside, then left. Rhona looked about, spotting the ship's decanter and crystal glasses behind a polished brass rail.

She poured a small whisky in a glass, downed it, and immediately poured another, knowing that this would be the only nice thing to happen to her on this boat.

Someone had pulled her from the water, undressed

her and put her to bed. Not the sort of good samaritan action she expected from Maley. If he had saved her from drowning, it was because he had something else planned for her. Something worse.

Rhona walked round the cabin, looking out of the windows, trying to recognise the coastline. They were well offshore, but she spotted the pinnacle that was Brochel to the south, which meant they were passing Sithearn Mór on their way north towards the islands of Rona and Eilean Tigh.

Rhona's heart sank. There was nothing but rocks and seagulls where they were headed.

She reached for the decanter again. Maybe being drunk wasn't such a bad idea after all. When the door opened five minutes later, she was ready for him.

Except it wasn't Maley after all.

'Dr MacLeod, I'm so glad you're okay.'

Dr Lynne Franklin came towards her, smiling that too perfect smile. Rhona was already on her feet.

'Okay?' Rhona didn't even try to control her anger. 'What the hell did you think you were doing? Your damn yacht drove us onto the cliff.'

Franklin's perfect smile disappeared.

'I assure you, Dr MacLeod,' she said sharply, 'we had no intention of harming you when we approached your boat. If you remember, you left me a text message saying you wanted to speak to me urgently. I was in Scotland on business and called your lab. Your assistant told me you were on Raasay. I have sailed these islands many times and keep a yacht up here with a friend of mine. I decided I would come and find you.'

Rhona sat down, feeling suddenly uncertain. It was true. She *had* sent that text message.

'But we thought this was Maley's boat,' she said stupidly.

Dr Franklin looked as puzzled as Rhona felt.

'I have no idea who this Maley is,' she said quietly, 'but this is certainly not his yacht.'

Rhona let that sink in.

If that was so, Spike needn't have panicked.

'Spike?' she asked.

'The boy with you? I'm afraid he is still missing.'

'Oh God.'

'I'm sorry.' She sounded as if she meant it. 'I've already contacted the coastguard and, of course, we'll keep on looking until it gets dark.'

Rhona felt like a fool, a stupid fool. Spike had panicked when he thought it was Maley, and she had joined in.

'Please don't worry. I'm sure we'll find him,' Franklin said. 'Look, can I get you something to eat?'

Rhona nodded blearily. Whisky on an empty stomach hadn't been such a good idea. Her body felt as light as her brain.

Franklin spoke on the phone, then sat down beside her.

'While we're waiting for the food to arrive,' she said, her voice full of concern, 'maybe you could explain what this is all about.'

*   *   *

Rhona decided to cut everything from the script except Maley and the drugs. Franklin didn't seem interested. But she had plenty of questions about Spike.

Where would he go if he managed to reach the shore?

How did Rhona know him?

Where had they been going in the dinghy?

Rhona looked at the impeccably made-up face. Asking questions; interested, but not too nosy. Lynne Franklin was a beautiful woman. Rhona wondered why she had never headed for Hollywood. She got the feeling that she was a very good actress.

'When did you say you phoned the coastguard?'

The slippage in the mask was momentary but Rhona saw it nonetheless.

Franklin rose to replenish her glass, which was still half full.

'As soon as we picked you up,' she said evenly.

'The helicopter would have been here by now.' Rhona's head was swimming, but she wasn't stupid. 'You may have come looking for me, but not, I think, to offer me a job.'

Lynne Franklin stood motionless, her back rigid. Rhona could imagine what was happening to the mask on that beautiful face. Then the woman turned and laughed. The sound should have been pleasant. It wasn't.

'You are right, of course.' She looked Rhona up and down.

'Actually, Dr MacLeod, I would have liked to have you work for me. Unfortunately I think we have incompatible scientific agendas.'

Rhona said nothing.

'The truth is, I came looking for you because I believe you have information I need.'

'What information?'

'The whereabouts of Dr Fitzgerald MacAulay.'

Rhona nearly laughed.

'MacAulay's dead,' she said. 'Bits of him have been washing ashore here for weeks.'

'You're wrong. MacAulay is not dead. And we believe Spike knows where he is.'

'Then it's you who are wrong,' Rhona told her. 'Spike and his father had an argument. MacAulay went overboard and drowned.'

Franklin glared impatiently. 'When was this?'

'MacAulay went overboard a month before his foot turned up in a fishing net,' Rhona repeated. 'The foot we found had a ReAlba tattoo just above the ankle.'

'We believe the body pieces belong to the man we sent looking for MacAulay,' Franklin responded.

'And who exactly is *we*?'

'The more I tell you, the more fragile your life becomes, Dr MacLeod.'

'I'll take that risk.'

'Very well. We are both women in a man's world, so I'll be frank with you. I tried to recruit you because you were directly involved in the forensic investigation of this case. You were coming to LA for the conference, which was convenient. Even better, Andre met you *en route* and . . . how shall I put it? Made friends with you.'

If the bitch thought she was going to react to that bit of information, she was wrong.

'Why do you want MacAulay?'

'MacAulay was being financed by my organisation to carry out some experimental work. We believe he has been hiding some of the results of this work from us.'

'He was working for ReGene?'

'Indirectly, yes.'

'You mean he was working for ReAlba.'

Franklin smiled. 'ReGene is not ReAlba.'

'And in which capacity are you here, Dr Franklin?' Rhona said angrily. 'ReGene representative or racist bastard?'

The other woman looked pityingly at her.

'Tell me, Dr MacLeod,' she said, 'where do you hide your blacks in Scotland? I don't think I've seen one since I arrived.'

Rhona was silent but Franklin wasn't finished yet.

'Of course, you do have incomers. Asians, plenty of them; Chinese, and then there are those English. White settlers. I hear the locals hate them so much, they've formed an organisation called Settler Watch to burn them out.'

Rhona ignored the taunts. 'What was MacAulay working on?'

'As you probably know from Andre, Dr MacAulay left his project for the British government at Porton Down to work for us,' Lynne Franklin said. 'We were keen to establish specific genes found in the families of Gaels who came from the west coast of Scotland.'

'The Men of the West.'

Franklin nodded.

'And MacAulay was working on that?'

'We believe he had completed the work before he disappeared . . . and that's where you come in.'

Rhona was fed up discussing a dead man as if he was alive.

'MacAulay is dead,' she said again.

But Franklin wasn't listening.

'Where would the boy go to hide?'

'You think Spike got ashore?'

Rhona's heart leapt. She didn't care if this woman or Andre had lied to her, as long as Spike was alive.

Franklin looked amused by the show of emotion.

'One of my men saw him swim into the cave. We sent the dinghy in, but unfortunately he had disappeared. The boy trusts you, which means you can deliver him to us.'

'Like hell I will.'

If Spike was alive and free, Rhona was going to make sure he stayed that way.

'Very well. You leave me no alternative.'

Franklin picked up the telephone. 'Tell Maley there's someone I want him to meet.'

32

AS HE RAN his footsteps echoed through the tunnel. At
every turn, Spike threw himself violently forward,
arching his back, expecting a hand to reach out and
grab him.

When he reached the cave opening, he hurled himself out into the night air and ran for the crevasse,
snatching at handholds, his knees scraping their way
down the narrow opening. At the bottom he stopped
and looked up at the sliver of sky, forcing himself to
wait and listen for footsteps above the snap of his own
frantic heart.

Nothing.

He ran along the rocky hillside and down into high
heather, disturbing midges that rose in a biting cloud,
scenting the blood that seeped from his skinned hands
and face.

When he reached the edge of the loch, Spike thrust his
face in the water, drowning the midges that encrusted his
wounds and washing the bitter salt from his lips.

It was still faintly light, the long day refusing to end.
Spike picked his way northwest, edging ever closer to
the sea.

He had made up his mind.

He would bargain for Rhona the way he had planned to bargain for Esther. He would give Maley what he wanted. He would give him that and more.

His damp clothes clung to him. His body had dropped into nagging exhaustion. Each swish of his feet brought more midges to feast on his bare skin. The woodland near the shore was no better, the maddening midges being replaced by fat black flies that buzzed tirelessly around his sweating face. Then he was on the edge of the wood and the soft sea breeze cleared his head of everything except his decision.

On his way to the black rock, Spike picked up the small dried sticks that would start his signal fire.

The drowned motor boat was thirty feet from shore in ten feet of water. Spike stood on the shingle and found his bearings, forty-five degrees east from the black rock, in line with the last deserted blackhouse of Screapadal. He'd picked up the knife, diving torch and some rope from his stash in the ruins of the castle. All he had to do was swim to the boat, release the stuff and get it to the castle. Then he would radio Maley to come and collect it.

But not before Maley agreed to free Rhona.

The water crept up his legs like the chill of death. But it wasn't the cold that was filling Spike's mind with horror.

He looked up, trying to judge how much good light he had left. An hour at most to get the cargo ashore.

He dipped his head and plunged into the water,

striking out towards the place that was etched forever in his brain.

When his head broke surface he was six feet away from the sunken boat. Spike took a deep breath and dived. The back of the boat was visible in the arc of his torchlight. It was lying upside down, the wooden stern driven deep into the sandy bottom, the long rent he'd dug in its side filled with the darting of small silvery fish. He flashed the torch, and the fish flew for the entrance, masking his face in a shimmering shoal, blinding him. Then they parted and the torchlight found the plastic container that held his father's notes.

Spike had just enough breath in his lungs to attach the rope before his body threw itself upwards, desperate for air. He struck out for shore, dragging the rope behind him, letting the drift of the sea carry him where he wanted to go.

On his second foray, a pale moon shimmered through a cluster of rain clouds. This time Spike wasn't so sure of his position and cursed himself for not releasing the orange buoy that was tied to the boat's stern. He looked to shore, checking for his landmarks, knowing he would have to trust his intuition.

He took a breath and sank, sweeping his torch through the sullen water, looking for the wreck. Something drifted against him, brushing his shoulder with a handless arm.

Spike flung himself round.

The head bobbed at him, eyes hollow and accusing. The rope he'd wound round his father's swollen body –

once, twice, three times, like a hangman's noose – cut through the decaying flesh.

Dr MacLeod had told him the body parts could not belong to his father, but Spike knew she was wrong. Bits of the corpse had made their way from here to the other side of the island even though he'd tried so hard to tie it to its watery grave.

Spike sliced frantically at the rope that attached Maley's parcel to his father's corpse, then rose kicking to the surface.

33

`MALEY AND I have already met,' Rhona said, 'Very recently, in fact.'

Maley's expression made her skin crawl.

Interestingly, he seemed to be having a similar effect on Lynne Franklin. Certainly Maley didn't fit her image of a big handsome Gael with a sing-song voice and something enticing under his kilt. But it was more than that.

'Joe didn't tell you he tried to kill me?' Rhona enjoyed scoring that point.

Franklin turned to Maley, 'You told me you couldn't find her.'

Maley was out of his depth. 'She's fucking off her head. I never saw her before.'

'That's funny, Joe. I distinctly remember the smell of your rotten breath, just before I twisted your wizened wee balls,' Rhona taunted.

'Bitch!'

Rhona's sidestep wasn't quick enough to avoid Maley's body as it smashed into hers. They fell together onto the fancy couch. Somewhere in the background a voice was screaming at Maley to get off. He did, but not before Rhona had snapped her teeth shut on his ear.

Maley howled. 'You're dead, bitch!'

But he wasn't to have his heart's desire . . . yet.

Franklin had recovered her sense of purpose. She stared unwaveringly at Rhona. 'You must see that your continuing survival depends on whether you decide to help us.'

Rhona looked at the two faces, one twisted with dumb hatred, the other devoid of emotion, and knew which she feared most.

'And if Spike takes you to MacAulay, what happens then?' she said.

'You have my word neither you nor the boy will be harmed.'

The voice was smoothly honest. Franklin might even believe what she was saying. But Maley's eyes told a different story.

'I need to think,' Rhona stalled.

'You can have ten minutes,' Franklin warned. 'After that Maley has my permission to do whatever is necessary to get us the boy.'

Rhona splashed her face with cold water. The ache in her head had eased, to be replaced by a pain in her chest where Maley had landed on her. She knew she had done her case no good by winding him up, but she couldn't help it.

Did Franklin know about Maley's little torture session with Spike? She doubted it. Maley wouldn't want his boss to know he had let the boy escape.

The drugs were top of Maley's agenda, above getting even with her. He wanted to know where they were before anything else. Maley was just a big fuck in a scabby wee pond. The politics of human genetics wasn't something his brain could handle, but he would carry on the charade until he got what he wanted. The drugs delivery and Rhona's death, in either order. Anything else would be a bonus.

Rhona didn't need time to decide. She had already made up her mind. She used the time to work out how to inflict the most pain on Maley with the glass stopper she'd taken from the whisky decanter.

If Spike had reached shore, surely he would have gone to Mrs MacMurdo by now. Even if he hadn't, she wouldn't wait forever before calling the police. Constable Johnstone would contact Northern Constabulary, who would contact Strathclyde Police and Bill Wilson. Somewhere in that chain would be Phillips and whoever he represented.

Rhona never thought the day would dawn when thinking about Phillips would make her happy.

They were passing the shielings south of Caol Rona. She could make out the broken stone walls clustered on the ribbed grazings. As far as Rhona knew, the nearest night anchorage was round the north point in Loch a' Sguirr. Anywhere else was too exposed. While she watched the passage between Raasay and Rona slide into view, she heard the door behind her open.

Esther was everything Rhona had imagined. Pale skin, big dark eyes, sexy in a waif-like way. Rhona remembered sitting next to Sean on the sofa, listening to her sing. She had felt the sound vibrate his senses, saw his excitement grow with every note. Music was sex to Sean. Playing it, listening to it.

In her imagination Sean was already fucking the owner of the voice. She had been wrong, she knew that now. Sean had accepted the girl for what she was, a singer with a problem. But had Esther betrayed Sean and helped Maley set him up?

Rhona had blamed Sean for screwing up her life. The truth was, her connection with Maley had screwed up Sean's life.

Esther closed the door quietly behind her.

Her voice shook as she whispered, 'Joe's strung out on speed. He's going to kill you.' She produced a small handgun from her pocket. 'Here, take this. I stole it from that woman's cabin.'

The gun felt light as a toy. Rhona stared at it. She had seen the results of gunshots. She had never imagined herself inflicting one. She slipped the gun into her pocket.

'There's a dinghy trailing the stern. You can make it ashore.'

'What about you?'

Esther shook her head vehemently. 'No. If I try to leave him, Joe will kill Spike.'

She turned for the door and Rhona saw the heart-shaped mole on her cheek.

Realisation dawned. 'It was you that day in the underground.'

Esther nodded, remembering. 'You were sitting opposite me. I was crying.'

'And I didn't help you.'

'You can help me now. Find Spike. Tell him I never wanted him hurt.'

The yacht rocked gently at anchor. The engine must have stopped while they were talking and they hadn't noticed. There was no one on deck. In the east, the sun was creeping over the horizon. Westward, the coast of Raasay was a dark pencil line.

Too far to swim.

They made their way towards the stern, every creak and shift of the boat playing their nerves. Rhona wanted Esther to leave, shooing her away immediately when they reached the rail, but Esther shook her head.

'You'll need help with the dinghy.'

They pulled it in as silently as possible. When it was close alongside, Rhona swung herself over the rail and found the ladder.

She dragged the oars into place, hating the grinding sound they made in the silence. When she looked up, Esther was no longer in sight. Then she heard her strangled cry.

'I'm sorry, Dr MacLeod, but we require the dinghy to get to shore ourselves.' Lynne Franklin was dressed for business, from the slim black trousers to the yellow waterproof. 'While you were contemplating your future, Spike very kindly radioed us and told us his location.'

She pointed southwest, where a dull red beacon fluttered in the darkness.

Maley had Esther's slight figure clamped to his side, and Rhona was sure that pain was being inflicted.

'Bring the girl,' Franklin told Maley, 'we might need her yet.'

They moved Rhona to the bow, alongside the guy who had brought her the clothes. He pressed his body hard against her, getting off on closeness and the scent of fear. Rhona sat her hands in her lap, the right one resting on the gun Esther had given her, and imagined blowing the creep's dick and balls all over the Inner Sound.

Esther sat next to Maley, her eyes vacant. Maley was on the engine, busy glaring at Rhona. She met him eyeball to eyeball, until Franklin reminded him to keep his eyes on where they were heading.

The wind was coming from the northwest, light but constant and the engine had to fight the small grey waves that pushed the dinghy east, away from shore.

The beacon fire hung on their horizon and Rhona tried to work out where it was, thinking at first that the rising blackness was cliff line before she recognised the shadowy outline of Brochel Castle.

As they neared the shore, Franklin signalled Rhona's minder over the side to pull them in.

Rhona wondered who the minder belonged to, Franklin or Maley? She was sure she'd spotted a look pass between him and Joe in the boat, and she suddenly wondered if Franklin realised how alone she was out here.

The air was thick with the smell of seaweed and the crackle of burning driftwood. The fire was on their left, just above the tangle of the high water line, and the drifting smoke nipped at Rhona's eyes. Beyond was a clump of whin bushes, then a flat porch of grass, before the land rose more steeply to the single track road that zigzagged across the island.

Spike was nowhere to be seen.

'Over there.' Franklin pointed at a cluster of rocks near the fire.

The minder dragged Rhona over, pushed her down roughly, jerked her hands behind her back and wound a thin wire tightly round her wrists. Then he shoved her knees up and wired her ankles the same way, making sure his fingers ran over her crotch as he did it.

Esther was standing beside Maley, a lamb to the slaughter. He had already twisted her arms behind her back and a thin rope linked her to him. Franklin was peering along the shoreline, searching for the change in the shadow that would be Spike.

Behind Rhona, the Gaelic whisper was like water on sand.

'*A' bheil thu 'gam thuigsinn?*' His tongue was badly swollen and he spoke slowly and as clearly as he could, willing her to understand.

'*Tha. Tha mi 'gad thuigsinn.*'

Yes, she understood him.

He emerged from the whin bushes. In the dancing light of the fire, Spike looked young and old at the same time. He walked

straight over to the American.

'I am Donald MacAulay,' he announced.

Franklin stared at him appraisingly, gun in hand. When she spoke, her voice was almost reverent.

'Yes, you are Donald MacAulay.'

'I have what you want.' Spike gestured at the ruins of the castle. He looked at Maley. 'What he wants is there too.'

Maley's eyes were pinpoints of greed. He made to move off along the beach, but Franklin held up her hand. She wasn't interested in the contents of the castle, not for the moment. She drew closer to Spike and touched his head, moving it sideways to expose a ReAlba tattoo etched in the pale skin of his neck, just under the hairline.

'He told us you died.'

Maley was getting impatient and Franklin was too interested in Spike to pick up on the signals being exchanged between him and the minder.

'You will come with me,' she was saying. 'You will come to America.'

'No.' Spike shook his head. 'You can take my father's work. It's all there. That is enough.'

'*You* are your father's work.'

Spike laughed, a desperate sound that tore Esther from Maley.

Maley jerked at the rope, sending the weeping girl sprawling at his feet.

Spike's expression betrayed the depth of his loathing, but he dragged his eyes away from Maley and addressed Franklin again.

'You said if I gave you what you want, Esther and Rhona would go free.'

She appeared bemused at his insistence.

'The girl and the woman go free when you come with me.

'Untie them and let them go,' Spike ordered, 'then I will go with you.'

'Spike, no!' Esther was crying.

'Let them go,' Spike repeated. 'Then you have my word I will stay alive. Otherwise I will do everything I can to kill myself.'

A flicker of fear crossed Franklin's face. She waved the gun at Maley. 'Untie them.'

'The girl's fucking mine,' Maley insisted. But if he was planning a move, it wasn't yet. The weasel eyes moved into submission. 'You promised me the gear.'

'Go and get it,' Franklin said. 'Bring everything you find.'

Maley was happy now.

'What about them?'

'I'll watch them.' Franklin told him.

When Maley and the minder disappeared into the darkness, Spike freed Rhona first.

'*Tha i trom,*' he whispered in her ear, with a swift glance at Esther. He pressed Rhona's hand, willing her to understand. She returned the pressure. If what Spike said was true, it changed everything. He moved towards Esther, untied her wrists, took her hands in his and rubbed the life back into them.

Franklin had watched his every move, but she hadn't heard the whispered words. Rhona was sure of that.

'Why take Spike?' Rhona tried. 'He doesn't know anything about his father's work.'

'You still don't understand,' Franklin smiled condescendingly. 'Donald *is* his father's work. The product of an adult male cell and a female egg. A human clone. The perfect Gael.'

'You're insane.'

Franklin looked irritated. 'You're a scientist, Dr MacLeod. You know what's really happening in the scientific world while governments argue about what they will allow to happen. MacAulay maintained his attempts at human cloning were unsuccessful. Until recently we believed him.'

Rhona's head was reeling. Perhaps there was some truth in what Franklin was saying. She thought about Phillips and the cloak and dagger stuff. If the British government knew about Spike, they would want to get their hands on him as well.

'But you said MacAulay was working on genetic profiling.'

'He was. Maley will bring us what we need to know about that.'

There was a shout from the direction of the castle and Franklin aimed the gun at Esther.

'Get in the boat,' she barked at Spike. 'Get in the boat or I'll kill her.'

Mute with terror, Esther clung to Spike, but he extricated himself from her grip. With one tender glance back he braced himself and headed for the dinghy.

The whin bushes were pushed apart and Maley and the minder appeared, carrying plastic containers.

Franklin looked relieved. 'Got it?'

'No problem.' Maley deposited a container at her feet. 'The notes.'

He threw Rhona a look. She saw the calculation behind the self-satisfied expression. He had the gear. Killing her would make his pleasure complete.

'Okay, let's go.' Franklin said.

'She knows me,' Maley whispered to Franklin. 'They both know me.'

Franklin thought for a moment. The two women were better dead, but she had to make sure Spike came with her.

Rhona strained to hear her reply.

'I'll send the dinghy back for you.'

Maley thought about that. The minder gave him a nod. He would take Franklin and Spike to the yacht. Then he would be back. They would cut the proceeds. It was a good deal. It also gave Maley access to both Rhona and Esther. A contemplative smile creased his unshaven cheek. He was already enjoying the pain he would inflict on the two women.

The minder followed Franklin to the dinghy.

Maley motioned Rhona towards Esther. 'Sit.' He pointed to a spot next to the fire.

He sat close to Rhona and told her what he planned to do once Franklin had Spike on board the yacht. He would fuck her in every available orifice. Mouth, ears, anus, cunt. He would fuck her so hard and so deep she would likely die before he slit her throat.

Esther had descended into a frightened stupor at Maley's whispered promises and Rhona knew she had heard them before. Rhona felt the anger she had seen on Spike's face. She could kill Maley and never feel the guilt of it.

The cold point of a knife pricked the small of her back.

'You know the human body, Dr MacLeod. If this knife goes in here, what organs will it slice through?

She didn't answer, although the internal map of her body was clear in her head.

'Esther liked the feel of the blade against her cunt. Made her excited.'

The tide had lifted the keel of the dinghy, bobbing it in and out four metres from the edge. The minder was already on board. Spike paused, ankle-deep in water. He glanced back up the beach, unsure.

'Maley won't harm them,' Franklin promised him. Rhona could see Spike wanted to believe her.

Maley was breathing heavily. Rhona thought how close the muzzle of the gun was to his genitals. She had seen a body once where the penis had been gnawed off. She visualised what a gunshot at this range would do to Maley.

One thing for sure. He would never fuck again.

Esther began mumbling words under her breath like a prayer. The knife-point left Rhona's back. She heard Esther's intake of breath and saw the flash of metal near the thin neck.

'Shut the fuck up.'

Rhona slid her hand into her pocket. Now was the time, while Maley was looking the other way. Just as her fingers closed around the trigger, a terse order came from the shadows. 'Get away from them.' A figure stepped into the firelight.

'Andre!' A rush of relief swept over Rhona.

Maley looked up, startled. He licked his lips, contemplating the firearm pointed at his head, then stood up slowly and stepped back.

'Drop the knife,' Andre ordered.

A second later, the blade clattered on the pebbles.

Rhona scrambled to her feet.

'Quick. They're taking Spike.' She ran towards the boat, slithering on the seaweed-strewn rocks.

But Andre wasn't following.

Franklin broke into a slow smile. 'What took you so long?' she called.

Rhona stared back at Andre in horror, hoping she was wrong.

Andre kept his gun on Maley. 'The boy stays here,' he shouted.

'What?' Franklin was obviously taken aback.

'The boy stays here,' Andre repeated. 'Rhona, take the girl to the jeep. It's up behind the castle.'

Maley glanced from Andre to Franklin, trying to figure out where he stood in all of this.

'Your father was ReAlba,' Franklin said. 'MacAulay's son belongs to ReAlba. You know that.'

Andre motioned Spike to come back.

'Where are you taking him?' demanded Rhona.

Andre ignored the question. 'Go to the jeep, Rhona, Norman will take you to Mrs MacMurdo's.'

The trickle of doubt was becoming a wave. Norman MacLeod was the man staying at her father's cottage. He had given her a lift on Raasay. Just how many people were involved in this?

'I'm not leaving until I know what's happening to Spike.'

'Spike is the property of the US government.' Andre's voice was calm and icily cold. 'He'll be returning with me.'

'You bastard,' Franklin spat.

The truth stared Rhona in the face. Andre wasn't there to help Franklin. He wasn't there to help Spike. He was an agent of the United States government come to retrieve its property. And she had helped him do that.

'Property? You're talking about a human being, remember.'

'Would you rather ReAlba had him?' Andre asked sharply. 'He's better off with us.'

'You're both the same,' Rhona shot back. 'To you he's a specimen, nothing more. What sort of life will he have?'

Above them, the sound of helicopter blades beat the air. Franklin glanced up as the swinging lights punched through the darkness.

Rhona prayed it was the coastguard, the police, Phillips . . . anyone but Andre's lot come to take Spike away.

The boy looked resigned to his fate, whatever that might be. Rhona wondered if either Franklin or Andre had noticed how haggard he looked.

The helicopter dropped on the grass behind them.

Maley grabbed his chance and scrambled down the beach.

The minder already had the engine running. Maley

splashed through the water and pulled himself over the side of the dinghy. Rhona heard him laugh. No doubt he thought they were stupid bastards, fighting over the kid.

'Kill Maley and I'll come with you,' Spike screamed at Andre. Andre took aim. 'Stop or I'll shoot!'

Maley didn't believe him. The propeller cut the water and the dinghy began to move towards the yacht. Maley turned and grinned as the bullet met him between the eyes. His body jerked backwards on impact, hung for a moment, then dropped over the side. The minder let go of the tiller and held up his hands.

Spike walked towards Andre.

'No, wait! Don't . . . I'll help you,' Rhona pleaded.

'Go home, Rhona,' Andre called. 'There's nothing you can do.'

But Franklin wasn't finished. 'The boy belongs to ReAlba. Dead or alive.'

Andre wasn't quick enough, but Rhona was.

Her shot thudded into Franklin's back. Franklin grunted with surprise and slumped forward. The bullet destined for Spike whined off into the bushes. 'Thanks,' Andre shouted.

'You're not taking him.' Rhona moved into position, the gun pointed this time at Andre. 'I won't let you.'

'It's no use, Rhona.'

He was right. Two armed men emerged through the bushes, their guns pointed straight at her.

It was the first light of a northern day and the long thin rays danced across the Inner Sound.

Spike stared out over the water, a last look, then he turned and climbed into the helicopter.

'*Cuimhnich dé thuirt mi riut,*' he called to Rhona from the open door. Remember what I said. '*Tha gaol agam oirre. A' bheil thu 'gam thuigsinn?*'

'*Tha mi 'gad thuigsinn,*' Rhona said. She understood him perfectly.

The helicopter rose, heading east out over the water, filling the air with the smell of grass and whin.

Esther was weeping quietly. Rhona put her arms around the girl's thin shoulders.

Now the helicopter was turning, heading northwest. Rhona imagined some US submarine sitting offshore, anticipating the return of its country's 'property'.

Spike must have waited until he was above the sunken boat before he threw himself from the open side of the helicopter. The body fell slowly, swooping the sky, a dark bird against the dawn plunging into the place he said was his father's grave.

34

PHILLIPS WAS TRYING to ignore the crying baby, standing with his back to the kitchen range. He looks different, Rhona thought, more like a real person out of the grey suit. But older, weary of life. Like Spike.

'I believe the boy spoke to you in Gaelic before he died,' Phillips began. 'What did he say?'

Rhona glanced at Esther, who sat with the baby in her arms, crooning to the puckered face.

'He said he loved Esther. He asked us to look after her.'

Mrs MacMurdo nodded. 'The boy shall have his wish.'

On the other side of the island, the MOD divers were already busy. They would bring up what was left of MacAulay's body from the drowned boat. They would search for Spike. Maybe they would find him, maybe not. The sea did not always give back what it took.

Rhona thought about the DNA sample she'd sent to Chrissy. She could give it to Phillips. Let his department compare it to MacAulay. Let them worry if the results showed what they suspected, that Spike was a clone of his father.

If MacAulay had achieved a human clone, who else out there had already done the same? And did it matter? A human clone would have no soul. That's what the papers had screamed when the first details of Dolly the cloned sheep were released to the world press. It would be a replica of its donor, with no soul of its own.

But Spike had a soul. A heart and a soul.

'I believe Spike was aging rapidly,' she said to Phillips. 'His father hated him. He told Spike he was a mistake. An abomination before God. A failed experiment. However Spike was created, or whatever his father did to him once he was born, it was wrong.'

Behind her Mrs MacMurdo muttered under her breath in Gaelic.

'Dr MacLeod,' Phillips said. 'This is a difficult business, with more at stake than a boy's life. You are an employee of the police service and a public servant. We expect your full co-operation.'

His face was stone. A public servant without a soul. Maybe the world should be peopled by clones instead of human beings. Clones like Spike.

'It wouldn't have mattered if Spike had gone with Dr Frith or stayed here,' Rhona said, 'He would still have been an experiment to be . . . monitored.'

Phillips had had enough moralising for the moment. He lifted his jacket from the back of the chair.

'Now that you have shown us where the laboratory

is, you may return to Glasgow,' he said. 'I will contact you there.'

Mrs MacMurdo left the door open after Phillips left, *to let God's own air back into the room.*

'What will we do about Esther?' Rhona asked.

'She and the baby can stay here for the time being.' Mrs MacMurdo paused. 'Donald said something to you in the Gaelic?'

'*Tha i trom,*' Rhona told her.

'*Mo chreach,*' Mrs MacMurdo put her hand on her heart. 'She's pregnant. By Spike?'

'There must be a chance, and he wanted us to know.'

A shadow crossed Mrs MacMurdo's face. 'If *they* find out . . .'

'I won't be the one to tell them.'

Early June air ruffled the strip of water between Raasay and the mainland. In the distance the Cuillin sat dark against the sky.

Rhona wondered what Spike wanted her to do if there was a baby. The natural baby of a clone. The next experiment.

Nothing, she thought. That's what he would have wanted me to do. Nothing. He wanted it to be over with him.

'I love her,' Spike had said. '*Tha gaol agam oirre.*'

Phillips was not interested in Maley's cast-off girl-friend anyway, or in how Spike had felt. She would give him Spike's DNA sample. That would keep him happy.

Rhona closed her eyes and let the Hebridean wind wash her soul.

'*Tha mi 'dol dhachaigh*,' she told the wind. 'I'm going home.'

35

RHONA STOOD OUTSIDE the flat. The taxi had dropped her at the door, but she didn't go in just yet. She wanted just to stand there.

She listened to the sounds of the city.

Glasgow. Big and brash and beautiful. She loved it.

The door buzzed open, even though she hadn't pressed the intercom.

Sean.

It seemed a long time since she had seen him, spoken to him, loved him.

She pushed open the front door.

Sean was playing the saxophone. The sound drifted down the stairwell, as tentative as herself.

Rhona climbed the stairs.

She had already been to the lab; wept about her cat; poured out everything that had happened. Chrissy had filled her in on the rest.

And all the time Rhona never asked about Sean.

Chrissy told her anyway.

'He's back at the flat,' she said. 'The only tunes he plays are sad ones.'

*   *   *

The door of the flat was open and through it came the smell of ginger, and something else Rhona didn't quite recognise.

Sean was in the bedroom. The window was open and he was playing to the sky.

'Hey, you're late.'

'There was a girl on the underground. She was crying.'

'You can't help everyone.' Sean placed the saxophone on its stand in the corner. 'But thanks for trying.'

He touched her lips with his.

'Hungry?' he said.

'Ravenous.'

EPILOGUE

IF THEY EVER found Spike's body, Rhona was never told. When the MOD took MacAulay's body parts and Spike's DNA sample, she was advised, in the interest of national security, not to discuss the case.

The baby's mother reported him missing the day after Spike took Esther from the hospital. Social Services already had him on the at-risk register. He was placed with foster parents and, because of the circumstances, Esther wasn't charged.

Esther took time to recover but Maley's death had freed her of fear. She stayed on in Raasay with Mrs MacMurdo. When Rhona went back six weeks later, she was helping out in the Post Office. They walked together towards Hallaig among the swaying birch trees.

Esther told Rhona about Maley and how the drugs she took when she was with him made her ill. The voices had become less frequent now and she hoped eventually for peace. As she saw it, Spike had saved her life.

'Spike loved you,' Rhona told her.

'I know.'

Rhona gave Esther the song Sean had written for

her. Esther promised to come and sing it at the club, soon. With a few carefully-worded enquiries about Esther's health Rhona ascertained that the girl wasn't pregnant, and she never told her the truth about Spike. Esther thought he'd killed himself because of the part he played in his father's death and Rhona let her believe that.

Two months later Esther sang again. In her green silk dress, she reminded Rhona of the birch trees in Raasay Wood. They both imagined Spike standing at the bar watching, a smile on his face.

ESTHER'S SONG

There's something inside me
A feeling so strong
No shadow can darken
It's here I belong
Dark clouds may gather
Rain start to fall
But I'll be here

When words try to hurt me
Lost dreams fill my mind
A vision of darkness
I left far behind
Love lifts me higher
Love shows me the way
And gives me a reason
To be here

And that something inside me
Gets stronger each day
I know I can make it
If love shows the way
The notes now are sweeter
'Cos I'm here with you

The shadows are gone now
It's here I belong
Love gave me a reason
To be here

Esther's Song – Words by Lin Anderson, music by Rage Music. Written for the 2001 STV drama *Small Love*, which told part of Esther and Spike's story.

A NOTE ON CLONING

The best known cloning technique is somatic cell nuclear transfer (SCNT). The nucleus from a body cell (male or female) is put into an egg from which the nucleus has been removed. The resulting entity is triggered by chemicals or electricity to begin developing into an embryo. If that embryo were placed into a woman's uterus and brought to term, it would develop into a child that would be the genetic duplicate of the person from whom the original body cell nucleus was taken – a clone.

Dolly the Sheep, the world's first cloned mammal, was born in 1996 at the Roslin Institute near Edinburgh and, apparently subject to an accelerated ageing process, was put to sleep in 2003. Her stuffed carcass is on permanent exhibition at the Royal Museum of Scotland in Chambers Street, Edinburgh. At the time of writing, no human clones are thought to have been born.

KATHRYN FOX

Skin and Bone

The corpse of a young woman is found bludgeoned, frozen and burnt to death.
Then the post-mortem reveals that she recently gave birth. And evidence suggests the baby may still be alive.

Detective Kate Farrer must find the missing newborn if it's going to have any chance of surviving, and catch the dead woman's murderer before her own personal demons overwhelm her . . .

'Comparisons with Patricia Cornwell and Kathy Reichs are inevitable . . . Fox holds her own, if not more, against the other two.'
The Times

'Will keep you gripped from start to finish.'
Jeffery Deaver

'Kathryn Fox has created a forensic physician who readers of Patricia Cornwell will adore.'
James Patterson

KAREN CAMPBELL

The Twilight Time

ANNA CAMERON is a new Sergeant in the Flexi Unit. On her first day in the new job she discovers she'll be working with her ex, Jamie. In at the deep end emotionally, she's also plunged headlong into the violent underworld of Glasgow's notorious Drag – the haunt of working girls, drug dealers and sad, seedy men.

CATH WORTH, Jamie's wife, watches jealously from the sidelines, having given up police work to raise their child. Anna's life could have been hers; hers could have been Anna's. When Cath attempts to get involved in a situation she is no longer equipped or entitled to tackle, the consequences for both women could be far-reaching.

Atmospheric, affecting and beautifully-written, THE TWILIGHT TIME is a stunning crime debut from a remarkably talented new writer.

'This is gritty as all hell, shot through with black humour and with enough pace and atmosphere to give the likes of Denise Mina a run for their money. All this and the chutzpah to create a seedy and unpleasant superintendent named Rankin!'
Mark Billingham

'Stiletto-sharp prose.'
The Herald

'Raw, real and so evocative you can almost hear the screams . . . if this debut is a true reflection of her talent then she's going to be huge.'
Daily Record